The shining splendor of our Zebra Lovegram logo on the cover of this book reflects _____ *inside. Look for the Zebra* _____ *orical romance. It's a tra* _____ *est in quality and reading* _____

PRAISE _____

"EXCITING PASSIONATE STORY . . . THAT FIRES YOUR IMAGINATION!"

— *Rendezvous* on *Gentle Warrior*

"AN EMOTIONAL TUG-OF-WAR, FULL OF HIGH ADVENTURE AND ROMANCE . . . WORTH READING!"

— *Rendezvous* on *Seductive Surrender*

SWEET CAPTOR

"Oh, Bliss . . ." He knew what he wanted and knew she wanted it, too. Some relief from the pent-up emotions bursting to be free. Moving forward, he touched her mouth with his.

Travis meant it to be a gentle kiss, but something—the danger, unresolved desire or the passion of the moment—turned the touch of their lips into a hungry probing. Time stood still as they explored each other with mutual passion. Then Travis dragged her roughly up against him, his mouth crushing demandingly against hers.

Desire coursed through both their bodies. The ground was hard, but they hardly noticed. Such a wild, beautiful madness, Travis thought. Pushing her onto her back, he slid his mouth sensuously down her throat.

"Travis. We can't. . . ." murmured Bliss. If they lost their heads now it could all have a tragic ending.

"Oh, Miss Harrison . . . but we can," said Travis. And he kissed her again, long and hard.

KATHRYN HOCKETT

ZEBRA BOOKS
KENSINGTON PUBLISHING CORP.

This story is for Bob Nicholson,
a very special man who has renewed my faith in men.
He is proof that friendship, trust, respect, and caring
are the most important elements of love.

To Alice Alfonsi, my editor,
whose expertise has proven so important
in molding these words into stories,
a heartfelt thank you.

ZEBRA BOOKS

are published by

Kensington Publishing Corp.
475 Park Avenue South
New York, NY 10016

First Printing: December 1992

Printed in the United States of America

Part One:
Wanted: For Love or For Money

Montana—1884

Good name in man and woman, dear my lord,
Is the immediate jewel of their souls:
Who steals my purse steals trash . . .
But he that filches from me my good name
Robs me of that which not enriches him,
And makes me poor indeed.

—Shakespeare, *Othello*, III, 3

Chapter One

Wanted dead or alive. *Dead* or alive! The words echoed over and over in Travis La Mont's brain as he guided the palomino through the great gaping gate of the stable. Right now he didn't know where he was going. Didn't really care. All he knew was that he had to get away from this town of Silver Bow or he'd end up with his neck in a noose, dangling from some tree.

Hell, he hadn't taken part in that bank robbery. Any half-witted fool would know that. He hadn't even been here long enough to settle down, much less mastermind such a plan. He had merely been standing in front of the bank building with his camera and tripod, taking a photograph of the new building to send to his newspaper. Suddenly all hell had broken loose. People were running to and fro, and he was caught in the melee. Like any good newspaperman, however, Travis had scouted out the story.

He had learned that a bank teller had been

killed during a robbery. It was just the kind of Wild West story that enthralled his Eastern readers back home. Hurrying toward a telegraph station, equipment and cases in hand, Travis had focused his thoughts on the events. Next thing he knew someone was yelling, "There he goes! After him." Looking around, he had been stunned to realize the man meant him.

The silver-starred marshal had pointed at Travis' tripod case, obviously mistaking it for one that held a rifle. There had been no time to explain, not when they were shooting before asking any questions. It was apparent that the marshal was after Travis' blood.

He hadn't had time to wonder. All his energy had been spent in getting out of the line of gunfire and losing his pursuers. As soon as they were off his trail he'd hurried to his hotel to hide out until things cooled down. Travis had been certain that once the marshal was aware of his credentials he'd realize his mistake. Newspapermen of good reputation just didn't rob banks and kill men. But it hadn't happened that way. As the hours passed matters hadn't changed one iota.

Travis owed his life to the boy from the hotel who had warned him of an impending trap. Thus alerted, he'd tied his bedsheets into a rope and had escaped from a second-floor window. Hurrying to the stables, he'd left the marshal and his men behind as they waited to corner him in the lobby. He took satisfaction in knowing that he had outwitted them. But for how long?

"It's all a mistake," he grumbled, and it was.

He wasn't an outlaw. He didn't even know those three men. How then could he have taken part in that robbery? The whole idea was absurd! Surely no logical man would believe such an obvious untruth. And yet, there it was. Tacked to a tree. A wanted poster with a drawing of his face and the name Travis La Mont emblazoned for all to see.

Wanted, dead or alive, it read. Reward two hundred dollars. The words leaped out at him from every post and building in sight as he thundered past. They sure as hell hadn't wasted any time in plastering the whole town with those things. They were even on the outhouses.

"Look, that's him." The shout came from a short distance away.

"There he goes!" The thundering of hoofbeats punctuated the exclamation.

"After him. Don't let him get away."

The yelling alerted Travis to the fact that he was leaving town just in the nick of time.

"Well, let them come. They'll have a hell of a time catching me." If it was the last thing he did, he'd lead them on a merry chase. Hell, he hadn't raced in the Kentucky Derby for nothing.

He rode northwest, urging his horse into a frantic gallop, quickly putting the buildings of Silver Bow far behind him. Only when he was well out of town did he let anger at the injustice of it all overtake him. He was in as much danger as a man could be.

"I'll demand my rights, insist on a fair trial." That is, if he was in any shape to demand anything after that ragtag posse finished with him.

Though Travis had always prided himself on his

bravery, fear surged through him at the thought that he was on the run. A group of angry, gun-toting men were chasing him down, killing him in mind. He felt insulted at being hunted by an uncouth, uneducated, unfeeling bunch of ruffians. If this was civilization he could only feel shame. And yet, recent experience had taught him that bullets whistled before questions were even asked. This wasn't the East. Men lived by a far different code out here. Only the strongest or the fastest with a gun survived, or so it seemed.

Well, Travis wasn't a sharpshooter but he had brains, that mass of gray cells beneath the skull. He hoped his intelligence would come to his aid now, for he had to outwit this band of burly drunken buffoons. He was fleeing for his life, about that he had no illusions. Nor did he have any hope that his being innocent would save him from a necktie party.

Thundering horses' hooves echoed violently through the stillness. The whole damned town must be in pursuit, he thought. Tension tightened his gut and shoulders. Seeking a firm grip on the reins, he bent low over the palomino's neck, a threefold purpose in mind: achieving more speed, being less visible and making himself a more difficult target to hit.

Travis urged the palomino on to an even faster pace, recklessly traveling the mountainous, rocky and rutted ground. More than once he looked behind him for any sign that he was still being closely followed. He sighed with relief when it appeared that he was quickly losing the posse. No doubt they had underestimated him just because he wore a suit.

10

Well, not all Easterners were dandies. He wasn't. Not by a long shot.

Riding hard and fast, doubling back, weaving in and out amidst the trees and scrub brush, Travis did his best to completely dodge his pursuers. With smug satisfaction, he paused to listen. He'd lost them. It was a victory he relished. Taking a deep breath, he at last had a chance to calm down and take a look around. Never had it felt so good to be alive.

"Beautiful. . . ."

It was a colorful world of unusual rock formations, trees of several varieties and clear twisting streams. There was a certain exhilaration in this vast space. The air was clean and fresh, the water cool and inviting. The only problem was, there were few landmarks to guide him. Even so, Travis would not admit to himself that he had no idea where he was headed. As he'd sometimes done in the past, he figured that determination and keeping a level head would work to his advantage. It always had.

Travis prided himself on the fact that he was a self-made man, the fourth son of a Vermont farmer with little or no inheritance. His had not been a life of luxury. No opportunities had come his way, except those he had forged for himself. No stranger to hard work, at fifteen he had left home, to roam the country in search of a direction for his life. There were few manual jobs he hadn't tried his hand at, including being a sailor and breaking horses on a Texas ranch. From Texas he'd gone to Kentucky to race horses, then, when he had become bored with that, had traveled to Omaha via the train. But it wasn't until he reached Denver, Colorado, that Travis had realized what he really wanted to do. He wanted to be a newspaperman. Not just a mediocre journalist and photographer but the best!

To that end he had apprenticed himself to the editor of the *Rocky Mountain News,* and quickly found a whole new world opening up for him. He now had a private window on other cities, states and even countries. He was at the hub of excitement, witnessing historic events as they happened and turning them into stories. A "pistol-toting, pencil pusher and shutter bug," his father liked to call him.

Currently he was a photographer and reporter for the Springfield, *Republican,* touring the West to satisfy his Massachusetts readers' hunger for reliable information about the vast terrain that even now remained a mystery to them. And, what a story this would make . . . if he lived to tell it.

It seemed he had been riding for hours, bouncing over the uneven ground. His head ached, his legs were stiff and sore. Even so, it was worth it. He was certain he had left his pursuers far behind. This place was completely isolated. Reining in the palomino and easing his weight in the saddle, he paused to study the terrain with care. Last Chance Gulch was scribbled on the wooden sign.

It seemed to be as good a name as any. Fitting actually. Even so he decided this wasn't quite the place he wanted to go. Where to then? He turned his head, wondering if he dared take a chance on going back now that he had dodged his pursuers. A dark blur on the horizon alerted him that it would not be a very good idea. They had found him again.

"Damnation!"

He gazed down into the dismal deep canyon. Looking searchingly in front of him, then turning to glance behind him, he was distressed to see that he was trapped. The pounding of horses' hooves, coming closer and closer, echoed in his ears like a funeral toll. Travis felt the last remnant of his self-control shatter. He didn't have to be an expert on strategy to know that he was nearly beaten. Nevertheless he gave his all to a wild, mad dash for freedom.

Drenched in perspiration from the strain and exertion of his hard ride, his heart beating like a drum, he cursed his circumstances. How then was it possible for those bastards to keep up with him?

The posse split up and came at him from two directions. As they said out West "he was done for." There was nothing more he could do now.

Gunfire! Well, let them go ahead and shoot. He much preferred stopping a bullet to being hanged. Hanging was an embarrassing way for a man to go, choking and gagging, his face red, his tongue sticking out, his feet dangling high up in the air.

"Go ahead. Shoot me, you stupid bastards!" He was so exhausted that his body was almost numb.

For just a moment he dared them to kill him, until a well-aimed bullet sent his hat flying from his head. Then the instinct for survival burst within Travis. If he had to sprout wings and fly, he'd get free of these stubborn nuisances. Just let them choke on his dust! With a muttered curse, he dug his heels into the mount's side and shot away like a bolt of lightning. Clinging to the palomino's bridle, he looked like a creature half-man, half-horse as he burst through the clearing with the violence of an explosion.

He could see the last rays of the sun fading behind the hilltops, and knew daylight would soon be gone. Darkness would be a blessing—and would give him at least a faint hope of getting out of this situation alive. Until it came, he had to be content with playing fox to these hounds, hoping he could survive.

Leaning forward in the saddle, stretching out his arms, he allowed himself to relax only for a moment. He had to formulate a plan. Had to!

The river! It wound through the canyon like a shimmering blue ribbon, surrounded by lush green trees. If he could reach that water far ahead of his pursuers he might be able to hide in the foliage, at least long enough to confuse the posse as to which direction he had taken. It was his only chance. Feeling the pulsating rhythm of the horse's flanks beneath his leather boots, he rode at a full gallop toward the river.

Reaching the bank, Travis recklessly urged his mount to plunge in. Luckily, the water level was low, the current lapping gently at the horse's body as he guided the animal across. He'd seek shelter in the dense foliage on the other side, double back, make a large circle and emerge from the trees to take a different route. He thought it to be an excellent plan.

A half-mile down he emerged from the water and guided his mount onto dry land, pushing into the greenery. Reining in his horse, he hid behind a tall, stout tree, scarcely daring to breathe. From his position he could see the dark shadows of the men on horseback as they rode past him. He could hear their shouts, the pounding of their horses' hooves, could nearly smell the sweat of man and beast as they passed him. The trouble was, instead of moving on they stopped.

"You're in here somewhere, La Mont! You're cornered. Give up!" the voice boomed, not more than a few feet away. "You're trapped."

So much for his well-thought-out plan of doubling back. He hadn't counted on them catching up with him quite so soon. Travis knew he had to come up with something else—and quickly.

"Do you hear me, La Mont! Unless you can become invisible we'll find you. If we have to root out every goddamned tree." As if to prove this was no idle threat, two of the men got off their horses and used their brawn to uproot a small dead tree and toss it aside. Far from terrorizing Travis, however, seeing the trunk and outstretched branches lying on the ground gave him an idea.

As the men in the posse crushed through the underbrush, Travis slipped off his brown tweed coat and tie. He'd just had another idea. An inspiration. He'd make a scarecrow, just like he'd done when he was a kid on his father's farm. A dummy. Sliding from the horse, he hurriedly sought out the discarded, uprooted aspen, tugging off all its branches except two. Using the branches as arms, he dressed the tree in his coat and tie, then tied the decoy securely on the horse's back with a long length of rope he pulled from the palomino's saddle. Not an exact likeness of his broad-shouldered, masculine form but close enough in the dusk to work if he was lucky.

"I hate to turn you loose. I really do," he whispered to the palomino. But he couldn't think of any other way of getting out of this one alive. With a slap on the horse's rump, he sent the palomino and scarecrow galloping on their way.

"Son of a bitch! There he is. After him!"

Travis nearly laughed out loud. His ploy had worked. For all their determination to track him down, they were going to come out of this one with more embarrassment than glory. Wait until they discovered they were chasing a tree.

"Ride. Ride you bastards!" he whispered. "We'll see what kind of reward you get when your mistake is discovered."

A thunderclap illuminated horses and riders, setting them in dramatic silhouette against the sky. A storm was coming. Just what I need, Travis grumbled to himself. As if things weren't bad enough already. Now he didn't even have a coat. Still he couldn't keep from mouthing a prayer of gratitude as he watched the posse riding away from him crest the top of a hill. For now he was alone and unmolested.

Chapter Two

Unfolding the piece of paper she held in her hand, Bliss Harrison scowled as she appraised the wanted poster. Travis La Mont. Now just what kind of a man was he anyway? She took note of the jawline, the cleft in the chin, the wide mouth that was set in a grim line. Probably a stubborn one. Handsome though. A real lady-killer. Certainly that face framed by dark wavy hair was interesting and caught one's attention. Those eyes beneath strongly arched black brows would undoubtedly be brown. Hooded eyes. The eyes of an outlaw if ever she'd seen them.

"Two hundred dollars!" A veritable fortune. Certainly enough money to be living comfortably for a while. Oh, how she needed that reward. Things had been mighty tough since the death of her father four months ago. Damned difficult. Pickings had been slim. But the capture of this man would be the answer to her prayers. Could she catch him? Of course she could. She was Oakwood Harrison's daughter, and hadn't he been the best damned

17

bounty hunter in the territory? At least until an outlaw's bullet had struck him down.

Bliss winced as she thought of that terrible moment. Her father had been shot in the back. She had witnessed the brutal act of revenge perpetrated by an outlaw, a man angered because her father had captured his brother and taken him back to a nearby town to meet his due. After that, she had vowed to take her father's place as the finest bounty hunter around.

Her father. Bliss made no secret of how much she had admired him. He had been more than just a parent. He had been confidant, companion and friend. Someone who had looked after her in more ways than she could count, as far back as she could remember.

Randolph Oakwood Harrison had been an adventurer. Of aristocratic stock, he had come West to make his way in the world after reading James Brisbin's *How to Get Rich on the Plains*. Having made his decision to give it a try, he took his twelve-year-old motherless daughter, Rebecca Bliss, with him. Their destination had been farther west than the plains. Montana Territory.

At first her father had bought some yearlings, planning to start a ranch as his friend Benton Winthrop had done. Yearlings sold for four or five dollars a head and could be resold for sixty or seventy dollars, bringing a good profit. But a devastating early winter storm had shattered all his dreams and wiped out his investment in the short span of two weeks.

Some of the ranchers in the area had found the

18

difficulties so crushing that they had gone back East. But had her father given up? Returned with his tail between his legs? Not at all. Instead he had gotten into the bounty-hunting business, which proved to be very profitable. The money from bounty-hunting was a sure bet because it was paid by the territory. And it was easy money with little investment required.

Her father had become a professional "wolfer," hunting and killing wolves and coyotes. The bounty was five dollars for each skin. Traveling in a canvas-covered wolfer's wagon pulled by two horses, and using two large wolfhounds as trackers, he had sought out his quarry. Bliss had gone with him. Following her father, always at his side, she had learned first hand how to handle the problems of life and survival. She had slept in a tent, survived weather that was forty degrees below zero, cut holes in the ice to get water, held off snarling animals, and she had churned butter, gathered eggs, skinned coyotes, and broken her own horse.

Her father had started "hunting" wanted men quite by accident when a ruthless man on the run had stumbled into their camp. In the stranger's attempt to kill her father, there had been a struggle for the gun. A shot. One man fell dead—but not her father. Loading the man onto a wagon, Oakwood Harrison had taken him into town, only to find there was a price of a hundred dollars on the man's head. That had added a new dimension to his bounty-hunting. One that had proved to be very lucrative at times and hopefully would again, for his daughter.

"Travis La Mont. . . ." It had been a while since

there had been such a large reward offered. Bliss had existed on the frugal payment offered for coyotes and wolves. She couldn't pass up this chance. "What do you think, Boru? Bard? Can we catch him?" As if to say yes the Irish wolfhounds beside her barked. Taking one last look at the poster, Bliss folded it in quarters, then stuck it in her belt.

"I think so too." Bard and Boru were more than just companions. Wolfhounds had been found to be the best dogs for bounty-hunting. Yep, she'd locate La Mont all right and when she did she'd haul him back to town for that reward money. Years of tagging along after her father had made her cunning, had sharpened her wits. She knew all the whys and wherefores of gunfighters and those wanted by the law. If this Travis La Mont had any idea of what was good for him, he'd watch out.

Getting up from the bed of dried leaves on which she had sprawled, she brushed off her canvas pants and tucked in her shirt. A wide-brimmed Stetson lay on the ground near her booted feet, and she bent over to pick it up. Before she plopped it on her head, however, she ran her fingers through her red hair. Silken fire her father had called it. A damned nuisance at times, she thought, tucking the braids under the hat where they wouldn't be a bother.

Bliss was used to the life of a Gypsy, making a home anywhere her bounty-hunting led her. She loved the romance and adventure of the outdoor life, the clear blue rivers, wide and wonderful, and the boundless land that stretched for miles and miles. Though the wagon she traveled in was crude and simple, she was proud of her strength and of her ability to survive without luxuries. Still, she wasn't averse to buying a few new things.

There was only one foreseeable problem. That damned posse. From the ridge where she was camped, Bliss had watched them chase the wanted man, had heard their shouts. All the while she had kept her fingers crossed, hoping they wouldn't nab him. Now, as the thunder of hoofbeats announced the posse's return, she anxiously counted the number of riders. Ten. Same number that had ridden by before.

"Nope."

They hadn't gotten him, but then she hadn't supposed they would. Whatever else his sins might have been, Travis La Mont was quite a horseman. She had to give him that. He'd sent the marshal's men on a merry ride. But she wasn't one of those fools. She'd go it alone and collect all the money for herself. That wily coyote of an outlaw might be able to lead the posse on a merry chase, but he wouldn't be so lucky with her. She was going to find him! She had only been waiting for the marshal's men to retreat before going in pursuit. The time had come to get going.

Bliss kicked dirt on the campfire, put the wolfhounds in the wagon so they wouldn't follow, then with long measured strides walked toward the wagon. It was going to rain. The thunder and lightning promised a severe storm. Putting on a rain poncho, she moved to the horses, tethering one beneath a tree, saddling up the other. She swung herself up into the saddle of her brown mare. Grasping the horse's bridle, she leaned over and crooned into Chocolate's twitching ear.

"Are you ready for some fun?" Ever so gently she touched the animal's gleaming, dark brown hide with her heels. "Then let's go."

Spiritedly Chocolate reared up on her hind legs, then plunged across the river. Bliss thought it to be great sport as she rode at breakneck speed, in hot pursuit of that bank robber. Wherever her father was, hopefully looking down from heaven and not up from that other place, he'd be proud of her. Female or not, she had always been said to be "a chip off the old block." Well, years of being at her father's side made her a match for any wanted man.

Oakwood Harrison had trained her well, so it didn't take her long to figure out which way that scoundrel had gone. No longer north. Now he was headed south. According to the tracks he had left, he was on foot. For some reason he had abandoned his horse. Most likely he had used that old Indian trick of divide and conquer, setting the pursuers after his mount while he gleefully ran in the opposite direction.

It was dark, getting even darker as clouds blocked the sun. That made tracking harder than it might have been in the sunlight, but Bliss managed to discover telltale signs of which way her quarry had gone. She could tell by the churning of the water in a nearly dry creek that someone or something had recently disturbed the placid flow. Several rocks had been overturned and a button was imbedded in the dry sandy soil.

"Yep, he was here!" She would bet her last dollar on that fact. He'd been in this vicinity not long before she had arrived. Probably looking for somewhere to get out of the rain that was even now sprinkling down. It looked as if a torrent was going to be unleashed at any moment, though, so he wouldn't be able to travel too much farther.

Bliss looked up to see that an eagle was circling the sky, likewise looking for a safe roost away from the rain. He finally settled down upon a large jagged rock, near the opening of an old abandoned mine tunnel. It was not too far away. Just up the hill a short distance.

"That's it! That's where he'll go," she whispered to herself. Maybe with a little luck she could catch up with him before he was safely sheltered inside. If not she'd get him anyway. Every inch of that tunnel was well known to her, for she had explored it time and again with her father. Yep, she'd get him all right. Bliss could already feel that reward money jingling in her pocket. Enough to ease the poverty she had experienced since her father's death. Moving silently, pistol cocked and ready, she headed toward the tunnel.

Chapter Three

Rain fell from the sky with a fury that gave the saying "raining cats and dogs" new meaning for Travis as he scurried along. The damned storm seemed to rend the very heavens, sloshing bucketsful of water on the earth below. Rivulets ran down Travis' hair to his face. Drops of rain glistened on his thick dark brows and lashes, and he reached up to brush them away. It was going to be a miserable night, particularly without his coat to keep him warm. Already he was shivering.

The wind howled about him, pelting his face, soaking him to the skin. "G-g-got to f-f-find some sh-sh-shelter," he said to himself, trying hard to keep his teeth from chattering. Oh, what he wouldn't have given to bask in the warmth of a fire, but it was out of the question. That posse might still be out there. He couldn't take the chance of alerting them to his whereabouts. But drat it all, he didn't want to catch pneumonia!

Darting from tree to tree, Travis sought a place to

24

wait out the storm, feeling all the more miserable as it raged on. There wasn't an inch of him that wasn't wet; not even the largest tree gave him much protection. He was just about to give up, to succumb to his ill luck when he spied the sign—The Red Sign Mine. By the looks of it abandoned. And where there was a mine, there were tunnels.

"The answer to my prayers!" With a muffled shout of glee, Travis hurried to the opening. Remembering that where there were tunnels, there were also shafts—and therefore danger—he was cautious as he entered. He hadn't escaped that posse to go plunging to his death. "Easy. Easy."

Reaching into his pocket, he found matches, but when he tried to light them he realized to his annoyance that they were wet. He'd just have to get used to the darkness and inch his way along until he found a comfortable place to settle down for the night. Fumbling along, testing each and every step to make certain there was solid ground beneath him, Travis made his way into the black, musty tunnel. Stopping when he found a spot just far enough away from the entrance to give him shelter from the wind, he found it to be a surprisingly comfortable area, not exactly warm but at least dry.

"Got to get out of these wet clothes," Travis murmured, stripping off boots, socks, shirt, trousers and underwear. Briskly he rubbed himself down, somehow managing to dry himself. Strangely enough he was more comfortable naked than he had been in his wet clothes. Once again he regretted that the matches were no good to him, but when he considered all that had happened since that morning he counted himself a very lucky man. He'd escaped with his life, at least for the time being.

Wringing out his garments one by one, and emptying the rainwater out of his boots, he thought about the matter of his being a wanted man. He came to the same conclusion again and again. He'd been framed, but for what reason? To the best of his knowledge he felt it just had to have something to do with the photograph he'd taken, and therein lay his only chance for clearing his name. He had to go back and retrieve his camera from its hiding place in the stable, then develop that picture and take it from there.

Go back! It sure as hell wasn't something he was looking forward to, especially after all that had happened, yet it undoubtedly was the last thing they would expect him to do. First, however, he'd have to hightail it to another town, get a horse, and outfit himself with a new wardrobe and some other accessories that would change his appearance. Spectacles perhaps. A new hat. And he'd find himself a lawyer, one with a genuine law degree and not some bogus certificate. An intelligent man who would be able to help him clear his good name.

Travis gave detailed thought to this plan as he laid out his garments to dry, but his optimism gave way to reality the longer he contemplated the matter. First and foremost he was without a horse, and unless he intended to capture a deer and ride it all the way to Helena, he was faced with the necessity of walking at least thirty miles. The alternative was to stay put. Hide out here? That was just as unpleasant an alternative. He had no food, and although he had learned to be a mediocre hunter he wasn't at all fond of raw meat and berries. The only answer seemed to be stealing a horse, that is if anyone ever came way out here.

"What a hell of a fix!" He was tired of even thinking about it.

Reaching up, Travis combed his long fingers through his dark brown hair. He had a roaring headache, brought on no doubt by that bone-jarring ride. Every muscle in his body ached, and he was dead tired. To add to his discomfort hunger was gnawing at his belly, and he had no way of satisfying it. Even so, Travis' sense of humor overtook him and he threw back his head and laughed, chuckling all the more as the sound of his mirth echoed in the tunnel.

"If the folks back home could see me now . . ." Here he was, a celebrated journalist, standing naked as a jaybird while he hid out from a posse in an old abandoned mine. An innocent man wanted by the law. Why, the entire story seemed a fabrication. Ludicrous. Unfortunately it was true. That reminder quickly silenced Travis' laughter.

Hoofbeats! Suddenly all his senses were alive as he paused to listen. He could have sworn he heard something outside the tunnel. Slowly reaching for his pistol, he flattened himself against the wall of the tunnel. If it was one of the marshal's men he'd soon let them know he would not be taken unaware. Hardly daring to breathe, he waited for what seemed a tediously long time.

"Your imagination, La Mont. You're hearing things." The truth was it was so quiet he could hear his heart beat.

Travis remained on alert for a few moments longer, then with a shrug settled himself down for what he knew was going to be a long, uncomfortable night. Finding an old length of canvas, he rolled himself within it as if it were a sleeping bag, stashing his gun inside for protection. Though his accommodations weren't as lavish as a hotel's, he was surprisingly comfortable. Closing his eyes, Travis tried to ignore his grumbling stomach as he counted sheep. By the two-hundredth he had drifted off, oblivious to the young woman who stood at the opening listening to his snores.

"Sleeping as peacefully as if he hadn't a trouble in the world," Bliss mumbled beneath her breath. "Well, he's in for a rude awakening." Lighting the small lantern that she always had tied to her saddle she stealthily moved forward. "There he is!" Snuggled up in the tarpaulin, the wanted man reminded Bliss of a caterpillar in its cocoon.

Setting the lantern down on a rock, she clutched her pistol with one hand, her lasso with the other. She'd tie him up right away, of course. There was no reason to take chances with such a big bruiser. Desperate men were dangerous. She carefully cocked her pistol, pointed it at the slumbering figure, then nudged him to wakefulness with the toe of her boot.

"Open your eyes, mister."

Travis was rudely jolted from sleep by something hard pressing into his side. "What the . . . ?" Startled, he bolted to his feet, forgetting in his haste that he was completely unclothed. He found himself looking into the bluest eyes he had ever seen. Thickly lashed, they were beautiful. His stunned gaze also took in the disheveled mass of flaming hair that tumbled from beneath the hat, the enchanting face that peered at him from beneath the wide brim.

"A woman!" He was immensely relieved. His capturer was a pretty girl and not one of the marshal's louts.

Bliss noted that he was surprised but not at all fearful. In fact, seeing a woman standing in front of him brought forth a wide grin. "But not just any damn female, buster! You've just been captured by a bounty hunter. R. B. Harrison by name." She stood with her legs apart, her revolver pointed straight at his heart. "The poster says dead or alive. If I were you I'd say my prayers." She cocked the trigger to punctuate her words. If that didn't put the fear of God into him, she didn't know what would.

Travis' smile faltered. He winced. Though beautiful, those eyes of hers were unrelenting. "Believe me, lady, I'm saying them." And he was.

The woman was staring at him, and it was in that moment Travis remembered he had just jumped up, forgetting he was completely naked. His canvas cocoon lay in a helpless heap at his feet. Bending down, he was anxious to retrieve it to cover his nakedness, but she would have none of that.

"Oh, no you don't," she said, kicking the canvas aside. "I've seen naked men before. I'm not interested in your body but whether or not you have any concealed weapons beneath that canvas."

"Weapons?" My God, he thought. This woman is unbelievable. She really means business.

"Just keep your hands up and don't make any false moves." Her tone was commanding.

There was no way of avoiding it. He had to do as she asked. His palms were sweaty. His mouth felt dry. But all he could do was wait. He didn't want to take a chance on being shot. While she turned the pockets of his wet clothes inside out, he just stood by and watched. After what seemed a very long time, she completed her search, confiscating his Colt .45, his ammunition, two knives and his rifle.

"There." Bliss felt secure, knowing she now had him totally at her mercy. She took time to appreciate the sight presented to her. A handsome man. The posters didn't do him justice. And his body was every bit as good as the face. A big man, he had wide shoulders and lean hips. His arms and chest were well muscled. Black hair covered his broad chest. "Well, well, what do we have here? I've heard of men being caught with their pants down, but this is ridiculous." Making light of the situation, she threw back her head and laughed.

Travis' face grew red at the sound of her merriment. He wasn't used to being humiliated, and he didn't like it one damn bit. "May I retrieve my covering?" he asked, trying to reclaim his dignity.

"Not just yet." Looking at the helpless man before her, Bliss made the most of the situation. She was feeling quite good about putting him in an uncomfortable position. Men usually did the ogling. She wondered how he liked having the shoe on the other foot.

Without averting her eyes, she boldly appraised him, seeing enough to know that he was well

30

endowed. Quite a specimen of male perfection in fact. But she wouldn't feed his ego. "Hmmmm . . ." She snorted. Picking up the canvas, she thrust it at him. "Here you go. I'll let you cover up your shortcomings."

The man pulled the canvas covering tightly around his unclothed body, looking sheepish the whole while. But even though he appeared to be vulnerable, she could not trust him. She didn't know that he wouldn't try something daring, like bolting through the mine's entrance to freedom. Or he might push her to the ground and try to wrest away her gun. She needed to make him respect her. Needed to make him properly afraid.

"Just to make certain you don't get any ideas of escaping . . ." Bliss placed the barrel of the gun to his head.

"For God's sake, ma'am!" He could feel the cold, hard steel pressed against his temple. All it would take to blow his brains out was one squeeze of the trigger.

Now he was afraid! She pushed the barrel of the pistol even harder against his head. He didn't move an inch. "Yeah, that's right. If you know what's good for you, you'll be a real good boy!" He was afraid of her now. So much the better. "Just stay as still as a statue! Don't move a muscle."

"Move? Hell, I wouldn't even breathe if I didn't have to." Travis eyed her with grudging admiration. She was a brave one to come barging in here. He took note of the way she held the Colt in her hands, with a practiced ease that drew his unwilling admiration. This young woman knew what she was doing.

31

"Put your hands together." When he didn't obey at first Bliss said curtly, "Do as I say!"

"Okay. Okay." Those blue eyes were spitting anger at him. He had never had a problem charming the fairer sex, therefore he had thought he would soon be free. Now he was not so certain.

Quickly Bliss secured the rope around his hands.

"You're making a big mistake!" In his own defense, Travis rattled off the story of just what had happened to him. "I'm not an outlaw. I'm as law-abiding as they come."

"They all say that!" Bliss laughed sarcastically. "I'll bet there hasn't been a wanted man alive that has actually admitted to being a low-down, ornery bastard." She remembered the outlaws she and her father had hunted. They had all said the same thing. Every one of them.

Travis tried to remain calm. Anger would only make the situation worse, he knew. "No, I don't imagine so, but the difference is I *am* innocent."

Again Bliss laughed, this time sarcastically. "I don't believe that for a minute." From under the shadow of her hat, blue eyes stared straight into brown ones. "The poster had your picture on it— and your name too."

"Then I guess it's up to me to convince you," Travis answered. The truth of the matter was that this whole episode was getting stranger and stranger. Trying to keep his calm, he said as politely as he could, "Now, now, ma'am, there's been some kind of mistake. I know you think I'm the man who robbed the bank, I know they say I did, but it was a setup, I swear it was."

32

"A setup." She eyed him up and down, coldly. "I don't believe you."

"I'm not the one who robbed the bank. I have plenty of money on my own." He nodded toward his belongings. "And there's more in a safe-deposit box back at Silver Bow."

Bliss scoffed. She wouldn't play his game. "Trying to bribe me will do you no good. No good at all. Matter of fact if I were you I'd try to get a good night's sleep. We've got a long journey ahead of us when morning comes."

"Sleep!" Travis held back an angry retort. He knew what she meant. She wasn't just toying with him. She really did intend to take him back. Sleep. Ha! It was the last thing he intended to do. His eyes flicked over her. She looked strong despite the slender softness her curves gave promise of. Even so he was determined to best her. He'd lie awake, watch and listen. She had to sleep sometime, and when she closed her eyes he'd be upon her like a hawk after a dove.

Chapter Four

The weather had become annoyingly treacherous. Rain fell in a downpour, sloshing through the opening of the mine. Wind howled like an angry beast. Thunder boomed like cannons. In the tunnel it was cold and gloomy. As he lay huddled in the canvas tarp, Travis La Mont couldn't help thinking how much the storm outside matched his mood. But it didn't seem to disturb the bounty-hunting woman. Oh, no. Adding to his frustration was the fact that she was cheerful. She even whistled a tune as she draped his garments over some rocks to dry.

"You told me to get some sleep. How can I if you keep up that infernal noise," he grumbled. It was annoying that instead of quickly falling into a deep slumber so that he could pounce, she seemed excessively energetic.

Setting her hat at exactly the angle she wanted, back on her head, Bliss walked around him, clicking her tongue. "Now, now, now. Kinda peevish, aren't we?"

He looked her right in the eye. "That's putting it mildly, lady."

Her look of sympathy was mocking. "Tell me what's wrong?"

"For starters I'm cold and hungry." As if to corroborate what he said, his stomach chose this time to growl. Loudly.

"Hungry?" To tell the truth so was she. Even so, she toyed with him. It would be well to keep him in his place. Too many men had tried to take advantage of her since her father had died. Now she was taking it all out on him. She wanted the satisfaction of making a man squirm. "So what if you are?"

Ordinarily Travis would have retorted with a caustic remark, but the truth was, he suddenly saw a chance for escape. She'd have to untie his hands while he ate, and when she did he'd lunge at her. The thought made him smile as he said politely, "Just hoping you had at least a little compassion, miss. After all you wouldn't want me to be weak as a kitten come morning, now would you? It might complicate the matter of your bringing me in."

"It might." Bliss shrugged her shoulders. Once she had been a lighthearted naive girl. But no more. Hard times had toughened her. Still, being strong was one thing, being heartless was another. "I have some coffee, hardtack and beef jerky with me. It will have to do."

"Right now it sounds like a feast to me." He couldn't help noticing again how pretty she was. Too bad she was such a bitch. What had happened to completely strip her of any softness?

Travis remained silent for the moment, but his

35

eyes seemed to be looking straight through her to her very soul. And that made Bliss very nervous.

"There's a mighty handsome reward for you, so I don't intend to let my guard down," she felt the need to say.

"I wasn't expecting that you would," Travis answered sourly. He had always been so sure of himself. Tough under pressure and able to handle any problem. Now he realized he was going to have a terrible time trying to keep up his image of himself. She was a strong, smart woman who, he was coming to learn, might just be a match for him.

In the tunnel were a few dry branches, leaves and enough debris to start a fire. Bliss had some matches with her, and she built a steadily burning blaze. Soon the tunnel was not only well lighted, it was also warm and cozy. Holding up her rifle, she slowly backed toward the mouth, where her horse was tethered. Keeping her eye on Travis all the while, she fumbled in her saddlebags for the necessary supplies.

"I always come prepared. My father taught me that." Just like he taught me so many other things, Bliss thought, feeling a stab of pain. Dear God, how she missed him!

"Then at this moment I thank your father," Travis retorted, watching as she filled a pot with water from her canteen, measured out some coffee, then put the tin utensil over the fire. The liquid made a sputtering sound as it came to a boil. "I don't know when the aroma of freshly brewed coffee has smelled so tantalizing."

Bliss didn't answer. She was staring at her father's cup, turning it over and over in her hand, remembering the last time he had used it. They had been sitting around an open campfire, talking and laughing. Little had she known that the next day he'd be taken from her. Shot in the back by a man just like this one. The memory hardened her heart.

"So what made you decide to become a bounty hunter, a fine-looking woman like you?" Travis asked, trying to start a conversation. If he was going to be sequestered he might as well make the best of a bad situation. Besides, maybe he could find out something that could be useful in securing his freedom.

"A fine-looking woman like me," Bliss mimicked, instantly putting up her guard against his flattery. "I became a bounty hunter to take the pleasure of cornering varmints like you and seeing them brought to justice."

Her answer stopped him cold. She wasn't going to succumb to any compliments, that was obvious. He tried another approach. "Justice? If you ask me you've appointed yourself as judge and jury. Doesn't it ever bother you that you just might be sending innocent men to their deaths?"

"Innocent?" Bliss laughed sarcastically. "If they were innocent there wouldn't be a bounty on their heads." Taking the coffeepot from the fire she filled her father's tin cup, then her own and stared at them for a long moment. Oh, how she wished she could catch up with the man who'd shot him. But even if she did, could that bring her father back? No. It was a sad truth she'd have to get accustomed to.

"I'm innocent, and there's a bounty on *me.*" Travis clenched his jaw. He had to try again to make her believe him. "If you take me back there you'll be making a dastardly mistake."

Bliss raised her head. "I'll be making a mistake if I don't. I can use two hundred dollars, mister." It was a painful truth. The past few weeks had been particularly miserable. All she'd had were her horses, dogs, wagon, a few meager supplies and the clothes on her back.

She sounded so blasé about it. As if she could just forget that what she was doing would most likely mean his life. "Blood money!" His tone was accusatory.

"If you are trying to make me feel guilty, you can just save your breath. I don't." Bliss refused to talk about the matter. She was going to do what she was going to do, and that was that!

Shadows danced upon the wall. The inside of the tunnel suddenly looked eerie, unnerving. The anger on the wanted man's face gave him a demonic look as shadows danced over his nose and chin. Well, she wasn't afraid. Not of him. Not of any man. Still, she was cautious as she moved to within an arm's length of Travis.

"Aren't you going to untie me so I can eat?" he asked, trying to suppress his hostility. He had just taken it for granted that she would; that was why he was so surprised when she shook her head.

"No!" She squinted her eyes as she put her face down to his. "You see, I can read your mind." She knew what she would do if she were in his place. As soon as her hands were free she'd take the cup of hot coffee, smile sweetly, and fling it in his face. It would then only take a minute to wrestle away the gun, turning captive into captor.

"No?" He was infuriated. "Then how in the hell am I going to eat?"

"I'll feed you," she answered bluntly.

"Feed me?" Travis was taken aback. "Oh, no." He was having none of that. He'd starve first. Turning his back on her, he curled up into a ball and closed his eyes, but the sound of her chewing was unsettling. Particularly so when his stomach was a gnawing reminder of what it was he wanted. Only stubborness kept him from giving in.

"Sure you don't want a bite?" Despite her resolve Bliss felt a small measure of sympathy. Even an animal deserved to be fed. "At least have a sip of coffee." Coming closer, she held out the cup.

Travis turned over on his side, only to find himself staring directly at the well-rounded breasts just a few inches from his face. A most tempting part of a woman's anatomy, particularly when they were just the right size. He wondered if they would be as soft to the touch as they looked, then shook his head to clear it of such a thought. Under different circumstances this might have been an extremely provocative situation, but not when a man faced such serious consequences. He pulled back.

"I told you, no. I don't want anything!" His pride wouldn't allow him to give in, even for a minute.

"Then have it your way." She'd offered, he'd rejected and that was that. Her obligation was ended. "Guess I'll bed down for the night." Pulling off her boots, she placed one foot upon a nearby rock, giving Travis a look at the slimmest ankle he had ever seen.

Just then a luminous burst of lightning lit up the entrance to the tunnel and a roll of thunder made the entire hillside vibrate. Tomorrow they would be lucky if they could make it down the slippery rain-soaked slope, Bliss knew. She scowled. How long would they be in here? She didn't want to be cooped up for much longer with this scoundrel. She wanted to take him back, get the money and forget about him.

"Nasty storm," Travis mumbled, more to himself than to her. The idea of traveling through the mud tomorrow wasn't a particularly pleasing one.

"A vicious storm." Not wanting him to think she was afraid of being alone with him, she purposefully formed her lips into a bold grin. "Don't look so grumpy. At least you're in here and not out there," she exclaimed. Seeing him shiver, she was reminded of his state of undress. His garments would dry much quicker if they were laid out by the fire. Bending over to pick them up, she moved them to a large rock closer to the flames.

"Ah yes, we're in here!" At the moment it was difficult for him to feel very lucky. He was naked beneath the canvas, hungry and tired as hell. Even worse was the future that loomed before him.

Chapter Five

Despite the fire steadily burning, the mine tunnel was chilly and damp. A wind whispered through the night, and even wrapped in the canvas, Travis was cold. So cold. The dampness and the chill were inescapable. They invaded his distrubing dreams.

He was riding through a storm, naked, trying to escape the marauding group chasing after him. They were shooting at him, calling his name as if he were an evil thing, threatening to kill him. But he'd get away! He'd leave them far behind.

"Bastards! Eat my dust!" He put his heels to the horse's flank, galloping down the ridge. But the wind, the rain, pushed him back. As if he were on a treadmill he kept his horse moving, but stayed in one place. Looking over his shoulder, he cried out as he saw that they were gaining on him. Then they were pulling him off his horse, dragging him to the ground. There was going to be a hanging. His.

"No, no, you are wrong! I have done nothing to be treated this way. I didn't . . . didn't . . ." But it was no use. Ruthlessly his hands were tied behind his back. He could feel the rope choking him. "No!" he called out again and again.

Hearing his rasping cries, Bliss hastened to his side and stared down into his face. Was he really having a nightmare or merely creating a scene? Was this a trick of some kind, or was he in the throes of a deep troubled sleep. "Hush," she chided, leaning over him. But seeing the way his closed lids were twitching, she decided he was dreaming, not playacting. She could see his lips move, but no sound escaped them.

Bliss looked at him as he slept and felt just a twinge of guilt at the way she had treated him. Perhaps he was right about her being judge and jury. Certainly in her mind she had already convicted him. But what if he was telling the truth? What then? The way he espoused his innocence was convincing. He was an able talker.

She had been surrounded by rough men, some of whom were positively distasteful, their mental capacity limited to woodchopping, their conversation diminished by whiskey-drinking and spitting chewing tobacco. Since her father's death she had long desired a conversation with someone who could meet her intellectual and emotional capacity. A gentleman. A man just like this one.

Looking down at the wanted man's face, reposed in sleep, she had a chance to really study him. Hair as dark as a pair of her father's best boots covered his head in thick abundance. His forehead was broad, his cheekbones high. The planes and angles of his face were perfect. Even his nose was straight, high bridged, and like the rest of him without a flaw. As to his mouth, the lower lip was slightly fuller than the upper, making it extremely enticing. Certainly he was handsome.

"And you're a damned fool!" she scolded beneath her breath, drawing back with a start. As if only ugly men were outlaws. Hell, lots of good-looking men had given themselves up to a life of crime. This man wouldn't be the only one. Well, this was one time when handsomeness wouldn't get him by. As if to reaffirm her stand, Bliss retreated to her side of the tunnel. Taking out the wanted poster, she stared at it for a long, long time.

The fire crackled and sputtered. Clouds of gray smoke curled upward. Blinking her eyes, Bliss fought hard to remain awake, but it was a losing battle. She had to get some sleep. She just had to. What shape would she be in without it?

Her eyes strayed to Travis La Mont, the only reason for her hesitation. What could he do? He could not escape, she had him securely tied. And if he did would he get very far on such a night? The steady pound of rain gave proof that it was a horrible storm.

"Nnnooo." Somehow she just didn't want to chance it. Thus she paced up and down, back and forth, this way and that, trying to keep awake.

At last, when an uncontrollable shiver passed through her body, when her brain felt as foggy as cotton, when her head kept nodding and her eyes closed to slits, she knew she had to give in. Just for safety, however, she removed the shells from the rifle she had confiscated from him. Then, to test him, she left it where he could see it. Her own trusty Remington would remain at her side, ready to be fired at the slightest provocation.

These precautions taken, she spread her blanket, settled down on the ground close to the fire, pulled her hat down over her eyes and relaxed for the first time that night. She'd catch a few winks, just enough to keep her strength up for the long trek ahead, she thought as she closed her eyes and drifted off.

Something, the silence perhaps, awakened Travis. The fire had burned low, but the light reflecting off the barrel of a rifle caught his eye. A gun! A chance for escape! So, she wasn't such an inescapable guardian after all. The rifle was well within reach, but first he had to rid himself of the ropes that kept him tightly secured.

Fumbling around on the ground behind him Travis searched desperately for something to cut his bonds. At last he came up with what he needed. A jagged rock that was almost as sharp as a knife. Slowly he maneuvered it so that it was touching the rope at his wrists. Moving them up and down in a sawing motion, he worked patiently until his hands were free. It was easy after that to remove his ankle bindings.

"You have a surprise waiting for you, Miss Bounty Hunter," he muttered. It was a victory he knew he would relish, considering the way she'd acted.

Travis' eyes darted to where his garments lay. Did he dare take the time to put his pants on? After the way she'd humiliated him it wasn't to his liking to be under her scrutiny once more, especially in the raw, yet he had to admit he couldn't take the chance now. He might make too much noise and spoil his chance. First the gun and then his clothes.

Ignoring his nakedness, he moved slowly, cautiously, crawling on his hands and knees toward his captor. Riveting his eyes on the rise and fall of her chest, he crept closer and closer, becoming as still as a statue when he saw her hand move. Damn! She was going to wake up, but no, she was merely brushing at her face. Her soft sigh gave proof that she was immersed in slumber.

"That's a good girl—get your beauty sleep." Ignoring the discomfort of the gritty ground, Travis slithered along on his stomach, inching his way toward the rifle. Stretching out his arm, he felt jubilant as his fingers closed around the cold steel of the barrel. Ha, he had her now. Wouldn't she be surprised to see that the worm had turned in his favor.

Grabbing his rifle, he took a deep breath. Rising to his knees, he let out a sigh of relief. So far, so good. Standing up, he carefully pointed the rifle, a smile upon his lips. He'd have a bit of fun taunting her, and then he'd make her listen to reason. Now that the gun was pointed her way, she'd have to hear him out. He was innocent; that was all there was to it.

Feeling overly bold when she didn't wake up with a start, he held out the rifle and, with the tip of the barrel, sent his captor's hat tumbling to the ground. With his finger firmly on the trigger, he loudly cleared his throat.

"Ahem!" For a woman who bragged about being

so alert, she slept as soundly as the dead. Travis cleared his throat again, feeling a deep satisfaction when she opened her eyes. At first they exchanged a series of glances. His skin became flushed. Perspiration made his hair cling to his forehead. He found himself wishing desperately that he wasn't in the nude. It was difficult to feel self-assured when you were naked as a jaybird.

"Ahem, yourself." Bliss stared him down, clutching her own gun tightly.

Travis was puzzled by her lack of fear. "Maybe you don't think I'll shoot. But I will—before you have time to take aim. Now be a good girl and throw me your gun."

"Give you my gun?" So, he had nibbled at the bait, proving he was sneaky. For just a moment she felt a stab of disappointment, but quickly she recovered her resolve. "I'd see you in hell first!"

Raising her weapon, Bliss took aim and purposely fired over his head. The bullet whizzed by. There was a whistling in his ears.

"The next one will be right between your eyes." And by God, she meant it.

Though Travis had no liking for shooting a woman, this was a matter of life or death, so he pulled the rifle's trigger. The moment he heard the impotent click, he knew he'd been tricked.

"The wanted poster says 'dead or alive,' mister. *Dead* or alive! The next time you pull a trick like this I won't aim so high." The flash of fire in her eyes told Travis clearly that she meant it. Bliss took his garments from the rock and, finding them dry enough, flung them at the ground near his feet. "Put these on." She stood watching as he picked them up.

"Aren't you going to at least turn your back while I get dressed?"

She sent him a quick assessing glance that piqued his masculine pride. Suddenly the whole situation made him feel ridiculous. "Why, you don't have anything I haven't seen before. Besides, if you think I'd turn my back on you even for a moment after what you just tried, you have another thought coming."

With an oath Travis threw the rifle to the floor of the tunnel, then hurriedly pulled on his clothes. Of all the women in the world, why did he have to meet up with this one? He felt stupid, humiliated at not having second-guessed her, and just downright foolish. Was it any wonder he was sullen as she tied his hands again?

Chapter Six

To say that he spent a miserable night was an understatement. Worse yet, as dawn came Travis realized his ordeal was just beginning. Before he even had a chance to open his eyes he heard a husky feminine voice ordering loudly, "Enough shut-eye, mister. Up and at 'em."

That was easier said than done. Travis had lain all night in a cramped position, his hands tied firmly behind his back. He was stiff and ached in every joint. As he carefully lifted himself up to lean on one elbow, he moved slowly. His hands were numb. It took several minutes of clenching and unclenching his fists to bring back feeling into them.

"Come on, we've got to hurry! We've got to make as much distance as we can while the sun is out."

"Hurry?" Travis laughed sarcastically. The last thing on earth he wanted to do was hurry to his doom. At least here, even if he was holed up with Medusa, he was safe from the posse.

"Up! Up!" Ignoring his plea that he was practically starving, she jabbed the barrel of the rifle into his ribs. "You had your chance last night. This morning we don't have time to dawdle."

"Can't I at least have a cup of coffee?" Travis nodded to where the tin pot was balanced over the fire. If it had smelled good last night, it smelled even better now.

She showed a moment of hesitation, brought on by distrust; then with a shrug she capitulated. "I suppose it wouldn't hurt. As long as you're a good boy."

Pouring the dark liquid into a cup, she blew on it to aid it in cooling a bit. Then, watching him warily all the while, she held the cup to his lips. It was warm but not hot. The best thing Travis had ever tasted, at least at that moment. Eagerly he gulped it down.

"Easy. Don't drown yourself!" Bliss pulled the tin cup away. "You're not quite as proud this morning, I'd say." She reached in her pocket and came up with a dried biscuit. Hard as a rock but good nonetheless. Putting it to his mouth she watched as he took a large bite, then another and another. After the third such biscuit she realized he had a big appetite.

Travis washed the fourth biscuit down with another cup of coffee, licking the remainder off with his tongue. He was not so remiss in his manners that he did not remember to say thank you.

She didn't respond, and he sensed that something was troubling her, though what he didn't know. But her mood didn't keep her from moving quickly about in the tunnel, gathering up her belongings. All too soon they were ready to travel.

"Come on!" Pointing the gun directly at his back,

49

she gestured for him to walk toward the entrance. Travis didn't give her any back talk. If he wanted to get out of this nightmare with a whole skin, it would behoove him to do exactly as she asked. Meanwhile he would hope against hope that he'd get a chance to break away before they arrived at their destination.

It was warm outside, belying the fact that clouds had shrouded the sky but a few hours before, but it was slippery. Travis slid warily along, falling several times in his downward climb. As he stumbled along he thought to himself how much for granted a man took his arms and hands. Now that he was virtually without the use of them—to break a fall, to grasp and to cling—he felt clumsy. Off balance. Powerless. Useless.

Behind Travis the female bounty hunter kept pace, leading her horse carefully down over the ridge. He darted a quick look sideways only to find that her eyes, visible beneath the brim of her Stetson hat, were steadily trained upon him. They were regarding him without any sign of compassion.

Travis had been in danger before, but never in a situation where one false move could cost him his life. Did he doubt that she would shoot him if he tried to get away? Not for a minute. She was as strong minded a woman as he had ever come across, tough and relentless in her efforts to take him in for the reward.

"All right, mister, stop right there." Travis paused and turned his head, relieved to see her pull herself up into the saddle. But while she intended to ride, that luxury was not to be afforded him. Instead he was made to walk ahead of her, straining at the length of rope she tied securely to the saddle horn.

"I feel like a dog on a leash!"Travis quipped. And he did. Being trussed up like this had stripped him of his last shred of dignity.

It was a grueling journey, stumbling over rocks, slipping in the mud, sloshing through puddles. Left, right, left, right—he kept putting one foot in front of the other.

"By the way," she said nonchalantly, "just what was it you did? To put a price on your head, I mean."

Travis paused in midstride. "I was supposed to have masterminded the bank robbery and to have shot and killed a man in the process." His look was earnestness itself. "But I didn't."

"No doubt you were just in the wrong place at the wrong time, is that so?" Despite the hostility in her tone she found herself suddenly curious. He intrigued her. He just wasn't the kind of man one met every day.

Travis shouted, his nerves already stretched as taut as a horse's saddle cinch. "Yes, that's so!" He couldn't help wondering what might have happened if he had been an hour earlier in his picture-taking or a half-hour later.

She hadn't found out the details and wanted to know more. "Just why were you there?" She hid her budding interest in him behind sarcasm. "Out for a morning stroll?"

"I'm a photographer and newspaper reporter," Travis answered truthfully. "I was taking a picture of the bank."

"You were what?" Bliss threw back her head and laughed. Of all the excuses she had ever heard that one was the damnedest.

Travis cringed under her disdain. "I said I'm a newspaperman. I was standing in front of the bank to take its picture. To send to my newspaper back East. The readers are very interested in anything that has to do with the 'rugged' West and all." He stared her down. "I witnessed the robbery, but I didn't take part in it."

"Uh-huh." She didn't believe him for a moment. It was a ploy. A sympathy pitch. But then, how many men would admit their guilt. "Better tell me another lie before that one gets cold."

"It's true!" Damn the woman. What did she want him to do, write his innocence in blood?

Bliss motioned for him to continue walking. "If I were you I'd be thinking up a much better alibi before we get back to town. That one will get you hung for sure." What did he take her for, a simpleton? Taking pictures indeed. And for just one moment there she had nearly been tempted to believe this might have been a case of mistaken identity.

The very mention of hanging brought a sick feeling to his guts. Of all the ways for a man to die that was one of the worst. A terrible way to end his brilliant career. "I didn't rob the bank, and I didn't kill anyone. I'm not that kind of man."

"Oh, of course not." Her sarcastic jibe put a quick end to the conversation.

Travis jerked his eyes back to the pathway from time to time as he walked along, feeling totally helpless for the first time in his life. This woman, though smaller by far than he, might well be the death of him. Of course, there was always the chance that she was bluffing, that she wouldn't really shoot him down, but he didn't think so. She seemed frighteningly determined. What's more, her constant reminder that he was worth just as much dead as alive was chillingly true. Though it seemed to him a most barbaric way to handle the law, that was how things were done in states and territories west of the Missouri River.

I won't think about it! Travis vowed. A lot can happen between here and the town. To soothe his burgeoning apprehension he forced himself to concentrate on the scenery as he trudged along. It was an area that had a subtle, mysterious beauty, a land with winding rivers and large clumps of trees. The scenery defied description. This was a one-of-a-kind type of place. He wished he had his camera, so he could capture the sculpted sandstone, the huge petrified tree trunks and the clay buttes which rose tier upon tier to the sky in uncompromising grandeur in the distance.

"Quite a place, isn't it?" Bliss stated proudly, taking note of the gleam in his eye and feeling extremely proud of the land she called home. She remembered how she had felt the first time she had viewed the area her father had said would be their very own Camelot. He had even promised her that someday she'd find a Lancelot to carry her away, but she had told him she didn't want a nobleman or a knight in shining armor. "I want a strong, hard-working and interesting man just like you," she had vowed.

Bliss and her father had often been away from

civilization for three or four months at a time, hunting wolves and coyotes. And later men. It was a time when she had proved to him her grit, her courage and her acceptance of the harsh life, unusual considering her well-born background.

"It most certainly beats being stuck in a crowded city." It was, in fact, a sparsely populated wilderness with only a sprinkling of horse, cattle and sheep ranches here and there. Travis assessed it purpose-fully, wondering just how many places there were that he could hide, were he to get away. Get away? More and more that seemed just a pipe dream. Every once in a while he would look over his shoulder to see how closely she was following. She was always just behind him, her Remington resting on her thigh, ready to be fired. God, how he hated to have that infernal gun pointed at him.

Travis was a healthy, robust man who had always considered himself in the very best condition. Even so, he was not immune to blisters. They slowed him down despite her urging. At last, when he knew he couldn't walk another step, he stopped and turned around. "I can't go on."

"Can't or won't?" Bliss knew she had to stay stern. Any breakdown in the forced discipline she had initiated could spell trouble for her later.

"I'm a person, you know," he said gruffly. "A human being. I'm not a wolf or a coyote or whatever the hell other kind of creature you're used to cornering." Perhaps if he could make her think of him in a more personal way she'd lighten up at least a little.

His comment provoked a threatening gesture with

her rifle. "Don't talk, just keep walking."

Travis tried another tactic as he forced himself to keep going. The rest of the way he cajoled her, not begging for mercy but merely asking her to have an open mind. "Let me go. You're going to send an innocent man to his death," he insisted, but she turned a deaf ear. "I know. Keep walking."

He stumbled on a little farther. "What are you, a man hater or something?"

His question surprised her. "I like men all right," she answered quickly. "I loved my father."

Loved? Travis wondered why she spoke in the past tense. "Is he dead?" It seemed to make sense.

Bliss's back stiffened. "That's none of your business," she snapped. Talking about her father was too much of a private thing.

"Hmmm!" The way she said it, Travis knew he had struck a nerve. Two things he had figured out by now. Her father had been a bounty hunter—he'd gathered that from her comment that the man had taught her all she knew—and he had been killed. Quite possibly by someone he was bringing in. Was that why she was so hostile toward him? Was she vicariously punishing all wanted men for what one of them had done?

Bliss caught him staring. "My wagon is just over the hill, at the other side of the gulch. About another mile or so."

Somewhere between the mine and the gully she relented on her vow not to let him rest until they reached her wagon. Down deep inside she at least had a thimble's worth of compassion, Travis thought dryly.

Whether to treat Travis to a feast or to give him proof of her shooting ability, the young woman took aim and fired at a rabbit, hitting the poor tiny animal right between the ears. And all the while guiding her horse at a steady trot. She roasted the hare on a spit over a hastily built fire.

"Too bad I don't have any onions with me, then you'd see some fancy cooking."

Travis didn't have any complaints, he was much too grateful for the chance to sit down. Besides, the rabbit was tender, delicious and filling. In spite of himself he grinned at her as she popped a piece into his mouth. Strange that in spite of all she was putting him through he really did admire her. Found her most appealing in fact. "Too bad we didn't meet under much different circumstances," he said softly, speaking his thoughts out loud. "I wonder what might have happened then."

Bliss was aware of the glow that sparked in the depths of his eyes as she looked at him. For just a moment she was mesmerized. A fluttery, spring-loaded tension began coiling in the pit of her stomach. "I couldn't imagine," she shot back, wishing that her voice didn't sound so shaky. She was attracted to him. It was a dangerous truth she had to admit, though it galled her. She responded to her alarm by pulling violently away. "You can save your breath."

"What?" The moment was shattered.

"Save your sweet talk and your might-have-beens. It just doesn't matter." She took her ill temper out on the fire, kicking dirt on the flames.

Why was she so angry? She had the answer in an

instant. Because he was expressing what she had been thinking all along the way. Watching him walk along, scrutinizing his manly physique had made her wish for things that just couldn't be—and that was frustrating. He was the kind of man she'd always longed to meet. The kind of man who might have been able to wipe her loneliness away. What a cruel hoax fate had played, making her the hunter and him the hunted. But that was the way it was. There was no getting around it.

"It's time to go." Bliss willed her face to remain expressionless. If he even guessed she had a soft spot for him she'd be in trouble.

"Yes, ma'am." Travis eyed her up and down. For just a moment there he could have sworn she was softening just a little. He had even thought she might have a heart. But he must have imagined it. The lady was tough as nails. As he wearily put one foot in front of the other he kept telling himself to remember that.

They reached her wagon at last, a dilapidated wooden vehicle with spoked wheels and a semicircular canvas top, but before Travis even had a chance to take a good look at it, two monstrous gray animals lunged at him. Their growls, snarls and barks gave warning that they were anything but friendly.

"Bard! Boru! Down, at least for the moment." Her tone of command brought them to heel as if they were tranquil lap dogs. "I'll keep them in line for now, but I think you can guess what will happen if you aggravate them at all."

Travis could well imagine. No doubt they could

do a man real damage were she to let them loose. This was one more way she would be able to keep him captive. He had a foreboding feeling, and wondered what was going to happen next. Unfortunately he didn't have long to wonder.

"The posse." Bliss could see them in the distance. She swore under her breath. "They've come back, looking for you!"

Travis felt his heart sink all the way down to his boots. With her, he had at least stood a chance. With them, he knew he'd be a dead man far sooner than he'd planned. "Well then, I guess I'd have to be the first one to admit my goose is cooked."

"Not by a long shot, mister." A broad smile etched its way across her face. "Duck inside the wagon. Quickly now. Let me take care of this!" She wouldn't give him up, especially not to them.

Travis did exactly as she ordered. Ducking inside the wagon, he kept as quiet as possible, hoping the hammering of his heart wouldn't give him away.

Chapter Seven

Holding her rifle up, primed and ready, Bliss met the three men who rode up to her encampment. "You boys here for a social call?" she asked with feigned cordiality. "Too bad you didn't let me know ahead of time; I would have tied a bow in my hair."

"We're not coming for a visit," the boldest of the three said sharply, a squat dark-haired man with a handlebar mustache, a bulbous nose and piercing eyes set beneath very bushy eyebrows. He quickly dismounted, but before he had time to get anywhere near her, the wolfhounds went crazy, barking and snapping. It was all Bliss could do to keep Boru from biting the seat of the squatman's pants. If it was true that dogs were good judges of character—and she firmly believed that it was—then clearly this man's must leave a great deal to be desired.

"Damned dogs!" Despite his facade of bravado the man was frightened of the snarling animals. "Keep them off me, I warn you, woman, or you'll regret it."

Though she would have liked nothing better than to watch Boru take a chunk out of the pudgy little man's hide, Bliss maintained stern control over the wolfhounds. "Now, now, now fellas. I'm sure these men intend to mind their manners." She cocked one eyebrow. "Don't you?" This time it was Bard who growled and Boru that answered. A snort came from the horses tied nearby.

"You want me to shoot them beasts?" Another of the men, a tall fellow with a cadaverously thin face and long straggly blond hair, reached for his revolver.

Bliss was determined to guard her animals. "Harm one hair on my dogs' heads and I'll aim for your kneecap. I swear that I will."

"Oh, yeah?" Eyeing her up and down with an outright cockiness, the man nevertheless backed down, putting his gun back in his holster.

"That's better. I really do hate it when conversations can't be civilized." Bliss settled the dogs down, then cradled her rifle in her left arm. "Now, what brings you out my way?"

"We're looking for a man," the shorter man said, coming right to the point. "Travis La Mont by name."

"Looking for a man, huh? One who sounds like he might be a Frenchie. Is he a friend of yours?" Bliss smiled sweetly.

"Of course not! He's wanted for robbing the bank and for cold-blooded murder." The mustached man seemed excessively gruff. "Have you seen him?"

Bliss crossed her fingers as she told the lie, "I haven't seen anybody hereabouts for days and days.

That's what I like about this place. The peace and the quiet." She shifted her weight to the other foot and gave him a look that plainly said she wished he would leave so she could have her solitude back again.

"Well, even if you haven't, I don't expect you would mind if we took a look around." The third man, gray-haired, dressed all in buckskin, and even more obnoxious than the others, dismounted. His long-legged stride quickly brought him to the wagon.

"Mind?" As he walked toward the back opening, she said sharply, "Of course I mind. You're invading my privacy, and I won't stand for that." She aimed her rifle again, this time at him. "I told you I haven't seen anyone. My word should be good enough."

From where he lay upon his stomach in the wagon, Travis could hear every word. He had to respect her. She certainly knew how to handle the situation. He started to relax until he heard a man's voice. "I don't care what she says; I think she's hiding something." There was a scuffle of feet, then gunfire. Travis held his breath, feeling a rush of fear as he imagined the worst. He just didn't want anything to happen to her.

The female bounty hunter's voice calmed his misgivings. "That's just a warning! Now turn around, get back on your horses and get the hell out of here, or you'll be all the sorrier for your intrusion."

If the tone of her voice didn't scare those men then they were fools, Travis thought, having experienced her anger firsthand.

"Now settle down, gal. Don't get all riled up. We're merely doing our duty." The mustached man tried to placate her.

"Your duty. Which is?" Though she had just met these three, she didn't like any of them.

The tall man's eyes were cold and ugly as he said, "Why to string him up of course!" Of the three, Bliss knew instinctively that this one would be the most trouble. It showed in his sneer, his swagger, and the way he kept reaching for his gun.

"Just as I figured." They intended to hang him right on the spot. Not surprising, since there was something about them that hinted they were violent types. This La Mont was a wanted man, true, but she didn't like the way these boys went about things. Lynching people was what seemed to be their definition of fairness. Well, it just wasn't hers. Despite her threats to shoot him, Bliss intended to take her captive into town and hand him over to the proper authorities.

The buckskin garbed man kept glancing at the wagon. In a mock dance he'd take a step closer, then pause when Bliss did likewise, then take another step and another. When it became obvious that he could not get the jump on her, he shrugged. "You say he isn't in these parts, so I guess we'll just have to believe you." He openly leered at her. "I'm sure we could find something else to keep us amused."

"A pretty little thing like you oughta be a mite nicer to us." The first man cajoled.

"Nicer? Hell." Bliss knew what type of men these were. The kind who saw all women as being put upon the earth to soothe their egos. Well, she just wouldn't play that game. She wouldn't pretend her head was filled with little more than fluff. Nor would she be fool enough to get within their reach. She'd had to fight off enough men since her father died to know what this kind of man wanted from a woman.

"Yeah, nicer. There's a killer on the loose, and if you were to ask politely like, we just might be willing to lend our manly protection so you'll be safe," the thin man said, riding up to within only two feet of her.

"And all we'd ask in payment is one little kiss, for each of us."

"Kiss?" The oldest man said. Suggestive laughter followed.

"I'd as soon kiss a sling of polecats!"

Travis' ego was soothed somewhat. At least he wasn't the only man this young woman insulted. These men would learn that pretty or not, she was prickly as a cactus.

"Well now, boys. It seems to me we have just been insulted." The man in buckskin stared Bliss down, obviously trying one last time to intimidate her, but her eyes were unwavering. She was deadly calm. Her confidence shook him. Suddenly he had no doubt at all that were he to overstep his bounds she would take it out on his hide. It was in her voice and in her unwavering gaze, which never left his face. And considering the determined manner in which she held her gun, she looked formidable indeed.

"Believe me, mister, you'll be worse than insulted if you and the others don't get out of here and leave me in peace." Bliss put her finger on the trigger.

"You gonna let her act this way, Jake? There's

three of us and only one of—"

"Shut up!" The mustached man stood immobile for a long moment as if deciding what he wanted to do.

"There may be three of you, but I can sure blow at least one of you all the way to Kingdom Come." Bliss took aim.

"Aw, hell, Boyd! We got better things to do with our time than jaw all day with a hellion like this one. Besides, she's not that pretty anyway. Too skinny for my liking."

The tall man licked his lips, and it was obvious she wasn't too skinny for him. Nevertheless, he turned his horse around, watching as his companions mounted up. Then, as quickly as they had come, the three men were gone, riding over the rocky hillside.

Travis listened to the thump of their horses' hooves, only daring to relax when the sound faded in the distance. For the moment he forgot all the indignities he had suffered at his captor's hands as the warmth of gratitude overwhelmed him. In essence she had saved his life, for he would have had to be a moron not to know what his fate would have been had he fallen into the hands of those men.

"You can come out now." Opening the back flap of the wagon, Bliss poked her head inside. Men like that made her ashamed of her profession, and for just a moment she couldn't look her prisoner in the eye.

"I don't know what else I-I can say but-but thank you. You saved my skin." Travis stuttered, suddenly at a loss for words, though using them was his profession. Despite the circumstances he was slowly coming to admire her. It must be hard for a woman on her own. Difficult enough to cause her to build a wall around herself to guard against hurt. She's had to be tough to survive, he thought to himself. If they'd met in a different place, a different time, he might actually have wooed her. He found that idea very pleasing.

"Yeah, I did." Why was it she felt so flushed all of a sudden? Twittery and jittery.

There was a long poignant silence. This time when the young woman looked at him Travis saw the hard glint in her eyes softening a bit. He thought she might just be coming to like him a little too, but she threw cold water on that theory suddenly and unexpectedly.

"Hell, I didn't save you from those men because I felt sorry for you." Bliss was incensed with herself as she realized she'd come perilously close to letting down her guard. "So don't go getting any ideas. I just didn't want to see them get the money for you, that's all," she said tersely. Not a flicker of emotion crossed her face. "Nor did I want to share."

Her words angered him anew. "And I was actually beginning to think you had something besides ice water in your veins." Well, she had proven him wrong.

Bliss stiffened. It wasn't the first time a man had accused her of being cold, nor would it be the last. But she was damned if she'd let her emotions get her into trouble. Not again! "Well, ice water or not we're in this thing together," she said. "Those men aren't going to be put off easily. They'll be back. This time with more men. I could handle three but not the whole damned posse. Therefore I suggest you make yourself comfortable as best you can. I'm going to hitch up the horses, mister. You're going to be treated to a real mean ride. But that's the way it's got to be. Unless you'd rather take your chances with *them*."

Above all, he didn't want that. "I don't care how rough the ride is if you can get me as far away as possible from them I'll be beholding." For the moment at least his adversary was to be his ally, but Travis was determined that at the first opportunity he'd get free of her watchful eyes and run as fast as his legs could carry him.

Chapter Eight

The old wooden wagon bounced, bobbled and bumped, its wheels rolling unevenly over the muddy, rutted road. It was the wildest ride of Travis' life, made even more harrowing by the fact that, with his hands tied, he wasn't able to balance himself or grab hold when he was tossed from side to side. Worse yet was the attitude of his "companions," Boru and Bard, who made it obvious with their stares and bared teeth that they were just waiting for him to make a wrong move.

"Nice dogs." Travis tried to keep as much distance between himself and the mammoth canines as he could, but every once in a while a jolt or a bump threw him perilously near them and they would growl. "Easy now . . ."

Damn those dogs, he thought as he tried to settle himself as comfortably as he could among the bags, boxes and sacks. Were it not for them he could easily have maneuvered himself toward the back opening and hurled himself to freedom. Instead he was cornered. As if they read his mind the wolfhounds watched him warily, giving him warning each time he moved an inch toward the flap. The pretty young woman had trained them well he grudgingly had to admit. It put him in a foul mood as the wagon bounced along, but as the road evened out and the ride became smoother, his state of mind eventually lightened.

Travis visually explored the confines of his surroundings. The wagon was made entirely of wood, except for the canvas stretched over wooden hoops. Boards added to the top and sides made it completely weather-proof for the animal pelts as well as the other assorted "treasures" stored within it. There were various items: a tent, guns of all shapes and sizes, ammunition, skinning knives, cooking utensils and foodstuffs, both canned and dried. The back of the wagon had two large hinged doors for easy loading and unloading, the front was open with curtains drawn across to give a small measure of privacy.

From the appearance of things, she traveled from place to place in this covered wagon, like a Gypsy. Everything she needed could be hauled inside the wagon. She even carried canvas bags of potatoes, cabbages, and onions with her. Whatever might be said about his captor, it had to be admitted that she was well prepared.

"She's an amazing woman," he whispered. The more he found out about her, the more she piqued his curiosity. No pampered miss this one, no hiding behind fluttering lashes and coy smiles. The only problem was, Travis was used to the pampered kind

68

and knew how to get his way with them. A woman like the bounty hunter he was not so sure of. How was he going to win her over? Make her like him? Convince her to listen to him? How could he change the look of wariness in her eyes to a look of trust?

Thinking about her made him uncomfortable. Thoughts of a sensual nature kept hampering more important pondering. What would Miss Bounty Hunter be like in bed? Spirited? Of a certainty. Passionate? Undoubtedly. Hot blooded? Just wondering was disturbingly arousing, thus Travis pushed any such thoughts far from his mind, or at least tried his best to do so. Yet every so often his imaginings got the best of him.

Closing his eyes, Travis let his mind conjure up a far different circumstance than what he was experiencing now. In his daydream she was *his* captive and he had her entirely at his mercy. But he wasn't holding a gun on her. Oh, no, he didn't have to. She was a willing prisoner, bending toward him, her hands touching his bare, muscled shoulders and then slipping around his neck. She was pulling him down, pressing her slender, well-shaped body against his, begging him to make love to her.

He was in the middle of a most vivid imagining when the wagon suddenly stopped. Travis braced himself, apprehensive that perhaps they might have met up again with some of the posse members, but Bliss's shout, "This place ought to do," calmed his fears.

It had been some ride, Bliss thought as she poked her head inside the back of the wagon, but she was certain now that the posse would never find them.

Just in case, she had traveled in circles for a while, then had crossed the river and doubled back. Shrouding the wagon amidst a tiny forest of trees, she had forged for them a perfect campsite.

"You can come out now, mister!"

She watched and waited as he moved across the wagon floor, then clumsily jumped out, the wolf-hounds at his heels. Damn, but he was handsome. Too bad he'd given himself over to a life of crime. But then, even if he hadn't they were much too opposite to have ever been attracted to one another. She knew his type, the kind of man who liked the silly-frilly kind of girl. A woman who would pretend that he could do everything much better than she. The kind who played up to masculine vanity. A twittering fool. She, on the other hand, always came right to the point and did not like pretense.

And she was not used to his kind of man. She was used to uncouth, swearing, swaggering men she could easily outwit. This man was intelligent. Dangerously so. She would have to keep one step ahead of him lest he outsmart her. He was like a fox, keen and cunning. She couldn't help but notice how diligently he was scrutinizing her wagon now. Undoubtedly he was already contemplating escape, certain that if just the right moment came along he could take her by surprise. But she'd fool him. Like her father, she had eyes in the back of her head. Just let him make a move.

"What do you think of my little home?" she asked, by way of conversation, trying to hide her thoughts. It probably wasn't up to his standards of luxury by a long shot.

70

"I like it better when it's not moving," Travis answered, trying to reclaim his balance. The ride had upset his equilibrium, at least for the moment.

In spite of herself, Bliss smiled. "I guess it must have gotten a tad rough back there."

"A bit. But wherever it is that we have stopped, I welcome it. I think I must be one big bruise." Travis stretched his legs and torso. It felt good to get out of the confines of the wagon and walk around again. *And it would feel even better if these damn ropes around my wrists were loosened,* he thought, looking over his shoulder. Somehow he had to think of a way.

Bliss read his mind. She thought again of how she'd have to keep on guard at all times. "We'll stay quiet for the rest of the day here and let the posse search for us a mite. You might want to get rested up while you have the chance, because as soon as I'm certain the posse isn't out there prowling, we're gonna have to make up for lost time."

"Yes, I'm certain you are in a hurry to turn me in for the money," Travis said dryly.

Bliss tossed her head purposefully, and making her voice sound carefree, she retorted, "Sure. There are a whole slew of things I need, and the money I get for you will help me buy them."

Business was business after all, she thought. Even so, she felt more than just a twinge of guilt at the thought of taking him in. But why should she? After all, he was wanted for robbery and murder. She doubted that he was a stranger to violence. Why, probably at this very minute he was contemplating just what he would do to her if he got the chance.

71

"Bard! Boru! Watch him. Don't let him get far from the wagon." The wolfhounds didn't have to be told twice. Eagerly they bounded up and positioned themselves to lunge if Travis made one false move.

Bliss crawled into the wagon. Everything she owned in the world was stashed inside. A camelback trunk held clothing, her father's and hers, shirts and pants mostly. The tools of her trade, including various knives and guns, hung from pegs on the sides. And there were the precious things her father had left her, including a tintype of her and him side by side. The only picture she had of him. Taking it out of the trunk, she stared at it for a long while.

"Oh, Papa!" Her father had built the wagon, and had done so with a loving hand. Therefore, the wagon meant a great deal to her. It was her legacy. In it she could freely conjure up memories. She and her father had traveled many miles in this home away from home. More miles than she could count.

"If you're preparing to set up camp I could help you if you'd just untie me for a while."

Bliss jumped at the sound of Travis' voice. "Untie you?" She was startled when he stuck his head through the opening. Hastily she put the tintype away, angered by his intrusion. How had he gotten past the wolfhounds? "Bard! Boru!" The dogs instantly reacted to her command snapping at Travis' heels. "I'll bet that would please you wouldn't it, mister? That I untie you."

Looking at the picture of her father reminded Bliss of the way Oakwood had died. A man like this one had shot him. And this one would shoot her if he had half a chance. Hadn't he proven that in the mine?

Travis tried to remain cordial, even though she was glaring at him. "It would make me feel more like a man and less like one of your trophies in there if you loosened my bonds." He nodded toward the coyote and wolf skins, a few of which had their feet tied together.

"A trophy?" Sliding down from the wagon, she circled him. "Well, you'd better get used to it, mister, because that is just what you are."

Mister. The way she referred to him was getting on his nerves. "My name isn't 'mister,'" he said quietly. "It's Travis."

"I know your name." She took out the wanted poster and waved it in his face. "Travis La Mont. Fugitive. Wanted man. It's written right here."

"Then why don't you use it?" He knew why. She didn't want to think of him as a human being, a man she was sending to an unkind fate. She was trying to be impersonal. But Travis hoped the first step out of his captivity might be forcing her to get to really know him, forcing her to deal with what she was doing. "Would it really hurt you so much to address me as Travis?"

"I don't suppose so." Every muscle in her body was tense. She held herself erect, flushing under his criticism. It galled her to give in, yet for some reason she did. "Travis. Travis, the wanted man."

What a stubborn woman, he thought, but he knew he'd won a tiny victory. "Thank you." He waited expectantly. "Our first introduction was . . . uh . . . quite informal. I don't remember what you said your name was."

Bliss paused for a moment, looking at the ground.

73

"I'm R. B. Harrison."

"R.B.?" Travis cocked one brow in question.

"The *R* stands for Rebecca and the *B* for . . . Bliss."

"Bliss . . . !" A sensual sounding name, Travis thought, his lips relaxing into a smile. "I'd shake your hand in greeting, but as you can see. . . ."

"We'll let formalities slide in this case," Bliss retorted sarcastically. She looked him over from the top of his head to the toes of his boots, openly and impersonally. "Gonna have to get you a change of clothing, mist—Travis. No offense intended but you look a mess." It was a lie. His garments were muddied and torn in places, his hair was tousled, a hint of a five-o'clock shadow covered his cheeks and chin; yet even so he was impressive-looking.

"No offense taken." He noted the way she looked at him. Hardly a cursory glance. No, she had regarded him with close scrutiny. Perhaps all was not lost after all. "I could use some clean clothing and a bath." And the opportunity to have his hands free if only for a few moments.

"The bath is out, but as to the clothes I can help a bit there." Bliss ducked inside the wagon, opened the camelback trunk to fetch a few articles of her father's clothing and was back within a minute. "These will have to do." He was a bit taller and longer in the arms and legs than her father, but it would be a close fit.

Bliss took a step forward, then another and another. She moved so close that the heady scent of his musky body enveloped her, tantalizing her senses. She liked his manly smell. Reaching out, she

74

began to unfasten the buttons of his shirt.

"What are you doing?" The touch of her fingers against his naked skin as she opened his shirt was arousing and made him remember his daydream of her.

Bliss concentrated on the small black buttons so she didn't have to look him in the eye. "I'm going to take off these dirty duds and then dress you." Oh, she could read his mind like a book. He had taken it for granted that she'd let him dress himself, had thought the time for escape was coming, but he had been fooled.

"Undress me? Oh, no you aren't!" He'd suffered just about all the indignities he intended to sustain from this woman. This was nearly the last straw.

"I am!" And just to assure that he would be cooperative she put Bard and Boru on alert again.

Surely she was bluffing, Travis thought. Most women were shy when it came to such things, particularly with a stranger. And yet she had been as bold as brass in the mine tunnel.

He doesn't think I'll do it, Bliss thought as she watched the change of expression wash over his face. But she did. With trembling fingers she completed the task of undoing his shirt, letting her hand slide down over his hair-roughened chest to the flat, hard muscles of his belly. Slowly she stripped the shirt from his shoulders, ripping it from his body and arms, then letting it fall to the ground.

"That was my best shirt!" And she had torn it to shreds.

She hesitated for an instant. Then her hands went to his belt buckle. Releasing it, she stripped the belt from his pants with a firm tug.

Travis' stomach was tightening. He could feel the beginning of an arousal as she moved to unfasten his trousers. "Good God . . ."

Bliss' hands moved inside his pants to unbutton them and slide them over his hips. He certainly filled those pants out well. The tight denim did more to outline the stirring of his desire than to conceal it. Fascinated, Bliss traced the outline of his hipbones as her hands moved to his buttocks. Then she ran her fingers down his thighs, grabbing the fabric of his pants as her hands traveled from thigh to knee, taking the denims with her.

Travis wondered if she was exciting him on purpose, but shrugged off the idea. Not this one. She had something else up her sleeve. "Are you enjoying yourself?" he said out loud.

She was! Bliss had thought she could remain unaffected while she stripped Travis of his clothing, but she had been wrong. Touching was much better than looking, and though she had seen him naked before and thus had no surprises, she was deeply affected as her hands slid down his well-shaped legs. Despite her determination to think of him as nothing more than reward money, profit from a man who had gone wrong, she couldn't help but think it was such a waste for this one to swing at the end of a rope.

Bending down, she tugged off his boots, pulled his pants over his ankles and cast the articles of clothing aside. Grabbing up the clean garments, she slowly began to dress him, pants first, then boots. And all the while she was fighting a temptation that nearly overcame her. Men took advantage of women in such situations all the time. Why shouldn't she take advantage of him? Use him to satisfy the urgings of her young healthy body?

"No!" The very idea of giving in to her desires enraged her.

"No what?" Travis eyed her warily. Her moods were as changeable as the tide.

Suddenly Bliss wanted to be as far away from this man as she could. Good Lord, he was more dangerous than she had suspected! He was making her think the strangest thoughts, tempting her to do things that were definitely against her best interests. Was it any wonder that she grabbed for the only security she knew, her rifle?

"I'm going to untie you just for a minute so you can finish dressing yourself, but I warn you . . ." To emphasize her threat she aimed the barrel directly at him as she undid the ropes. "Now, you have three minutes to get dressed before I tie these ropes again."

His hands were free! Travis' eyes darted to his right, then to his left. It might be the last chance he had to make an escape.

Chapter Nine

Travis felt the cylinder of the rifle pressing into his back as he slowly slipped his arms into the sleeves of the red and black flannel shirt. Purposely he took his time, moving in slow motion, hoping all the while he could catch Bliss Harrison off guard. If he could take her unaware and somehow grab the rifle, then the only things between him and freedom were those damn dogs.

"Come on. Come on. Move it." Even watching him dress proved to be a sensual experience. Bliss's eyes were riveted on his broad shoulders and taut muscles. She secretly enjoyed looking at them, really looking. He was as fine a specimen of a man as she had ever seen. "You're as slow as molasses. The three minutes are almost up!" Bliss hid her growing attraction to Travis by pretending impatience.

"I can't move any faster. I'm tired!" Travis countered, all the while weighing his options. He could slam into her and hope the wound he incurred wouldn't be fatal, but that was risky. Or he could collapse and play possum, then find a way to knock her unconscious; but doing physical harm to her troubled him. Or he could hope against hope that she would drop her guard, at least for a second, until he got hold of the rifle. Then he could take off. That seemed to be the best plan. Of course he'd have to shoot the dogs before they tore him limb from limb. And the young woman, if the need arose could he shoot her as well? No. He had best hope that it didn't come to that.

"I've got a hundred things to do to set up camp." Bliss didn't trust him, not one iota, even if he was pleasant to the eyes. She was going to feel a whole lot better when he was trussed up again. Only when she was in complete control of the situation could she relax. "Hurry it up."

She was watching him like an eagle. "I told you I'd help you move some things." Damn, this isn't going to be easy, he thought as he fumbled with the shirt's buttons. She wasn't giving him an inch. She was, in fact, prepared to shoot him the moment he sneezed suspiciously. But he had to make a try or die in the attempt. Better to go down fighting like a man than wait for the worst.

"And I told you I could do everything myself. I don't want you helping me." Bliss had learned to be self-sufficient at an early age. Only the strong and the wily survived in this man's world, she knew. She was never inactive or bored. Indeed, there were more than enough things to keep her occupied as she tried to keep body and soul together. It was doubly

79

difficult now that her father had died, for she had to do the chores he used to do as well as her own.

Her father. For just a moment the wanted man's head was down, and she could almost imagine that Oakwood himself was standing in front of her. She had made that shirt for him for Christmas two years ago when she had seen him admiring the bolt of cloth at the general store. Her father had prized it, ignoring her uneven stitchery and the slightly mismatched sleeves. Now somebody else was wearing it.

The rifle's barrel jiggled slightly, and Travis knew the young woman's concentration had momentarily wavered. If he was going to make his move, it had to be right now. So thinking, Travis swung his elbow inward, knocking the rifle aside. At the same time his right hand fastened on the barrel, wrenching it free. Grabbing the gun with both hands, he hastily aimed it at her as the wolfhounds growled and snarled, preparing to lunge.

"Call the dogs off! Now! Or I'll shoot them both."

She didn't want that. "You bastard!" The thing she had most feared had happened, and Bliss was furious with herself, with him. She wanted to rebel against this turn of events. Still, he was a killer. If she didn't do as he said he would most likely kill her dogs and then murder her. "Boru, Bard, down!"

"That's a smart girl." Travis circled around her, all the while thinking of what he was going to do next. He didn't want to seriously harm her, that kind of ruthlessness wasn't in his character, but he had to keep her from following him.

Bliss was bitterly disappointed. At the back of her mind had been the hope that maybe he was innocent, but clearly he was crafty—and an outlaw. He knew just the right moves. "I'll follow you. I swear, you won't get away!"

He'd have to keep her from following him. "Pick up those ropes." There was no other way.

Bliss was all too aware of her rapidly pounding heart, the queasy feeling in the pit of her stomach. Was that all he was going to do to her, or was he going to kill her? She looked him full in the face, trying to read his intent, but his features were expressionless. "You're going to tie me up."

"You are very astute." Even though she had called off the dogs, the way they were eyeing Travis made him nervous. All she had to do was say the word and they would be hot on his heels. "Lock those . . . those animals in the wagon."

"What?" It was the last thing she wanted to do. Bliss looked upon Bard and Boru as her last hope.

"Lock them up!" His voice was harsher than he had intended.

She wanted to tell him to go to the devil, but she wouldn't chance her dogs getting hurt. She whistled shrilly. "Into the wagon."

Travis wanted to make certain she didn't trick him in any way; therefore, he held her in a viselike grip as he hauled her toward the wagon. He supervised as she closed the hinged door and latched it. Knowing the wolfhounds were out of the way gave him an immense sense of relief. As a matter of fact his confidence was swiftly returning.

"That's a good girl. Just do as I say and you won't get hurt."

Good girl! The way he said it, as if she were a witless child, infuriated Bliss. Well, he was in control, but only for a little while.

"Now, for those ropes. . . ." Travis' hand touched the small of her back, stroking soft strands of her hair. It was all he could do to keep his hand from wandering, but he held himself in control. I ought to do to her just what she did to me a moment ago, he thought. He wondered what she would do if he made her stand naked before him, but shrugged the idea off. Though it would have delighted him to seek revenge for her humiliation of him it was too risky.

Bliss eyed the rope haughtily. If he thought she was going to let him get away with this he was crazy. Defiantly she glared at him.

Travis had the sudden need to taunt her. "You underestimated me, Miss Bliss . . ."

His tone was infuriating. Bliss looked up to see his white teeth flash in a smile. His grin was the last straw. Hard and swift her knee shot up, smashing into his groin with perfect aim. Howling, Travis released her. He doubled over as an explosion of pain tore through his private parts. Sinking to his knees, he writhed in agony. "No, to the contrary, you underestimated me, Mr. La Mont," Bliss answered, quickly reclaiming her rifle. She pointed it at his head.

Misery etched Travis' face as he lay in a heap upon the ground. She'd humiliated him once again. "Go ahead and shoot. It's a quick death and sure as hell beats hanging."

She couldn't. Not in cold blood. But that didn't keep her from bluffing. "I ought to, and take your hide back to claim the reward."

The reward again! It seemed of the utmost importance to her. She was a mercenary, that was for sure. His fists clenched at his sides. "Have you ever happened to think that there might be something more important than money?"

"Like what?" Since her father's death she had faced a constant struggle. If she hadn't known how important money was before, she knew it now. Without it, life was unbearable.

"Integrity. Honesty. *Compassion.*" Slowly he staggered to his feet.

"Compassion? For someone who just did what you did?" To her, his escape attempt was proof that he was guilty, although the thought tickled at the back of her mind that had their roles been reversed she would have tried to get away too.

"I had to at least try!" Now things would be doubly hard for him. "I didn't do it! I didn't rob that bank."

Bliss scoffed. "No, of course not." Reaching behind her, she unlatched the door of the wagon. "Bard, Boru. I just might give you to them for their supper," she threatened. Certainly having him as a prisoner was becoming more and more troublesome. Not only did she have to tie his hands but his feet as well. That made him a nuisance, dependent on her for his every need.

Travis watched as Bliss Harrison hurriedly gathered firewood and then stared a fire. Hurriedly she set up camp. He'd just learned that she threatened to be more than a match for him, and the thought was anything but pleasant. He'd had a chance to get away. He'd bungled it. And all because of some slip of a girl who had a grudge against men.

"I didn't kill him, you know," he said softly.

"What?" Bliss threw a tree branch on the fire, watching as the flames shot up to the sky.

"I didn't kill your father, Bliss. It won't do you any good to punish me."

How did he know what happened? For just a moment Bliss could only stop and stare. But time and hard knocks had made her mentally agile. "Punish you?"

"Whether you fully understand it or not, that's just what you're doing." Travis had finally figured it out, though he lacked all the facts about what had happened to Oakwood Harrison.

Bliss paled. "I'm not! I'm only seeing justice done." The law declared that all wrongdoers should be turned over to those in authority. That was just what she was going to do.

"Justice?" Travis pulled against the ropes that tied him once again. "I think I'd call it something else if I were you." But what was the use of arguing anyhow? They were at an impasse. Travis doubted she'd ever believe him, particularly when he couldn't really say for sure why he had been accused, why he'd been so hotly pursued? He suspected somebody feared that he knew something. And if so, what?

The picture he had taken of the bank just when the

robbers were exiting probably would expose the culprits. That must be why they were determined to get him out of the way.

If he could get back his camera and develop the picture, then with visible proof of the robbers' identities, perhaps he could clear his name. There was one problem, however. And it was a doozy! Unless he could convince Bliss Harrison to go along with his plan he would fail.

Chapter Ten

Not even a flicker of emotion crossed Bliss's face as she stared across the campfire at the man she was keeping prisoner, but deep inside she was in turmoil. Travis La Mont hadn't done anything to earn her trust, yet despite her usual stubbornness and his attempt to escape, she was beginning to weaken. Damned if she wasn't. His accusation that she was punishing him because of what had happened to her father had gotten to her. Was she taking revenge on him because she couldn't get her hands on the real culprit? Was that why she had become a one-woman crusade against all perpetrators of crimes?

"Surely in the few days we have spent together you must have learned something about me," he was saying now in that earnest tone of voice that elicited her sympathy. He was lying on his side, his head pillowed on a sack of flour, but he didn't look in the least relaxed. "Can you really think, then, that I'm a cold-blooded killer?"

Bliss grabbed a potato from the burlap sack next to her and began peeling it with her knife. "I don't know what to think." At least that much was clear. Since she was a little girl she'd met all kinds of men, those like her father who had the courage to dream and those whose only purpose was to destroy and all those in between. Just what kind of man was this Travis La Mont? He defied categorization. "All I know is you're wanted and there's a posse after you. Not very good credentials, I'd be thinking."

"Well, then let me come to my own defense since there is no one else to do it." Travis raised himself up, swearing beneath his breath when Boru growled. Since his escape attempt the largest of the dogs was doubly threatening. "Easy! Easy. Nice dog." He remained motionless, looking in Bliss's direction. "Will you listen?"

His intrusion on her concentration caused her to look up and nick her thumb with the knife. She sucked at her wound grimly. "Say anything you want," she replied coolly. "I haven't put ropes on your tongue. At least not yet."

Although he had little freedom of movement with both hands and feet tied, Travis somehow maneuvered himself into a kneeling position, as if pleading for clemency. "I didn't kill *anybody*. I wasn't even holding a gun."

Bliss didn't feel like arguing again. It had been a long wagon ride. She was tired, hungry and grumpy. "Uh-huh, I remember you told me you were holding a *camera.*" His constant banter about his innocence had become irksome. "Well, guess you know now

87

just what people out West think of newspapermen."
Her tone was sarcastic.

Travis rocked back on his heels, more than a little
irritated by her reaction to his sincerity. "If you want
to make light of my situation I can't stop you, but let
me tell you, being on the run is not any fun."

In a frenzy, she wielded the knife, peeling the
potato in a matter of seconds. "I didn't think it was. I
was just making a statement. Some people just don't
like those who go poking their noses in other
people's business just for the sake of a story." She
reached for another potato and, after peeling it, for
another.

"Does that include you? Do you resent men who
earn their living by taking pictures and using
words?" Travis could tell this pretty young woman
had a lot of anger and frustration pent up inside her,
and he wanted to know why. Her father's death, of
course, but for what other reason?

Bliss couldn't help but bristle as she remembered
the outrageous manner in which she had been
treated by the local newsmen after her father's death.
They had hounded her, ignoring her grief. Sensa-
tionalizing the situation, they had soon made her
father's murderer into a legendary figure, ignoring
the fact that he was a cold-blooded killer. She'd
learned then and there how unscrupulous some
people could be. "I don't resent them as long as they
tell the truth!" Bliss threw the potatoes into a large
cooking pot filled with water, then set the pot on top
of the fire.

Travis closed his eyes for just a minute. Although

he liked this feisty woman he had to handle this situation just right. He could tell that her feelings about him were slowly changing in his favor, and he hoped to make full use of that. "I always tell the truth, Bliss. Just as I am doing right now." He repeated slowly, "I did not have anything to do with robbing the bank. I didn't even fire one gunshot."

"Then why are your name and face on a wanted poster? Why is a posse out looking for you at this very moment? Why has the marshal put a price on your head?" She was trying very hard to convince herself that he was not telling the truth, for otherwise her life would be fraught with complications. "Hearing you say that it's all a mistake just isn't good enough for me."

"All right then, I'll tell you what I think." Travis clenched and unclenched his hands, which were tied behind his back, trying to control his rising anger. "I think someone is trying to frame me," he blurted out.

"Frame you?" It seemed to be a ridiculous accusation. "Who and why?"

Travis shook his head. "I don't know the answer to either question, but it's the only thing that makes sense." He tried to re-create the scene for her. "I was standing about three feet beyond the boardwalk, focusing my camera, when I heard a noise inside the bank. Gunshots. Shouting. I think I must have shot a picture instinctively when I realized there was trouble."

"So?" Bliss shrugged her shoulders.

"I was a witness. And what's more, I tangibly

captured the happenings." Travis was trying hard to fit all the pieces of the puzzle together, but it was confusing to him. He mumbled, more to himself than to her, "That photograph must be the reason I'm being hunted. Can't you see?"

"No, I don't see." Bliss snapped several carrots in two, throwing them into the pot with the potatoes.

"Someone involved in the robbery knows I took that picture and thinks it is incriminating. That's why they want me out of the way." Travis looked her right in the eye with what he hoped was pure sincerity.

"Now, let me get this right." It was the damnedest thing she'd ever heard, yet as she chopped up an onion she repeated it. "You're saying that while you were busy taking a picture there was a bank robbery and that you must have captured an image of one of the robbers on your film. It worried and angered him so much, he fabricated the story that you were involved in the robbery and shot one of the bank tellers. Is that what you're saying?"

It sounded ridiculous the way she said it. "In a manner of speaking that's what I mean but—"

"Uh-huh!" The onions made her eyes water, and she wiped them with her sleeve. "Well, let me give you a piece of good advice."

"Which is . . . ?"

"Don't tell anybody else what you just told me. It just doesn't wash, mister." Even Bard and Boru seemed to doubt his alibi, for as he sat back down they glowered at him. Their bared teeth looked like ominous grins.

90

"Well, it must be true, nonetheless! There just isn't any other answer."

"Yes, there is!" Bliss exclaimed, punctuating her words with a jab of her knife. "You got yourself in with the wrong kind of men, needed some easy money and thought you could get away with robbery. It happens all the time."

"Not with me, it doesn't! I am and always have been an honest man."

Disgruntled, Travis kept silent for a long while, watching as Bliss prepared some kind of stew, making use of vegetables and chunks of some kind of dried meat she carried with her. The appetizing aroma that wafted through the night air gave promise that she was a good cook. He certainly hoped so, he was famished.

Bliss quickly took note of Travis La Mont's silence and was strangely uncomfortable with it, though she didn't know why. She should have welcomed the respite from his arguing, but found herself saying, "Look, I just don't want any hard feelings, mister. I'm just doing what I get paid to do, yōu know. It's not for me to be your judge and jury. It's for the law to say whether or not you're guilty or innocent." Never had he looked more handsome. A brisk wind was blowing his dark hair around his face. His shirt was open at the neck, exposing the hair on his chest; his trousers hugged his muscular thighs. But she couldn't afford to let her thoughts get out of hand; she hurriedly turned them elsewhere, concentrating on the stew.

"What if I proved the truth of my story to you?"

91

Travis said suddenly. "What then?"

"Proved it, how?" Bliss eyed him warily.

"We could go back to get my camera." If his suspicions were correct then it would be an easy matter to corroborate his version of what had happened. In this case a picture would be worth far more than anything he could say. "I'll develop the film, and if I don't miss my guess the photograph will prove to be very intersting."

"Yeah, I'll bet." The truth was she didn't think there really was a picture, of the bank or anything else. Undoubtedly he was lying through his teeth, thinking up stories that would get her to set him free. And once she untied him he'd run off like a rabbit.

"Please, Bliss!" Never in his life had he come so close to begging. "Give me just one chance to clear my name. Keep me tied up if you want to, only let me take you to where I hid my camera."

She thought about his request for only a moment. "I can't do that."

"Why?" Travis couldn't keep the edge out of his voice. Damned woman, she was going to be his ruination.

"Well, for one thing the posse might catch up with us and shoot you on sight. We would both come out losers then." She bit her lip as the troubling image of Travis La Mont lying dead on the ground whisked through her mind.

"Yeah, you just might miss the chance to cash me in on the reward," Travis said beneath his breath.

"Precisely."

Never had he met such an uncompromising,

stubborn woman. Well, this little episode in his life wasn't over yet. The night was still young. "As you said, dead or alive."

Her heart jumped up in her throat at the thought of his death, still she acted cavalier. "Dead or alive, mister." My God, her emotions were beginning to play tricks on her. She was starting to have feelings for this man. Had traveling alone really made her that lonely? She had better hurry to their destination and turn him in before her heart intruded on her best interests. "The last thing in this world I would ever do is to turn you loose."

"So it seems." Travis could see that she was set upon her course of action. As the minutes passed the tension grew. Apprehensive that she might mean what she said about dead or alive he made no attempt to overstep his bounds. "Well, then so be it!" He settled himself back down, wondering if this woman would ever show she had a weakness.

Bard and Boru were eyeing Bliss with the woebegone look that meant they wanted to be fed. "Okay. Okay!" Retrieving four tin plates from the back of the wagon, she gave them large scraps of the meat she had thrown into the stew. The appreciative sounds the wolfhounds made as they gobbled them up reminded her that she was likewise famished. Dipping a spoon into the bubbling pot, she decided it had cooked long enough.

"Are you hungry, Travis?" She used his name before she had even realized it. Now she blushed despite her resolve.

He raised his head. "Yes, I am!" But even so the

idea of her feeding him rankled. As she came forward he defiantly shook his head. "I'm so hungry I could eat my shoe, but I also have pride. I won't be spoon-fed."

"Pride doesn't fill an empty stomach." She offered him the first ladled-out portion, passing it under his nose to tempt him. "But give it time to cool, it's hot."

The fact that she had him totally subdued gnawed at Travis. Looking her full in the face, he asked, "Don't you even have a thimble's worth of humanity flowing with that ice water in your veins? Can't you even untie my hands long enough for me to eat something?"

"Untie your hands. Ha! You'd like that, wouldn't you?" Bliss put the plate on the ground in front of him. She'd done her duty in giving him food. It was his choice how he was going to eat it.

Slowly Travis lowered his head toward the plate, then snapped it back up. "I'm a man, not one of your dogs."

Bliss dished out a portion of the stew for herself and heartily looked forward to eating it, at least until she glanced over at Travis. True to his word he hadn't eaten a bite. If it was a war of wills she knew he had won. She couldn't let him go hungry.

"All right! All right!" She must be softer of heart than she thought. Or more precisely soft in the head to think she could trust him even for a second. Yet there had to be a way.

Bliss solved the problem. She unbound only one of his hands, his left, and tied the other securely to one of the wagon wheels. It gave him a tiny measure of freedom while at the same time assuring her own safety. There was little he could do to escape, unless he could take the whole damned wagon with him.

"Here!" Picking his plate up, she held it forth like a peace offering.

"Thank you." Travis took it, but too hungry to be cautious, he burned his tongue.

"I told you so." Bliss took a spoonful herself, waiting for it to cool. The meat was tough, the broth weak and thin, there wasn't enough salt or pepper, but she had to admit for a hastily concocted dish it wasn't too bad.

Travis eagerly cleaned his plate and held it out for a refill. "Very tasty."

"My father taught me to make good use of all supplies," she answered, pleased by his compliment. "I can honestly say I seldom let anything go to waste."

Travis took a bite, trying to figure out all that went into the stew. Potatoes, yes. Cabbage, onion, carrots and strangely enough apples. "What kind of meat is this?" It had a strong flavor and was certainly stringy.

"Wolf meat!" Bliss answered.

Travis' expression showed his disgust. "Wolf meat!" It was much too close to dog meat for his liking. Suddenly he lost his appetite.

"After I took those wolf pelts I couldn't see being wasteful," she answered defensively, stung by his abhorrence. The truth was she hadn't had the money for any other kind of meat. It was either dried wolf meat or none at all. Bliss shuddered as she remembered what it was like to suffer deprivation, to be cold and hungry, with nowhere to turn and no one you could count on but yourself. Travis La Mont who dressed in pin-striped suits wouldn't have any comprehension of just how poor that was.

It was the first time Travis had seen vulnerability written so clearly on anyone's face. That it was etched on the features of the woman he had up to now thought perfectly self-controlled and sure of herself made it all the more potent an observation.

Not as strong as she pretends to be, he thought, realizing his hope that she would reveal a weakness might not be an impossible one. She erects a tough shell, a barrier to guard herself from hurt.

Now when he wished both his hands were unbound, it wasn't because he wanted to break free but because he wanted to comfort her, to put his arms around her, stroke her hair and tell her everything was going to be all right from now on.

"Bliss . . ." His voice was low and husky as he called her name.

She was somehow compelled to look at him, but as their eyes met and held she was gripped by a sudden shyness. There was an intent yet tender look in his eyes, a look she hadn't seen before on any man's face when he was looking in her direction. In that moment it was as if they were enclosed in an isolated world, one in which only they existed.

"You're beautiful, you know. Especially with the firelight shining on your hair." There wasn't a woman alive who didn't eventually weaken under prettily spoken words. Travis knew himself to be skilled at amorous approaches, yet that wasn't why he had just complimented her. For some reason he'd wanted her to know.

A smile crinkled the corners of her eyes and softened her whole face. Combing her fingers through her hair, she asked, "Do you really think so?"

"Yes, I do," he answered sincerely.

Her huge blue eyes looked nearly violet in the light, the well-sculpted contours of her face appeared even more perfect, but it was her hair that held him spellbound. It was exactly the color of the flames, such a vivid hue that it was silken fire. She fascinated him as no other woman ever had. He found himself wondering what it would be like to hold her in his arms, to kiss her and caress her. He wanted to hear her say his name softly, wanted to see her eyes sparkle with an inner fire that burned because she wanted to make love to him.

"Bliss . . ." He felt as if they were sharing a very intimate moment, one that could very well be a beginning and not an ending. Though he didn't want to stare, he was unable to prevent his eyes from roving where they chose. His gaze touched on the pert tips of breasts thrusting against the cloth of her shirt, then moved to her firm stomach and thin waist, a longing in it that could not be hidden.

She liked the way he said her name. The softness in his voice touched the hard core deep inside her and turned it to jelly. For just a moment she forgot the whys and wherefores of their being together and allowed herself to dream. What if . . . ? Suddenly the truth of what he was doing struck her like a blow between the eyes. He was sweet-talking her. Trying to gain his freedom by the most treacherous way of all! "Why you sneaky bastard!"

Her words stung him. Looking up, he saw her lips tighten grimly, saw a look of anger come into her eyes. "What do you mean, sneaky?" He hadn't made even one attempt to get away.

"Your flattering words!" Reaching for his hand, she yanked it brutally from his lap and once again tied it with the other one. "Well, I won't fall for such shenanigans, mister. I'm not some dewy-eyed maiden waiting for some handsome stud to whisper in my ear."

"No, I guess you're not," Travis retorted. "I humbly apologize. For a moment there I was deluded into thinking you were a real woman. But you aren't, are you? You're too busy trying to act like a man to ever be soft or feminine. It was just an illusion, that's all."

Bliss was instantly defensive. "I have to act as I do. I don't have anyone but myself! No one!" She hastily added, "And I don't need anybody. I particularly don't need any man."

"Ah, but that's the sad part about it, Bliss. You do." Travis resumed his previous position, once more cradling his head on the flour sack. "If there was ever a woman just made for passion and tenderness, it's you. But your anger and resentment are wrapped as tightly around you as a cocoon, keeping you isolated and all alone."

"I don't care!" Bending over, she snapped up his

tin plate, nearly scouring it into nothingness with sand as she cleaned it. How dare he tell her what she needed, as if she were some prim old maid who languished for a male's attentions. "I don't need anyone, him in particular," she mumbled to herself as she cleaned up the campsite. And yet if that was true why did she feel such an aching void in her heart? It was a question that troubled her as she took out her bedroll and lay down upon it to sleep.

Chapter Eleven

Bliss lay awake, staring up at the stars. She just couldn't sleep no matter how hard she tried. Thinking about Travis La Mont and what he had said, that she was too much like a man to ever be soft or feminine, bothered her. *I deluded myself into thinking you were a real woman, but you aren't, are you?*

"I am a woman. I *am!*" Bliss said aloud, clenching her fingers and beating at the hard ground. Just because she didn't want to dress in frills and lace or drop her drawers every time a man looked at her didn't mean she didn't have "those" feelings. "What do you know about it anyway, Mr. La Mont?"

The only answer she got to her question was the loud rasp of his breathing. Unlike Bliss, Travis wasn't bothered by his thoughts. He was sleeping soundly. It irritated her that he could sleep like the dead while she was left tossing and turning, and all because of what he had cruelly stated, that he thought her to be less than a woman. Was she? Had she shielded herself against hurt so fiercely that she had lost all hope of ever feeling those tender emotions?

In the moonlight Bliss appraised herself, trying to view herself as others would see her—a slim, red-haired woman in faded britches, an old flannel shirt and nearly worn-out boots. A woman who had isolated herself and who rarely trusted anyone. A loner. A woman who had once been capable of deep emotions but who now purposely guarded her feelings. A woman more comfortable with anger than with passion.

"It doesn't matter! I like the way I am," she said aloud, coming to her own defense. But did she? Weren't there times when she did long for the comfort of a man's love and protection? His company? She had no one to talk to except herself or Bard and Boru. No one with whom she could share her adventures. No one who really cared if she lived or died.

It was better that way, she told herself, trying once more to bury such thoughts. Her father was the only one who had ever loved her. Now that he was gone she was better off alone. Hadn't she learned that by now? Hadn't her naivete taught her anything at all? Travis La Mont had said she needed a man. In a pig's eye she did!

Bliss closed her eyes, but opened them again quickly as an unwelcome image hovered before her eyelids, Rufus Barker's leering face. He was one among many men who had taught her how important it was to always be on guard. No matter how much a man pretended to be sympathetic, there was only one thing he had on his mind when it came to a woman. She had learned that lesson when she had nearly been raped by a man who supposedly was her father's friend, a pitiful excuse for a human being who had pretended to understand her grief. He had offered her comfort while all the time he had been plotting the foulest crime that could be committed against a woman. His touch had filled her with revulsion when he had fondled her breasts and pressed his legs between hers to part them.

Like an all too familiar nightmare, Bliss remembered the moment and the atrocity that had nearly been perpetrated against her. She remembered her struggles as the man had torn away her clothing, leaving her vulnerable and exposed. With calculated brutality he had been forcing her to the floor so he could proceed with his lustful quest. Only Bliss's feisty nature had saved her. Doubling up her fist she had struck a blow to her would-be rapist's male parts. That had been his ruination and her liberation.

The nausea and terror she'd experienced that night had haunted her since then. Bliss had escaped Rufus Barker's drunken embrace, but it had been a shattering experience all the same. Now as she looked over at Travis La Mont she wondered if that ugly assault had done something to cripple her natural desires. Was it true? Did she have ice water in her veins? No! The very sight of Travis La Mont thawed her, had from the very first no matter how she fought against the desire he inspired. She remembered the sight of him, naked and defenseless but still heart-stirringly handsome.

102

Frightened by the feelings this particular man kindled, Bliss forced herself to harden her heart. "Men!" She didn't want one! Didn't need one. Experience had taught her well.

The men she had met were unscrupulous and dangerous. They had proven beyond a doubt that they could not be trusted, that they were an unwanted element in the settlements, taking advantage of honest folk. And they were lustful creatures, always pawing and pinching. Uncouth, swearing braggadocios who filled her with disgust. Bliss had made it a point to keep them a safe distance away and had been very happy with that arrangement until now. Something about Travis La Mont drew her, despite the fact that he was a wanted man. Drew her dangerously, mindlessly.

Turning her head, she stared at him a long, long time at last admitting the truth to herself. Since the first moment she'd taken him unaware in the mine tunnel she had fantasized about him, had imagined being held in his arms. Perhaps that was why she always made it a point to be sharp with him, taking her anger at her own weaknesses out on him. She had hoped her feelings would just go away, but instead her imaginings had intensified along with her curiosity. What was he like as a lover? It was the question she had at last put into words.

"Why shouldn't I find out?" She wanted to know, perhaps more so now than ever before, particularly after what he had said: *If there was ever a woman just made for passion and tenderness, it's you.* Travis La Mont had looked at her as if he pitied her, as if she were cheating herself of something wonderful.

103

As if he were the one who was her salvation. Was he?

She was goaded on by her frustration. How easy this world was for males. Were their roles reversed, however, were it he who had her tied up, she knew very well what would have occurred, he would have had his hands all over her, would have made her a slave to his desires. But fate had a good sense of humor. He was the captive and she the one in control. He was tied as securely as was possible; thus, he would pose no menace to her. No matter what she did, he couldn't retaliate. Oh, how she relished that thought.

"I'll bet it's the first time a woman has had him at her mercy," she said to herself, feeling awe at her own power. And most certainly she did hold all the aces. It was a perfect opportunity to assuage her curiosity about him and yet at the same time be safe, from physical as well as emotional dangers. Just a kiss at first. She could stop any time *she* wanted to. Why not do it then?

A strange glimmer came into her eyes as she thought about what she was going to do. A brazen act to be sure. A daring and bold turn of the tables on a man who undoubtedly always had such situations under his control. Should she? Did she dare? Did she even want to? Puzzled and troubled by conflicting emotions, Bliss just sat watching him for a long, long time, but then she made her move.

Scrambling out of her bedroll, she slipped from her place by the fire and walked barefoot over to where Travis La Mont lay sleeping. Kneeling down, she reached out and touched his shoulder, fighting against the sudden urge to go scurrying back to her bed. When he didn't move, she felt emboldened. Slipping her arm around his neck she bent forward so that her mouth was just inches from his. It would be so easy to appease her longing, so very easy. She slowly lowered her head. When her mouth was aligned with his she moved her lips gently but insistently over his mouth. His lips were molded to hers in the same moment his eyes snapped open.

"What in blazes?" he mumbled, drawing away. There was something in her eyes that both fascinated and unnerved him. What was she planning?

"Keep still!" She moved closer.

"What idea is spinning in that pretty little head of yours?" Something out of the usual, that he could tell.

"If you think it's something sinister you have misjudged me! I just want to show you that I can act like a woman when I want to," Bliss whispered in his ear, doing her best to make her voice sound provocative.

"I'm sure that you can . . ." He had feared she might have some sort of punishment in mind, but if this was punishment he'd hasten to it gladly. "By all means, continue!"

Bliss held his face in her hands as she once again kissed him on the mouth, a deep kiss of exploration. His mouth was warm, soft, despite the firmness of his lips and she had to admit that it was an enjoyable encounter. Tracing the outline of his lips with her tongue, she lingered a long moment, then slipped inside to stroke the edge of his teeth. His mouth opened to accommodate her quest, accepted her seeking lips and tongue with a groan she interpreted as a sign of pleasure. Bliss chose that moment to pull away.

"Well?"

Realizing she was expecting some kind of appraisal, Travis said softly, "That was very good for a start." He wouldn't have admitted to her for anything the way that kiss had affected him. Her mouth was sweet beyond his wildest dreams.

"A start, ha! You liked the way I kissed you just now, and so did I. Kiss me again," she ordered, bending her head. His mouth sought hers, drank her in. Teasingly, caressingly he moved his lips against hers. The pressure of his mouth parted her lips, and she felt the tip of his tongue gently dueling with her own. The sensations he unleashed made her feel weak, and she sagged against his strong frame. She was right. Travis La Mont was an expert in the preliminaries of making love.

This should be the end of it. A kiss, just a kiss. She knew she should quit before anything else happened, but far from quenching her curiosity, Travis La Mont's kisses intensified it. She could never have foretold her reaction, but suddenly she was totally caught up in seducing him, and it was a wonderful, liberating feeling.

She wrapped her arms around his waist and pressed her breasts against his chest. Tilting her face, she smiled up at him. "Still think I act too much like a man?"

"No . . . !" His answer came in a tormented whisper. Dear God, she felt so good. Too good. A fierce longing, a nearly out of control desire began to stir in Travis' body at the feel of her soft curves writing against him.

"Any objections if I open your shirt, Mr. La Mont?" she asked softly.

"None at all," he whispered, shifting his body slightly to form a more comfortable cradle for her. Although he now knew her actions to be driven primarily by anger and not passion her body was nonetheless still strangely magical in its power over him. Tenderness rushed through him. The touch of her hands, the scent of her hair, overwhelmed him. He wanted to make love to her fiercely, yet with such tenderness that he could forever banish her hurt and resentment and replace it with contentment and fulfillment.

Her fingers moved down to open his shirt, her hands clumsy as she snagged the material with her nails. She touched his smooth shoulders and neck, her fingertips roaming slowly, tantalizingly. As her hands roamed she remembered in her mind's eye just what he looked like nude. He was hard, lean, virile and strong, his stomach flat, his legs long and well shaped. A magnificent male. Such a pity he was going to be jail bait!

The moon shone on his face, and she could see that look of mixed pleasure and pain. Passion. He'd taunted her, but before the night was over she'd prove to him that she was a woman! Her intent was to make him squirm. "Ha, what a strange change of events. This time I'll be getting money for you, rather than you offering it to me for my services. This time you'll be the one with the price attached," she teased.

"If you want to get your full money's worth, set me

free, Bliss," Travis responded. She was just toying with him, punishing him in the cruelest of all possible ways for what he had blurted out about her femininity, but still he gave it a try. "Do it and I swear you will never be sorry. I'll take you with me. It's a big world—"

Bliss once again denied his plea. "No!"

Travis, however, was encouraged nonetheless. A woman didn't initiate lovemaking with a man only to give him up to the law. Despite what Bliss Harrison pretended she was beginning to have feelings for him. It was only a matter of time. Until then he'd just close his eyes and give himself up to the ecstasy she was bringing to him with her lips and hands. And what ecstasy it was. She was taunting him with them.

"Touch me," he urged her when she withdrew from him. "I like to feel your hands on me."

Bliss wasn't certain what possessed her, but as she gave herself up to the enjoyment of caressing him, sensuality assumed dominance over her mind. She let his warmth penetrate her limbs, bent her head and nuzzled his bare chest.

Travis had thought to himself that she would probably be a passionate woman were her feelings unleashed, but she was outdoing his suppositions. She was passionate, responsive and exciting. Travis drew a deep breath, then let it out in a long, drawn-out sigh. "Yes, oh yes!"

Bliss smiled, her blue eyes flashing mischief at him. All too quickly she was learning just how primitive and powerful desire really was. Even more important, she suddenly realized the power a woman had over a man like Travis La Mont if she learned how to use it. One more potent than holding him at bay with a gun. It was an interesting revelation, one that soothed all the hurt she'd experienced from other men in the past.

Her eyes were irresistibly drawn to the area of his maleness, now stiffening under the manipulations of her questing fingers. Instead of feeling repugnance as she had many times before, Bliss was strongly aroused herself. She stared at the hard spear rising beneath his trousers wondering what it would be like to feel that strength inside her. But no! It was not her purpose to actually make love to him, only to experiment so that she could learn what made men tick. And she had found out all right. More disturbing, she had found out something about herself as well. She was all too human. The wanton, abandoned feelings he brought to life in her told her so. Bliss hadn't counted on the flame that was steadily growing inside her. A fire she had to quickly cool.

"Well, mister, I guess I showed you!" she said, pulling away.

"Showed me?" Bliss Harrison didn't fool Travis even for a minute. She wasn't as blasé about the whole episode as she pretended.

"You can't say I'm not a woman now . . ."

"So that was the game. You're merely a tease. And to think you so coldheartedly dashed my hopes of becoming your lover." Desperately he tried to curb the aching, unfulfilled desire raging inside him. "But it is just as well. I don't want to make love to you, Bliss. Not until I'm free and can act like a man!"

Travis forced himself to sound angry, but he wasn't. He knew now that there was a chance for him. He had found her Achilles' heel, and before too long had passed he'd make good use of that knowledge. Oh, yes indeed, he would.

It was a dark night. Men with unfriendly eyes scanned the horizon.

"How in the hell could she just disappear, Barlow? She has to be out there somewhere, and if I don't miss my guess she's got La Mont in tow," the meanest of the three said sharply. The squat dark-haired man with the handlebar mustache, bulbous nose and bushy eyebrows, quickly dismounted.

"Yep, she's got him all right! She didn't fool me for a minute. But if she's smart she won't be counting that reward money yet." The tall thin-faced man with long straggly blond hair touched his revolver, then decided it was premature to draw.

"Reward money, hell! That's not what's at stake here. If we don't silence him permanently and bring his carcass back to town, the boss will have our hides for sure. You know how *he* is." It was obvious that Jake Heath was feeling testy. Things just weren't going the way he wanted, and his companions knew that when he was unhappy he could be dangerously mean.

"Yeah, we know how he can be." Boyd Withers, the third man, gray-haired, dressed all in buckskin and even more obnoxious than the others, grimaced, loosening the belt that pressed in upon his huge bulging stomach. "That sharp-talking hellcat showed

110

more feistiness than I've ever seen in a female—and I don't like it at all. She needs to have her claws clipped, needs to be taught a lesson."

"She will be." Tom Barlow was ruthless. He had a nasty crooked smile and dark brooding eyes. Eyes that could ferret out a needle in a haystack if need be. Now he saw something of great interest. "Look, over there beyond the ridge. That's either the largest firefly I've ever seen or the embers of a campfire."

"A campfire!" They all looked at each other, huge smiles upon their faces, then in unison they said, "Come on!"

Chapter Twelve

It was cold. Travis opened his eyes and lifted his head from the sack he was using as a pillow. The fire had long since burned to embers. Even so there was enough light to illuminate the sleeping figure less than two feet away. The bright red hair that fell across her shoulders like a crimson flame had a natural curl, beautiful hair, but it was the face that held his eyes. Asleep it was cherubic. Bliss looked serene, innocent, even vulnerable lying there. She could be a hellion, that was for sure, but now as he watched her sleep he knew she had a softer side.

"Well, well, well. Miss Bliss Harrison, bounty hunter. You certainly are a surprise," he whispered. She was the kind of woman he'd been looking for, strong and independent, with a mind of her own. She was smart, brave, cocky and beautiful. What better companion could he have. He admired such women and had little interest in the clinging-vine type. What an irony it was that he had found her looking at him from above the barrel of a gun.

Could he really blame her for not believing his story of what had happened at the bank in Silver Bow? Would he have believed anyone else had they told such a tale? A slight smile curved Travis' lips when he thought of the way she had cornered him in the mine tunnel. She had acted as cool as you please, with no evidence of embarrassment at having a naked man in her sights.

"You're quite a woman."

As if sensing his gaze she stirred sleepily, brushing at her face, then turned on to her back. She made a charming sight. He stared at her so earnestly, and for such a long time, that he began to feel as if he knew each feature, every curve and angle of her face and figure. He took note of the thickness of her lashes, the curving line of her eyebrows. Her nose was straight, her slightly parted lips soft and full.

Ah yes, Bliss was a very pretty young woman, though he wondered if she even knew how pretty. Unlike most women who made use of their physical attributes, she seemed prone to hide hers. Why? What had happened to her to make her want to hide behind threats and curses. Her lips were made for laughter and kissing, not for swear words and taunts.

"What I wouldn't give to hear you call out my name in passion, just once," he murmured.

How did he feel about this woman who had him at her mercy? Until last night his most frequent responses to her had been frustration and anger, but that had quickly changed. He had been attracted to her right from the first, that he couldn't dispute; but his lustful yearning had softened. Now he found

113

himself wanting to know all about Bliss Harrison, wanting to know just what made her tick.

That she had veritably worshipped her father was obvious. He could nearly see her in his mind's eye, a little minx with bright red braids tagging after the foremost bounty hunter in the territory. Now she was all alone, and that thought tugged at Travis' heart. Whether Bliss Harrison knew it or not she needed someone who cared about her. Everyone did. Somewhere deep inside him he sensed now that he was the someone for her. The problem was, how was he going to prove that to her, especially trussed up like he was?

Travis flexed his numb hands over and over again to bring back feeling into them and to try to loosen the bonds. Rolling over and over, he worked his way across the hard earth, feeling prickles of gravel and small stones, but he had no luck in getting free so he stopped struggling. Even if he did get free where would he go? What could he do? As Bliss had so bluntly told him he would be target practice for the men in the posse. At least with her he had a chance.

That was not to say that Bliss Harrison had turned him into a docile lamb. It was not in Travis' nature to give up or give in. It was just that what had happened last night seemed to call for a change of plans. Now his scheme must include Bliss Harrison as friend, not foe. He couldn't help hoping that somehow, some way, he'd be able to at last convince her of his innocence. More than anything in the world he needed someone who believed in him, someone who could help him prove his suspicions.

Travis didn't really know just how long Bliss held

114

his attentions, but he was still staring at her as the sun crept up to peer over the horizon. The pink haze of dawn began to push out the darkness of the night sky. Another day. Mentally he marked off the time that had elapsed since that bank robbery. Three days. It seemed like an eternity.

"Bliss . . ." Her name escaped from his lips before he even knew what he was doing. Why?

Her awakening was instantaneous. She was quickly on alert. Sitting up, her heart pounding, she grabbed for her gun and turned her head sharply from left to right, searching for Travis La Mont. She was only satisfied when she had ascertained that he was where she had left him.

"I'm still here! You've seen to that," he said, holding up his tightly tied wrists and nodding his head in the direction of Bard and Boru, who were eyeing him warily. "Of course I'm not certain I want to leave now, not after last night."

"Last night . . ."

Bliss recalled what had happened very vividly. The kisses still seemed to linger on her lips, causing them to tingle. Remembering the intimacy of her fondling, she hastily looked away. Their destinies lay in different directions.

"Surely you haven't forgotten."

"No." Last night had been enjoyable and she wouldn't soon forget it, she couldn't argue with that, but she was far past that time when she'd believed in happy endings. Nothing serious could come between this man and herself. She'd take Travis La Mont in, that was that! It was for the marshal to see to his fate after that. If La Mont was innocent as he claimed, it

115

would be up to him to prove it at his trial. It was highly unlikely that she and this man would ever meet again. "But for your information, only the money concerns me," she said, perhaps a bit too quickly.

"The money!" Well, what had he expected?

Bliss stood up, cursing the lateness of the day. It seemed the best-laid plans of mice and men were doomed to alteration. She had wanted to ride out at dawn, but restless hours of tossing and turning had taken their toll. She might have slept the entire morning away, as a matter of fact, if she hadn't been awakened by the sound of her name. That didn't mean she exhibited her gratitude, however.

"Get up." She recalled again the intimate contact between them last night and blushed. What in the world had gotten into her? "We're moving out of here."

She stood as still as a stone, absorbing the familiar morning sounds, the restless neighing of the horses, the song of the birds, the faint whisper of an early morning breeze. She cautiously surveyed the area with knowing eyes. Nothing moved. Why then did she have a gut feeling that something was wrong?

Travis didn't move.

"Come on. Come on. Gotta get going. We have a long steep road ahead of us." Bliss tugged at his bound wrists to pull him to his feet.

"Without as much as a cup of coffee to get me started? You're a cruel, hard woman, Bliss." She was emotionally closed. Guarded. He wondered if she would ever share her innermost feelings with anyone. "Silver Bow isn't going anywhere. It will

116

still be there regardless of what time we arrive."

Maybe he was right, she thought. They had to take time to eat. She had a duty to perform, but surely time out for coffee and a biscuit wouldn't slow them down too much. "All right, but I'll be sitting here with this rifle pointed right at your head, so don't try anything. I'll keep you bound 'til I get the coffee made."

She gathered sticks, piled them high, then lit the fire, poured water from a bucket inside the wagon into a tin coffeepot, put in a heap of coffee, placed the coffee on the fire and got out two tin cups. All the while she was thinking, *I have to see that he doesn't try to escape. I couldn't stand his death on my conscience. But I'm going to have to be hard nosed so as not to give myself away.* But it was difficult to pretend that everything was the same, that last night hadn't happened.

"What I wouldn't give to have eggs and bacon," she said, hastening to fill the silence with conversation. "Pa used to say a day hadn't begun until after breakfast."

Searching the wagon she found some stale sourdough biscuits. Once again she tied one of his hands to the wagon wheel so that he could eat. "Hard as a rock, but edible if you dip them in the coffee." She handed him a tin cup of the strong brew and became flustered when their fingers touched.

"Your fingers are soft."

"Soft?" She laughed, a nervously strained sound. "Hard work has made them calloused."

"They're soft just the same." She had rolled her shirtsleeves up, and her exposed arms were tanned

117

and more muscular than any lady back East would have allowed, but Travis found them very appealing. "I liked having your hands on me last night."

"Oh, is that so . . . ?" She tried to hide her own feelings about what had happened. "Well, it won't happen again. I was just mad as hell at you and wanted to make you squirm."

"You did."

They ate in silence, each immersed in thought. When Travis had finished she gave him another biscuit without his asking.

He watched as she went about the morning chores, working swiftly and efficiently in flowing easy motions. She was graceful, not at all mannish in the way she moved, and he found it enjoyable to look at her. Her breasts were round and full. He remembered all too well how soft they had felt against his chest. The neck of her shirt had opened far enough to allow a tantalizing glimpse of the valley between, and he feasted his eyes.

Travis found it strange that while most women relished the idea of looking at themselves in the mirror, he had never witnessed Bliss Harrington showing a weakness for such vanity.

"You're staring a hole clean through me," she challenged. Looking down at the men's britches that she wore, she found herself foolishly wishing she were wearing a dress and chastised herself for such a thought. Travis was staring—and thinking that he liked the way her pants clung tightly to her hips.

"I'm sorry. But men always stare at beautiful women, Bliss."

She acted as if she hadn't heard the compliment.

"I wish it would rain!" she said out of the blue.

"Rain?" Remembering the storm that had sent him into the tunnel of the mine, Travis shuddered. The last thing he wanted to see right now was clouds.

"Yes, rain. That would make it impossible for the posse to track us. As it is we're hidden, but not so well that somebody good at looking for the right signs can't find us."

"Well then, let us hope that they aren't." He also hoped that when his newspaper back East didn't hear from him they'd do some searching. A man of his reputation didn't just up and disappear.

Leaning back against the wagon, Travis sipped his coffee as if he hadn't a care in the world. Westward as far as he could see were mountains, glorious snow-capped peaks, gigantic, rising to meet the sun. Under different circumstances, he thought, this mountain wilderness would be an ideal place to settle down. Whoever could want for more? No wonder Bliss loved it so.

Bliss hitched up the horses grazing nearby, thinking her own thoughts. Being in such close company afforded them little privacy or modesty, thus Bliss was beginning to know intimate details about him. She knew the location of every mole, every freckle—

"Was it just you and your father, Bliss?" he found himself asking.

Immediately suspicion flickered across her brow. "Why do you want to know?"

"Just making conversation. I just want to know something about you."

Bliss sighed. There was no reason to be secretive.

119

"Yes, it was just me and him." She refused to talk about her mother. "What about you?" Somehow she imagined him as an only child, the pampered son of wealthy Easterners. No doubt, Travis La Mont had been born with a silver spoon in his mouth.

Travis looked down at his cup. "I'm the youngest son. Three older brothers preceded me. Antoine, Boyce and Gaylord."

"None of them wanted men I hope."

Travis couldn't help but grin. "No, seems I'm the only one with that distinction." He took a bite of the biscuit and, finding it still too hard, dunked it in the coffee again. "But they're prisoners just the same."

Bliss cocked her head. "Prisoners?" She was bewildered.

"Trapped working at the family farm, just as I would have been if I hadn't made up my mind up to escape. Undoubtedly they'll live out their entire existences there, marry there, have children there, die there and be buried in the family plot." As if he should criticize. For all his newfound sophistication he'd ended up in quite a pickle.

Travis couldn't help but notice how quiet Bliss was this morning. Usually bold and talkative, she was making it a point to keep her distance.

"Are you afraid of me?" He sensed that she was.

"Afraid of you?" Her head snapped around. "Of course not! I'm not afraid of any man."

"Then why do you say you don't want to repeat what happened last night when I know that you do."

"I don't!" He had a masculine magnetism that was difficult to ignore, but she forced herself to do it,

120

busying herself with routine matters. When she'd finished with them, she tidied the camp, putting all the supplies back into the wagon. Looking out of the corner of her eye, she caught Travis giving Bard part of his biscuit. "If you think you can make friends with them, mister, don't even try. All I have to do is give a command and they'll be on you like flies at a picnic."

"I'll bet . . ."

Travis started to say something else, but with a finger to her lips, she shushed him.

Thank God for the dogs! Had it not been for their alert ears and sudden barking Bliss knew very well she might have been caught unawares. As it was, she peered through the rocks and foliage and saw *their* silhouettes. "Damn!" The three men of the posse had tripled into nine. The odds were not at all encouraging. "They're back and this time with friends."

Travis looked and saw them too. They were there all right.

"What are you going to do?" Once again Travis felt the sweat of fear. Death was stalking him, and his only salvation was a slim, red-haired woman toting a gun.

Chapter Thirteen

It all happened swiftly—a shout, a second of pulsating silence, then the tramping of feet. A shot blasted a signal that these men meant business. The horses whinnied, the dogs put up a fierce ruckus and Travis and Bliss looked at each other in horrified astonishment.

"Get down!" Just to make certain he obeyed, Bliss threw herself against Travis and sent him toppling to the hard ground. They'd kill him, of that she had no doubt. Even her own life was in danger. Crossfire targeted everyone. Crawling on hands and knees to the wagon, Bliss reached for another rifle, a Winchester repeating model.

"What are you going to do, use one in each hand?" Travis asked sarcastically.

"No, one's for you!" she shouted out. "It's your neck *and* mine. I can't do it all alone." Quickly untying his hands and feet, she thrust a rifle at him. "I'm going to have to give you a chance to defend yourself."

Travis grabbed the weapon before she had a chance to change her mind. His finger curled on the trigger. "You mean you trust me with a gun?" It was a challenge he was determined to meet.

"Have to. You're an intelligent man. We've got our hands full." The staccato pop of gunfire reverberated through the air. Bullets spattered around them. Wild shots! The posse was sending lead in all directions. "I don't think you'll be going anywhere!"

"No, I don't expect that I will," Travis responded, watching as Bliss fired her rifle without shouldering it, shooting from the hip as if her weapon were a pistol. Her skill won Travis' admiration for he knew how heavy the weapon in her hands was, knew too that few men could have shot it well.

"Hurry!" Her shooting had taken their attackers by surprise, but she knew they had to get ready for the onslaught before the posse recovered and started firing again. "Take cover, mister!"

Quickly Travis heeded her order and selected a strategic spot behind a large rock, one that would keep him sheltered from gunshots, offer him a gun-barrel rest and at the same time give him a good view of his adversaries' slowly advancing figures. Hunkering down he settled into as comfortable a position as possible on the sharp stones that covered the ground. With an outwardly cool facade, he began firing.

"Bard, Boru, into the wagon." The dogs instantly obeyed. "It's going to be a real dangerous turkey shoot," Bliss said as she ducked behind a tree. Despite her bravado she had the feeling that she might have bitten off more than she could chew. Had she?

"Yeah," Travis agreed, "but just who is going to be the one to end up wearing the feathers?" Taking careful aim he fired at the dim form of a man, saw him fall only to be replaced by two more.

"Not bad, for an Easterner," Bliss complimented. Inwardly she felt as if a fist were squeezing her stomach. Was that how he'd shot that poor fellow in Silver Bow? Better by far he'd proved himself inept with a gun. Perhaps then she would have believed his story of innocence, but he was skilled all right. Too much so for a man who professed to be a newspaperman.

Bliss began snapshooting, working the lever of her Winchester as fast as she could. "Not bad shooting yourself," Travis said, in awe. He'd actually thought at one time that he could be a match for her, but when it came to guns he was just a novice.

A bullet thumped the dirt near Travis' arm, a reminder of his mortality and the danger he was in. He hugged the ground, his eyes searching. Shots came from directly in front of him, just over the ridge. They were moving in.

"Stop shooting! We don't have no quarrel with you, lady," a loud voice cried out. "It's Travis La Mont we want, and we know you've got him. Just put down your guns and we'll act real polite in settling this thing."

"I'm not putting down anything, most of all my rifle. As for your acting polite, I don't think there's a one of you who would know how," Bliss shouted back. The intruders answered with a ragged volley of shots. She kept her eyes on the spot where she had seen movement, waited for just the length of a heartbeat, then fired in that direction.

"How long do you think we can hold them off?" Travis' blood surged with adrenaline.

"All depends. Why?" Bliss cast a quick look at him over her shoulder. "Do you want to surrender, mister?"

"Definitely not!" He wasn't anxious to wear a rope as a necktie. "I just . . . well . . . just don't want anything to happen to you." There, he'd said it.

"Me." Bliss laughed with feigned joviality, trying to hide her own apprehension. "Don't worry about me. I can take care of myself."

The number of gunshots increased. Bliss and Travis matched them bullet for bullet. They heard the scream of a man in pain, the frightened whinny of a horse. Travis swore and levered another cartridge into his rifle's chamber. Out of the corner of his eye he saw Bliss move from her cover.

"Be careful!" He knew for a certainty that seeing her hit would be more than he could bear. Hoping to distract the posse gunmen, he fired a hasty shot. The answering bullet shattered chips of rock right where Travis was sprawled. He dropped to such a totally flattened position that his nose was just inches from the ground.

She stealthily came to where he lay and knelt down. "You hit?" For just a moment she felt the nausea of fear.

"No, but they almost got me!" He looked her full in the face. "Would you care?"

"Of course I would," she said all too quickly, then

125

tempered her show of emotion by adding, "I prefer to bring you back alive! Hauling a body back into town can be tedious work. You look as if you'd be heavy."

"Don't worry, I plan to cooperate," Travis said dryly. Didn't this woman ever think of anything else except her bounty-hunting? Didn't she have any sympathetic feelings? Was he just a hunk of meat to her? The idea was deeply troubling.

"They'll circle around us and come at us from both sides, if they have any brains that is. That's what I'd do. Keep us turning in circles trying to pick them off until we're both dizzy." Clamping the butt of the rifle in her armpit she began propelling herself forward on hands and knees. Closer, she had to get closer to where they had gathered. "'Course now we have a slight advantage. Anyone who comes up behind us has to come up a slight incline."

Staccato snaps and booms filled the air with sound. Gun smoke hung in the air. The shoots were coming nearer, bringing death with them. "What do you suggest we do?" He glanced at the evidence of the bullets that had only by chance missed him.

"I suggest we create confusion when they make their attack." Bliss's eyes darted to the wagon. It was the only thing besides her dogs and horses that she possessed, yet she knew she had to sacrifice it now. "We'll set the wagon on fire and roll it down the hill. That way we'll only have to worry about the men harrassing us from the front."

"The wagon!" It sounded reasonable to Travis. "Let them come. We'll be ready for them."

"Yeah, we'll be ready." Bliss heard a loud buzzing

126

by her ear, then her wide-brimmed Stetson fell to the dust.

"Bliss!" Travis was petrified, thinking she had been hit.

"I'm all right." In retaliation she opened fire again, then paused. "Cover me while I make a dive for the wagon." It was a daring move. Bullets whizzed over her head, imbedding themselves in the wood of the wagon frame just as she threw herself beneath it, scarring its sides. One bullet caught an iron hinge on the door and made a clinking sound before it careened erratically into the air.

"One more chance! Give up Travis La Mont and we'll let you walk right out of here," a loud voice boomed out.

"Go to hell!" Bliss opened up with her rifle, aiming carefully sighted shots. She reloaded hastily and began firing again.

Meanwhile Travis pressed his shoulder against the rock he was hiding behind, braced his arms and hands against it, bent his legs and began to push. With a burst of angry strength he gouged his heels into the earth and forced the boulder to roll down the incline just as one of the gunmen was trying to sneak up on them from behind the way Bliss had predicted.

"Just like a game of ten pins!" he proclaimed. The only problem was he had to find other shelter. With little time to choose he picked a tree this time. The wooden shield did little to bolster his nerve. He felt vulnerable. Even so, his fears were more for Bliss than for himself as he watched her douse the wagon with lamp oil. Just in time too, for it appeared the posse was gathering to make an attack.

"Bard, Boru, into the trees!" Bliss hastily retrieved the tintype of her father and herself and tucked it inside her shirt. Then, lighting a match, she set the wagon on fire. Wood, rope and canvas burned with a fury, flames shooting from the canvas top. She choked back a sob of sorrow. So many years, so many memories all up in smoke. It was, however, the only way. "Signal me when it's time to push it," she called out to Travis, waiting with indrawn breath. What if she was wrong? What if the men didn't use the same strategy that she would? What if she'd sacrificed her wagon and still lost this dangerous game?

Apparently she hadn't, not yet. The shooting from in front of them had died down. That could only mean one thing. The men were moving to the rear of the campsite. Travis watched and waited; then when it seemed the time was appropriate and the men had made their formation, he called out, "Now!"

The flaming wagon rolled down the hill, scattering the members of the posse here and there. "Look at them. What cowards," Bliss gasped. "They aren't even going to continue the fight. Must think I have something even more sinister in store for them if they rile me up too much."

As he saw the men running toward their horses for a getaway, Travis knew he'd won at least a small victory. As a precaution he fired into the air over their heads. "We beat them!" He was so occupied with shooting that he forgot all about Bliss until she stood directly behind him.

"Yeah, we beat them all right, at least for a while.

128

Now, put the rifle down." Travis felt the hard tip of a gun barrel pressed against his back. "What the—"

"You did your part, impressively I might say, but now it's time for us to get back to status quo."

"Which means?"

"You're still my prisoner, and I aim to take you in." Certainly his life wasn't worth a nickel to him with those men roaming about. They'd lick their wounds for a while, but they would be back. Bliss knew that all too well. She wanted to get Travis into town without any lead peppering his body. If, as he said, he was innocent there would be time then to see about his defense.

"You can't mean it!" He had thought that after proving his courage she would have a change of heart.

"I do!" Her tone was purposely sharp as she fought her inner emotions.

Travis threw the rifle on the ground in a fit of outrageous anger. "If you aren't the damnedest female I've ever met," he said through clenched teeth. "You're stubborn clear through."

"And right proud of it!" Bliss replied. She was doing what was right. "Besides, now that my wagon has gone up in smoke while saving your hide, I need that reward money twice as bad."

"Reward money!" Sullenly Travis stared at her as she tied his hands, knowing for the first time in his life what it truly felt like to be defeated.

Part Two:
Guest at a Hanging

Watersville, Butte and Surrounding Territory

And naked to the hangman's noose
  The morning clocks will ring
A neck God made for other use
  Than strangling in a string.

—A. E. Housman, *A Shropshire Lad*

Chapter Fourteen

Bounty hunting was a nasty business! But somebody had to do it, no matter what inner turmoil it might cause. That was the thought runing over and over through Bliss's mind as she continued the last leg of the journey. Though she wouldn't admit it to herself, she felt more than a little guilty about what she was doing. Several times she had even been tempted to just let Travis La Mont go, and might have had it not been for her father's well-meant teachings. Oakwood Harrison had always been adamant in his insistence that the law had to be obeyed or the territory would explode into anarchy. Thinking about that made it just a little easier for Bliss to haul her quarry toward the town of Watersville, the site of the marshal's office and jail.

"One thing I can say is that at least you're being treated to some pretty good scenery," she said to Travis. And it was true. The territory of Montana was a sparsely populated wilderness of spectacular canyons and valleys, sprinkled with forests and rock formations, the domain of soaring eagles and bighorn mountain sheep. In addition there were the prairie lands and large areas of wild grass with streams cutting through them. Bliss was very proud of this beautiful place and of all that had been accomplished here in the territory since its development had begun twenty years ago.

"I'm being treated?" As Travis strained at his bonds he was anything but grateful. He had actually begun to have feelings for this young woman, had worried about her during the posse's attack, yet all she thought about was bringing him in. She had trussed him up without even a blink. Was it any wonder he felt betrayed? "Well, you can see it that way if it soothes your conscience any. I'd as soon ride through here blindfolded."

Bliss was stung by the nastiness of his tone. He'd hardly said two words to her since she had tied him back up, loaded the two horses with whatever had been salvaged from the wagon fire and told him they were heading out. Bard and Boru were much better company as they tagged along behind. "Suit yourself. You can either appreciate the view or close your eyes for all I care, mister!"

Travis responded with a silent scowl. He would never admit to her that what his eyes beheld did give him a feeling of awe. It was beautiful! Uncrowded. Bountiful. Desolate in places but subtly alluring. As the huge expanse of Montana opened up before his eyes, he felt his heart surge. Seeing this area made him remember the first time he'd set eyes upon it. He had felt then as if his life were just beginning.

The area they passed through now was heavily

forested with many varieties of trees, including cottonwood. Behind the trees, in a clearing, were numerous cottages, mostly of wood. Some with granite trim. They presented an entirely different appearance from the dwellings he had seen so far. Squinting his eyes, he could see that far away to the north were snow-capped peaks. One could see for miles, as far as Helena in the distance.

Bliss told him they were five thousand feet above sea level. "Over there is Bear's Tooth," she said pointing to a huge peak in the distance. "That is where the great Missouri River has its origin."

There were smokestacks and evidence of mineral dumps scattered all over the hills. Travis tried to act nonchalant, but he knew she'd caught him looking. "It looks right down there as if this used to be an old mining camp."

"Yep. Millions of dollars came from these mountains. But most of it was spent in Helena." She pointed in a northerly direction. "Over there, nestled in that gulch is where it is." Right now they were at the top of the heavily forested Moonlight Mountain, five thousand feet above sea level, looking out at the towns and the little valley below. "And close at hand is Silver Bow and Watersville."

"Wonderful!" he exclaimed sarcastically. Taking a critical look Travis was astounded at how far he had ridden in his attempt to get away from the place. Now he was back. To clear his name or fall victim to treachery? Only time would tell.

Casting his eyes on the sprawling grandeur as they rode along, he thought of how he loved this land. It was so different from the cultivated and cultured

East. There was a sense of freedom here that even his bondage could not quell. The very air was stimulating, as were these pioneering people so unlike the more established New Englanders he had known. These folks had pulled up their roots and traveled West by prairie schooner or wagon. They were proud and self-sufficient. A few were argumentative, even a little trigger happy and quick to action, and many were vagabonds too fond of drink, but there was much to admire about most of these folks nonetheless. They had the kind of strength that came from the soul and not just the body. Bliss's kind of people.

"If only things were different," he mumbled. Now, thanks to this female, he'd soon be cooped up and all this would be just a memory. A somber ending, not the wondrous beginning he had first supposed when he'd come to Montana Territory.

There were several new buildings popping up, new since Bliss had come this way. Now horse, cattle and sheep ranches dotted the land that had once been unsettled. "Look there. A new ranch. Two. Three." The chimney smoke was as thick as clouds.

All along the way Travis' mind had whirled with schemes for escape. Now a new one came to him. "A ranch, huh?" A place where he might be able to steal a horse faster than the nag he was on. Bliss Harrison wouldn't think she was so smart if he just up and disappeared. "Don't suppose we could stop and have a cold drink. It's been a long, nasty journey."

Bliss sensed he intended some sort of mischief. "We're traveling straight through. I'm not taking any chances with you, mister!" Already he had tried ten times to get away, even going so far as to chew the ropes around his wrists. Now she had him secured with thick rawhide.

What a fool he was to think she would agree. All the way she had watched him like a hawk. "So, that's that!" Travis nudged his horse into a faster gallop, thankful his hands were tied in front of him and not behind. "Well then, if you're so hellbent on getting to our destination let's not waste any time."

Travis remembered another journey that now seemed long ago. He had come this route by stagecoach on a venture that had taken him over the Rockies, tough miles that had tempered his strength as if it were the precious metal strewn over the mountain sides from mines and mills. Everywhere along the way he had been faced with unusual scenery, vast open spaces just waiting to be tamed. Nowhere had he found the crowded cities and tall buildings that were reminders of the East. Here houses and corrals were far apart as they dotted the hills.

He smiled as he saw a large board sign in front of one of those houses advertising pies, coffee and pistols for sale up ahead.

"The answer is no before you even ask!" Bliss said sternly, though the idea of a cup of coffee and a piece of gooseberry pie made her mouth water.

"Okay! Okay!" Once again Travis cast her a frown, wondering what might have happened if. He had wanted to make a strong impression on the people of the territory, but certainly not by being hauled into town.

"We'll be there in two shakes of a tail. The town is

just around the bend. You can get something to eat and drink then," Bliss announced, then paused before saying, "Too bad you have to reside in jail. It's an interesting place. I went there with my father once. I could show you around." And she suddenly wished that she could. Like it or not Travis La Mont was any woman's dream. If only he had stayed on the right side of the law!

Watersville was in a cool canyon surrounded by high hills. Dotted with shanties, tents, fragile-looking stores and shops with false fronts and several substantial buildings, it and its neighbor Silver Bow fit the description of places right out of a dime novel. The main street was narrow and dusty. Everywhere there were horses, carts and people, mostly men. Their dress varied, the miners wearing baggy pants, the ranch hands denim and flannel, the others the uniforms of their professions—butcher, baker or barber. They were rough looking, not fashionably dressed, and everyone carried a gun, even the females in town. All seemed to be in a hurry.

"Guess it's time to dismount, mister. And join these folks for a stroll." Though she tried to sound stern Bliss felt a knot forming in the pit of her stomach. Hunger no doubt. Well, she would get something to soothe the emptiness just as soon as this business was over.

Tying the horses to the hitching post near the water trough and telling Bard and Boru to stay, Bliss walked behind Travis, urging him on at the point of the gun poked in his ribs.

"Come along!" It annoyed her that people were staring so. Hadn't they ever seen a woman leading a

138

prisoner down the street before? She pulled her sleeves down over the gun to hide it, at least a little. Smiling and saying a polite good morning to the few people she passed on the boardwalk, she tried not to draw attention to the fact that she had a prisoner in tow. She had no desire to bring forth a large crowd of onlookers.

"The jail has got to be somewhere hereabouts!" Bliss looked to the left, then to the right, then straight ahead. A pity, she thought, that the town had fallen on hard times. Once it had been a well-populated place, but when some of the mining claims had proved disappointing, many had left never to return again.

"Ah yes, the jail," Travis mocked. It was hard to believe that he was here. A small part of him had hoped against hope that Bliss Harrison would have second thoughts about what she was doing. "Wouldn't want you to miss out on your blood money!"

There were several children meandering in the street, all seemingly of the age to attend the one-room school. Bliss asked them about the layout of the town. She was told by a little girl that there was one small, two-story boarding house, a one-room school building, a general store and a saloon, mixed in among the other buildings of less importance. Behind the school was a log cabin where the school marm, her husband and two children undoubtedly lived. Farther up the mountain were groups of cabins for the townsmen, most of whom seemed to have been miners at one time. The jail was in the opposite direction.

Thanking the child, Bliss continued down the boardwalk, but now going east and not west. It took awhile for Bliss to spot the marshal's den, but at last she did. Wedged in between two shorter buildings, it nearly went unnoticed if you blinked. The marshal's office was in the front part of the jailhouse. Bliss's sharp eyes all too quickly found it.

"Shall we go?"

"After you, ma'am." Travis nodded with feigned politeness but Bliss insisted on staying behind. Following him across the street, she pushed open the door and they both walked in.

The marshal's office was what would definitely be called plush. Wood paneling covered the walls, the five leather hairs scattered about all matched, there was a huge oriental rug, the bookshelves were crammed with gold-lettered books and there was even a chandelier. It seemed overly opulent when compared with the rest of the town. Bliss eyed the interior with a critical eye as she and Travis walked across the floor.

A burly, tawny-haired man hurriedly pulled his feet down from a marble desk top, got up from his well-padded swivel chair and approached the two people before him. "What do we have here, ma'am?" The way he addressed Bliss held just a tinge of smugness.

He's a shifty-eyed son-of-a-bitch, Travis thought, feeling an instant dislike. *I wouldn't trust him as far as I could throw him.* Something about the man clicked in Travis' head. But what?

Blisss took the folded wanted poster out of her shirt pocket. "Him!" Having been taught by her father to assess every man she met, Bliss looked the marshal up and down. He was large boned, with features that were prominent yet not unattractive. A mustache hid the large distance between his nose and lips. As for his hands they didn't have a callus on them. As if he'd never done an honest day of work. Somehow he didn't seem like a marshal. He was too debonair, in a sinister kind of way.

Hurriedly he snatched the poster from her hand. He looked at it, then at Travis, then at the poster, then at Travis again. Then he grinned. "I'll be damned! Looks like that bank robber-killer, the one with a price on his head."

"One and the same." Bliss grabbed the poster and carefully folded it up.

Though he pounded her on the back his beady brown eyes seemed to mock her. "You caught him! Guess that makes you a hero to this town and to Silver Bow."

A sudden lump formed in Bliss's throat as she looked at Travis out of the corner of her eye. "I guess it does!"

"And believe me, we are beholding." He slapped her on the back again.

Bliss waited for him to mention the reward. When he didn't she said, "Well I'm glad you're grateful, but gratitude won't fill an empty stomach or put a roof over a body's head." She held out her hand, palm up. "Now that he's been delivered into your hands I want to collect my two-hundred-dollar reward."

"Two hundred?" The marshal forced a smile.

"Yes, the two hundred dollars," she repeated emphatically, bringing forth the poster again. "This

141

is Travis La Mont, the man on this poster. Just as you said. And see here, it plainly says 'reward—two hundred dollars.'"

"So it does." He shrugged. "And I'll be more than happy to honor that." He circled Travis clucking his tongue. "Well, well, well. Travis La Mont. A thief and a killer. Dangerous!"

Up until now Travis had kept silent, but how could he remain still in the face of such an assault on his character? "I'm neither! It's all a damned misunderstanding. I had no part in that robbery, and for sure didn't kill anyone!" He was indignant in his own defense.

"Uh-huh!" The marshal's cold glare made it obvious that he was anything but sympathetic. "Well, there are people who say differently."

Hurriedly Bliss put in a good word for Travis. "Mistakes happen all the time, Marshal. People can see one thing and think they see something else." Her eyes softened for just an instant as they touched on Travis. "All along the way he's been a model prisoner. Hell, he even had a chance to shoot me, but he didn't. I've seen a lot of outlaws, working with my pa, and this one just doesn't fit the mold."

The marshal wasn't even listening to Bliss's testimonial to Travis' good character. As for Travis, every time he tried to speak he was told to keep quiet or suffer the consequences, that being a brutal stab in the ribs. "Come along!" Travis was put in a cell close to the door. One with only a tiny window, located about nine feet up. As for furniture, it held a small cot with a lumpy mattress, nothing more. Hardly a comfortable-looking place.

"I want a chance to send a telegram to my lawyer! It's my right!"

"You don't have any rights!" was the angry retort.

Bliss didn't like the marshal's attitude toward Travis in the least. Taking a deep breath, she tried to bring her temper down to a manageable level. "It would seem to me that he does. Innocent until proven guilty, isn't that the way it works? Even the worst desperado deserves a trial."

The keys jangled. The thick iron door creaked open; then Bliss was told to say her goodbye. She had done what was right! She had brought in a wanted man to assure that justice was done. Even so, her thoughts tormented her as she heard the cell door bang shut.

Damned if she didn't suddenly feel the urge to cry. What in the devil had come over her? Had Travis La Mont gotten under her skin more than she had realized? For a woman who never like to admit she was wrong, Bliss was having some serious second thoughts.

"Marshal, he says he didn't do it!"

"And just what would you expect him to say?"

"But it could be true." Wasn't that what he had insisted all along? That he was innocent. "Don't you think he deserves a chance to be heard?"

The marshal patted her on the head as if placating a child. "Of course! Of course."

"I think you *should* hear him out. He said he was framed. Claims he took a photograph of the robbery that will prove it! Anything is possible."

The marshal stared at her long and hard, but didn't reply. Then, before she knew it, he had taken

143

her by the arm and was propelling her away from the cell, toward his office door. Suddenly it seemed he was anxious to get rid of her. Opening his safe, he took out a sackful of money and thrust it into her hands. Before Bliss could count it out, he said, "I need some time to put that reward money together. Come back tomorrow. Meantime you just take that as a gift from the grateful citizens of Silver Bow and Watersville. You're our 'guest'. Enjoy."

"But . . ." Bliss didn't like the way this was turning out. Most importantly something about the marshal deeply troubled her. She wasn't at all certain that she trusted him.

"Thank you, little lady. Justice has been done today, don't have any second thoughts on that."

"Justice?" Doubt flooded her as she followed him through the door. Then it was shut abruptly in her face. "Justice . . ." Bliss looked down at the money, feeling exactly like Judas must have felt. The gold was heavy, but nowhere as heavy as her heart.

Chapter Fifteen

The gold coins jingled in Bliss's pocket as she strode the boardwalk of Watersville aimlessly. Bard on one side and Boru on the other. Perhaps seeing another face or even a group of faces now would help heal her loneliness, get her mind off the awful biting conscience that tormented her. She simply wasn't sure about Travis.

Damn him. Why did he haunt her thoughts? Why did she have to care? Well, it was out of her hands now. Besides, she had a whole slew of things to do before she finally rode out tomorrow. She had to stable her horses, find a place to stay for the night. And she must choose an eatery, maybe one that would let her bring in her dogs. She and Travis had only been able to load a few things on the horses, so she needed to replenish her supplies. First on her list, however, was a visit to the blacksmith. Chocolate, her brown horse, had thrown a shoe.

Bliss reclaimed the large animals from where they were hitched and led them down the wide dirt street toward the slightly dilapidated livery stable, which was conveniently located right next door to the blacksmith's. It was dark inside and smelled strongly of horses and mold, but the tall young curly-haired man who took her horses seemed pleasant enough.

"Are you new around here? Don't remember seeing you before." He winked at her flirtatiously, trying to ignore the protective hovering of Bard and Boru.

"I was here once before with my pa, but it was a while back." Somehow it seemed like a lifetime ago.

"Are you going to be here long?" he asked hopefully, eyeing her up and down.

Bliss quickly quenched his optimism. "I'm only here for the night. I've got business in town tomorrow; then I'll be riding out."

His disappointed look was flattering. "Too bad. Pretty girls are a scarcity in Watersville. I was looking forward to calling on you."

Once Bliss might have responded to the young man's attentions. After all, he was reasonably attractive and not as long in the tooth as the men she usually came across. But somehow when she compared him to Travis La Mont he came up short, thus she quickly got down to the business at hand. "I need to put these two up for the night. Chocolate and Straw Boy are their names." She put the ends of the leather reins in his hands. "They've had a long, hard ride."

That he patted the head of each horse fondly was a favorable sign. Likewise, the fact that Bard and Boru were wagging their tails.

"Yep, I rode a long way all right." Bliss aided him as he slipped off the saddlebags, saddles, and bridles, carefully avoiding Straw Boy's hind legs because he sometimes kicked when approached from his hind quarters. "I brought a prisoner in, you see. A wanted man. Travis La Mont. Ever hear of him?"

He shook his head. "Nope, but then I seldom keep track of such things. Best to mind your own business, my mother always says, and I believe her."

"Well, he's the prisoner I caught and brought into town." Seeing a sack of apples on the ground, she picked up two for each hand, then proceeded to give the two horses a treat.

"You brought in a prisoner?" He stiffened and looked at her warily. "Are you in the marshal's employ?"

"No." Bliss took note of the way he sighed in relief. "Why?"

"Just . . . just making conversation." Turning his back on her, he busied himself with the horses, currying them, feeding and watering them, then securing them in their stalls.

"No, you weren't just making small talk. The look in your eyes just now when I mentioned the marshal wasn't a very good recommendation for his character." Remembering the way he had treated Travis, she asked, "Is he a bully?"

"No . . . no!" But the way he said it clearly stated that the marshal was.

"Well, I don't care just how he acts. I won't let him intimidate me." At first Bliss had been perfectly

147

willing to hand over all her rifles and guns to this young man for his safe-keeping, figuring she had no need of them for her short stay. Now, however, she changed her mind. There was no telling what could happen.

"One of the horses threw a shoe, so I need to visit with your neighbor. I'll let you two work out the arrangements." Hefting up one rifle and a handgun, she whistled to her dogs, then had second thoughts. "Would you mind keeping the dogs with the horses until I talk with the smith?"

"Not at all." He smiled at her congenially.

"Thanks." After paying for one night of her horses' board she took her leave.

It was just a short jaunt to the blacksmith's shop; a large wooden building that looked to be a combination shed and house. The most important place in town, so her father had always said, and Bliss knew that hadn't been idle talk. No town was complete without a blacksmith because no one else could shoe horses and oxen, sharpen plows, repair wagons or do the other tasks involving skills in handling iron and other metals. And the smithy was always a friendly place for conducting business and exchanging gossip. But where was this blacksmith? There was no fire in the forge, the water tubs were empty, the hammers and anvil were left untended. A strange way to do business.

More than a little annoyed, Bliss knocked at the door that separated the shed from the house. It took five knocks before the door was opened, but just a crack. "What do you want?" a gruff voice called out.

"What do I want? I want your services, that's what!" Bliss thrust her booted foot in the crack, forcing the door open a little wider. "You are the blacksmith I presume."

"I am!" And an unsociable one it seemed.

"My horse threw a shoe. I need to have a new one."

"Is that so?" Only one gray eye was visible and it was burning a hole right through her. "You can make an appointment. Tomorrow afternoon is free."

"Tomorrow afternoon?" It certainly didn't look as if he had more business than he could handle or else the tools of his trade would have been in use. Was there something wrong with him? "Are you ill or indisposed?" Or was he just lazy.

The door was thrown open and she could see for herself that he was, to the contrary, very robust. A huge man dressed all in black with shoulder-length gray hair, enormous shoulders, a hook nose and a patch over one eye, he did in fact look more like a pirate than a man who plied the blacksmith's trade. Bliss thought to herself that she had picked a bad time to have left her dogs behind. "As you can see, I have my good health, at least for the moment."

"You look extremely healthy," Bliss answered taking a step backward. She pointed to the unused tools behind her. "You don't appear to be that busy, why then must I wait until tomorrow? You see I planned to leave Watersville late tomorrow morning." Taking the moneypouch out of her pocket she held it up and shook it. "Couldn't I persuade you to

149

change your mind?"

"Maybe. It all depends."

"Depends on what?"

"On who you are, where you're going and what you're here for."

Bliss took off her hat, allowing him a clear view of her long bright red hair. "My name is Bliss Harrison, to answer your first question first."

"Harrison!" Though he wasn't making much attempt at being friendly, the blacksmith at least stepped outside, shutting the door behind him.

"As to where I'm going I can't rightly say. I just delivered a prisoner to the marshal."

"The marshal?" Anger furled the gray, bushy brows. It was obvious the blacksmith held the marshal in contempt. "If you're working for that weasel then it might be into next week before I can shoe your horse. I have honest customers to accommodate!"

Bliss was stunned, hardly expecting this sort of reaction. She searched for the right words to say. Obviously she had to be careful how she handled this man. "I . . . I don't work for him. I've never even met the marshal before. Hell, I don't even know his name."

"And yet you delivered a man into his hands?"

"A wanted man, yes!"

His lips curled up in snarl. "Wanted for what?"

"For robbing a bank and . . . supposedly well, killing a bank employee." To corroborate her story she reached for the wanted poster and held it out for him to read. "Travis La Mont."

150

Seeing the poster didn't lessen his hostility. Instead it seemed to antagonize him. "And just why would a woman take it upon herself to turn a man in? Was he a wayward lover who wronged you?"

Intuition told her not to mention her profession, therefore she gritted her teeth and said, "Yes." After all, they had exchanged a few kisses.

"Huh!" Clearly he disapproved. "And now that you've thrust him in the lion's den you plan to leave." He snapped his fingers. "Just like that."

He made it sound so terrible, as if Bliss didn't feel bad enough. "What do you mean 'lion's den'?"

"Marshal Taggart isn't known for administering justice! If you ask me, the people made a big mistake in choosing a man like that to enforce the law hereabouts. Though it seems that I'm the only one brave enough to speak out. Ah, well!" He turned his back and headed for the door.

"What about my horse?"

Turning around he grumbled, "The offer is the same. Tomorrow afternoon."

Bliss was doubly in a hurry now, though not for the same reason. The blacksmith's attitude toward the marshal had really made her think. She needed her horse, but not for the same reason now. Travis had made some accusations and Bliss was determined to check them out.

Travis felt like a caged animal as he clung to the bars of his cell. It was cramped inside, with barely enough room for a man to move around. A

151

miserable way to be treated. Worse yet was the fact that the jail seemed impregnable, thus any thought of escape was little more than a dream. No, he was trapped all right, there was no getting around it. The thought that at least he was alive didn't quell his anger.

"Damn that stubborn woman!" He wondered what Bliss Harrison was doing right now and figured she was undoubtedly out celebrating somewhere, telling all who would listen about her daring deed in bringing him in. Well, he hoped her conscience bothered her, at least at little.

What hour was it? The minutes passed so slowly that he wasn't really certain of the exact time. He didn't have a watch, and there was no clock near the cell. He looked out his window. The sun was still out. Must be around two o'clock. He couldn't have been in the cell more than a few hours. A few hours! And already he was going loco. Still, he tried to keep calm. It would all come out in the wash, as his father used to say. His attorney, Aric Wesley would make arrangements to bail him out, that is, if he was contacted.

Wesley was a man Travis had always trusted, a soft-spoken Bostonian with shrewd green eyes and grizzled gray hair. He had handled business and legal affairs for Travis for the last six years. There was no one better at the game.

"Has anyone wired my lawyer?" Travis asked the man who mopped and swept the floor of the narrow corridor between the cells and the outer door. Ellis Jones, an incessantly chattering little man with a bald head and large ears, talked to himself as well as to Travis.

Pausing in his sweeping, Ellis asked, "Done what? What has he done?" His expression couldn't have been more befuddled had Travis spoken in French. For a moment he seemed at a loss for words.

"Telegraphed my lawyer," Travis shouted, taking his frustration out on the funny little fellow. "I asked the marshal if he would, even gave him the lawyer's name and told him where to reach him, but he didn't commit himself." Clenching the bars, he said in a calmer tone, "Did he?"

"Did he what?" There was a sparkle of fear in Ellis' eyes, as if he were confronting some kind of monster. He was quiet; then he broke into senseless chatter.

"Did he wire my attorney?"

Taking up his broom again, Ellis worked it hurriedly over the floor outside Travis' cell. He seemed in a world of his own. Travis regretted having asked at all.

"Oh, for God's sake!" Travis' threw up his hands. His patience was being sorely tested. He was beginning to wonder if this elflike simpleton was part of his punishment. Plopping down on the cot, he put his hands behind his head and stared up at the ceiling.

"Don't know." Ellis Jones snapped out of his trance. "I'll go ask!" Anxious to please, he put down his broom and scurried off through the door to the marshal's office. When he returned he didn't come back alone. Marshal Owen Taggart was with him.

"Ellis here tells me you're raising a ruckus. Is that

153

so?" Though his tone was pleasant, there was something in his eyes that hinted of danger.

Travis sprang to his feet, taking his place back at the bars. "I merely inquired if Ellis knew whether or not you had wired my attorney so that he could help me get out of this mess!" Travis ignored his instinct for caution. This overbearing lawman was being totally unreasonable, but he was sure that Wesley would come and by the time the lawyer was through with the marshal, Taggart would be begging his pardon. He was innocent, by God! "You've made a big mistake, and I intend to prove it, with his help."

"I've made a mistake? I've made a mistake!" Taggart's eyes narrowed to angry slits.

Taking a deep breath, Travis was determined to act civilized about the matter. "Look, I don't want hard feelings. I don't blame you for what occurred. Mistakes happen. All I ask is that you give me a chance to prove I'm innocent, and then you can go after the real villains."

"Sure. Sure." Marshal Taggart made it a point to smile. When he left Travis imagined he had won a victory. That is, until the marshal returned, this time with four ugly men accompanying him. "This one is too big for his breeches, boys. What are you going to do about it?"

Travis looked at the men the marshal called "boys," a rough-looking bunch if ever he'd seen them. The one with red hair was lanky, trigger happy and had the face of a mischievous monkey. The black bearded man with the gap-toothed smile looked undeniably mean. Then there was the pair who walked so close together that they reminded Travis of bookends, a humorous fumbling duo as stout as they were tall.

"Teach him some respect." Suddenly four guns were pointed right at Travis, as if these men feared he could walk right through the bars.

Quickly Travis held up his hands in a gesture conveying that he surrendered before any trouble began. "I'm a peaceful man. Let's just let bygones be bygones."

"Too late for that!" The man with the black beard pushed forward while the others aimed their guns to cover him. As if Travis would be fool enough to pick a fight. Using his own set of keys, the bearded man wrenched open the door.

"What are you doing?" Though Travis had wished to be set free, he wasn't foolish enough to think that was what was going to happen. He was going to be set upon. He could only hope they would give him a chance to defend himself.

They didn't! While the bearded ruffian held his arms behind his back, the others took aim with their fists, turning him into a human punching bag. Searing pain tore through his stomach, his chest, his arms.

"Be careful with his face. Don't want to mark him where it can be seen!" Marshal Taggart cautioned, though he didn't call them off. Not yet. Travis bit his lip to help him bear the burning agony of the continued beating. Moving his body left and right, back and forth, he heaved and bucked against his attackers, doing what he could to lessen the impact of the blows, but he suffered nonetheless. So, this was the kind of man he was up against. A man violent when crossed, a total bastard! It was a lesson he learned all too brutally.

"Oooooooooh!"

He fought against the awful blackness that hovered before his eyes as one punch left him winded. Would they never stop? For a moment he closed his eyes fearing they might go too far and cause his death. Then, from somewhere in the darkness, he heard Taggart say, "That's enough!" The arms that held him suddenly loosened and Travis slumped to the floor.

Chapter Sixteen

Marshal Samuel Taggart listened to the groans coming from the man in the jail cell, but didn't feel one iota of sympathy, nor did he regret the brutality he had instigated. The word "sorry" wasn't in his vocabulary. Long ago he had hardened his heart to such feelings. Only the strong, the cunning and those without scruples survived way out here. Had he not lived by that belief, he wouldn't be wearing a star.

"Marshal Samuel Owen Taggart," he said aloud, reaching up to polish that silver object of his affection. The name and title he liked very much.

There were some who said the badge of a lawman was just a piece of metal, but being a marshal had given him unrestrained power. Among other things he was a tax collector, a server of foreclosures and eviction notices, a collector of license fees for saloons and places of prostitution. He kept the official records of arrests and of the property taken from prisoners in his custody. Even more important, he was a protector of the more influential and moneyed citizens of the town. If that cut him in on quite a few deals, well, that was one of the advantages of the job. He smiled.

"It was a case of timing, pure and simple." That coupled with his gunslinging abilities and persistence, and the fact that Watersville, Silver Bow, Butte and the surrounding area had wanted a law enforcement officer who could give law breakers a run for their money, had given him the inside track on a new profession.

Peace officers were usually hired by a newly incorporated community when the settlement grew big enough to acquire a town charter.

Now he had at his disposal a small force of "friends," made up of an assistant marshal and a few deputies, all men he could count on to follow his orders. In addition he could call upon ordinary citizens in an emergency.

Oh, yes. It had all worked out very well. If he sometimes worked both sides of the law he doubted that very many people in the town had the guts to stir up trouble for him. And even if some did he'd soon make them look like fools. One of the advantages to his position was that he was in control of the law and what went on in his "territory."

Taking out an expensive cigar, one of the bonuses of his position, he lit it with a match, then puffed at it with great relish as he shuffled through the stack of wanted posters on his desk. Travis La Mont. For a while there he had feared the man might well be on his way out of the territory, and La Mont might have been had it not been for that flame-haired slip of a girl. She'd brought him back and saved Taggart a hell of a lot of trouble.

"Ah, yes, La Mont." Right from the first the newspaperman had gotten on Taggart's nerves. He was the nosy type, the kind who asked too many questions. It had been a worry. But then one incident had put him right in the palm of Taggart's hand. The bank robbery.

For a long while Taggart just sat there thinking about that fateful moment and smoking, until his cigar ash measured more than an inch. The gray dust drifted to the desk top like dark snowflakes. Taggart brushed it away, then smiled. No need to be so fastidious. His wife Josephine wasn't here to nag him. Not yet anyway.

Josephine. She was the kind of woman a man wouldn't mind being nagged by. Curvacious, buxom, spirited, charming and pretty, she was the possession he treasured most of all. The perfect consort for a man like him. A cattle baron's daughter, she had brought not only wealth and business contacts to the marriage but a measurable amount of class. Something even the largest amount of money couldn't buy.

"Josephine . . ." Her name was on his lips as his deputy, Jake Heath, pushed through the door.

"I hear you got him!" Heath ran a pudgy finger over his mustache in a nervous gesture that was always irritating.

"Him . . . !" More than a little peeved that Jake and his posse had been unable to accomplish what a female had done, he decided to toy with his deputy. "Who?"

"Him. La Mont." Jake Heath's eyes darted to the

159

door that connected the cells to the office. "It's all over town that she brought him in." There was venom in Jake's voice when he said the word "she."

"And suppose she did?" Taggart eyed Heath disdainfully. Once he had been one of his very best men. Tough. Bold. Daring. Now it was obvious that Heath was no longer in the pink of condition. He was getting soft. So soft that he had let a woman best him and had thereby complicated matters.

"I . . . I wanted to explain—"

"How you tripped up on an important assignment?" Taggart was gratified to see that the threat of his anger could still bring a cold sweat to his cohort's brow. "Now I'll be obliged to give her two hundred dollars. Two hundred dollars, Jake. Money I'd like to take out of your hide, but I'll settle for taking it out of your earnings."

Stuttering and stammering, Jake Heath tried to make excuses, but his telling of the confrontation with the female bounty hunter only made him sound ridiculous. "She's trouble with a capital *T*. Have no doubts about that."

"Trouble?" Taggart shrugged. "She seemed amiable enough. But then of course I'm not such an idiot that I let her get the best of me." Already he was wondering how he could keep the reward money from her hands. "But perhaps your warning isn't just hot air after all. I'll be on guard. And if Miss Bounty Hunter knows what's good for her, she won't get in my way."

Chapter Seventeen

The words of the blacksmith had jarred Bliss into doing a bit of inquiring around town. Was Marshal Taggart the brute the "old pirate" smithy had said or was that an opinion based on a grudge? It was a question she was determined to ask the young man at the livery stable when she returned to collect Bard and Boru. She found him trying to play a game of catch with them, throwing a stick and telling them to fetch it.

"You're wasting your time. I've trained them to obey only my commands. That's so they won't be distracted while we're out . . . uh . . . hunting."

"I thought they were just being stubborn." Bending over, he picked up the stick and passed it from one hand to the other as he admired the magnificent gray, wiry-haired animals. "They're fine-looking dogs. What kind are they? I've never seen any like them before."

"Irish wolfhounds. The best hunting dogs ever created!" Reaching down she gave each dog an affectionate pat on the head. "Their ancestors once belonged to the kings of Ireland."

"Fancy that!" He was obviously impressed by the dogs' pedigree and lineage. "Did you finish your business with the smithy?"

Bliss nodded. "I made arrangements all right, though I must say he's not a very amiable fellow. As a matter of fact he acted as if he didn't care a whit whether or not he shoed my horse. I'm surprised he gets any customers. Why, his tyrannical looks are enough to frighten a body away, not to mention his surliness."

"He's been that way since his wife died." The man shook his head. "Took it pretty hard. I think if he had his way he'd be a hermit."

"Looks to me like he already is," Bliss said wryly, then changed the subject abruptly. "Is the marshal hereabouts a bully?" she asked him point-blank.

Her question took him by surprise, and though he said no very vehemently, the expression on his face negated his reply. "Why?" A look of distrust glazed his eyes.

"Just asking." Bliss looked down at the young man's hands and noted that they were shaking. Marshal Taggart inspired fear. That was not a very good sign. Either this young man was a coward or something wrong was going on around this place.

Her curiosity heightened, Bliss inquired of everyone she met just what they thought of the marshal. She was answered by a great deal of stuttering and lots of hems and haws. Though no one admitted to being afraid of the marshal, it was obvious by their mannerisms and the looks that came into their eyes

162

at the mention of his name that everyone was. And this was the man into whose clutches she had obligingly thrust Travis La Mont.

"What if he told me the truth right from the first. What if he wasn't involved in that bank holdup. What if . . . ?" The fact that she was talking to herself made her the object of a few stares as she headed toward the general store, Bard and Boru at her heels. Until she got a new wagon there was no use in getting many things now, but she did have a hankering for a bar of rose-scented soap, a new shirt and a piece of hard candy.

Bliss reached her destination in no time at all. Hattie's General Store, the sign across the false facade read in erratic lettering. On either side of the door were windows haphazardly crammed with goods. Unlike some stores, this one didn't seem to be suffering from any shortages.

"You two be good and I'll bring you back a bone," she said to the wolfhounds, leaving them behind.

The bell over the door jingled as she went inside. Quickly she scanned the large room. A variety of provisions was heaped in bundles just like the goods in windows, occupying every inch of available space. A large cracker barrel stood in the middle of all this, propped against it a sign that read, One Free Cracker To A Customer. On one side of the interior was a counter for groceries, on the other counter and shelves piled high with dry goods. Hardware was located in the rear.

The store smelled of fresh ground coffee, kerosene, dried meat and pickled fish. Hams, sausages and slabs of other smoked meats hung from the rafters along with cooking pots and pans. Kegs and barrels brimmed with sugar, flour, molasses and vinegar. But it was the glass jar on the counter that became the focus of Bliss's attention. It was filled to the brim with red-and white-striped peppermint sticks, horehound drops and licorice. Sauntering up to the jar, Bliss tapped impatiently on the glass.

"A woman after my own heart!" Materializing as if from out of nowhere, an amply bosomed, dark-haired woman in her late thirties came up behind Bliss.

"You're Hattie!" It seemed to be a reasonable guess. "My name is Bliss. Bliss Harrison."

"Hattie Dodd, to be precise." She handed Bliss a piece of licorice. "On me, just a little gesture of welcome to our town."

Bliss took the offering, but before taking a bite felt the need to be truthful. Besides, she didn't like to be beholden. "I won't be staying in Watersville long so if you think you'd be lining up a regular customer your generosity is in vain." She reached for the money pouch.

"Oh, pooh!" Hattie stayed her hand. "Let's just say it's a gift from one female to another."

Bliss was instantly suspicious. No one gave anything to anyone without a catch. "I'd be more comfortable paying for what I get, but thank you just the same."

Hattie Dodd was not so easily put off. Chattering of town gossip all the while—the latest weddings, births and scandals—she followed Bliss around the store, determined to strike up a friendship. At last Bliss gave in. Though she preferred being a loner, there was something about the woman that struck a responsive chord deep within her. Because Hattie seemed so motherly? Perhaps.

Bliss's first purchase was a bar of pink soap, though it smelled more like violets than roses. Heading toward a counter piled high with cotton and flannel shirts, she paused for just a moment as she passed by the bolts of colorful calico. How long had it been since she'd worn a dress? She really couldn't remember.

"I could have it made up for you and even trim it with lace. I have some fashion plates from England that are only a bit out of date." As if to tempt Bliss she held a bolt of blue calico up beneath her chin.

Bliss felt herself weakening, but was able to respond with a firm no. Instead she chose a dark blue cotton shirt, then on a sudden impulse bought a shaving mug, soap and a razor for Travis, the kind her father had used. A peace offering? It was. She only hoped he wouldn't fling it in her face after the high-handed way she had treated him. Which brought her to the subject of the marshal.

"I suppose being new in town and all, a body really has to tow the line. Isn't that so? The marshal doesn't look like anyone a smart person would want to cross."

"He's not!" Just like the others Hattie didn't seem to find the subject of the marshal among her favorite topics of conversation. Her stance, the way she looked down at her shoes and her fidgeting gave that away.

Bliss touched her arm. "You seemed to be offering me friendship. Please, there's some information I'm badly in need of. Can you help me?"

"Information about what?" Instantly Hattie was on the defensive.

"About Taggart. Just what kind of man is he?" Once more Bliss was direct as was usually her way. After all, what good did it do to beat around the bush?

"He's a powerful man. A man who has this town, Silver Bow and several of the others right in the palm of his hand." Hattie's voice lowered to a whisper as she looked around to see if anyone had come in. Deciding it was safe, she said, "Look, honey, you seem like a nice kid. Take my advice and just put any questions about the marshal from your mind. If he hears any talk that you've been asking around about him you might—" Instantly she stopped talking when the bell over the door jingled. Someone had come in. The bearded man's intrusion put an end to all conversation.

Her curiosity now merely whetted not appeased, Bliss had to content herself by sharing chitchat with Hattie as she gathered her purchases and paid for them. Then she was on her way, heading for the hotel Hattie had recommended. A combination hotel-boarding house with an eatery that was run by Hattie's sister. People on the boardwalks on both sides of the street were elbow to elbow. She hoped she wasn't too late to get some food and a room for the night.

The planks under her feet creaked as Bliss hurried along the main street. Coming to a clean, newly washed building, she stopped for a moment to read the room rates posted in the window; then, leaving

166

Bard and Boru once again, she stepped inside the Watersville Wanderer Boarding House and Cafe. The smell of newly baked bread and good home cooking filled the air. She took her place in line, hoping that the rooms would not fill too rapidly.

"I've come from a long way off," she said as soon as the three people in front of her had been taken care of. "I would like a room for the night."

"The rooms I have left are pretty small," said a woman who looked so much like Hattie that Bliss knew she was her sister.

"I don't care about the size." She was in need of a bath and the luxury of clean sheets. After sleeping out of doors anything would be fine.

"The price is four bits a night."

"That will be fine."

The woman noted she had no luggage save her guns. Bliss explained that she had left her saddlebags and possessions at the livery stable.

It was a small but clean-looking room. The shades were drawn, and because the stairway to the second floor was outside and not indoors Bliss figured it would be easy to sneak Bard and Boru into the room. With that thought in mind she opened the window wide, then whistled. As soon as the dogs slipped through the window she closed it and drew the shades, then hung a Do Not Disturb sign on the door just to make certain there weren't any troublesome visitors.

"Now you boys try to be quiet so you don't get us all thrown out of here," she cautioned. As an incentive for them to be good she put the oval rug in the room by the bed, gave them each a bone and settled them down.

There was only one bathroom on the second floor, so Bliss had to wait in line. At last her turn came, however. The big brass tub she now filled with warm water and powdered soap was well worth waiting for. She stepped into the frothy suds and sighed with pure pleasure. Lathering herself good, hair and all, she put the pink soap in a wire holder and leaned back. Tomorrow, when she visited the jail, Travis La Mont couldn't help but notice how good she smelled. At Hattie's urging she had even purchased a small bottle of cologne.

"Pure foolishness," she scoffed, yet somehow the eccentric item made her smile. As for Travis La Mont, Bliss was now determined to do what she should have been doing all along. Help him. Somehow if she could get him alone she'd ask him where he'd hidden those photographs, find them and bring them back as evidence. If he was telling the truth she'd do everything she could to get him out of jail—the law-abiding way. And if he wasn't? Well, the was a bridge she'd cross when she got to it. One thing was certain, though, Travis La Mont had come into her life like a thunderbolt and she knew now she wanted him to stay.

Bliss took as long as she could in the bath, just relaxing, dreaming and thinking, but the loud pounding on the door all too soon put an end to her warm, wet cocoon. She had to be fair and let the others take their turn. Hurriedly dressing, she went back to her room, relieved to find Bard and Boru curled up on the rug, asleep. So far they hadn't caused any trouble.

Downstairs in the cafe while Bliss waited for her pork chops and fried potatoes to be served, she thought things over again. What would her father do in a case like this? Somehow she knew he, too, would want to come to Travis' aid, though not for the same reasons. Like it or not, Bliss had to admit that she was smitten.

"The marshal told me the little filly brought that La Mont fella in for the reward."

"I bet the boss was mad as hell about that, wasn't he, Jake?"

Even if the words hadn't gotten Bliss's attention the voices would have. Two men at the table behind hers were talking, and she recognized the nasal twang in one voice immediately. One of the members of the posse who had come to her campsite in search of Travis was speaking. Bliss shifted in her chair and pulled her long, hair back behind her ears in order to hear more clearly.

"What if they find out the truth? That bank fella was shot in the back."

"Who's gonna tell 'em?"

Bliss was fidgety. She knew if they saw her they would remember her and right now she thought it best for Travis if she stayed as far away from troublemakers as she could. Obviously some skullduggery was going on. If she made herself as invisible as she could, and kept her eyes and ears open, she just might find out what it was. Meanwhile she didn't want to draw any unnecessary attention to herself.

The voices behind her quieted to a hushed mumble; still she was able to pick up a few words of what they were saying. They were talking about Travis La Mont and the bank robbery, of that she had no doubt.

"He's going to have to be silenced—and quick—before the truth comes out, that much is certain," she heard the member of the posse say.

"It's all planned, and it will be done the legal way." The deep-throated chuckling that followed sounded ominous. What exactly did they mean? Just what kind of danger was Travis in?

"Well, we'd best be on our way. I've got a meeting with Taggart. Planning a little homecoming party for his wife, who's due in tomorrow."

"Are you acting as his host now?"

"Among other things."

There was a rustling sound as they got up to leave. The men had to pass by Bliss's table to get to the door, therefore she purposely dropped her knife on the carpeted floor and stooped down to pick it up. Just in time. They never even noticed her!

Bliss put her hand to her mouth. "Oh, Travis!" Her stubborness had gotten him into a horrible fix. It appeared that it was up to her to get him out.

It was dark in the jail except for the flickering light of the lone lantern hanging from a chain outside the cell. The silence pervading the small barred room was broken only by a low groaning. Travis slowly pushed himself up into a squatting position and examined his torso carefully, gently. It felt hot and swollen and painful. His lower back was almost too tender to touch, and he couldn't move

170

without every muscle and joint protesting. His body was a mass of bruises and welts, but obeying the marshal's instructions, the men who'd beaten him had left his face alone. No black eye, no broken nose, no split lip to give their brutality away.

He leaned his head against the bars, aching in every muscle and bone. The marshal's "boys" had done a good job on him all right. He closed his eyes against the pain, then counted slowly to three. Using the bars to brace himself, he tried to stand up. It was a foolhardy thing to do. He pitched forward onto the cell floor, landing heavily and painfully. For a long while he lay on the wooden planks gathering his strength, then slowly, his teeth clenched, he pulled himself upright again. This time he was able to make it to the bed. Sitting on his cot, leaning against a pillow, Travis stared into the lantern's flames.

A bitter gleam lit his brown eyes, an angry flush stained his cheeks when he thought about his beating. Though she hadn't actually been the one to throw those punches, Bliss Harrison was guilty in his eyes nonetheless. Could he ever forgive her? At the moment he wasn't so sure.

"All I asked for was a chance to prove my innocence, but she was more concerned with getting the money," he wheezed. His nostrils flared in anger as he remembered. Well, tomorrow she'd be at Taggart's office bright and early to grab her reward. He hoped the money made her happy.

Travis put up a hand to touch his shoulder, and winced. He couldn't decide which hurt the most, his stomach, his back, his ribs, his legs or his buttocks. He was unable to take a deep breath without feeling pain, and his stomach rumbled with hunger. Starvation seemed to be part of the marshal's plan too. Why else would he have left Travis alone without providing any supper?

"Oh, who cares?" If he didn't meet his end that way he was certain the marshal had something else in mind for him. But why was Taggart acting as if this were a personal vendetta? He'd never even laid eyes on him until coming to Silver Bow. Or had he? Something teased at the back of Travis' brain, but though he sorted through his thoughts, he just couldn't remember.

Once more his thoughts turned to Bliss Harrison. Oh, why couldn't he get her face out of his mind? Every time he thought of her something moved inside him, tore at him, gripped him so hard he couldn't let go. The truth was, although he was loath to admit it, he'd fallen hard for the girl. That had kept him hovering around her when he could have used force to escape while he'd had her rifle. He could even have taken his chances and escaped during the melee with the posse, but no. He had hoped to prove his integrity to her, had wanted her to see him as a hero. His reward? She had coldly betrayed him. Well, maybe it served him right.

Travis eased his aching body down onto the mattress. He didn't want to think about her anymore. Closing his eyes, he sought the oblivion of sleep and was able at last to fall into a troubled slumber. He was awakened by a voice telling him breakfast had arrived. Ellis Jones.

"Black coffee. And eggs and potatoes."

Travis opened his eyes and tried to focus on the

man bending over him. "Take it away. I'm not hungry."

"Are you sick?" There was a genuine note of worry in the voice. "Try and take at least a few bites. You gotta keep up your strength."

"For what? My hanging?" Travis was beginning to doubt that he would even have a trial. After all, wasn't this Marshal Taggart's town?

"Hanging?" The little man paled. It was obvious that he was not of a violent nature. To the contrary, he seemed to be very kind.

"Oh, never mind. It's not your fault." Travis sat up. He hurt in a dozen places, but the little elf-man was right. He had to keep up his strength. One thing for sure, he wasn't going to just sit back quietly while they tried to destroy him. Marshal Taggart would find out he had a real fight on his hands. That thought brought back Travis' appetite.

After wolfing down the entire plate of food and washing it down with coffee, Travis slept again. This time he was awakened by the sound of a woman's voice. Muffled, it was coming through the door. It was her!

Bliss called on every ounce of self-control she could muster as she followed the marshal through the open doorway that led to the jail cells. How she acted was of the utmost importance. She had to let Travis know she was on his side and try to find out where he'd hidden that photograph without letting the marshal in on the same information. It was going to be tricky.

Sunlight streamed in through the high, barred window to illuminate the narrow bed. Sitting absolutely still on that small cot, his legs drawn up to his chest and his head resting on his knees, Travis looked strange somehow. Distant. Even the marshal's loud ahem didn't cause him to look up.

"Hey, mister . . . ?" She tried to act bright and cheerful, but her heart was aching. Travis looked as if he felt miserable. For the first time since she had met him he seemed whipped. Tired.

Travis raised his head, and Bliss knew the moment she looked into his eyes that something was terribly wrong. The set of his shoulders, the way he was curled up on the cot reinforced that impression. Even so, he rolled from the bunk and crossed the small distance that separated them, clinging to the bars. "Come to gloat, Miss Bounty Hunter?" He turned to the marshal. "Get her out of here."

Marshal Taggart put his hand on Bliss's shoulder. "Now, now, now. Is that a way to treat a lady?"

"Lady? She's anything but that," Travis retorted angrily. Then he asked, "Have you gotten your blood money yet?"

"Not yet . . ." At the moment she didn't care a fig about the money. She could only stare at him mutely, withering under his glare.

"I want to speak to him alone, Marshal," she said tersely, but the marshal was having none of that. He insisted that he stay by the door, just in case there was trouble. Had she expected this would be easy?

Bliss had the feeling that her world was about to crumble. "What's wrong, Travis?" Pride stiffened her back and held her head erect. Anything he said

174

she had coming.

"Wrong?" Despite his aching body he managed to stay on his feet. "How could anything be wrong, Miss Harrison? The food here is tasty, the pillow soft and the rest of the accommodations beyond reproach. I only hope you get the chance to stay here sometime."

Their gazes locked and held. In his eyes she saw a flicker of affection mingled with a sorrow that swiftly passed as he clenched his jaw. In its place was an icy glare that chilled her to the very bone. Struggling to break the hold his eyes had upon her, Bliss looked down at her hands, clasped tightly together.

"Please don't hate me . . ."

"Hate you!"

In all her life she'd never felt such anguish. She told herself this was no time to cry, nevertheless the moisture of humiliation and sincere remorse welled behind her eyelids. "I'm sorry, Travis," she whispered softly.

"Sorry. But you will take your share of the money!" His eyes were bright shards of anger.

Seeing the marshal look their way, she threw back her head. She had to keep him thinking she was against the prisoner or all would be lost. "Yes. I'll take the money, all right. It's a hard, cold, cruel world, Travis La Mont. I need it."

"Blood money!" he said again.

A sudden trembling caught at her lower lip. Bliss thrust her hands into the pockets of her pants. Her heart was beating so frantically she thought for a moment she just might choke. A fiercesome debate

175

warred in her mind. Dear Lord, she had never felt so helpless. What could she say? How could she make him understand that she had been taught to live by her father's rules?

"Travis, I want to help you." She breathed the words out softly, so the marshal wouldn't hear.

"Help me?" he said aloud, wondering if this was some sort of a game.

"Tell me where the photograph is, so you can use it in your defense," she whispered frantically while the marshal's attention was occupied by a tiny little man who was standing in the doorway. "I'll get it and keep it safe."

"Sure you will." What game was she playing now? Whatever was on her mind, he'd be a fool to trust her.

"I will!"

"Forget it." From now on he had to view everyone as his enemy, including her. It was a matter of survival.

"But . . ."

He looked down hard into her eyes, his features chillingly devoid of expression, his lips clamped tightly together. So much so that lines showed on each side of his mouth. Then, with one final look, he turned his back.

"Travis!" Oh, why couldn't he see that she had had a change of heart.

He didn't look at her, but said very plainly, "Go to hell!"

A stricken silence followed as they maintained a grotesque pose. At last Bliss found her voice. "Marshal, I'm ready to leave now." There was no use

176

in trying to make him understand. Better to leave before her emotions got out of control.

Closing his eyes, Travis could hear her boot heels strike the hard wooden floor. Moving farther and farther away. Well, let her go. He shouldn't care! And yet he did, so very much. It took all his resolve not to call her back.

Bliss tried to keep her face expressionless as she faced the marshal in his den. "My reward!" If she was going to help Travis she had to have money. Later, when everything was straightened out, she could give it back.

"Well now, about that reward." Suddenly Taggart's attitude changed, and he looked at her like the cat who has the canary by the tail. "I got word that the posse caught him, but you interfered. Seems you contrived to have the honor of bringing him in. In that case the offer of money is dissolved."

"The hell it is!" Bliss folded her arms across her chest, stood up on tiptoe and thrust her face within inches of the marshal's. "I captured him all by myself, the posse be damned. The two hundred dollars is all mine. Mine."

"How'd you capture him?" Taggart reached out and patted her head. "You're just a tiny little lady. He's a pretty big man. Surely you had help at least."

"I caught Travis La Mont all by myself and made damn asses out of that posse to boot! I gave them a run for their money."

"How about if I give you fifty dollars?" He grinned as if his offer was magnanimous.

"Fifty dollars?" He was trying to cheat her. Bliss just wouldn't have it. It was the principle of the thing. "No, I want the full amount," she repeated, touching the handle of her gun, "or I take Travis La Mont and hightail it out of here!" At this moment that was just what she wanted to do. Take him and run. "He hasn't had his trial yet. How do you even know he's guilty?" That ought to make the marshal think.

A mask of anger came over his features. "Because he is. There are at least six men who will testify he was with the men who robbed the bank."

Yeah, I'll bet, Bliss thought, and all of them in your employ. Somehow she smelled a skunk, the two-legged kind.

Holding up his hand, the marshal silenced her before her annoyance could be put into words. "All right, I'll give you the money." He was anxious to get rid of her. Opening the safe, he took out a handful of bills and thrust them into her hands.

"Paper money?" She would have preferred gold, but decided it was best to settle for what she could get. "Oh, well!" She couldn't stand by and let Travis stay cooped up in that prison very much longer. This money would be a big help. After all, everyone knew that money talked.

Leaving the jail, Bliss fled back to her room at the hotel and closed the door. She could cry freely now, without any thought to pride. Cry! It seemed the only thing left to do. Flinging herself down on the bed she let all her grief out in a flood. Tears came in an overwhelming flow, pouring from her eyes, rolling down her cheeks, drenching the pillow beneath her head. In an attempt to stop the torrent she put her fingers to her eyes and pressed hard.

178

"Get hold of yourself! Stop crying, I say." All her troubles had been of her own making, she realized that now. Right from the first he had professed his innocence but she, pigheaded fool that she was, had refused to even listen. Because she'd been hurt, Travis La Mont had borne the brunt of her anger. Now he was caged, and it was up to her to set him free.

Chapter Eighteen

Puffs of dust rose up from the road in a thick cloud as the carriage lurched and bounced into Watersville. Marshal Sam Taggart put a hand to his mouth to keep from choking as he hurried across the street before the horses ran over him. But he wasn't the least bit angry at the erratic driving. He was much too happy to see Josephine's face for that. Two months. Two long months without her while she gave in to her wanderlust. Now she was back—and arriving in a style that made him proud.

"See that, Jake," he said coming upon his henchman. "No plain old stagecoach or buggy for her. No siree. Not for my girl." His eyes flashed with pride as he watched her alight. The carriage was an hour later than Josephine had promised. Taggart had checked his pocket watch nearly a hundred times, telling himself all the while to calm down. She'd come, he knew. It wasn't like Josephine to break a promise.

"Yeah, she's sure as hell creating a scene all right,"

Jake jealously grumbled. "Coming in here like some princess or somethin'. But don't you worry just a little about what the townsfolk might say. Don't you think they might wonder just where she gets all her money when her husband is a lawman and not a king? Don't you?"

"I don't care about that!" No matter what he had to do, he'd make certain she was able to have what she wanted. He just couldn't take the chance that she would leave him. "All I want is to be able to give her the best. That's all that's important to me."

Oh, he'd showed them. Showed all those who had looked down on him from their lofty perches, whispering behind their hands that he had taken on a wife he couldn't afford. If that had meant branding a few cattle that didn't belong to him, well, a man had to make his own opportunities sometimes.

"Yeah, and just what are you going to do someday when she starts asking questions? Have you ever thought about that?"

For just a minute Taggart's composure faltered. What would Josephine do if she ever found out he wasn't who or what he'd said? If his past caught up with him? "She won't." At least she hadn't up to now. Her head was too filled with the usual feminine clutter. "She's more interested in dresses from Paris than in the events of the town."

"Then if I were you I'd keep it that way," Jake offered.

"What do you mean?" Taggart's eyes narrowed to angry slits. He didn't like getting advice, particularly from one of his hirelings.

"Only that I've heard tell your new prisoner has

181

been chattering. So much so that even the hellcat who brought him in has been asking questions. She's going all over town asking about you."

"The Harrison woman?" Taggart had thought giving her the money would get rid of her. Well, she had better not become too much of a nuisance.

"If you ask me we're going to have to do something—and fast—about La Mont. He's the type who's going to shoot off his mouth once too often. Trouble is, there just might be someone nearby who will listen. Such as your wife."

Taggart stiffened. "I don't want her anywhere near him!"

Jake Heath shrugged. "It's up to you to control that situation. All I'm saying is things can happen."

"Make certain that they don't!"

"Dead men don't tell no tales, or so I've heard." Jake Heath grinned evilly, but when he opened his mouth to say something else, he was silenced by a brutal nudge to his ribs.

Taggart's joyful mood had been spoiled. Even so, he watched intently as his wife stepped down from the carriage. How could he have forgotten how beautiful she was? Bright, sunny and smiling. A dream. A mirage.

The crowd was thick, and for just a moment he couldn't see her. The women were full of exuberance, asking questions, pushing around her. It made him proud, yet at the same time he wanted her all to himself. They had some time to make up for.

"So what do you want me to do about La Mont?" Jake Heath was anxious to get the matter settled once and for all. "A little accident in his cell, like

182

with Ruppert Davis and John Oliver?"

Taggart fiercely shook his head. "No. That would look too suspicious, happening for the third time."

"Then?"

The question went unanswered. Taggart's attention was diverted the moment he realized that his wife had spotted him. He watched, fascinated, as she smiled and then, picking up her skirts, started toward him. His heart lurched like a lovesick boy's as he heard her high, tinkling, feminine laughter.

"Josey!" She was absolutely glowing, and for a moment he was envious that she could be so happy when all this time he had been so miserable.

"Samuel!" She placed a dutiful kiss on his cheek, then straightened his hat. "You look a bit pale. Hasn't Bertha been feeding you?"

"A man needs more than food." His words and the look he gave her made her blush.

"Sam!" She looked at her husband then at Jake Heath, then at Taggart again.

"Oh, don't be so shy. He's a man. He understands." Taggart barked out an order. "Jake, see to her bags."

Josephine didn't speak until Heath was out of hearing distance. "I don't like him, Sam. I never have. There's something sinister about the man. I do wish you would get rid of him."

"We've been all through this before, Josey." Putting his arm around her, he nestled his chin in her hair. "He's loyal and good at what he does. I need him."

"But . . ." Seeing the grim expression on his face she shrugged. "Oh, all right. I'll leave men's business to you." She smiled. "San Francisco was just wonderful. You really must come with me sometime. I brought back the most marvelous things . . . !"

For just an instant Taggart stiffened. Knowing Josephine, he feared she had spent so much money he would be impoverished. At least for a while. "Let's go home and you can show me." Taking her arm, he tugged at her gently.

"Home, of course. But first I want to stop by your nasty little jail. I hear you have quite an infamous prisoner on your hands, and I want to get a look at him. It isn't just any day a female bounty hunter brings such a man in."

Taggart's face froze. "So, you heard about that!"

"The moment my feet touched the ground. I must admit to being more than a bit put out that another woman stole my thunder. Oh, the women asked me questions about my trip to San Francisco all right, but I had to share the limelight with her. This Bliss Harrison, whoever she is, is the talk of the town. And so is this man she brought in." She reached up to pat his cheek. "I hear he's handsome."

"All the more reason for me to want you to stay away from him, my dear." It was difficult for him to keep the smile on his face. His jaw ticked as he forced his lips into an upward slant.

"Oh, don't be jealous. It's just that I would so love to see him and *her.*" Her eyes sparkled. "At first I had thought she must be some sort of ruffian. Homely, husky and as tough as a nail, but I hear she's very pretty."

"Not at all. Certainly she isn't the kind of woman for you to waste your time with. Now, come along."

184

This time he was forceful in his urging; practically dragging his wife along behind him. As he passed Jake Heath he hissed in his ear. "There's going to be a hanging. See to it and quickly." Then, with a congenial smile in his wife's direction, he continued down the street.

Perspiration glistened on the blacksmith's bulging muscles as he stood close to the forge to get the iron for the horseshoe red hot. Holding the metal in long pincers, he laid it on the anvil and raised his arm again and again. The small shed was filled with a clanging sound as he pounded a new horseshoe into shape.

Bliss sat on a tall stool, both feet resting on the wooden rung, as she watched him. Oh, he was strong, all right. The kind of man who would be better as an ally than an enemy, she thought. The type of man who could aid her in helping Travis. That he didn't like Marshal Taggart was an added plus. But how on earth could she win him to her side when he wouldn't even talk to her except to say what needed to be spoken to conduct his business?

"It's a nice day," she offered, trying to make a start.

"Yep." The blacksmith was a man of few words.

Bliss looked around the shed, trying to find something that could be a subject of conversation. Talk about his business. Since a man's profession was the center of his universe that was usually the best way to start up a lively talk.

"You must do a lot of shoeing, what with everyone

hereabouts owning at least one horse." She took off her hat and rotated it from hand to hand. "Lots of wagons, buggies and farm machinery. Must keep you busy."

"Yep." The blacksmith didn't even bother to look at her.

"Was your father a blacksmith too?" Usually a man followed a family profession.

"Nope." The clanging grew louder.

"Then what made you decide to take it up as a trade?" Bliss smiled, knowing she'd asked a question he couldn't answer with one word.

"I needed the money." He paused in his pounding. "The town needed a blacksmith."

"Oh!" Bliss stood up and came closer to the forge. It had a blower to intensify the heat of the glowing bed of soft coal, shining bright red pebbles against the black of the forge's sides. "Do you ever get burned?"

This time he looked at her, his uncovered eye shining nearly as brilliantly as the coals. "And just why would you want to know?"

Bliss stiffened, proceeding cautiously. "I was just curious."

"Well, you ask too many questions!" Taking the horseshoe off the anvil, he cooled it in a tub of cold water, then dipped it in a tub of oil to temper the hot metal.

Stung by his rebuke Bliss stomped off. What a rude fellow he was. The gruffest curmudgeon she had ever had the misfortune of coming across. He certainly had a few things to learn about manners. A blacksmith shop was usually a friendly place, one for conducting business and exchanging gossip. Ha! Well, it would serve this one right if he lost all his trade. Bliss clenched her jaw as she watched him finish her horseshoe, hoping to hold her temper in check. Alas, her anger won out.

"I've come across a lot of men in my lifetime, but you have to be the worst of the lot!" She kicked at a clod of dirt. "I lost someone I loved too, but I don't use it as an excuse to treat people badly."

"What?" Her outburst got the blacksmith's attention.

"I said that grief isn't a reason to be rude." Bliss didn't care if he was three times her size, she was determined to stand up to him. That was undoubtedly what he needed.

"What do you know about it?" For just a moment his surliness gave way to a look of pain.

"My father was killed by a renegade gunman not long ago. He was the only family I had. Since then I've just wandered about on my own." Instantly Bliss succumbed to her own troubled memories. "I can understand your wanting to be left alone. I felt like that too. But a person can't forget that he or she is a member of the human race. Other people have troubles too."

The blacksmith thought about that for a while, then said, "To answer your question, I have gotten burned." Holding out his hands, he showed her the scars. "Carelessness, I suppose."

Bliss cringed as she looked at the scarred red welts. "It must have hurt!"

He looked down at the anvil. "It did, but I've found that the agony I suffered from the wayward iron was nothing compared to the pain I felt when *she* died."

Bliss spoke from experience. "I know. After Pa was killed I was certain I couldn't survive. But somehow we do." She moved closer. "How . . . ?"

"There was a gunfight in the street, a shootout between a gunman and one of the marshal's men. Martha was killed by a stray bullet from the lawman's gun."

"Ohhhhh!" It was not an uncommon tragedy. "I'm sorry! Really I am."

As quickly as his reverie was sparked it passed and he seemed to close up again, but Bliss knew that at least she'd made a start. She felt a bit easier around him as she followed him next door to the livery stable.

"Which horse is yours?"

Bliss pointed to the brown mare. "I traversed some pretty rough roads coming in to Watersville, but she'll be good as new with your help."

Now it was the blacksmith who asked the questions. "That man you brought in. Wanted for robbery. Is that what you said?"

Bliss shook her head wearily. "Yep, that's what I told you, and I was sure-fired obstinate about his guilt. Now I'm not sure at all. I think I just might have made one hell of a mistake! He's always insisted he was innocent, but I just wouldn't listen. After taking a closer look at that marshal, I'm having second thoughts. I wish . . ." She left the sentence unfinished. Wishing was silly. Her father had always said that if wishes were horses then no one would need legs for walking.

"You wish you'd believed him," the blacksmith finished for her. "But you didn't, and it's too late to cry over spilled whiskey!"

"It can't be too late!" Her voice quivered with remorse. She remembered the way Travis had looked that very morning. He hated her—and with good reason. No matter how he felt, however, she had to make certain he got a fair chance. Remembering that Travis had asked the marshal to telegraph his lawyer, she asked the blacksmith if he knew of a lawyer in Watersville, one who was skilled.

"An honest and competent one?"

"Of course."

"Nope!" Carefully approaching Chocolate from in front, he lifted up the horse's back left hoof, put the horseshoe in place, then started hammering in the nails.

"Not even one honest lawyer?" Seeing that the blacksmith now had his mouth full of nails, she held her question back until he was finished, then asked again. "Isn't there even one good lawyer in this town?"

The blacksmith wiped the sweat off his brow with his bare arm. "There used to be when they could earn a few hundred dollars just settling land and mining claims. But Taggart has scared off the reliable and knowledgeable ones. Now the only ones you'll be seeing are on his payroll. And the judge as well."

"I see!" Travis' fate was looking blacker and blacker. Bliss was not of a notion to just give up, though. She owed it to Travis La Mont to get him out of this fix, and get him out she would. Taking her leave of the blacksmith, therefore, she strolled around the town, asking what questions she could. Just like before she was met with frightened stares and sealed lips. Whatever power Marshal Taggart wielded, it seemed to be awesome. In defeat Bliss headed back to the boarding house, afraid if she was gone too long Bard and Boru would get into trouble. She could only hide them in her room for so long before their barks or an inquisitive maid gave them away.

There were several ways to go, but Bliss picked the longest route, the one that took her past the jail. Even from a block away she could hear the sounds of sawing and pounding, not unusual in such a town, so she gave them little notice until she turned the corner. That was when she saw it.

"A scaffold!" She watched as one of the carpenters raised a large two-by-four and attached a rope to it. There was going to be a hanging. The question was, whose? Running across the street Bliss put her apprehension into words as she approached one of the workmen. The answer stunned her. The gallows were being built to hang a bank robber who had killed a man over in Silver Bow. A man by the name of Travis La Mont!

Chapter Nineteen

Weary from the ordeal of the past night, Travis sat down on the cot and put his face in his hands. He had to get out of here—and fast—before Taggart's apes paid him another visit. And they would. He had no doubt on that score, and he was certain that this time they wouldn't be quite so "gentle."

"Damn that woman!" Bliss Harrison had told Taggart about the photograph. He knew that was true because about an hour ago the marshal had smiled and inquired if Travis would like to have him send one of his men to fetch it. Travis had of course said no. If anyone was going to lay hands on that undeveloped negative it would be him, for the simple reason that *he* was the only one he could trust. Oh yes, he'd go after his photographic equipment all right. That is, if he could get out of jail.

"I have to escape!" But how? As if second-guessing him, Taggart had placed two men on guard outside the door connecting the marshal's office to the cells and one guard inside. Unbribable men. Men who glowered. Loyal men who obeyed the marshal's every whim.

What about Ellis Jones? Travis watched as the little man moved his mop across the floor. Was it possible he could get Ellis to help him? Somehow he had to, for Jones seemed to be his only hope. Certainly Bliss Harrison had deserted him. Gotten her reward money and run. She was undoubtedly halfway to Helena by now.

"Good riddance!" He didn't want to be reminded of her betrayal or the cold way she had traded him in for gold. Even so, a knot of pain in his throat made it hard for him to swallow when he thought about her. Hell, he even missed hearing her call him mister.

Trying to get free of his thoughts, Travis paced up and down in the small cubicle of a cell, trying to ignore the soreness of his body. He had to forget her. There were more important things to dwell on than a flame-haired ruffian who acted like a man. Things like how he was going to get the guards to open the door. Could he do it? Could he maneuver a way to escape?

"Yes, By God." Nothing had ever defeated him before, and nothing would now. Especially not a man like Taggart.

"Hey, you!"

Travis looked up to see the man named Jake Heath regarding him. Heath was a squat dark-haired man with a handlebar mustache, a bulbous nose and piercing eyes beneath very bushy eyebrows. Travis remembered seeing him with the posse that had come to Bliss's wagon.

"Are you talking to me?" Travis returned glower for glower.

"Don't see nobody else in here, besides ole Ellis. Now what do you think?" Walking over to the cell, Heath took out his gun and ran the barrel back and forth across the bars creating an unnerving sound. "Don't know if you have noticed it or not, but they are mighty busy outside. Building something. Wanna guess what?"

Travis wasn't at all certain that he did.

"Hey you, Frenchie. Cat got your tongue or what?" It was obvious that Heath intended to be as annoying as he could. "I said they're building something. Take a little peek so you can see."

Deciding at last that this would be the way to get the man to stop pestering him, Travis stood up on the cot and looked between the bars of the small window. Squinting against the sun, he scowled at the view of the town that met his eyes. A dusty little hole, made up of sagging storefronts and badly painted wood, he thought in frustration, an average Western town. Not the kind of place where he wanted to spend so much time.

"I don't see . . ." But in that minute he did. All afternoon he'd heard thumps, bumps and grinding. Now he knew why. My God, it was! He'd been out West long enough to know what that platform with the inverted L-shaped beam was. But who was that rope meant for? He was the only person in the jail, but he hadn't even had his trial yet.

"That contraption is for you!" Jake Heath seemed to take great delight in being the one to break the news.

193

"You can't hang me! I didn't do anything." Travis jumped down from the bunk, wincing against the pain such exertion caused. "I demand the services of my lawyer."

"You don't say!" Jake Heath grinned.

"And I demand a fair trial. If I don't get one, this will be a lynching."

"Oh, there'll be a trial all right. And a judge, Clayton Owen. The hanging judge he's called in these parts." A deep belly laugh shook Jake Heath's paunchy frame as he walked off.

Travis had a dazed look in his eye as he resumed his sitting position on the cot. A terrible numbness came over him. A hanging platform was being built for him, proof that he was already convicted and condemned. Even though he'd been running away after that wanted poster had been plastered all over the territory, he had somehow assumed he could win. He just hadn't figured on losing his life in such an unjust manner. Burying his face in his hands, he tried to shut out the truth of his discovery, but the picture of his lifeless body hanging from the rope wouldn't disappear. He would never be allowed to prove his innocence.

Did Bliss know his fate? Had she turned him over to these men, knowing full well what was going on? Shaking his head he had to believe she had not. Bliss was stubborn, yes, boisterous at times, but he didn't think she really had it in her to be cruel. Hadn't she told him she was taking him in so he could stand trial? He wanted to believe she'd thought the marshal would be fair, wanted to hope there was still a chance she might have second thoughts about what he'd said and come back. If she did he wouldn't chase her off this time.

The worst part would be the waiting. Travis had never waited for anything. He had always taken a hand in his fate. He had wanted an education and had worked hard to get the money to achieve that goal. He had wanted a job at a large newspaper and had found a way to get hired. He had wanted to travel West and had managed to do it. Now, suddenly, he was as helpless as a leaf adrift in a windstorm.

No! He couldn't give up now. That was exactly what they wanted him to do. Slowly he thought about his alternatives and came up with a plan, one that might well get him out of jail so he could hide out for a while until he could gather together the proof that would exonerate him. "Ellis!"

The little man came shuffling to the cell immediately when he heard his name. "Yes!"

"I feel the urge for a smoke. Surely even a condemned man has a right to a few cigars and some matches."

"Well . . ."

Travis said a silent prayer. "Please . . ."

The little man cocked his head to the side. "Don't see that it would hurt." He shuffled off, returning with one cigar and one match. Fewer than what Travis had wanted but better than nothing.

"Thank you, Ellis." Striking the match on the sole of his boot, Travis lit the end. Puffing, he blew the smoke into the air. "Ahhhhhhh . . ." Leaning back he watched until Ellis was gone and Jake Heath had settled down in a chair, put his hat over his face and slipped into a nap. Punching a hole in the cot, he held the hot tip of the cigar to the straw inside, then blew on it, igniting a fire. A fire that spread slowly. Nonetheless, it would be his salvation, or so he hoped.

The smoke choked him as the flames turned into a blaze. "What the hell . . . ?" Jake coughed. His eyes bugged with anger. "Why you . . ." He ran forward, the ring of keys in hand. There was no way for him to put out the fire without opening the cell, which was exactly what Travis was waiting for. The moment he stepped inside, Travis jumped him.

"You bastard!"

Jake swung his fists, but Travis was stronger. He was fighting for his life. He had nothing to lose.

"I'll kill you for this!"

"No you won't, not if I have my way."

They rolled over and over on the floor, first Jake on top and then Travis, struggling for the gun. Pinning his adversary around the neck by way of a stranglehold, Travis choked Jake until he gagged. "Give me the gun. Quickly. Do it or I'll squeeze until your tongue hangs out!"

Fearful that Travis might well make good on his threat, Jake Heath gave up his revolver, throwing it to the far side of the cell. And all the while the flames grew higher and higher. "For God's sake, let me out of here."

Travis' jaw ached where Jake had hit him, but he ignored that as he crawled on hands and knees on the floor toward the gun. His hand touched it, grabbed it, and he held it up.

"We'll burn to death!"

"Not we, you. I'm going, but I'll leave you here," Travis threatened, but not being a cold-blooded murderer he reneged on his vow and therein came his defeat. Reaching down to give Jake a hand up, he was caught in a bear hug. His hope of escape was soon put to an end when Jake yelled at the top of his lungs. The marshal and the other two guards heeded the call in an instant. Travis was easily overpowered and beaten and kicked into submission. He could only watch from his sprawled position on the floor as the marshal doused the flames. Then he was shoved back against the wall of the cell.

"Sleep on the floor, damn you!" Marshal Taggart shouted. "If you know what's good for you, you won't try that again."

Travis' lips curled into a rebellious smile. "To the contrary, Marshal, if I know what's good for me, I will." It was either that or dance from the end of a rope. And he did try to escape, over and over again, using every scheme he could think of, from playing possum to using subterfuge, but unfortunately Taggart was a cunning captor who seemed to anticipate his every move.

Finally Travis lay on the floor and stared up at the ceiling, trying hard not to give in to despair. He felt a flicker of hope at knowing that he was going to have a trial, a chance to openly air his side of the story. Or so he hoped.

Jake Heath made certain Travis was securely handcuffed before he entered the cell, then ordered, "Come on, La Mont." Completely surrounded by a circle of the marshal's men, Travis was pushed through the jailhouse door, taken to an alleyway and marched to a large wooden building four doors away.

Though usually a trial drew the curious, there were very few people in the courtroom. Travis was quick to notice as he was pushed and shoved into the chamber. But then, had he expected this to be a normal proceeding? Forced to take a seat between Jake Heath and Marshal Taggart, he watched as the judge lifted his gavel and brought the court to order.

"The accused, Travis Stephen La Mont, is charged with robbery and the murder of one Frank W. Whitewood, bank teller and citizen of this community. Is the prosecution ready?" A beady-eyed, hawk-nosed man with no hair on top of his head nodded. "The defense?"

Travis' head snapped up and he took a look at the man who had been assigned to defend him. A weak and ineffectual-looking sort if ever he'd seen one. Hardly the kind to inspire confidence.

"I do not want this man to represent me." Bolting to his feet he made his opinion known. "I have a lawyer, Aric Wesley from the firm of Wesley, Lord and Brandbrith. I have repeatedly requested that he be contacted. To my knowledge he was not." If only the judge would grant his request it would buy him some time.

"Oh . . . ?" The judge's brows furled. It was whispered that he was unquestionably a harsh arbiter of justice.

The marshal quickly stood up. "That man is from an Eastern law firm. He did not respond to our attempt to contact him. Your Honor. Perhaps he was out of town or—"

"Liar!" Travis knew Aric Wesley's habits very well. He was a man thoroughly dedicated to his profession, one who never even took a weekend off. But when he tried to make this known, as well as to reveal the abnormalities in his imprisonment, he was roughly silenced.

"We appointed another counsel. A man very well qualified," Taggart stated.

Travis mumbled beneath his breath, angered that he had been muffled. But he would find a chance to have his say. Or would he? As the trial proceeded it was all too obvious that he would not. Taggart had seen to that. As to his defense, there really wasn't any. Bowing and scraping to Taggart, the defense lawyer made it glaringly apparent to Travis that he was not only woefully inexperienced but biased against him as well. But wasn't that the plan?

"Your Honor!" Once again Travis stood. He just couldn't stay quiet any longer. In what he hoped was his most eloquent oratory, he spoke in his own defense, outlining his credentials and just why he had been at the scene of the crime. He had taken a shot, all right, he said, but with a camera and not a gun. "All I ask for is time so that I can prove I'm telling the truth. Time!" It was a request the judge pondered but in the end denied. Had he been bribed? Travis could only wonder.

To say that the trial was a living nightmare, a mockery from start to finish was an understatement. Had Travis held any hope of justice it was shattered right away. The prosecutor walked up and down smiling at the witnesses like some ghoul, goading them into telling outright lies. Travis doubted if some of them had even been anywhere near Silver Bow the day of the robbery. Certainly they didn't look familiar to him. No doubt some money was going to change hands after this farce.

Travis could only watch as his character was besmirched and the story of the robbery became an outright lie. It was much like a dime novel about the old West, with him cast as the villain. And so well planned that had it been any other man on trial, he would have believed him guilty. As to Clayton Owen it soon became apparent why he was called the hanging judge. He was stern, uncompromising and seemingly biased against all he considered transgressors. He included Travis among them. Was it so surprising then that he handed down a verdict of guilty?

"No! I'm innocent." Travis shrieked indignantly. "This is a travesty of justice, sir."

Frowning, the judge pounded with his gavel so loudly that the taps sounded like gunshots. "Order. Order," he shouted angrily. His expression gave Travis little comfort. "The defendant, Travis Stephen La Mont, has been found guilty."

Travis listened to his sentencing in a daze. He felt his heart stop, then start beating again. Frantically. Death, that was to be his punishment. Marshal Taggart hadn't built the scaffold for nothing. Tomorrow, when the sun was straight up in the sky, Travis was condemned to walk up those steps.

Chapter Twenty

Night cloaked the town of Watersville in black, but the light from kerosene lamps and hearth fires glittered like fireflies through the darkness. Boisterous laughter and spirited chatter carried through the air on the wind, drifting through the open window of Bliss's room.

"How can anyone be happy tonight?" she lamented, staring out the window toward the jail. The scaffold beside it was a gruesome reminder of what awaited Travis La Mont.

It couldn't be true! Dear God, she didn't want to believe it. How could she live with herself, knowing she had sent an innocent man to his death? Travis La Mont deserved better than a kangaroo court and swinging from the marshal's gallows. Taggart had proven to her that the law wasn't cast in stone. Her father's idea that it was always right didn't apply in all instances. Moreover, things were often not what they seemed. She had learned this last only recently.

The more she had found out about the marshal,

the less she liked him. He was cruel, greedy and as stubborn as a mule. She had hurried to his office the minute she had seen the framework for the scaffold, planning to beg for Travis' release but changing her mind after hearing the marshal's conversation with one of his deputies through the open door. He had spoken of Travis being a danger to him, of his desire to get him out of the way. Though she didn't know exactly what he'd meant or what part the marshal played in the scheme, to her this was proof enough that Travis' suspicion of being framed was right on target. Hopefully she hadn't learned it too late.

"Oh, Pa, what am I going to do?" Leaning her head against the window glass, Bliss scorned her self-imposed isolation. The marshal ruled the whole damn town, but she had no one to turn to. No one to give her consolation. Not one soul could she count on for help in this time of need. Everyone was beneath the marshal's thumb. "Everyone?" Raising her head, Bliss knew this wasn't exactly true. "The blacksmith!" He had shown his loathing for Marshal Taggart soon after she had knocked on his door. But could he be persuaded to come to her aid?

A knock on her own door shattered her musing. "Bard! Boru!" she rasped before they sounded an alarm. "Quiet!" If it was discovered that the dogs were in the room, she'd be thrown out into the night and then her problems would be multiplied. "Quick. Under the bed!" With one full swoop, she grabbed the bedspread and held it up. Used to obeying her command to get into the wagon, the wolfhounds hurried to comply. "Just a minute," she called out.

Always cautious, Bliss picked up her revolver

before opening the door a crack. She breathed a sigh of relief to see the familiar face. "Bliss . . ." It was Hattie Dodd. "Won't you let me come in?"

Bliss was hardly in a mood to be sociable. "I was just going to put on my nightshirt," she said bluntly, hoping to rid herself of the overly friendly woman's company. It was a ploy that didn't work.

"Go right ahead." Hattie Dodd pushed into the room. Reaching into a large wicker basket, she pulled out a razor and held it forth. "I just came to give you this. It's yours. You paid for it, then left it behind."

Bliss blinked back tears. It was the razor she had purchased to give to Travis. She had neglected to take it with her, and in all the confusion of finding a place to stay and settling in had forgotten it for a time. Now he likely wouldn't need it. "Thank you."

"I was afraid I wouldn't get a chance to give it to you, what with you leaving town so soon and all. I'm glad to see that you're still here." She closed the door behind her, signaling that she meant to stay.

"I've had a change of plans," Bliss admitted sourly, laying the razor on the nightstand.

"How delightful!" Taking off her bonnet and shawl and hanging them on the doorknob, Hattie moved toward the chair by the bed, looking ready for what Bliss feared might be a long visit.

Seeing a telltale bone in Hattie Dodd's path, Bliss hastily kicked it under the rug. "It looks as though I'm going to stay a few more days." Or however long it took to initiate a plan of action.

"Then we'll have a chance to get better acquainted." Hattie settled herself into the chair.

Without even a pause she started in on her favorite subject of conversation. The town's gossip. Hilary Applegate had gout again. Flora Cummings' baby was overdue. Ralph Spensor's wife had thrown him out into the street for spending too much time in the saloon. Meaningless chatter, considering Bliss didn't even know these people.

At first Bliss hardly paid her chattering much attention; she was too occupied with making certain that neither of the dogs poked its head out from under the bed. Then she heard the name Taggart. "What did you say?"

"I asked if you saw all the hoopla on Main Street this afternoon. Such an exciting day, what with Josephine Taggart coming back to town and all."

"*Josephine* Taggart?" Bliss raised her brows in question.

"The marshal's highfalutin wife," Hattie explained, making no secret of her envy. "Arrived in a carriage drawn by four white horses. As if she were some kind of queen! Dressed to the teeth, she was. Wearing a maroon dress of silk with puffed sleeves and a huge bustle." She patted her own. "A tall hat heavily trimmed with feathers and ribbons. And would you believe it? A fur boa." She rolled her eyes.

"So, the marshal's wife has expensive tastes," Bliss said to herself, making a quick mental note. She wished she had seen the woman. It was obvious that Taggart's wife had made quite an impression on Hattie Dodd. "Where had she been?"

"San Francisco!" Hattie reached down into the crevice between her big breasts and came up with a hankie. Mopping her brow, she said, "It's rather warm in here, don't you think?"

"No, I don't." It was, but Bliss didn't offer to open the window, hoping that if it got uncomfortable enough the woman would leave. She wanted to be alone with her thoughts.

"Well, at least it's not as warm as it was in the jail late today!" Hattie leaned forward, watching as Bliss picked up a brush and ran it through her hair. "There was a fire, you know."

"A fire. Where?"

"In one of the cells."

Bliss panicked, imagining the worst. Travis would have been trapped, unable to get out. A gruesome fate even worse than hanging. "The prisoner . . . ?" Her heart pounded, her throat went dry. She almost feared to hear the answer.

Hattie stuffed the hankie back in its nest. "He was the one who set the fire. A way to make an escape, they say."

Transfixed, Bliss could only stare, moving the brush harder and faster. "And did he?" Pray to God he had and was now far, far away.

"No. Marshal Taggart and his men quickly subdued him before anyone was hurt, and they put out the fire. But it was an exciting moment nonetheless."

"Oh." It was impossible for Bliss to hide her disappointment that Travis' attempt had failed. "So he's still in jail."

Hattie nodded. "Surrounded by a dozen of the marshal's men. I would dare to say he can't even sneeze without bringing them running. Poor soul. All he got for his bravado was to have his hanging moved up a day."

"His hanging . . ." Bliss shuddered. "But what about a trial?"

"Already been one. Marshal Taggart just isn't one to waste any time."

Bliss could imagine just what kind of trial it had been, if indeed there had even been one. There would have been a hurried gathering of the marshal's men, a crooked judge and bogus testimony. What more proof did she need of Travis' innocence than the way he had been railroaded into a date with the hangman.

"When is it to be?"

"Tomorrow, at high noon."

"Tomorrow!" Her hands and knees trembled in unison. Her stomach coiled up in a knot. Now she was the one who was hot, then suddenly cold. So little time.

Bolting to her feet, Hattie was all motherly concern. "Why, honey, you're as white as a sheet. You look as if you're going to faint. What on earth?"

Bliss forced herself to remain calm. Dissolving into a blubbering, quivering, emotional display of womanly weakness wouldn't do Travis any good at all. "It's . . . it's just that it *is* too hot in here, that's all." Hurriedly she opened the window, breathing in the night air that was her only salvation. Oh, Travis! Oh, God! Forgetting Hattie for just a moment, she stared out into the night. How deceptively normal the sky looked, as if it wasn't about ready to fall.

"Oh, Travis," she murmured under her breath. She had wanted to make it up to him for being so unreasonable, had wanted to help him clear his name; but what good would it do to prove his innocence after he was dead? My fault. Mine! she wanted to scream.

Suddenly there was an outcry, but not from Bliss's lips. "What in the name of God?"

Bliss whirled around to see Hattie down on hands and knees, nose to nose with Bard. Apparently searching for a fallen hairpin. "Oh, no!" The game was up. Hattie would tell her sister, and Bliss would be looking for another place to sleep. Just what she needed. But perhaps it was better to face the situation head-on. "Don't be afraid. It's just my dog. One of them."

"One of them?" Hattie slowly backed away, then rose to her feet. "How many do you have?"

"Two." At the sound of her whistle, Bard and Boru slipped from their hiding places wagging their tails.

"And just what *are* they?" Guardedly Hattie eyed the big, sleek gray dogs.

"Irish wolfhounds," Bliss announced proudly. "They're hunters."

Drawing herself up to her full height, the older woman asked, "And just what do they hunt?"

"Wolves and coyotes mainly." Bliss patted her thigh. "Bard and Boru, say hello."

"I'm sure that won't be necessary." Hattie moved toward the door. Quickly whisking up hat and shawl, she opened it, preparing herself for a hasty retreat.

"I suppose you'll tell your sister," Bliss exclaimed, laying a hand on the woman's shoulder. Well, what did it matter? She wouldn't be here much longer anyway. The only thing that had held her this far was Travis.

Slowly Hattie turned her head. "I should! Dogs are nasty animals who chew everything in sight and are prone to make . . . messes. Sophie will have a fit."

"Not my dogs!" Bliss said, coming to their defense as well as her own. "They're trained to mind their manners." As if proving that fact, both dogs sat down in unison. "See."

Hattie was less than convinced. "Yes, yes, I see." Her stern expression softened. "All right, I won't say a word. It doesn't look as if they've hurt anything in here." The room was, as a matter of fact, fairly tidy. Cleanliness was one of Bliss's attributes.

"You won't be sorry." Bliss felt a surge of affection toward the dark-haired woman. She had thought herself friendless, now she was not so sure. Still, she was not prone to trust Hattie about the matter of Travis. Perhaps because it was just too private a matter. She stood in the doorway, tempted to call Hattie back, but in the end let her leave. When the woman was safely out of sight Bliss plucked up her hat, picked up her rifle and vanished into the night.

Bliss wasn't the only one taking a late night walk. Taking a respite from the frivolities of his wife's homecoming party, Marshal Sam Taggart strode the boardwalk with one of his men. "It's all set for tomorrow, Tom. It went even smoother than I had planned."

"Because you got the judge in your pocket." Tom

Barlow chuckled.

"Let's just say that we saw eye to eye and came to a mutual agreement." There was no misunderstanding his meaning.

"Blackmail."

"The judge has some things in his past, some indiscretions he wouldn't want spread around." Taggart paused in his stride. He knew just how such things could haunt a man, surfacing when it was least convenient. Just as that damned newspaperman had. With his camera. That photograph he had planned to send back East was threatening for more reasons than one. Taggart knew all too well that the picture's falling into the wrong hands would be his undoing. It could prove once and for all who he wasn't and, most dangerous of all, who he really *was*. Was it any wonder he was anxious to get Travis La Mont out of the way? A snoop in town made things far too perilous.

"So tomorrow is hanging day." Slapping his thighs with both hands in a mock drumbeat, Tom Barlow made light of the situation. "I'll practice the drumroll so we can give the poor sucker a lively send off. What do you say?"

"I don't need a drummer. What I do need is someone to keep tabs on that Harrison woman. Jake says she's been asking around, involving herself in things that are better left alone. Things that are none of her business, like how I run my town."

"The bounty hunter? The one with those damn dogs?" A look of pure hatred replaced Barlow's expression of joviality.

"That's the one. Holed up at the boarding house

for her stay here. Seems like she's having second thoughts about having brought La Mont in. I don't want to chance her making a scene tomorrow."

"She won't. Not if I can help it." Barlow gritted his teeth. "I got a score to settle with her. This will be one job I look forward to."

"I want her out of town. After noon tomorrow La Mont will be out of my hair. She's next, if you know what I mean."

"I do, and I'm more than happy to oblige." Sticking out his index finger and thumb, curling the other fingers up, Tom Barlow made his hand into a gun and pretended to shoot.

"No. I don't want violence if there is another way. But if she makes trouble. . . ."

"I hope she does. I'll be waiting!"

Chapter Twenty-One

The lights of the town were slowly being extinguished. An eerie silence had fallen over Watersville in the late hours of the night. Only the faraway tinkle of the saloon's piano and the tread of Bliss's boots on the boardwalk sliced through the quiet. She had never felt so alone, so desperate, in all her life.

"They're going to hang him. The marshal is going to make him swing." She repeated it over and over until at last the reality pounded into her head. *It was really going to happen.*

Less than twelve hours, that was all she had to figure out a way to get Travis free. So little time to successfully thwart the mockery of justice that had been planned, and yet she had to do it. Either she found a way to undo the wrong she had done in handing Travis over to the marshal, or by her own stubbornness she had condemned Travis and had broken her own heart.

How long or how far she walked Bliss didn't know; she was oblivious to reality. But she suddenly realized she was at the site of the jail. Passing by the scaffold, she averted her eyes, not wanting to give in to the despair such a sight initiated, but the image danced before her eyes nonetheless—Travis dangling from the rope.

"No!" It tore from her throat on a mournful sob. She forced herself to concentrate on the image of Travis safe. Travis free. Travis alive and in her arms. "There must be a way. There just has to be." With that thought in mind, she blended into the shadows to make a quick investigation of the cell's outer wall. It was thick. Solid. Impregnable. "How am I going to get him out?" That question plagued her.

Oh, she could try bravely barging into the jail, her rifle primed and ready, but that would be a stupid and pointless thing to do. During the shooting someone would invariably be killed, perhaps even Travis or herself. She contemplated tying one end of a rope to the bars of Travis' cell and the other to the saddle horn of a horse and tugging until the bars pulled free, but that could prove too noisy. She could slip Travis a gun through the bars, but from what she had heard from Hattie, they were watching him every minute, just waiting for him to make another attempt at escape. The moment he tried to leave the jail he would be a target. Shot or hanged, he would still be dead.

Several other ideas flitted through her mind, from dynamiting the wall of the jail to using the marshal as a hostage. One by one Bliss cast them aside. From what she had observed, the marshal just had too many people in his employ. Even if she did get Travis

212

free, they would be followed immediately. If they failed to get away, Travis would be caught by the posse and hung from the nearest tree. No, the odds of being captured were much too great.

As she walked aimlessly about, she realized that freeing Travis from the danger he was in was not something she could do alone. She had to have a foolproof plan. There could be no blundering. She needed help. For once in her life she had to admit that. But who could she turn to?

"The blacksmith!" He was the only answer, the only one she knew for a certainty had little liking for the marshal. The question was, would he give her aid? Knowing she had to take a chance, Bliss started running in the direction of his house. Though all the lights were out, she hurried to the door and pounded anyway. There would be time enough later for apologies.

It took several knocks before the blacksmith was roused. Standing in the doorway in his red-and-white-striped nightshirt and cap he looked like anger personified. He was not wearing his patch, and she could see the horrible scar that gouged the lid of one eye as he scowled. "By God, you had better have a good reason for awakening me at this hour," he thundered, his tone nearly as frightening as his expression.

"I do. A matter of life and death." Outwardly she was calm, but inside she was trembling. So much rested on the outcome of this midnight meeting.

"Life and death?" Bending down, he looked her full in the face. Something he read there convinced him she was serious. "Then by all means, come in."

Lighting the kerosene lamp by the door, the blacksmith led her through a small hallway into his widower's abode. The parlor was sparsely furnished with a dark blue settee and matching chair, two lamps and a small rectangular table strewn with nails, scraps of paper, a hammer and wire. Dust everywhere gave evidence of the lack of a feminine occupant.

"Well?" The blacksmith made no sign that Bliss should make herself comfortable.

"Tomorrow at noon the man I brought in to the marshal is going to be hung!"

"So?" There was no sympathy in either voice or face. "What else did you expect?"

Bliss hung her head. "Not that! It's little more than a lynching."

"It isn't the first time, nor will it be the last." Folding his arms across his chest, the blacksmith signaled that he was not interested in listening to a full account of the story. "There is nothing that can be done."

"There has to be. Otherwise . . ." Her lips began to tremble as tears sprang to her eyes. She had spent too much time concealing her emotions. Suddenly, like a shattered dam, her pent-up control burst. Mentally and physically she was at the end of her rope. "Please, you have to help me."

Flinging herself on the settee, Bliss sobbed out her fear and grief as she told him the whole story, from the first time she had cornered Travis in the tunnel to the moment she had turned him in. She hated herself

214

for her weakness, yet she was unable to keep in her feelings anymore. This man was her last remaining hope. Now it seemed that she had failed.

"I thought I was right. But I was wrong. Travis said all along that he was framed, only I didn't believe him. Now he's going to die because I was so smug in my certainty that the law was always just. Well, it isn't!" Setting her jaw, she continued her tirade of self-condemnation. "I traded a man's life for money, and there's no way I can rectify what I've done unless I save his life. I have to! I have to, don't you see? No matter what happens I can't let him be hanged, because . . . because . . ." Because somewhere along the way she had fallen in love with him. Strange that only now could she admit that she had strong feelings for the man. "Oh, it's hopeless, I know it is, but what does it matter to you?" Bliss buried her face in her hands.

The blacksmith reached down and stroked her hair very lightly, tentatively. "It's not as hopeless as you think."

"What did you say?" For a moment Bliss was afraid to believe her ears.

"I said it's not hopeless. Difficult. Harrowing. Fraught with dangers. But not impossible."

Bliss looked up at the blacksmith through a veil of tears. "Not impossible. You will help me then?"

The blacksmith pulled his hand away. "It's none of my business. Taggart is a devil. If he found out I had anything to do with it he'd be mad as hell. He'd retaliate in an instant."

"So, when it comes right down to it you're afraid

215

of him, too?" How could she have been so silly as to think she could count on a total stranger? She didn't even know his name.

"Not afraid. Just cautious."

"And after all, why should you help me." Though for just a moment Bliss had shown herself to be vulnerable, had let the wall she'd built around herself slip, she now regretted her brief show of weakness. Hastily she threw the barrier back up. She was brave and she was tough, she didn't need him or anybody else. Moving toward the door, she said over her shoulder, "Well, to hell with you, I'll do it myself!"

"And get yourself killed." Grabbing her arm, he kept her from storming out.

"What does it matter!" She inhaled, sucking air into her lungs, then straightened her spine as she reached for the latch, but she didn't have time to open the door.

"All right. You win." For the first time since she had met him, she heard the blacksmith laugh. "And perhaps I can find others brave enough to assist us. It's about time Taggart was taught a lesson."

Bliss nearly sagged with relief. The blacksmith *was* going to help her. "About time indeed." She hooked her arm through his, feeling a genuine surge of affection for the burly man.

"Come, I'll fill you in on my plan." Once more he led her into the parlor.

What followed was an intense lesson in the molding of discipline, patience and duplicity into what they both hoped would be a successful rescue.

4 FREE BOOKS

TO GET YOUR 4 FREE BOOKS WORTH $18.00 — MAIL IN THE FREE BOOK CERTIFICATE T O D A Y

Fill in the Free Book Certificate below, and we'll send your FREE BOOKS to you as soon as we receive it.

If the certificate is missing below, write to: Zebra Home Subscription Service, Inc., P.O. Box 5214, 120 Brighton Road, Clifton, New Jersey 07015-5214.

FREE BOOK CERTIFICATE

4 FREE BOOKS

ZEBRA HOME SUBSCRIPTION SERVICE, INC.

YES! Please start my subscription to Zebra Historical Romances and send me my first 4 books absolutely FREE. I understand that each month I may preview four new Zebra Historical Romances free for 10 days. If I'm not satisfied with them, I may return the four books within 10 days and owe nothing. Otherwise, I will pay the low preferred subscriber's price of just $3.75 each; a total of $15.00, *a savings off the publisher's price of $3.00*. I may return any shipment and I may cancel this subscription at any time. There is no obligation to buy any shipment and there are no shipping, handling or other hidden charges. Regardless of what I decide, the four free books are mine to keep.

NAME _____

ADDRESS _____ APT _____

CITY _____ STATE ____ ZIP ____

TELEPHONE ( ) _____

SIGNATURE _____
(if under 18, parent or guardian must sign)

Terms, offer and prices subject to change without notice. Subscription subject to acceptance by Zebra Books. Zebra Books reserves the right to reject any order or cancel any subscription.

ZEBRA HOME SUBSCRIPTION
SERVICE, INC.
P.O. Box 5214
120 BRIGHTON ROAD
CLIFTON, NEW JERSEY 07015-5214

AFFIX
STAMP
HERE

But it was much more as well. As Bliss learned bits and pieces of his life—that his name was Jonathan Price, that he had lost his eye while fighting for the North in the war, that he was a decorated war hero whose home had once been in Kentucky—the beginning of a friendship blossomed as well. By the time Bliss left in the wee hours of the morning, she took something with her that she hadn't had when she had come. A warm sense of hope.

Chapter Twenty-Two

Lying lethargically on his makeshift cot, Travis contemplated a great many things he'd hoped not to have to think about until he was into old age. Life. Death. Hell. It looked as if he was going to find out sooner than he had expected just what happened when a man's breath was stilled. Just a few more hours. The rays of early morning sun peeking through the window were an ominous greeting and although he had spent the late night hours preparing for what was to come, Travis knew he wasn't ready. Not yet. He had only tasted of life. There was so much more to enjoy.

"Hanging day, La Mont," Jake Heath announced cheerily, eyeing Travis' discarded hat as if already laying his claim.

"Yeah, hanging day," Travis answered. As if he had to be told.

At high noon, when the handle of the gibbet was pulled and the trap door dropped, he would be plummeted to his death, dangling like a side of beef for all to see. Would the fall through the trap break his neck or would he suffer slow strangulation, a grisly end even for the most deserving outlaw. He could only hope that God in his mercy would make his death quick.

Travis had hoped for a miracle, but now as the hours dwindled so did his faith. He suspected that his execution, like his trial, would be a muddled nightmare. Oh, he had had a trial all right. Even Taggart had been forced to give a prisoner that, but the outcome had been a foregone conclusion. No one had testified for Travis, yet a parade of people he didn't even know had pointed in his direction and insisted that he had done things he knew he never did. Was it any wonder the harsh sentence had been handed down?

Hanging. It would be the culmination of this low point in his life, the time spent in a cramped jail cell for doing nothing but taking a damning photograph while a robbery was going on. He'd tried time after time to escape, but it was useless. He was trapped. Even now he had trouble realizing it wasn't all just a horrible dream. Oh, that he would wake up and find it was.

"You didn't eat your last meal, Mr. La Mont." At least Ellis Jones looked sympathetic.

"I've lost my appetite." Food was the last thing on Travis' mind at such a time. Besides, where he was going he wouldn't need it.

"Are you sure you aren't hungry?" The little man was always anxious to please. "I can bring you something else."

"How about a gun?"

"Pancakes and sausage or—"

"He said he isn't hungry, you little monkey!" Coming up behind Ellis, Jake Heath roughly pushed him aside, sending the little man toppling to the floor.

"Leave him alone, you bastard! Don't take your dislike of me out on him. He hasn't done you any harm." Travis wanted to beat Heath's smirking face to a pulp. If, after he died, something went wrong and he ended up in hell, he knew the devil would look just like Jake Heath. But he would not give in to mournful speculation. "As a matter of fact I only have a few hours left, and my dying wish is for you to go the hell away and leave me alone! Why don't you go back to your corner and resume your game of solitaire."

"Turn my back on you so you can start another fire? Not on your life." Making it a point to be purposefully annoying, Jake Heath stood right by Travis' cell, pulling on the ends of his mustache. He was still standing there when Bliss made her entrance. "Well, well, well, that lady bounty hunter who brought you in. Bet you're glad to see her, aren't you, La Mont?"

Strangely enough Travis was, despite the circumstances, though he felt the need to hide his true feelings. "Did you come to gloat?" he asked.

"No, of course not!" How could he think she wanted him dead?

Travis grimaced. "Then why?" Standing up, he

raked his hands through his hair, swearing softly.

"To . . . to say that I'm sorry things turned out the way they did." Bliss looked nervously toward Jake Heath. How could she follow through on her plan with him hanging around? Not even trying to mask her irritation, she elbowed the scowling man aside. "I need a little privacy if you don't mind, so I can make peace with Mr. La Mont before he dies."

"Mr. La Mont is it now?" Jake Heath guffawed, yet in the end he grudgingly gave in to her firm determination. Resuming his position in a chair in the corner, he began playing another card game.

"I don't have much time, so listen carefully," Bliss whispered, motioning Travis forward. "I'm going to save you. All I'm asking is that you trust me."

"Trust you. The way you trusted me?" Though he was trying not to sound bitter, he just couldn't keep the words from coming out.

Bliss took a deep breath. She had been afraid of this. But then, could she blame him? Swallowing her pride, she looked him straight in the eye and said, "Travis, I'm sorry. What more can I say than that? I've been wrong and pigheaded, and because of that you're in a whole heap of trouble." Knowing how deep her pride ran, Travis should surely realize how much the apology cost her. "I can't ask you to forgive me because I don't think you could, but I can ask you to listen and to believe me when I say I have come to help."

He looked into her determined face and in that instant felt a fierce upsurge of emotion. "I believe you." It was obvious that she did care. "So, how are

221

you going to get me out of this jail before the hanging?"

"I'm not." Jonathan Price had insisted that it was much too predictable. Marshal Taggart would be expecting a jailbreak.

"What?" For just a moment Travis thought she was playing a game, but she quickly shushed him. "Explain."

"I don't have time to tell you all the details. That guard with the mustache keeps looking this way. All I can tell you is the plan won't become apparent until after you're on the scaffold."

Travis gasped. "That's cutting it kind of close, don't you think?" What if something went wrong. Then it would be too late to save him.

"It's the only way. Taggart and his men are watching you like a wolf after a flock of sheep. One false move and you'll be shot as full of holes as Swiss cheese." Casting a glance over her shoulder she contented herself that Jake Heath was occupied for the moment. "But if you can fool them, just for a time, into thinking you're dead, then we figure that will give you a little bit of breathing room."

"We?" For just a moment Travis felt a stab of jealousy.

"Jonathan, the blacksmith and I." Reaching under her shirt, she brought forth an object and thrust it through the bars. "Take this quickly and hide it until just before they take you out of here."

It looked like a big leather dog collar. "What . . . ?"

"There's no time to tell you the details. Just put it on before they take you to the scaffold." Seeing Jake

Heath coming she said merely, "Just do as I say. And Travis be careful!" She wanted to tell him that she loved him, but suddenly she was just too shy. Little did she know that the look in her eyes said it for her.

"Same to you." Travis stuffed the collar under his shirt, tucking it safely in his belt just in the nick of time. Once again Jake Heath exploded onto the scene.

"Time's up. If you haven't already made your peace, then that's just too bad." Brazenly he patted Bliss on her well-rounded bottom, forcing her to move along. "Of course now, if you'd like to come back after the hanging and pay a call on *me* . . ."

Bliss cringed at the very idea. Was it any wonder she hurried along? Still, as she reached the doorway she couldn't keep from looking back. "I love you, Travis," she said so softly that no one, not even he, could hear. Only now could she say it. Maybe one of these days she could say it aloud. Crossing her fingers, she could only hope that all would go well. If not, then she would revert to desperate measures. She was prepared to use her rifle if all else failed. One thing she had vowed, no matter what happened, she wouldn't let Travis die.

Watching Bliss walk through the door, Travis felt more exultation than a man due to hang should experience. He wasn't alone after all. Someone did care about him. It had shown in Bliss's voice, in her eyes, and most importantly in her dedication to saving him.

*   *   *

So many things to do and so little time. Was it any wonder that Bliss felt harried and nervous. When it came right down to it, this plan hinged on her, and there were moments when she was just plain scared. One false move, one miscalculation, and the consequences would be more than disastrous, they would be fatal. Travis would hang.

Trying to put her apprehension from her mind, she hurried about her tasks, buying dynamite and blasting caps from the Watersville Powder Company, visiting the dressmaker to purchase an already made-up, new blue calico dress, stocking up on a few important supplies; yet every so often reality intruded and threatened to destroy her self-imposed calm.

The more she thought about it, the more impossible and unpredictable the blacksmith's plan seemed, and yet it had worked before, more than twenty years ago. Jonathan Price had fooled his jailers by using a leather collar with spikes just like the one he had hurriedly fashioned for Travis. It had made it possible for him to be hung and not meet his final end. He had then pretended to be dead, even managing not to wince when he had been kicked in the ribs. Having been loaded on a wagon and driven to the undertaker's, he had nearly frightened the poor mortician to death when he had sat up in the coffin.

It worked once, but would it work again? It all hinged on Bliss's being able to replace the hangman and not being found out. A delicate matter of subterfuge and impersonation.

Lugging her purchases to the livery stable, she hid the dynamite and caps so they'd be handy when needed and packed the other items in her saddlebags. Hearing the church bells toll eleven times, she felt a moment of panic. It was nearly noon.

Hurrying to the boarding house, she squared her bill, then raced to her room to gather her belongings together. Bard and Boru greeted her at the door, their enthusiastic welcome making her feel guilty at the thought of temporarily leaving them behind. If everything worked according to plan, she and Travis would be on the run, so she couldn't even think of bringing them along.

"I'll miss you boys, but I'm sure Todd will take good care of you while I'm gone." The arrangement had been made with the blacksmith's help. Even so, parting with the wolfhounds was an emotional drain on Bliss. As she left the livery stable after taking Bard and Boru from the boarding house, she was crying.

"Don't you worry. I'll take good care of them." Todd, the young man from the livery stable, patted her arm to reassure her, even so Bliss felt a moment of loss. The dogs had been her only companions since her father had died. It was as if she were leaving part of her family behind.

This sentimentality gave way to another emotion, however, as she passed the hangman's house and caught sight of him walking out his front door. Leaving home to go about his grisly task.

George Haladon! A man who was said to have performed ninety executions. A former deputy sheriff, he was said to be almost as expert with pistols as with a rope. He had shot four prisoners who were attempting to escape. A treacherous opponent. Even so, Bliss couldn't afford to falter or even pause to think about the consequences of what she now intended. The only thing she allowed herself to concentrate on was Travis as she fell into step behind the hangman.

Chapter Twenty-Three

The clock on the jailhouse wall displayed the time as a quarter to twelve. Just fifteen minutes left, Travis thought as he sullenly stared at the hour and minute hands. Tick tock, tick tock. Each minute that passed brought the moment of reckoning closer and closer. Would Bliss be able to keep her word and save him from strangling to death? He had to believe that she could. Bliss Harrison was his only hope.

Opening his shirt, Travis pulled out the collar she had smuggled to him through the bars and stared at it for just a moment. It was a strange-looking contraption that might have looked like an ordinary leather collar were it not for the three-quarter-inch curved nails that poked through the leather. Put it on right before they came to take him to the scaffold, she had instructed, and though he had misgivings, he had little choice but to obey.

Travis had just finished cinching the buckle and was tucking the collar beneath the neck of his shirt when Jake Heath came up behind him. "What are you doing?"

"Just making sure I look presentable," Travis answered sarcastically.

"Yeah, well ain't that nice," Jake mocked loudly.

Moving his hand upward to his chin, Travis ran his fingers over the stubble. "Don't suppose you'd let me take time for a shave. So I'd look nice for the ladies present?"

Coming up behind Jake, Ellis Jones nodded. "I'll get you a razor."

Jake reached out and grabbed Ellis by the shirtfront, holding him immobile. "No you don't, you little runt. Where he's going it won't matter if he's clean shaven or not." With a grunt he sent the little man sprawling.

"Back off, Heath! He was only trying to be kind. But then that's something you probably wouldn't understand." Travis looked at Ellis and smiled. "Thanks anyway, Ellis." He made up his mind that if he got out of this in one piece and cleared his name he'd repay the little man in some way.

"Thanks anyway!" Jake Heath mimicked. "You'll think 'thank you' when your tongue is hanging out and your face is purple." With a nod of his head, he brought four gunmen running, their weapons pointed in Travis' direction. Bliss was right about one thing. Escape from the jail would be impossible with so many guns and eyes trained upon him. But what was her plan? And just what part did the collar play? He had a pretty good idea that it was to guard him from the noose, but what then?

"So nice of you all to escort me." Travis assumed an air of bravado as he got up from the cot, but inside he was anything but sure of himself. Even the best-laid plans were prone to failure. Intellectually he was prepared for the possibility that there would be no last-minute reprieve, but emotionally he could not help but be on edge lest something go wrong. He didn't want to die! Hadn't prepared himself to meet his maker just yet. Above his head he could see a spider hanging from its web, and he shuddered as it reminded him of his own fate.

"Would you like me to say a prayer?" One of the guards pulled out a Bible, but Travis shook his head. It was too much of a sacrilege. "Then let's go, La Mont." Roughly his hands were tied behind his back, though to his relief that was the only place they touched him. At least for the moment the collar had not been discovered.

Jake Heath took out his keys and opened the creaking door, then Travis was led out to the corridor. Sandwiched in between the men, he joined their gruesome procession. It was a death march, and it felt and looked like one, but Travis walked as slowly as he could. He needed more time, had to buy himself as many extra minutes as he could.

A jab to his ribs hastened him along. Though it was hot outside, Travis shivered as he stepped through the outer door. The sun was at its zenith. It was a cloudless day. "A fine day for a hanging," Travis heard several people declare as he was walked to the scaffold, "a mighty fine day, indeed." Ladies in calico, some tugging children by the hand, and men dressed in the style of their trades, be they miners, ranchers or shopkeepers, all followed in a small parade.

"Ghouls!" Travis exclaimed. He wondered how these ordinary-looking people could so calmly assemble around the gallows as if awaiting an entertainment. Even so, there was no anger in him now, only a feeling of suspense. At any moment something was going to happen, but he didn't know what, when or how.

"Up the steps, La Mont!"

He walked up the twelve makeshift wooden stairs of the scaffold very slowly, searching the crowd that was quickly gathering. There was no sign of Bliss, yet strangely enough he didn't panic. She had told him to trust her, and he did. Somehow she'd get him out of this predicament.

"Travis La Mont, you have been tried and found guilty of robbery and murder by the territorial judge of Montana. May God have pity on your soul!" Marshal Taggart sounded authoritative, the very epitome of justice, but his composure faltered for just a moment as he looked around him. "Where the damn hell is Jericho? Where's my hangman?" He relaxed as he caught sight of the short rotund man coming up the steps, dressed all in black as was appropriate. Travis tensely watched as the hangman stumbled forward.

"Take all the time you need. Don't hurry on my account," Travis quipped, trying to hide the apprehension that was slowly building within him.

"Do you have any last words?"

Any last words? A rapid succession of emotions stormed through his brain. Hell, Travis thought, he had enough of a speech planned to take all day, all of it on the injustice of a system that allowed a law-abiding man to be cheated of his life. "People of Watersville, I declare to you that I am innocent, but I wonder if your marshal can say—"

"Enough!"

Travis was quickly silenced, though at least he had caused a few people to stare.

"Jericho, the rope."

It seemed they were in a hurry to hang him. Travis looked around for Bliss, again didn't see her. Had something happened? Worry brought beads of perspiration to his brow. He looked at his executioner, trying to see the face of the man whose job it was to kill him, but the wide-brimmed black hat was much too low. What the hat didn't hide a black neckerchief did. But wait. The eyes! Travis gasped as the hangman winked at him. It was Bliss. If his life had ever been in her hands it most assuredly was now. Her name was on his lips like a whispered prayer. They looked at each other, joined in something far beyond the excitement of the moment.

Hardly daring to breathe, Bliss waited. Would she be discovered? It had been so absurdly easy up to now. She had set upon the hangman from behind and hit him on the head. Then, using a pillow from the boarding house to simulate his girth, she had wrapped it around her waist, secured it with a belt and put on the hangman's garments. Only now did she have any second thoughts. Would there be two with their head in a noose and not just one? No. It appeared that all was going according to the blacksmith's plan. Taggart and the others were

231

much too busy making certain the hanging would be a spectacle that they weren't looking at her very closely.

A drum roll sounded as she looped the rope over Travis' neck. Carefully she secured the thick hemp beneath the curve of the nails on the collar to cushion his throat so that the fall wouldn't break his neck or cause him to strangle. Then, as the marshal gave the signal, she pulled the lever that sent the trap door falling and Travis as well.

Travis felt the pull as he slid into empty air, felt as if his neck was going to be stretched beyond its limit, but despite his discomfort he played his part well. Having seen men hung once or twice on his assignments he now mimicked their bug-eyed expression. Holding his breath, he prayed that Taggart would believe he was dead.

"We'll let him hang there a while as an example," the marshal was saying. Travis only hoped it wouldn't be too long. Already he was agonizingly uncomfortable with every ounce of his weight straining the muscles of his neck. Even so he was amazed that everything had gone so well. Who would have thought that the marshal would have been taken in by such a wild scheme. He wished he could see Taggart when he found out later that he had been duped and by a woman!

One by one the townspeople tired of gawking and started to disassemble. Likewise, the marshal's men slowly sauntered away from the scene. So far, so good. Suddenly from down the street came frantic yelling.

"Wait! Wait. Something strange is going on." The

shout came from a chubby man who was running down Main Street in his long johns.

"By God, it's Jericho. Then who?" All heads snapped around to look at Bliss.

"Damn! I should have hit him harder. It almost worked." Frantically she gave a signal, then drew her revolver. "Stay back. Don't anyone make a move." But she could only hold them off so long. "Ten, nine, eight, seven . . ." Now it was time for the blacksmith to initiate plan two.

"Get her. Get him. She can't shoot us all!" Taggart was livid with rage, though not so angry that he wanted to call her bluff.

"Four, three, two—"

The loud, booming explosion shook the platform. Splinters of wood, roofing and stone flew everywhere.

"Someone's dynamited the jail!" Like frightened ants, the marshal's men scattered, running in every direction.

Bliss used the moment of confusion to whip out Travis' razor and hurriedly cut the rope from which he dangled. He fell with a thud. "Travis, run! Around the corner by the barbershop the horses are tethered. Meet me there."

Travis didn't have to be told twice. Taking to his heels, he ran like a man with the devil following. And the devil was! Having recovered from the shock of Bliss's "surprise," Marshal Taggart was coming after them.

"Travis, hurry!" Running a deadly footrace, Bliss passed him and then paused for just a moment to let him catch up. Again she used the razor, this time to

233

cut the ropes that held his hands behind his back, and together they sped around the corner. Hurrying to the horses, they grabbed the reins and vaulted into their saddles in a daring show of horsemanship Travis knew he could never duplicate. Leaving the marshal behind in the dust, they headed East and to freedom.

Marshal Sam Taggart was coldly furious. He felt like a goddamned fool. He'd been duped. Bested. His jail had been blown to the high heavens, his hangman had been assaulted and his prisoner had escaped. The question was, how had it happened and who had been the instigator? At the moment it didn't matter. All he could think about was bringing Travis La Mont back.

Waving his arms about, he yelled to his men, "Don't just stand there gawking. Go after them!"

Oh, they were a comical sight. Running about every which way in confusion. Taggart might have laughed if the situation hadn't been so all-fired serious. Travis La Mont was a walking stick of explosives just primed to go off. He had to be caught right away, before he revealed what had happened to him here in Watersville. Before he laid his hands on that photograph and sent it to every newspaper east of the Mississippi River.

"Someone's head is going to roll!" His, if Travis La Mont and his cohort weren't caught. Taggart's life unrolled in his mind, as if he were a man drowning. All he'd worked so hard for these many years could be wiped away in an instant, because of this one man. "No!"

His name wasn't Samuel. Wasn't even Taggart. He would be found out. Daniel Quentin Plummer, that was who he really was. A man who had served time in a Boston jail for larceny and worse. An escapee. A wanted man, whose face had been plastered on more billboards than Travis La Mont's. Not the cowboy he had pretended to be, a well-intentioned drifter who had married the boss's pretty daughter.

"Heath, you go to Silver Bow. Barlow to Butte. Tremayne, you stake out Centersville. Jenkins, the mountains. Withers, you check everywhere in between."

"What about you, boss?" Boyd Withers, a man dressed all in buckskin wasn't in a hurry to get on his horse.

"Me? Why, I'll stay here. Got some investigating to do." His eyes took on a dangerous glow. "La Mont had help, and I aim to find out just who it was. And when I do . . ."

Tom Jenkins flinched. He didn't envy Travis La Mont's accomplice in the least. Whoever had taken the place of the hangman was in far more trouble than he knew. But he would soon find that out.

Chapter Twenty-Four

If horses had wings they couldn't have covered as great a distance and traveled at as frantic a speed as Travis and Bliss did in their effort to get away from the marshal and his men. Their determination, coupled with the fact that they had a head start, made it possible for them to leave their pursuers behind, at least for the moment.

"No sign of them," Travis said as he looked behind him for the umpteenth time. He heaved a sigh of relief as they left Watersville behind, but Bliss was quick to warn him that the danger was just beginning.

"The explosion took them by surprise, but once they get reorganized they'll be hot on our trail. There won't be an inch of ground between here and Canada they won't search, Travis."

Taking off her hat and kerchief, she freed her long red hair, which blew with untamed abandon around her face as they rode. Riding up beside her, Travis leaned over and gently touched the silken strands. "I owe you a debt of gratitude for saving my life, Bliss. No matter what happens now, I want you to know I think you're very brave."

A smile crinkled the corners of his eyes.

"Oh, it wasn't anything spectacular." She tried to sound modest, but the truth was, she felt warmed by his compliment.

"To the contrary, it was. I don't know of very many people who could have gotten me out of that fix, male or female." At this moment he felt a special bond with her, a surge of feeling so intense he was nearly frightened by it. This young woman was becoming so important to Travis that he couldn't imagine being without her. Was it the danger that made him feel this way? Partly. But he knew deep in his heart it was something else as well.

"I didn't do it all alone. The blacksmith helped." She swiveled in her saddle to look at him. He needed a shave and was streaked with dirt and sweat, nonetheless his face was very dear to her. Was there a chance that once they got out of this mess they might have a future together? It was a question she had little time to think about. All her attentions were centered on one thing. Getting away!

They rode all day at a punishing pace, splashing through streams, kicking up dust, galloping through the wild grass. They passed ranch houses, corrals of livestock, abandoned mining claims; dodged in and out of the trees, rode over rough gravel and rocks. Uphill and down they rode, ignoring their discomfort. They forced themselves to go on until their bodies ached for rest. Only then did they dare to stop. Helping her down from her horse, Travis was attentive, showing his appreciation for what she had done in small ways. Trying to ignore the stiffness in his sore neck, he picked her up and carried her to a spot beneath a shade tree. It was he who took care of the horses while she rested. Taking her canteen from the saddlebag, he gave her the first drink.

"Thanks." Bliss took a long gulp, then pulled her mouth away. "Now you." Unfastening her belt and opening her shirt and pants, Bliss took out the pillow and hurled it on the ground.

The muscles of Travis' neck were sore. At first it hurt to swallow, but his thirst was greater than his discomfort. He took a mouthful and forced it down his throat. "I don't want to ever have a rope around my neck again, even for a moment."

"No, I don't suppose you do." It seemed so natural for her to reach up and gently knead the pain away. "There, does that feel better."

It did. Her fingers had worked magic. "Um-hmm . . ."

Wetting her neckerchief, he gently wiped the dust and dirt from her face, returning her gesture of caring.

"You're very beautiful." He liked the slight curve of her brows, the tiny mole by her eyes, the proud set of her chin and the way her eyes always widened whenever she was listening to him.

"Naw . . ." Bliss was flustered, hardly knowing what to say. Once when he had said the same thing she had accused him of false flattery. But now the circumstances were different and for the life of her Bliss wasn't sure how to react. She wasn't holding a gun on him now, wasn't in control of the situation.

"You are. Very pretty and probably the spunkiest woman I've ever met." His fingers replaced the neckerchief, then traced the curves of her face. With infinite care, he brought his mouth close to hers. "You're very special to me, Bliss."

For what seemed to be an endless moment she stared back at him. "I . . . I like you too, Travis." Like him. She was crazy about him. It was all she could do to maintain any semblance of poise.

"Oh, Bliss . . ." He knew what he wanted and knew she wanted it, too. Some relief from the pent-up emotions bursting to be free. Moving forward, he touched her mouth with his.

Travis meant it to be a gentle kiss, but something—danger, unresolved desire or the passion of the moment—turned the touch of their lips into a hungry probing. Time stood still as they explored each other's mouth with mutual passion. Travis dragged her roughly up against him, his mouth crushing demandingly against hers, but she didn't complain. To the contrary, she returned kiss for kiss, awakening to the awareness of her own sensuality. Her arms locked around his neck, her hands kneading the upper muscles of his back and neck as if committing them to memory.

Desire coursed through both their bodies as their fingers explored, their senses enjoyed the nearness. The ground was hard, but they hardly noticed. Lying side by side, they banished coherent thought as they gave themselves up to a more primitive need, ruled now by emotions. Such a wild, beautiful madness, Travis thought. Pushing her onto her back, he slid his mouth sensuously down her throat, then, unbuttoning her shirt, moved his attentions lower. Compulsively he kissed the soft mounds of her breasts.

Bliss embraced him eagerly. She wanted more. Wanted . . . But no. Danger still lurked on the horizon somewhere. The marshal's men would be following. And yet, as the hot ache of desire for him coiled deep inside her, it was so difficult to pull away. "Travis . . ."

"Hmmmmmmm?" She was so warm, so responsive. At the moment all he could think about was having her naked against him. He wanted to do such wonderful things to her.

"Travis. We can't . . ." If they lost their heads now it could all have a tragic ending.

"Oh, but we can." As she started to protest he kissed her again, long and hard. Sliding his hand down her shirtfront, he touched her breast. His warm seeking fingers teased and stroked, bringing forth a moan of pleasure from her throat. "Ohhhh, Miss Harrison . . ."

Bliss was lost, totally ruled by her womanly emotions for the first time in her life. Her body aflame with needs she had barely envisioned before now, she convulsively clenched his dark hair pulling his head even closer to her. No matter what happened she would have this moment to remember.

"Wait!" Taggart's sneering face hovered behind her closed eyes, so vividly that when she opened them she nearly expected him to be staring down at them. "No! Travis. We don't have time . . ."

Through the haze of passion, Travis heard her

words, heard the tone of panic and knew she was right. With an agonizing effort, he brought himself back to reality. "Damn!" For just a moment they had shared such a wonderful dream.

"We've got to get moving again. We can't think, not even for a moment, that we've lost them. Remember that time when the posse surrounded us."

He did. "Yeah!" Taking a deep breath, he forced his breathing back to normal, forced his brain to think logically again and willed his hungers to cool. But it wasn't easy.

"We can't let that happen again." The need to protect him was nearly as obsessive as her desire had been. More so perhaps. Standing up, she brushed herself off. "We've got to mount up again."

Travis groaned. "You're the boss—and a cruel one, I must say." Even so, he smiled at her. "But once we're safe . . ."

Her heart seemed to stop, turn over, then start beating again. "Yep, once we're safe." It was a promise she wanted very much to keep.

"Now, I suppose I should ask you just where we're headed. I hope you know of some little cave or cavern where we can set up housekeeping." Travis assumed that like before they would have to stay just one step ahead of the marshal's men. Live life on the lam, at least until he was able to clear himself of the wrongful charges.

"Nope. The marshal will be expecting that. He knows this neck of the woods much better than I ever could, being it's his territory. He'd find us no matter how cleverly we hid. And when he did . . ."

Travis shuddered. He knew he'd never forget the experience of being marched to a scaffold for his execution. "Then what do you have planned?"

"We're headed for Butte."

"For civilization? But—"

"Marshal Taggart won't be expecting that. Most wanted men stay away from large towns and seek the refuge of the wilderness."

Travis wasn't so sure he wanted to be elbow to elbow with people. "But those wanted posters will be plastered all over. Even there. Surely Taggart will telegraph the lawmen. They'll be on the lookout."

"For two men!" Throwing back her head, Bliss gave vent to laughter. Oh, she and the blacksmith had been clever.

Travis looked at her appraisingly. Her hangman's garb reminded him of her ploy. No one would know who had rescued him. Certainly with that pillow stuffed in her shirt, the hat and neckerchief to hide her face, she had hardly resembled Bliss Harrison when she'd ridden out. "By God, you're right." At least she would be safe from discovery.

Bliss headed for the horses. Digging in the saddlebags she pulled out yards and yards of calico, along with other feminine paraphernalia—hats, scarves and gloves. "Two men, Travis. They won't be on the lookout for two *women.*"

"Two women?" It was obvious from his expression that he had reservations. "Oh, no!" He wasn't dressing up in skirts for love or money.

Ordinarily Bliss would have taken the time to convince him, but as she had already said they were running out of that commodity. "Do it!" she ordered, throwing him a dress of pink calico. "It's the only way. The blacksmith, brawny as he is, pulled it off during the war. It saved him from Andersonville."

"So it was his idea." Though he grumbled all the while, Travis picked up the dress.

"That dress belonged to his wife. She died a while back. I hated to take it, but he insisted." Bliss hurriedly put on the blue dress she had purchased from the dressmaker Hattie had recommended; then, seeing that Travis was all thumbs, she came to his aid. "She was a tall woman, thank God! It fits you remarkably well. But there is something missing."

Travis immediately knew what. "Breasts."

Bliss laughed at the humorous picture he made. "Of course!" But the problem was solved at once. This time it was Travis who used the pillow. Bliss pushed, patted and pinched it into place so that he looked like a pregnant woman. That way it would not seem strange that "she" kept to her rooms when they took up lodgings. A hat with a veil was the finishing touch. "We'll say that you are in the 'family way'. Then people will be more willing to leave you alone."

"Despite my first opinion I have to admit that it sounds plausible. As long as I don't have to talk." Travis knew that his baritone voice would immediately give him away.

"I'll do the talking for you." She nodded toward the horses. "Now we had better get riding. There's no telling where Taggart might be lurking."

"Riding, ha!" Travis was having a hard enough

time just getting into the saddle. "How in the hell do women manage?"

Bliss answered matter-of-factly. "Why do you think *I* prefer pants? I'm not at all partial to dresses myself. They're a damned nuisance. But we'll just have to do it."

"Ride into town like this?" As he plopped his now-unwieldy body into the saddle, Travis was dubious.

He did look strange. Sprawled atop the horse, he looked anything but womanly. Bliss thought for a moment. "We'll have to steal a wagon or carriage along the way. Women in 'your condition' shouldn't be on horseback."

There was no more time to say anything else. Putting her foot in the stirrup, she hauled up her skirts and pulled herself up. Then she gave the signal that set them off down the road toward Butte.

Chapter Twenty-Five

The first glimpse of Butte that Travis had was startling. The distant city seemed a gigantic gray mirage floating between barren earth and distant mountain peaks. A haven. Safety. Or at least so he hoped.

"I came here once with my father at night," Bliss said wistfully. "Its lights twinkled like jewels on black velvet." She looked over at him, wanting to judge his mood. "But then, compared to the cities you're used to, it probably isn't impressive."

Travis' eyes grew large with surprise as he viewed this city in the midst of the wild Western surroundings. It was the only city of any size he had seen since leaving Denver. "To the contrary, it is."

"Well, cross your fingers. Here we go!"

It had been an exhilarating ride in the buggy Travis and Bliss had stolen at the first house they had come to along the way. Travis had held his breath from time to time, certain the buggy would be upended or topple over the bank. He had felt every rut and jolt, but had to admit to a sincere admiration for the skill Bliss had exhibited. The same skill at the reins she showed now.

"Remember, you're Mrs. Abigail Humphrey and I'm Rebecca Thomas your niece."

Travis forced his voice into a falsetto. "I'll remember, dear."

The buggy groaned down the mountain road, affording Travis a full view of the sprawling metropolis that was a mosaic of headframes and shafthouses, ore dumps and ore trains. Between Watersville and Centersville were several mining properties as well as some beautiful homes that had been built by wealthy miners in the days when this area was a thriving mining center. Owners of the Comstock Lode had invested their riches here, Bliss told him.

"Gold?" Travis asked.

"And copper."

Due to the steep streets, the houses were built in tiers along the hillside. From the north approach, called "the Hill," the fugitives could see a gridiron of crisscrossing streets lined with homes, rooming houses, stores, churches. Travis could tell at a glance that it was a town of sizable population.

"I see what you mean. It will be easy to get lost in the crowd here."

Mingling sounds permeated the air. Thumping stamp engines, whining cables, whistles, clattering hooves, squeaking ore carts, plodding feet. As they drove the buggy down Park Street, the thoroughfare that went through the center of town, dividing the residential from the industrial area, Travis feasted his eyes. He wanted to get familiar with Butte as quickly as he could, just in case something unforetold happened.

"Silver Bow Creek runs right through the middle of town. If you remember that you won't get lost," Bliss instructed, parroting the advice her father had once told her.

"And a railroad!" In case things got really dangerous Travis had it in mind to leave by that sophisticated conveyance. "Where does it come from, and where does it go?"

"It's the Utah Northern Railway. Links Butte with Ogden, Utah. There's also the Northern Pacific." Bliss noticed that there were some additional buildings since she'd been here with her father. "Everything is changing from day to day here."

Seeing a wolfhound accompanied by its master, Bliss's thoughts darted to Bard and Boru. Travis read her mind. "By the way, what happened to those two brutes?"

"The young man at the livery stable agreed to take care of them until I returned. He'll probably have his hands full, because I'm sure after the luxury of the hotel they're spoiled rotten." Strange how much she missed them already.

Remembering the hard time they had given him, Travis muttered beneath his breath, "I wish him luck."

All kinds of vehicles clogged the wide road—wagons, buckboards and carriages—and many people walked the crowded streets. Ore wagons squeaked through the town, drawn by six horses. Bliss swore loudly as one of them rumbled down the dirt road right toward them. "Hang on!" She guided the buggy out of the way, missing the wagon by little more than an inch. "Whew!"

"It's a busy place, that much I'll say," Travis stated, wondering if, like Chicago, this was a city that never slept. The numerous saloons, gambling houses and other evidences of vice seemed to hint that it was. So much the better for their anonymity.

Boardwalks on each side of the street were crowded with people of every shape and size. Gamblers, miners and tradesmen rubbed elbows as they walked along. Well-dressed matrons stuck up their noses as they carefully avoided physical contact with those they considered their inferiors. Women of ill repute displayed their "charms" very freely.

"Don't you dare look or you'll give yourself away," Bliss cautioned.

"How can I not?" Travis said in his newly cultivated high-pitched voice. "It's shocking, my dear. Simply shocking." He feigned an attitude of prim abhorrence, which brought forth a giggle from Bliss.

"Over to the right is the baker's, the butcher's and a boarding house. To the left is the liverer's, the barber's, the gunsmith's and a hotel. What do you think?"

"It's too run down. Abigail Humphrey would never approve. Let's find another."

248

Bliss continued down the road, but thought the next hotel was just too grand. "I only have one hundred and fifty dollars with me." A large portion of the bounty. "It might have to last a while."

"Keep going." They came to three more hotels in all before they settled on the Highland. Since there was a livery stable behind and well out of sight, it was a perfect choice.

Putting the horses and buggy into the hands of the old man who ran it, Bliss took Travis by the elbow and led him inside. "You wait over there, in that shadowy corner. I'll take care of us."

A tall bespectacled man with a mustache was behind the counter. "Well, little lady, you're in luck. We only have one room left." He winked as if he had saved it just for her. Was he flirting or did he just have something in his eye?

"Yes, I am lucky. I'll take it, thank you," she said, smiling sweetly. "Will you be going to the dance tonight?" the desk clerk asked as he handed her the key.

"Dance?" Hurriedly she shook her head. "Oh, no. I'm with my aunt, you see."

"Oh." He sounded extremely disappointed, then craned his neck in Travis' direction.

"She's extremely strict. Never allows me to go out with men."

Taking note of the pillow he envisioned as a protruding stomach, the bespectacled man sniffed indignantly. "Looks as if she should have extended that rule to herself."

Anxious to clear her "aunt's" good name, Bliss

said hurriedly, "She's a widow, poor dear. Such cruel timing. Her husband had a weak heart."

"Ohhhh?" Now he was extremely sympathetic. "I'm so sorry." And to prove it he leaned closer, patting her hand.

Suddenly a large-boned, blond woman with her hair piled high upon her head appeared as if out of nowhere. "Lloyd, you just get any ideas of philandering out of your head," she said, grabbing him by the ear and stepping in front of him. Despite his actions it was obvious who wore the pants in that family. "I'm Lloyd's wife, Gertrude. If you want anything come to me."

"Of course." Bliss could see right away that any friendliness she might show toward the woman's husband would get her in trouble.

"Sign the register!" The woman named Gertrude said stiffly, pushing it forward.

Bliss picked up a pen and scrawled the names. Rebecca Thomas. Abigail Humphrey.

"Come, miss, I'll show you and your companion to your room."

Bliss and Travis followed the woman up the stairs, both of them trying very hard not to trip on their long calico skirts. The room was the fifth one down the hall. Number twenty-five. Travis took smaller steps than usual, determined to affect a matronly air. Anxious to avoid the woman's staring eyes, he hurried inside the moment she opened the door.

It was a pleasant room. Bright and sunny. There was a big double bed in the middle of the floor, another smaller one that was more like a sofa against the wall. "I'll let you decide upon the sleeping arrangements," Gertrude said with forced politeness. "I hope this will do. If not, then I daresay you'll have the devil's own time finding another. The dance has brought people from all around. The rooms hereabouts will all be taken."

Bliss eyed the bright blue drapes and bedspread, the tiny vanity, the two chairs and table, and nodded with approval. "It will be just fine." She did have one request. "Is it possible to have a tub? My aunt is very shy, what with her condition and all. She requires complete privacy."

"A tub? There's a bathroom down the hall." Gertrude shrugged. "Oh, all right. There's a wooden tub that could be used for bathing. And I suppose you'll want hot water." When Bliss said that she would, the woman grunted in exasperation. "It will cost you extra."

"I don't care." At that moment she would have given practically anything for the luxury of warm water and soap.

Talking to herself the hotelkeeper cursed all those who expected special services, but as she left she said, "Have a pleasant stay in Butte."

"Thank you." Bliss closed the door just as soon as the woman stepped away. Collapsing against the safety it promised, she breathed a deep sigh of relief. "I don't think she suspected that anything was amiss."

"I certainly hope not." Without even bothering to look around, Travis closed the windows and the curtains, then tore off the veiled hat and threw it on the bed. "A damnable annoyance!" Reaching behind him he fumbled at the fastenings of the dress, frustrated when he had to beg for Bliss's help.

"What would you do without me?" A smile trembled on her lips.

"I'd be lost," he answered simply, then rubbed his jaw. "A bath and a shave. What I wouldn't give." The thought of scraping Bliss's poor face with stubble was disturbing. "I'm as scratchy as sandpaper."

"A shave is it?" Pulling over a chair Bliss pushed him into it. Taking out the razor she had purchased in Watersville, she used her scented soap and a little water from the pitcher on the table to lather his face.

"Are you sure you know what you're doing?" Travis was hesitant. Good barbers were hard to come by.

"I used to shave my father all the time, when he didn't grow his beard for the winter that is." Slicing through the foam over and over again she proved her ability. "I can do anything when I set my mind to it."

"Yes, you can, I dare say. As I've always known, you are a remarkable woman!" Travis tightened his upper lip as she finished the last spot on his face.

"There." She handed him a small mirror from the vanity. "Without even one nick." Reaching up to touch his cheek, her fingers couldn't resist a gentle exploration of his jaw.

"So I see," he said, looking at his image. As Bliss looked into the glass her eyes met the reflection of Travis' heated gaze. "Now what can I do to see to your comfort."

Slowly Bliss turned so that her fastenings were in view. "Oh, I'm sure you could think of something."

"I'm sure I could." Reaching up, he played lady's maid, unhooking her all the way down the back. The dress slid down her body, falling in a heap at her feet. All that covered her now were a chemise and petticoat. Pushing the thin fabric of the chemise aside he let his appreciation out on a deep sigh. A full breasted, hourglass figure met his eyes. Her body was even more perfectly proportioned than he had imagined. "Bliss Harrison, I think I love you."

"Think?" She wasn't certain she should take that as a compliment. She wanted him to say it with conviction, the way she could—and would if he said it that way first.

Capturing a handful of her hair, he wound it around his hand, bringing her face toward his. He brushed her lips with his, not once, not twice but three times. "I love you," he amended.

"Love me or lust after me. There is a difference." Coyly she dodged away from him.

"Lust and love." The tightening in his loins was blended with a warmth he felt deep in his heart. "With your cooperation I can show you how well the two go together." Quickly he stripped off his female garments, thankful to be quit of them. "Now, do you come to me or do I come after you?" At last their thoughts could be turned to mutual desire, or so he'd thought. A knock on the door intruded.

"Who is there?" Instantly Bliss was on guard, fearful that one of Taggart's men had found them.

"I've brought you a tub!" a voice called from the

other side of the door.

"So soon!" Bliss picked up the discarded dress and put it back on. Travis hid behind the curtains as she unbolted the door. A tall strapping youth lugged in a large round wooden tub, and behind him came another boy dangling a water bucket from each hand. Making several trips, the lads soon had the tub filled to the brim.

"Be careful not to slop!" As if to guard against such an infraction the older boy put an old blanket down and molded it around the bottom of the tub, then held out his hand.

"Here. Don't come back for it until tomorrow!" Bliss thrust a quarter into each boy's hand and they smiled in appreciation.

"Tomorrow. Ten o'clock."

"Eleven." Closing the door behind the boys, she called to Travis. "You can come out now!" But though she had thought she was prepared for the amorous moment that was to come, she suddenly felt awkward. Once she had had Travis totally in her control. Now they were on equal ground, and it was strangely unsettling.

Travis eyed the tub. He felt grimy. "You'll never know just how tempting that water looks."

"Oh, but I do!" The thought of sharing the tub with him was extremely arousing. Looking at his naked body, she was just as fascinated as the first time she'd seen him. He was just flesh and bone like any other man, but everything was put together so well.

They faced each other, both strangely silent. Bliss

254

made the first approach. Going to him, she put her arms around his neck. "Oh, Travis, what if . . ." Her voice caught and she pressed her face against his naked chest, only now succumbing to memories of his near hanging.

"It didn't happen. Because of you . . ." His eyes turned from brown to a darker, smokier hue, mirroring his desire. Bliss's heart hammered as she saw the glitter of desire in them. His lips nuzzled the side of her throat.

"Then I'm forgiven for putting you into Taggart's hands in the first place?" If not, she realized she had set herself up for a perfect kind of revenge.

"Forgiven, yes." He muttered a moan as her hands moved over the smoothly corded muscles of his shoulders. "Oh, how I love you to touch me . . ." His breath seemed trapped somewhere between his throat and stomach. He couldn't say any more. The realization that she was finally to be his was a heady feeling that nearly made him dizzy as he brought his lips to hers. Such a potent kiss. As if he had never kissed her before.

When at last he drew his mouth away his eyes were sparkling. "You know, in spite of everything I wouldn't trade one minute of what happened to me if it meant I wouldn't have met you."

"Really?" It was the nicest compliment she could have had.

"Really." He stepped forward, standing so close that there was barely an inch between them. Just enough space for her dress to slip from her body and fall once again to the floor at her feet. Tugging at the chemise, Travis watched as it, too, slipped to the floor, then gazed at her a long time. The sight of such womanly beauty was well worth his ordeal. "Perfect."

It was her breasts he liked the best. Bending down, he kissed each soft peak before picking her up in his arms and depositing her in the warm water. She leaned back in the soothing depths and closed her eyes to the tantalizing sensation of his scrubbing her back. When his fingers moved to her breast, touching the sensitized skin, Bliss shivered with pleasure, the warm, pulsating feeling in her loins becoming stronger and stronger.

Watching her in the bath aroused Travis and he joined her quickly, the water nearly overflowing as he settled into the already brimming tub. "Careful, you know we promised not to make a mess," Bliss cautioned.

"We won't." With an impish grin, he handed her a washcloth that had been draped over the side of the tub. Bliss tugged it out of his hand and set about lathering him with soap. "I'll smell like flowers."

Bliss's eyes devoured him, noting once again with pleasure his broad chest, the muscles of his abdomen, and the throbbing maleness that seemed to have a life of its own. He was highly aroused, that was certainly obvious, and in that state he was most impressive. Yes indeed. It made his having posed as a woman all the more ludicrous.

"See what you do to me," he said huskily, noticing her stare and liking her rapt fascination.

In a bold move, Bliss reached out, taking his maleness in her hand. Strange, how men seemed to think having "that" made them so superior. All her life she had been subjected to men's crowing about their prowess, but she had coldly turned her back. Now, however, her resentment melted as she held him. Suddenly she viewed things differently. Man and woman. God had had a perfect plan when he created them.

"Oh, Bliss . . ." The expression he wore was akin to pain. A torment she realized only she could take away. Her hands closed around his shoulders, pulling him to her. In the small confines of the tub it was difficult maneuvering her body, but she managed, crushing her breasts against the wet sleekness of his chest in the ultimate caress at the moment their lips met in a kiss. The warm water intensified her feeling of pagan abandon. Exquisite torture. A sensual, all-encompassing, glorious dream.

Every inch of Bliss's body tingled with an arousing awareness of his. Travis' slightest movement sent a shudder of ecstasy rippling deep within her. Driven by emotions she'd felt before but never so intensely, she arched up to him as he kissed her. When at last his lips reluctantly left her mouth to travel like liquid fire along her jawline to her ear, she knew she was totally lost.

"Come," he whispered in her ear. "I think we're steaming up the room. It's growing much too hot in here." Reaching for a large linen towel the boys had left near the tub, he drew her to her feet, then began caressing her with the soft length of the linen. Slowly, leisurely, he dried her off, before using the towel on himself. His hands cupped her buttocks, pulling her against him as his mouth passionately found hers.

All memories of other women faded from his mind as Travis made love to Bliss. Hers were the only arms he wanted around him, hers was the only mouth he wanted to kiss, her softness was the only reality in this world of violence and deceit. Burying his face in the silky soft strands of her hair, he breathed in its fragrant scent and was lost to any other thought.

Bliss caught fire wherever he touched her, burning with an all-consuming need. Travis! A shudder racked through her. She, in turn, appraised him. His broad, bronzed shoulders, wide chest, flat belly and well-formed legs would forever be branded in her mind. Reaching out, she touched him, her hands sliding over the hard smoothness of his shoulders, moving to the crisp hair of his chest.

"Travis . . ." Closing her eyes, Bliss awaited another kiss, her mouth opening to him like the soft petals of a flower as he caressed her lips with passionate hunger. She loved the taste of him, the tender urgency of his mouth, the seemingly endless onslaught of passionate kisses. It was as if they were breathing one breath, living at that moment just for each other. They shared the joy of touching and caressing, arms against arms, legs touching legs, fingers entwining and wandering to explore.

Mutual hunger brought their lips back together time after time. She craved his kisses and returned them with trembling pleasure, exploring the inner softness of his mouth. The most enticing experience of all was the feel of his lips, on her mouth, at her throat, on her breasts, on her stomach.

"Bliss . . . !" he cried out, desire writhing almost painfully within his loins. He had never wanted anything or anyone as much as he did her at this moment. Lightly he stroked her all over. Then his hands were at her shoulders, pressing her gently down on the bed. His breath caught in his throat as his eyes savored her. "Lovely . . . !" Bending down he worshipped her with his mouth, his lips traveling from one breast to the other in tender fascination. His tongue curled around the taut peaks, his teeth lightly grazing until she writhed beneath him.

Then he raised his head to savor the expressions on her face, where the wanting and the passion for him were so clearly revealed. His fingers entwined in her flaming hair. Drawing her face closer, he gently nipped her lower lip. Holding her tightly, he rolled her over until they were lying side by side, and the warmth and power of the firmly muscled body straining so hungrily against hers gave her great pleasure.

He kissed her again, his knowing, seeking lips moving with tender urgency across hers, his tongue finding again the inner warmth and sweetness of her mouth. As his large body covered hers with a blanket of warmth, Bliss felt the rasp of chest hair against her breasts and answered his kiss with sweet, aching desire. But kisses weren't enough now that she was fully aroused.

"Travis, love me," she urged.

"In due time . . ." His hands caressed her, warm-

259

ing her with their heat. They took sheer delight in the texture and pressure of each other's body. Sensually he undulated his hips between her legs, and every time their bodies caressed, each lover experienced a shock of raw desire that set off fiery, pulsating sensations. Then his hands were between their bodies, sliding down the velvety flesh of her belly, moving to that place between her thighs that ached for his entry. His gentle probing set a sweet fire to curling deep inside her in spirals of pulsating sensation. Then his hands left her, to be replaced by the hardness she had held in her hand, entering her just a little, then pausing. She tingled with an intense arousing awareness of his body.

Bending his head to kiss her again, he quickly moved forward, pushing deep within her fusing their bodies. There was only a brief moment of pain as she got used to his invasion, but the other sensations diminished it. Soon Bliss was conscious only of the hard length of him creating almost unbearable sensations as he began to move within her. Capturing the firm flesh of her hips, he caressed her in the most intimate of embraces. His rhythmic plunges aroused a tingling fire, and pleasure burst gloriously inside her like fireworks on the Fourth of July or the lightning of a summer storm. She arched herself up to him, fully expressing her love.

Travis groaned softly, blood pounding thickly in his head. His hold on her hips tightened as his throbbing shaft entered her again and again. Instinctively Bliss tightened her legs around him, certain she could never withstand the ecstasy engulfing her. It was as if the night shattered into a thousand stars, all bursting within her. Arching her hips, she rode the storm with him. As spasms overtook her she dug her nails into the skin of his back whispering his name.

A sweet shaft of ecstasy shot through Travis and he closed his eyes. Even when the intensity of their passion was spent, they clung to each other, unable to let this magical moment end. They touched each other gently, wonderingly.

"Your lovemaking is as fiery as your hair." Indeed, she made love with the same daring that she lived. She was a sensual woman who was more than his equal in passion, the perfect mate. For a long, long time he was content to just look at her. That is, until his eyes grew heavy. It was late, and he knew they were both exhausted.

"Try to sleep, Bliss," he said, settling her into the curve of his arm. "It's been a harrowing day."

She laughed. "Making love *is* strenuous. You should have told me."

A smiling kiss touched his lips. Then she cuddled up against him closing her eyes.

Travis stroked her hair. "Tomorrow I'll have you send a message by telegraph to my lawyer to get him started on my defense . . ." The soft whisper of her breathing told him she was asleep. Strange, he thought, how fragile, how vulnerable she looked in slumber. A woman who could wield a gun, impersonate a hangman, instigate an escape from the most ruthless marshal in the West and make love with all the abandon of a practiced seductress despite her innocence looked as soft as a kitten now. "I love you, Bliss Harrison," he said, and he meant it. She had given him hope for the future and a renewed faith in the goodness of mankind. Grasping the sheet and blanket, he covered her up, then closed his eyes to seek his own sleep.

Chapter Twenty-Six

Bliss awoke to the sound of the maid cleaning outside the door, bumping the dust mop against the wall. Stretching out her hand, she made contact with the thick hair of the head resting on her breast. "Boru, get away. I've told you not to get on the bed!" Thinking herself to be back at the Watersville boarding house, she yawned and sleepily opened her eyes. It was not the wolfhound nestled against her, however, but a familiar dark-haired head.

"Travis La Mont!"

In a whirlwind of remembered sounds and visions the events of last night came back to her. A flush of color stained her cheeks. Oh, she had been brazen, and yet she didn't regret one thing that she had done. To the contrary, she gloried in the memory of what had transpired. She and Travis had made love, and it had been a truly fulfilling experience. He knew just how to touch her, knew all her sensitive spots. In a tender assault of kissing, stroking and teasing her with his tongue, he knew how to bring her again and again to a heart-stopping crest of pleasure.

Travis' arm lay heavy across her stomach, the heat of his body warming hers as she lay entangled with his legs and arms. "You lusty devil, you!" she whispered, smiling to herself. But then she couldn't give him all the credit. She'd stoked up a flame or two herself last night. That thought brought forth a smile as she again stretched languorously.

Shifting from Travis' embrace she turned so that she could watch him as he slept. He looked mighty contented for a man who had just had such a close brush with death. Could it be that she was the reason? *I love you.* He had said it, and though she had always been taught to be wary of those impassioned words she believed him. Last night had just been too special, too out of the ordinary. She had felt it, and she knew that he had too.

The feelings that stirred inside her breast for Travis were certain to plunge her into turbulent waters, yet wasn't he worth the risk? Determinedly she shoved aside the misgivings that entered her mind and clung to her optimistic feelings. She did love him. Right now that was the only important thing. Her mind, her heart, the very core of her being longed for him.

"So where do we go to from here?" she said softly. Clear him so that he can go on with his life, a voice inside her head whispered. It was up to her to do it. Travis La Mont was in some ways more at her mercy now than he had been at the end of her gun. "Clear you, but how?"

There would have to be undeniable evidence that proved a conspiracy, since the marshal had used the deplorable practice of bringing in witnesses who had been paid to lie. The photograph of course was the key, but she had another idea as well. If Taggart had framed one person odds were that he had likewise used such foul means before. Maybe if she did enough investigating she might come up with someone who would be willing to squeal.

"Before this is over Taggart will regret what he did to you, Travis. That I promise," she whispered, though her vow was wasted. Travis slept the deep sleep of the contented. Indeed, he looked like a happy man at this moment. The pleasant sound of soft snoring told her how deeply he slept and she smiled, reaching out to touch a lock of his dark hair. "We'll get your reputation restored and then we'll be free to travel. Oh, Travis, there are so many places I'd like to take you. Why, we could buy a wagon just like the one I had before, only bigger, and ride all over Montana as free as you please."

But would he go? Or would he insist on going back to his prestigious position at that Eastern newspaper? "Ha!" Bliss scowled as she thought how out of place she would be in the East. Like a fish out of water. Somehow she'd have to convince him of the joys of a Gypsy style of life right here. "Making love beneath the stars."

Love. What a potent word that really was, encompassing so many things. Bliss didn't think she would ever forget the way Travis had looked at her, his eyes bright with desire. He had learned every inch of her body, had whispered her name with a husky cry of passion that had made her heart sing. But what they shared went even deeper than that. Their love went beyond the physical gratification of the moment. She deeply cared about Travis, enough to risk her life and well-being, and she knew he felt the same way about her. They were friends now as well as lovers. They were a team. What had happened between them last night was right, was meant to be. Now there would be no more loneliness.

Above all she wanted to make him happy. Was she? It certainly seemed so. His face had the calm peace of a delightedly satiated man. Breathing a sigh, she remembered his kisses, his caresses, the awe-inspiring moment when he had made her a woman. She remembered his eyes bright with desire, his lips trembling into a smile as he kissed her. Leaning forward, she touched his mouth lightly in a kiss, laughing softly as his lips began to twitch.

"Bliss?" Travis cherished the blessing of finding her cradled in his arms, her mane of red hair spread like a cloak over her shoulders. He felt an aching tenderness and drew her closer. "Good morning. What a welcome surprise."

"Good morning." A bird was trilling a song outside the window, and she mimicked the melody.

"You sound happy."

"That's because I am!" She snuggled into his arms, laying her head on his shoulder, curling into his hard, strong body. "I trust you slept well. After that hard cot at the jail this feather bed must have seemed as soft as a cloud."

"I slept very well. The enjoyable activities we participated in last night made me sleep like a babe." He did in fact feel quite warm and content. His hand moved lightly over her hip and down her leg as he spoke. Weeks of frustration and worry just seemed to have melted away. Her body had been pure heaven, her genuine outpouring of love a precious gift.

"I'd like to wake up every morning and find you next to me," he confided, nibbling at her earlobe playfully. But he was not sure just what destiny had in store for him. "Bliss, we need to—"

"Hush!" She didn't want to spoil the morning by letting reality intrude upon her dreams. "I already have the morning planned, but before we both have to face reality, don't you think we might just stay in bed a little while longer?"

"It seems we could. Come here, Miss Bounty Hunter." He reached for her, a primal growl in his throat. Cupping her chin in his hands, he kissed her hard. Pleasure jolted through him, a rush of emotion. As she arched her body and sighed he knew it to be the same for her. Her response to him gave him a heady feeling. He had been able to bring her deep satisfaction, not once but several times during the night.

Travis moved his hands over her body, stroking lightly—her throat, her breasts, her belly, her thighs. As they caressed her breasts, gently and slowly, the tips swelled beneath his fingers. He outlined the rosy peaks, watching as velvet flesh hardened.

Bliss closed her eyes to the sensations she was becoming familiar with now. Wanting to bring him similar sensations, she touched him, one hand lightly running down over the muscles of his chest, sensuously stroking his flesh.

Their eyes met and held as an unspoken communication passed between them. He was ready for

267

lovemaking and so was she. In a surge of physical power he rolled her under him. Then they sank into the warmth and softness of the bed. Bliss sighed in delight at the feel of his hard, lithe body atop hers.

A flicker of arousal spread to the core of her body. Being with Travis encompassed every emotion she had ever known. She was passionately in love, recklessly so.

"Bliss . . . oh, Bliss . . ." he said again, his voice thick with desire. But kissing didn't satisfy the blazing hunger that raged between them. Slowly, sensuously Travis let his hand slide up her thigh, his fingers questing, seeking that most intimate part of her. His legs moved between hers and pressed to spread her thighs.

Bliss moved her body against him, feeling the burning flesh touching hers. He inflamed more than just her body. Indeed he sparked a flame in her heart and soul. The touch of his hands caused a fluttery feeling in her stomach. A shiver danced up and down her spine. She leaned against his hand, giving in to the stirring sensations.

Caressing her, kissing her, he left no part of her free from his touch, and she responded with a natural passion that was kindled by his love. Her entire body quivered. She would never get tired of feeling Travis' hands on her skin, of tasting his kisses.

Before when they had made love Bliss had felt just a little bit awkward, holding a small bit of herself back from her pleasure. Now she held nothing back. Reaching out she boldly explored Travis' body as he had hers—his hard-muscled chest and arms, his stomach. His flesh was warm to her touch, pulsating with the strength of his maleness. As her fingers closed around him, Travis groaned.

Desire raged like an inferno, pounding hotly in his veins. His whole body throbbed with the fierce compulsion to plunge himself into her sweet softness, and yet he held himself back, caressing her once more, teasing the petals of her womanhood until he could tell that she was fully prepared for his entry. Her skin felt hot against his as he entwined his legs with hers.

"Now, oh please. Now!" she whispered. Her frantic desire for him was nearly unbearable. Parting her thighs, she guided him to her with an ardor she had never shown before. Her body arched up to his, searing him with the heat of her passion. Warm, damp and inviting she welcomed him as he entered her.

Writhing in pleasure, she was silken fire beneath him, rising and falling with him as he moved with the relentless rhythm of their love. They were spiraling together into the ultimate passion. Climbing together. Soaring. Sweet, hot desire fused their bodies together, yet there was an aching sweetness mingling with the fury and the fire. They spoke with hearts and hands and bodies words they had never uttered before in that final outpouring of their love.

In the aftermath Travis placed soft kisses on her forehead. She mumbled sleepily and stretched lazily, her soft thighs brushing against his hair-roughened ones in a motion which stirred him again. "That was pure heaven. Shall we try it again," he breathed mischievously.

A loud pounding at the door interrupted their pleasure.

"Damn!" Travis' oath was muffled by Bliss's hand. Rising up from the bed she cast a worried look in the direction of the sound. Was it always going to be this way? The fear of discovery, of being cornered, of having the marshal's men right outside.

Hurriedly Bliss got dressed, mussed up the small couch so that it would look as if she had slept there and pulled the covers over Travis' head. Then crossing her fingers she went to the door and opened it. The hotel clerk, the one who had flirted with her, stood in the corridor.

"Well now, little lady, just how was last night's bath?" His eyes roamed toward the wooden tub as if he wanted to jump right in. "Thought I'd just come and empty it out with the buckets myself. No need to trouble my boys." Though Bliss blocked his way he sidestepped her, brushing much too close as he passed by. "I just might say that I'm a very good back scrubber," he whispered in her ear.

"So is my aunt," Bliss replied pointedly. She nodded toward the bed with her head, just to let him know that she wasn't alone. "Poor dear, she's just exhausted from our journey. I thought it best for her to sleep in."

"Your aunt! Oh, yes. The large woman." It was obvious the man had forgotten she shared the room. He'd needed to be reminded. "She conveniently slipped my mind." Nervously he cast a glance toward the bed.

"Well, believe me, I can't forget about her. Her temper is just fiercesome in the morning. Particu-

270

larly when she is awakened by uninvited visitors!" Bliss pushed him roughly toward the door. "So, if you would be so kind . . ."

"Of course. Of course." Reaching out, he patted her cheek with overt familiarity. "You are so pretty. Has anyone ever told you that?"

"Yes, someone has." Last night as a matter of fact, she thought with a smile. She had little need of this philanderer's attentions. Opening the door she gave him a nudge. He took the hint and walked into the corridor, then turned his head.

"I'll be back," he said cheerily.

"Don't be in a hurry," Bliss answered peevishly. The man was a danger to Travis. She didn't want him popping in now and again. Even so, she didn't want to give him any hint that anything was wrong. "With my aunt feeling as she does we . . . we would appreciate our privacy."

"Oh, your aunt. Yes, poor woman." He leaned on the door. "But how lucky she is to have a niece who is so devoted. Surely she loosens the chain once in a while. They say there is going to be a full moon toni—"

Bliss slammed the door in his face, thoroughly irritated. He was the kind of man she always seemed to run across, at least until she'd met Travis. Well, hopefully after her rejection of his advances he would have the good sense to leave her alone.

"Rebecca, dear . . ." Travis' falsetto cut into her thoughts.

Pushing off the covers, he bounded from the bed, a scowl of annoyance on his face. "I wanted to throttle him, and I would have were it not for this

271

masquerade. Aunt indeed!" Reaching beneath the bed, Travis pulled out the trousers he had worn under the dress and put them on.

"Well, I can tell you one thing. He'd better not show his face around here again or Aunt Abigail just might break his nose! He'd think good back scrubber then," Travis grumbled beneath his breath as he put on his boots and shirt. Having to play possum while some married Romeo tried to get overly friendly with Bliss had gotten on his nerves.

"Oh, I think he's probably harmless. Just a hen-pecked husband trying to be a rooster." Walking over to him, she put her arms around his waist and laid her head against his back. "Once we clear your name this is one of the instances we'll laugh about."

It took only a moment for his mood to soften. "I suppose." Turning to face her, he smiled with sincerity. "Besides, how can I blame him for finding you so pretty. You are." He punctuated his opinion with a slow, leisurely kiss. Only with great reluctance was he able to pull away. "Oh, Bliss, I could spend eternity in your arms, but we can't forget about the outside world forever."

"No, we can't." It was only a matter of time before Taggart's men would sweep through Butte. In the meantime they had to try to outsmart him.

Chapter Twenty-Seven

The sun was shining but not brightly enough for Bliss to be uncomfortable. She adjusted the brim of her hat with a twofold purpose in mind—to shade as well as hide her face—as she stepped outside the hotel. One just couldn't be too careful.

It was a pleasant walk down Main Street, one Bliss didn't mind taking at all. It gave her a chance to familiarize herself with the surroundings and to learn the whereabouts of the important establishments. Butte's general store of course, the meat market, drug store and the dry goods business. On the way back from her errand she'd visit them so that she could get everything needed to make the hotel room a little hideaway. Since Travis had to stay cooped up, she wanted to make their quarters as comfortable as possible. Real homey.

Butte seemed just the kind of place she and Travis could settle down in when all this furor was over. But before she could even think about that she had to make contact with Mr. Aric Wesley so that the wheels of Travis' defense could start turning.

The farther she walked, the more she decided she really liked Butte. It housed a variety of residents, their occupations just as varied. Between Main and Colorado Streets in the midst of the city, people wore their native dress. Cornish, German, Irish, Scandinavian, Italian and Bohemian garb all mingled, affording Bliss a colorful display. The town was certainly a melting pot. But so much the better for Travis. "Aunt Abigail" could easily get lost among this crowd.

Hiking up the long skirt of her blue calico dress and clutching the handwritten messages that Travis had dictated, Bliss walked down the boardwalk heading for the telegraph office. She was about to work a little magic, or at least that's how she thought of it.

"Hmmm. Imagine being able to communicate with people so far away."

Travis had explained this new-fangled contraption to her. He said the electrical current generated through a wire in one city switched on and off a small magnet in another city. That magnet attracted and repelled a key. The key clicked as the current switched on and off, its clicks following a code devised by a man named Morse. Opening and closing the electrical circuit with the key controlled the messages sent over the wire. The longer the man kept the key pressed down, the longer the click, or dash. A short click created a dot. Used in different combinations these signals made up a kind of alphabet.

"Electricity is how it's done, huh? Well, it sure

beats sending up smoke signals," she had quipped, "or beating a drum."

The question was, would it work? Would Travis' lawyer even care what had happened to him? And if he did, would he be able to do anything about the situation? So far, from what Bliss had seen of lawyers they weren't worth spit in a beer, but Travis seemed to have faith in this man Wesley. Right from the first he had wanted to get him involved. Well, now was the time to put this lawyer to the test.

Sandwiched in between the *Daily Miner Newspaper* office and a bank Bliss found the small post office that housed the telegraph equipment. Inside, a tall, dark gray-garbed and -capped man was busy sorting a stack of letters and placing them in tiny pigeonholes. He was so wrapped up in his work that he didn't even notice her until she loudly cleared her throat.

"I'd like to send a wire. Two in fact."

"A wire." Putting down his pile of mail, he led her over to a large table where a strange-looking machine of wheels, switches, wire and a lever was set. Pulling up a chair he took a seat, then tugged the pieces of paper from her hand.

"The contents are to be kept confidential. Do you understand?" She hoped that like doctors, telegraphers had a code of ethics, for she and Travis would be in danger if the information she was relaying was deciphered and fell into the wrong hands.

He seemed insulted that she had to remind him. "Confidential, of course." Quickly he set to work.

It never ceased to amaze Bliss that a message

could be sent over thousands of miles just by this system of dots and dashes. She watched in fascination as the telegraph operator clicked out the words of the brief message Travis had dictated to her. It simply said that he had been wrongly accused, named Taggart as his antagonist and requested that Aric Wesley make contact with the territorial judge on his behalf. It was signed simply T. La Mt.

There were telegraph wires connecting the principal cities. Bliss instructed that the message from Travis be sent from Butte to Ogden, Ogden to Denver, Denver to Kansas City and so on until it reached his lawyer, Aric Wesley in Boston. In the same fashion Travis was having her send an explanation to his newspaper editor, Howard Vickery, at the Springfield, Massachusetts, *Republican*. As far as the people at the paper knew he had just disappeared. He wanted them to be aware of the situation so that perhaps they could use their influence to thwart Marshal Taggart in this deadly game he was playing.

As soon as the messages were sent, Bliss tore them into pieces, paid the telegrapher, then with a polite thank you, walked out the door. Accosted by a boy selling newspapers, she paid him for one and hastily scanned it to see if Travis' escape was mentioned. She breathed a sigh of relief at seeing that it wasn't. They still had a little more time. In fact, she was quite pleased with herself and her insistence that they use Butte as a hideout. So far so good.

That feeling of optimism quickly faded as a shadow fell across her path. Looking up, she found herself face-to-face with a tall man who had a cadaverously thin face and long straggly blond hair. She recognized him at once as being in the marshal's employ, a member of the posse. He, along with Jake Heath, had been one of the three who had accosted her at the wagon. She would never forget that this man had threatened to shoot her dogs. And she had threatened to shoot *him*.

"Are you lost?" His voice was friendly as was his smile.

"Lost?" Bliss was certain at first that he would recognize her, but it was too late to hide. "Wellllll, no! Why?" She tilted her face downward, so he wouldn't get a good look at her features. She could only hope that the dress and hat would fool him.

"Just hoping." He eyed her up and down, taking in every inch of her figure, including her full breasts. Bliss had a hunch he had more in mind than just being helpful. "I thought if you were I'd help you out."

"Well, I'm not," she said quickly. Knowing there was an enemy close at hand did little for her peace of mind. If he recognized her he might get that information to Taggart. She didn't need the marshal snooping around.

He took her arm before she could protest. "Well, I'll accompany you anyway. It's not safe for a lady to be upon the street alone."

That was for sure, Bliss thought, particularly when she met up with a man like him. Keeping her thoughts to herself, she said merely, "Thank you."

"My name is Barlow. Tom Barlow." He said this with the flair of a politician. It was obvious that he held himself in high esteem, an opinion that wasn't

277

mutual. She didn't like him. "And just where are you going, miss?"

"Miss Smith. Taking a stroll. Just taking a stroll." Purposefully she headed in the opposite direction from the hotel, wishing all the while that she could just drop from sight. The longer she stayed in his company the more chance there was he might remember her.

"You're going to think it strange, Miss Smith, but I get the feeling I've seen you before."

Aha! Bliss thought. There it was, just as she had feared. She had sparked his memory. The red hair no doubt. Too bad she hadn't hidden it under the hat.

"Have we met?" Pausing in his long stride, he looked her full in the face before she had time to turn her head.

"No!" she said a bit too quickly. "I . . . I'm new in town. Just came in yesterday as a matter-of-fact." Well, that much was true.

He didn't seem to be convinced. "Are you sure?"

"Positive!" Bliss pretended to be interested in one of the shop signs. Anything to keep him from looking at her face again, or he might remember the time she had her rifle pointed at him.

"Hmmm." He was dubious, but didn't push the matter. Hiding his true character from her, he chatted conversationally as he walked beside her, trying to get into her good graces. And all the while Bliss was beginning to feel more and more ill at ease. She had to get away from him before he recognized her.

Alas, before she could manage an exit a man

278

coming up the boardwalk with an Irish wolfhound at his heels triggered just what she had feared.

"I remember now. Those damn hounds!" This time when he looked at her his expression was anything but pleasant. "The bounty hunter."

Bliss didn't even pause to reply. Picking up her skirts, she did something she would later regret. She ran! Not because of fear for herself but for Travis.

Darting between two oncoming wagons, she braved a collision to get to the other side of the street. She had to get away from Tom Barlow before he started asking questions. With that thought uppermost in mind she ducked around the corner, ran through an alley and didn't stop running until her sides were heaving. Only when she stopped to catch her breath did she realize the implication of what she had done.

"You fool!" By running she had implied a feeling of guilt, of fear. Her fleeing might well make Tom Barlow wonder what was going on. It might make him start asking questions. Questions that just might implicate her in Travis La Mont's escape. "Damn!" All of a sudden Butte wasn't safe anymore. Bliss had to face the reality that no place was. Clearing Travis seemed an even more pressing matter now, and worst of all they were running out of time.

Chapter Twenty-Eight

Sam Taggart strode the boardwalk like an angry bull. Damned if this whole mess hadn't kicked up his ulcer again. His stomach burned like fire. That he was surrounded by incompetent fools only added to his frustration. He had fifteen men snooping around, trying to find out who had impersonated the hangman and masterminded the escape. Fifteen men. And that was just counting the ones in Watersville. Even so, he had yet to find out one little thing about who was responsible.

"Damn. I'll fire them all. Take them off my payroll," he blustered. Alas, he knew he couldn't really do that, much as he would have enjoyed turning the lot of them out to pasture. Each and every one of them knew too much—or at least enough to get him in hot water if all the pieces of the puzzle were fit together.

Doubling over with pain as a spasm hit him, Taggart wondered fleetingly what might have happened to him had he sought an honest way of life, but the thought quickly vanished. He had no desire to earn his money the hard way, by working for it. He'd tried that briefly while toiling for Josephine's father, and that one attempt had been enough to last him a lifetime. No, his forte was in using his head, in scheming. That talent had made it possible for him to get a cut from just about every transaction of value taking place from Butte to Rawlins, Wyoming, thereby making him a wealthy and powerful man. But was his influence so strong that it couldn't turn from gold to pewter in his hands?

"Bah!" Clutching his stomach, Taggart forced himself to stand up straight. He was being silly to worry. He was impatient, that was all. Hell, he'd faced adversity before. Escape or no escape no damned Eastern dude was going to rain on his parade. He'd find him. Find the both of them. Something would turn up. Didn't it always?

"Sam!"

The musical sound of his wife's voice caused Sam to whirl around. "Josey . . ." She had her arms full of packages that reached from waist to chin, but she promptly set them down and gently took his arm.

"It's your stomach again."

"Something I ate, that's all." He couldn't confide in her or chance telling her of the turmoil the jail escape had created. "Too many damned dill pickles from the general store."

"Or too much whiskey from the saloon." Her voice was softly scolding. "You know Doc Roberts told you to stay away from that terrible poison and to take your tonic."

"I know. I know." As he looked down, the cleavage of her breasts was in his line of vision. "But I can tell you there is something else that will do me a lot more good." He chuckled.

"Samuel!" As he started to swat her on the behind she pushed his hands away. "Behave."

"I try, but there's just something about you that turns my brains to mush. When I'm near you, Josey, I just can't think of anything else." Being married to her was like possessing his own living doll. From the top of her feathered hat to the tips of her toes, she was perfection.

"Well, try." Her gloved fingers touched his badge in a circular motion, shining it, reminding him that he had a job to do. Taggart knew that Josey looked upon his profession with pride. Little did she know that the man she perceived to be straightforward, honest and heroic wore a star that was more than a little bit tarnished.

"All right. All right." Taggart shrugged, determined to put Travis La Mont out of his mind, at least for the moment. Bending down, he picked up the packages. Damned if it didn't seem she'd bought out the whole town. Strange that with four closets filled with dresses, coats, hats and shoes she felt the need to buy more, but that was a woman for you. Oh, well. He'd just rejuvenated his safe with his cut from a cattle rustling deal up near Helena. "I can see that you're having a lucrative day."

"Just a few things." She looked up through her lashes coquettishly. "To go with my purchases in San Francisco." Her voice silenced to a whisper. "And a flannel shirt, a Stetson, denims and boots."

"What?" It was so out of character that he was stunned. Josephine was the epitome of femininity. In all the days he'd known her he had never seen her in male attire, even while she was living on her father's ranch.

"I saw your bounty hunter. She made quite a fetching sight in her . ... well . . . comfortable clothes. I was inspired."

He grunted, his congenial mood spoiled. The mention of the Harrison woman reminded him of La Mont and of his failure. "Inspiration indeed. Listen to me, Josey. Stay away from her. A woman like that is far beneath you. Trouble."

She pursed her lips. "Oh, Sam, you sound so stuffy when you talk like that, but it's water under the bridge now. I did go to the hotel to meet the woman, but she's long since gone."

"Gone?" At least in that he could feel some relief.

"Vanished and under the strangest circumstances." Her brows formed a V.

Taggart stopped in his tracks. "What do you mean 'strangest circumstances'?"

"I talked to Hattie Dodd who owns the general store. Her sister, who runs the boarding house, told her that the young woman left most of her possessions behind. Including her clothes. As if she took off in a hurry." Seeing that one of her packages was going to take a tumble, Josephine hurriedly reached up to rescue it. "No woman worth her salt would just up and leave like that." She snapped her fingers. "Strangest of all, she also left her two dogs behind. Thoroughbreds. Wolfhounds. Now why do you suppose she'd do such a thing?"

Why do you suppose? Why? The wheels of his brain started clicking. Could it be? No. La Mont had been rescued by a man, hadn't he? A man just as paunchy as Jericho the hangman. And yet the fact that she had left in such a hurry seemed to hint that she shared some guilt. A conspiracy?

Taggart's head pounded as he walked along beside his wife. Now there were three fugitives he was obsessed with locating. La Mont, the dark-garbed "hangman" and a certain lady bounty hunter.

Chapter Twenty-Nine

Bliss bounded through the door of the hotel room like a cat with a dog on its tail, only to find it empty. A sick feeling gnawed at the pit of her stomach as she tore at the curtains, searching. Travis wasn't hiding. And if he wasn't, that meant only one thing. He was gone.

"Oh, no!"

Falling to her knees, she looked under the bed, hoping against hope that he might be squeezed under there, but the only living thing was a small mouse that squeaked in anger at her intrusion. Bolting to her feet, she didn't leave even one pillow in place as she tore the room apart in her search. Had he left on his own? Gone off on some hairbrained attempt to redeem himself without telling her first? The fact that his boots were by the bed made that possibility doubtful. What then?

"Stay calm."

Good advice, but an impossibility considering that the bottom had just dropped out of her world.

Travis was gone! She was too late. Something had happened. Dear God, she never should have left him alone. This time they would kill him quickly, without even a pause.

"Tom Barlow," she said, loathing the name as she spoke it. Somehow he'd figured it all out and had gotten here before she did. Barlow, yes, that was it. He'd known who and where she was hiding all along and had just been toying with her. Now Travis was his victim.

"Where did they take him? What am I going to do?" All sorts of images flitted before her eyes, not a one of them pleasant. They'd hang him, of course, if they didn't shoot him. Running to the window, Bliss threw it open wide and leaned so far out that she nearly lost her balance. It was then that she saw him, balanced on the ledge between their room and the next like some tightrope walker from a circus.

"Hi!" Travis tried to act nonchalant, but the truth was, he felt more than a bit foolish.

"Hi, yourself." Bliss felt her heart flutter in relief. If anything had happened to him she knew she would have been distraught. As it was she tried to hide her true feelings with feigned cockiness. "What are you doing out here, keeping the sparrows company?"

"Your friend the would-be backscrubber came up while you were gone, to empty the tub and God knows what else. I didn't have time to put on that silly dress. This ledge was the only refuge I had." His grin was sheepish. "Then I . . . well, I couldn't get the window open from this side. I was trapped. What took you so long?"

Bliss grabbed him by the shirt, pulling him back inside. "I ran into one of Taggart's men. Tom Barlow."

Travis' usually tan face paled. He didn't want anyone to tie Bliss in with what had happened. If it came out that she'd helped him escape from the scaffold, Taggart would make her suffer, and he didn't want that. More and more he was coming to feel protective of her. Perhaps because his brush with death had made him see things in a different light. Until then he had thought it possible to control one's fate. Now he knew otherwise. He worried about Bliss. Despite her bravado he knew she wasn't as invincible as she thought. No one was.

"One of Taggart's men?" he asked.

"One of the three who came to the wagon with the intention of lynching you. The skinny one who threatened to shoot my dogs. Remember?"

How could he ever forget. Bliss had angered them all by refusing to back down. "How well I do recall."

Quickly she related the incident of being cornered by Barlow after coming out of the telegraph office, of his having asked if he had seen her before, of her insistence they had never met. "But seeing a man on the street with a wolfhound brought it all back. He was reminded of Bard and Boru, and recognized me, Travis."

"Damn!" In a show of frustration he hit his fist against the wall. He had been hoping to keep Bliss out of this, but now he feared she might become hopelessly entangled. "Did he follow you here?" His eyes darted to the door as if he were expecting someone to barge in.

"No, I made sure he didn't do that. I led him in the opposite direction, then left him far behind." Bliss had repeatedly looked over her shoulder just to make certain Tom Barlow had been outdistanced and outsmarted.

"That's a relief." He had a good feeling about this place. And no one would suspect a pregnant woman of being Travis La Mont. Even that simpleton of a hotel clerk was taken in by the scheme. "Then we're still safe." Plopping down in a chair, Travis put his feet up on the table. He was tired of running, and this room was a welcome respite from all he had endured lately.

"Safe for the *moment*." Bliss silently started packing up their meager possessions. There was no way she was going to take a chance on Travis' being caught. "But probably not for long." Tom Barlow would start asking questions. It wouldn't be long before he located her and thereby, Travis. They had to get out of Butte and quick, before they were cornered.

She was buzzing about like a bee in flight. Travis asked quickly, "What are you doing?"

"Getting things together so that we can get out of here, of course." Bliss threw him a canvas saddlebag so that he could help. "Those men of Taggart's are like roaches. They can creep out from almost anywhere. Where there's one, there'll be a whole slew." There, she thought, that should settle the matter. Surely by now Travis knew enough to trust her instincts about such things.

"Then what you're saying is I won't be safe here or

288

anywhere," he said, letting the saddlebag slip from his fingers to the floor. And as long as she was with him she would be in danger too.

Bliss nodded. "That's what I'm saying."

Travis stood up with such force that he knocked over the table. "Then it's time we split up!"

"What?" She hadn't been expecting this. "You can't mean that Travis La Mont." It was as if her heart fell right down to her toes. She had made so many assumptions, one of them being that they were going to be together from now on, his words struck her like a blow.

"I do." For her safety they would have to separate now. Once he'd cleared himself, if he cleared himself, they could come together again, on a permanent basis.

"Split up, just like that." She snapped her fingers.

He knew he had to explain or she would misunderstand. "Bliss, being in my company puts you in peril. You saved me from hanging, and for that I will always be grateful, but—"

"Grateful?" The word drove a painful wedge between them. "Grateful?" Was that why he had made love to her? Out of a sense of thankfulness? Obligation? "Is that what all that mooning and spooning we shared was about?" Hastily she looked down at the floor so that he wouldn't see the pain his words had brought her. "Well, you can take your gratitude and—"

"Bliss!" As she turned her back on him, Travis grasped her by the shoulders and forced her to look at him. In the bright light streaming through the window he could see the stricken look on her face and knew he had hurt her. "I didn't mean it that way."

She had allowed her protective shell to slip, but now she thrust it up again. With a proud toss of her head, she jerked her shoulders from his grip. "Then just what did you mean?"

For a man who made his living from writing words, suddenly Travis found himself in a quandry, wondering just what to say. How could he let her know how much she meant to him and at the same time make her see that he had to go it alone? "You came to my aid, and I'll always be thankful. What passed between us had nothing to do with that. I . . . I wanted to make love to you."

"Really?" Pride stiffened her back and made her hold her head erect.

"Really." And to prove it he bent his head and kissed her in a manner that could not be misconstrued. There was no hint of obligation in the caress of his lips. Passion flowed from his mouth to hers, blocking out conversation and all thought.

For a long time they clung together, the kiss exploding into feelings that left them both hot and breathless, but finally Bliss pulled away. "This is no time to lose our heads."

Powerful urges were throbbing in the area below her stomach. She and Travis were like sparks to tinder when it came to lovemaking. Even now it was all she could do to keep away from that bed. But that sort of activity drained the body of energy and the mind of coherent thought. Both assets to them right now.

Being a sensible man, Travis had the same

thoughts, although it took him much longer to ignore the sensual pain gnawing at his vital parts and gather his composure. "We have to carefully make plans as to where we go from here."

On that at least they were in agreement. "We can't make even one mistake."

"Our plans will have to take us in different directions." He had to make her understand. "At least until all this is sorted out."

They started to talk at the same time, but Travis quieted to let Bliss have her say. "All right then, if that's what you want." She tried to sound calm, but it was tearing her up inside. "You go where you want to, and I'll follow my own road."

The look in her eyes made him nervous. Bliss could be hotheaded, that he knew from experience. Hotheaded and at times a bit too big for her britches. "Which takes you where?"

If he thought she was going to obediently stand by and watch him go, then sit calmly in a rocking chair until he came back, he was wrong. Bliss was much too impatient for that ballyhoo. "I think it's time I went to Silver Bow and got that camera of yours."

"You?" At first he thought he hadn't heard her right. "Did you say that *you* should go to Silver Bow and get my camera equipment?"

"That's what I said." She could see that got his attention. "Of course, you're welcome to come with me if you want."

She had him. He knew it, and so did she. With or without him, she was determined to go headlong into trouble. "And if we go together, what then?"

Seeing that he was weakening, she felt just a little

bit smug. "We'll hide you out in an old mine or an abandoned mill along the way, where Taggart can't find you. I'll get the camera, then come back to get you." They were looking for him, not her. She could make it safely into town and accomplish the necessary goal without being intercepted, while he could not. It was the only sensible way.

"You'll hide me away somewhere?" Travis' pride was pricked, thus he was surly. "No, I refuse to hide behind a woman's skirts."

Bliss laughed impishly. "All right, I won't wear skirts. I'll put on pants."

Travis bristled. "That's not what I meant, and you know it. To put it bluntly, I won't let you go to Silver Bow, with or without me. It's too dangerous!" He didn't want to chance Bliss's getting hurt. She was too important to him. Besides, it was about time he made a few of the decisions. Sometimes she was just a little too impetuous.

"You won't *let* me?" She looked at him, incredulous. Why was it that the minute a man got in a woman's drawers he started acting as if he owned her? Started asserting his dominance. Well, she had never liked being bossed around, and she wasn't going to start taking it now.

"Someone has to temper your actions, Bliss."

Her cheeks were suffused with red, her balled fists evidence of her frustration with him. "I've been on my own for a long time now, and I can damn well carry on all by myself without you poking your nose in."

"And go running headlong into danger." His voice crescendoed. "I don't want you going up against Taggart and his men. That's for me to do."

"Alone!"

"Yes."

"You'll get yourself killed! Taggart will have you in his clutches before you're a mile out of Butte." Bliss lost all patience with him. "What is it with you men? Why are you so bravely stupid and stubborn."

Her words riled him. "Stupid and stubborn?"

"That's what I said. And what's more, whether I go to Silver Bow or not, Travis, is my own decision." Though her stance and voice spoke of defiance, she was already starting to feel remorse. How had their difference of opinion so quickly escalated into a full-blown argument? She was on his side, not his enemy, yet they were dangerously close to shouting at each other.

"Your decision, yes. And whether or not *I* go is mine." Hotheaded little spitfire. Well, he at least had one ace up his sleeve. "There's no way I'm going to let you take that burden upon yourself. I should be the one to go and get it. *I* know where the camera is, Bliss, and to put it quite bluntly I won't tell you. Going to Silver Bow will be a waste of your time." Picking up the saddlebag, he started packing his own belongings for the trip.

"Of all the pigheaded . . . !" The words exploded from her lips. Was it any wonder the territory was in such a mess when it was run by men? "Taggart knows just where you'll be headed. He'll be waiting for you." She clucked her tongue. "For a man of intelligence, Travis La Mont, your thinking's not very clear. You'll get ambushed along the way, and I'll have to rescue you all over again."

He folded his arms across his chest in a manner that clearly annoyed her. "And just what makes you think you'll be in any less danger?"

She sighed in exasperation. "My face isn't plastered from here to Utah on wanted posters, that's what."

Bliss was right and he knew it, but his male ego wouldn't let him admit it. "You'll find yourself in trouble just the same." He threw up his hands in exasperation. "Taggart isn't an idiot. He'll put two and two together and come up with four; then he'll be looking for you, knowing that you can lead him to *me.*"

They stood there looking at each other for a long time, then all of a sudden Bliss laughed. "Listen to us, Travis. Fighting tooth and nail like an old married couple." She held out her hand. "Truth is, we care about each other. That's the point, isn't it? So let's call a truce."

Travis reached out to her, but instead of shaking her hand he gathered her into an embrace. "Oh, Bliss, what am I going to do with you?"

"Take me with you. I'll be miserable if you don't, and so will you. Admit it."

He was just about to say the words, but footsteps outside their door alerted him to someone's presence. Putting a finger to his lips, he gestured for Bliss to keep silent.

"The girl with the red hair is up on this floor, all right. I couldn't forget her. Pretty as a picture. She and her aunt are in the room right here." It was the hotel clerk.

"She's with her aunt?" Tom Barlow's voice.

294

Bliss looked up at Travis, her heart in her eyes. They had spent too much time foolishly arguing. Now they were trapped. The worst had happened.

"Yep. Big woman."

"Open the room with your key."

Bliss and Travis exchanged glances; then, taking her by the hand, Travis headed for the window and pushed it open. It was their only way to escape. "Follow me," he whispered in her ear, "and don't look down."

She didn't. There were few things she was afraid of, but heights was one of them. Nevertheless she put her faith and trust in Travis. Without even a sigh of protest, she hoisted herself out on the ledge. Climbing up to the roof, they slowly crawled across it, working themselves to the other side and to the livery stable behind the hotel. Dropping to the ground, Travis cushioned Bliss's fall as she jumped.

"If you can't find our horses, saddle anything that moves," Bliss called out. "We've got to get out of here."

"My boots!" Travis had had to leave them behind.

"Surefire proof that Aunt Abigail is a man." Bliss had the feeling it was only a matter of time before someone pieced together just what had happened.

Despite their nervousness, they quickly saddled two white horses and rode out through the stable door, galloping down the road and leaving the hotel and Butte far behind them.

All alone for the first time in several days, Sam Taggart assessed the situation he found himself in as he paced back and forth. "If La Mont processes what's in that camera I might well be in a real mess." Reaching for the bottle of tonic on his desk, he took a swig. The liquid cooled the fire tormenting him. "I was in a predicament like this once before. Can't afford to let him find out the truth."

He laughed to himself, almost as if laughter would chase away the fear and doubt he was feeling. How was he to know that when that red-haired woman came into town she wouldn't be solving his problems but adding to them. But in what way? Just what was her part in all this? Why had she turned La Mont in, then changed her mind and requested clemency. Most puzzling of all was why had she just suddenly vanished?

Seeing Boyd Withers through the window in his office, he hurried to meet him, hoping Withers had some information that could be useful or even the news that La Mont had been captured. "Well? What's happening?"

Sticking his head around the door, Withers dashed Taggart's hopes by asking the same question. "I came to ask you what's going on."

"Nothing!" How that riled him. "I haven't heard a word from Heath, Barlow, Jenkins or Tremayne. Inept fools. I've never been so furious in my life. What do they think I pay them for?"

"If you're so angry why didn't you go looking for La Mont yourself?" Withers was the only one who would have dared to pose such a question.

Taggart eyed him with disdain. "Shooting people isn't a marshal's job. That's what I pay you boys to do." He didn't want to dirty his hands by killing

296

anyone. And why would he have to when there were so many men willing to take money to do it for him?

Taking out his handkerchief he wiped his sweaty brow. Lord Almighty, it was hot in the office, or was it just his conscience getting the best of him at last? Going outside, Withers following, he breathed in the fresh air. He wanted to rid himself of his frustrations, to relax. If he didn't his stomach would start troubling him again. He didn't want that.

"So what do you want me to do about La Mont?" Withers was saying.

Taggart shook his head. "I don't care. I want to think about something else for a while." That was an impossibility as circumstances were soon to prove. A telegram delivered to him by a freckle-faced boy proved that the chase was just beginning. "Barlow's located La Mont."

"In Butte?" Withers seemed surprised. "Then he caught him?"

"No." Taggart scanned the telegram, then read it over again more carefully. "That bounty hunter woman was with him. Staying together in the same hotel." So that explained it. They were lovers, though when that had come about Taggart couldn't say. "It's all her fault, I should have known. I thought she was showing too much concern after she brought him in. Well, she won't get away with it."

The pair had been seen climbing out the window of the Highland Hotel in Butte. Apparently they didn't have money to pay their hotel bill. Hell, La Mont didn't even have boots on.

"You're sure it was him." Withers was skeptical.

"Barlow says so and I believe him." Of all his

deputies, Barlow as the most ruthless and the most dependable.

"Says he got a glimpse of him from the hotel window."

"What now?"

"I want you to take ten of the men stationed here to Butte." That should be the end of the matter, once and for all. At least he hoped so, but it wasn't. Somehow the news had leaked out. That night at dinner even his wife, Josephine, had heard the gossip.

"So, Travis La Mont wooed the very woman who brought him in. It almost sounds romantic." Josephine sighed.

"Josey, bite your tongue." He didn't want any of that kind of talk.

"That man's handsome as all get out. Never saw anyone with eyes like that before."

Taggart winced with sudden jealousy, but right now was no time to start an incident. "He's a thief and worse!"

"She doesn't seem to care."

"Well, she will when her foolishness gets her killed!" He spoke in the heat of the moment and regretted it the moment he saw his wife flinch.

"You wouldn't shoot a woman, would you, Sam?"

Though he shook his head no, he was thinking that if the woman had done what he thought she had, he would be very tempted. Accidents did happen now and then. But no, when the shooting started he wasn't going to be the one firing. It would be Barlow, Heath, Tremayne, Withers or one of his other hired assassins.

"Then what are you going to do. With her I mean?" Unfortunately for Taggart, Josephine was interested in the woman's fate.

"She's done wrong, Josey." He affected a pious pose. "And as you know, those who disobey the law have to pay." Oh, she'd pay all right. She would pay in spades.

Chapter Thirty

Hatless and bootless, Travis rode his horse at as fast a gallop as the old nag could manage. Wasn't it just his luck, he thought, to have picked a horse that was on its last legs while Bliss's choice had been a spirited filly. Time constraints and the pressing matter of getting away had forced him to take the nearest horse at hand, that being a poor old mare he now decided wasn't up to pulling a milk wagon.

"Hurry up, Travis!"

Bliss's constant urging did little to soothe his bad mood. This whole episode was starting off badly, and frankly he wasn't at all happy about it. Oh, they had gotten out of Butte by the skin of their teeth, but despite his better judgment he had been forced to give in to Bliss's cajoling to save his skin. That rankled him. She had him in the palm of her hand, and she knew it. Damn!

Once he had been an independent man, taking control of his life and never giving in to anyone. Suddenly that had changed. Now he had his hands

300

full. She, too, was an independent person. And yet he couldn't really say he didn't like that. She was so vibrant, so full of life that she gave him hope for the future no matter what kind of fix he was in. Besides, they really were alike in some ways. Headstrong, perhaps. Set in their ways. Strong personalities. Stubborn, though each of them seemed to be weakening a little on that point.

Perhaps he'd weakened just a little too much. For all his attempts to assume control, she was slowly winding him around her little finger. She insisted she knew just how to out play Taggart at his own game, but could a woman really be capable of outsmarting the marshal and his hired guns. Well, so far so good. Or so it seemed.

"Travis!" Motioning with her hand she urged him to keep pace with her as they made their way down the hill into the valley of Silver Bow. "Travis!"

"If I make this horse go any faster it's going to keel over on me," he answered back. It was seven miles from Butte to the small town, but to Travis' mind it might as well have been seventy. He was hot, tired and as cranky as a bear.

"If you can't make it go any faster you might as well get off and walk." Despite the peril they were facing Bliss was in a teasing mood, brought on in part by the fact that Travis had been forced to capitulate to her plan that he hide out in a mine or mill house. She'd nagged him all along the way, and at last he had agreed to let her get the camera.

Not that convincing him had been easy. From the minute they had left the Highland Hotel he had been trying to take manly command of the situation. Only

301

having a close call when someone on one of the side streets recognized him and sounded the alarm had made him see the light. There was a wooden watch tower on Fire Tower Hill. A triangle hung from the corner of the building on Bridge and Water Streets was used to bring men running with buckets full of water in case of a blaze. Today, however, it had rung for another purpose. To alert the town that there was a wanted man on the loose.

Travis and Bliss had led their horses up Glena Street, down Mercury street and round and round the town, taking refuge in alleyways. Nearly colliding with wagons and buggies on the crowded roads, overturning carts and stands, and quite literally causing havoc, they had left an angry mob behind. Even so some good had come of it. At last Travis had admitted that he would have to be crazy to chance showing his face in Silver Bow.

"On to Silver Bow, Travis," she called out now, a gentle reminder of her victory.

"On to Silver Bow," he echoed, though not with as merry a tone. "Remember, you be careful," he was insisting now, advice that made her smile. He did care, and though she knew very well that she could take care of herself in any situation, it warmed her heart.

"I will, I promise." On impulse, she put her hand to her mouth and blew him a kiss.

Actually despite her air of daring it didn't seem to be a very dangerous quest. Travis had hidden his photographic equipment in a pile of hay in the loft of a stable, the one right behind the Gold Nugget Hotel. How difficult could it be to retrieve it? Simple

302

really. After the skirmishes she'd been in with her father, digging out a camera would be easy. The hardest part was going to be getting the items he needed to develop the photographs. Items on the list he'd scribbled.

"Photographic paper, glass plates and gold chloride." She remembered a few of the items by heart. Hopefully the needed items would be available at the Silver Bow General Store.

It was a tedious journey, made more so by the necessity of stopping every so often to hide and make certain no one was following. At last, however, they stopped to water their horses on the bank of Silver Bow Creek, the halfway point in their short journey. The tiny stream was overshadowed by a canopy of full-leafed cottonwood trees. As Bliss bent to splash cool water on her face Travis could not help but admire her well-rounded breasts and slim, lean hips. Oh, but she was tempting.

Hurriedly he looked away. "God, will I ever be glad when this is over," he said, mopping his brow. Then perhaps they could get on with their lives.

"Just beyond is Silver Bow," she said, pointing. "The next few miles will be steadily downward toward the valley below. The road will be rocky and rutted—slow traveling—but we're nearly to that old mine where I first found you."

"Oh, great," Travis espoused this information dryly, cupping his hands to drink the cool water. "That should bring back some colorful memories."

"It will for me," Bliss confided. "It was there I first got you in my sights, in more ways than one."

As she arose they exchanged nostalgic smiles.

"Well, I guess I have to admit that first meeting with you was one of my more memorable moments," he said softly. "How was I to know then that our meeting would lead to such pleasant things?" His smile revealed even white teeth.

Bliss knew just what he meant, and the very memory of their lovemaking caused such a stir within her breast that she had to catch her breath and steady herself. Their gazes locked, he reached out to touch her cheek, her hair, and then he leaned toward her, drew her to him and settled his lips upon hers in a passionate, demanding kiss. When they finally separated it took several minutes before they regained their composure. Neither spoke, each knowing that time did not allow for further lovemaking to consummate their desire.

"I know. Later," Travis whispered.

She lowered her lashes in a coquettish manner. "Later. Soon you'll be a free man, Travis. We'll have forever then. Right now we have work to do to accomplish that goal."

It took every bit of strength she had not to submit to him. Her hands trembled as she threw herself into the saddle and recaptured the reins. Travis followed her example, but as he thrust himself into the saddle his heart was skipping a beat and he had a woebegone look on his face.

"Oh, lady, what you do to me," he whispered. Then he cleared his throat and attempted to clear his head of the sexual thoughts still lingering there. Well, maybe if he stopped thinking about how different things might have been had he not been at the wrong place at the wrong time and started to face the reality of their situation, he could calm the terrible ache in his loins. "Come on, Methuselah," he said, nudging his horse in the ribs.

They reached the Red Sign Mine much sooner than Travis had expected. His senses reacted to the sounds, smells and visual reminders very strongly. "Bliss, I don't know about this . . ."

"I do. My woman's intuition tells me you'll be safe here."

He shrugged. "Then by all means, I will be." He was determined to be a good sport about the situation. "At least it's not raining this time, so I won't have to take off my clothes."

Bliss rode up and gently touched his hand. "Not until I get back." There was no mistaking what she meant. Her smile was seductive as she winked.

"In that case, do hurry," he said softly. As before a storm, there was tension in the air. But of a sensual kind. Alluring. And another emotion lingered between them as well. Though they intended to say goodbye for only a few hours experience had taught them both that anything could happen. What if the worst occurred and they never saw each other again.

"Travis . . ." The words she wanted to say got stuck in her throat. She had never told a man she loved him, because she'd never loved anyone but her father before. Was it any wonder then that forming the words was so difficult? "Travis, I . . ."

"I feel the same way," he said, reading her mind. "After this is over, Bliss, I'll be able to make some promises. Promises I know I'll be able to keep. In the meantime, be careful. You're very special to me." It was the closest he could come to saying I love you.

"I'll be back before you know it." There was a blanket on her horse. She took it off and handed it to him. "Now, go on in there and make yourself comfortable." She watched as he hid his horse in the shrubbery, then carefully made his way into the mine tunnel. Once she was certain he was safely settled, she rode off.

Though the rest of the trip was the same distance as the first part of the journey, it seemed much longer without Travis' company, but at last Bliss reached the outskirts of Silver Bow. She glanced about. Up ahead several travelers on horseback cantered lazily over the narrow bridge which spanned the creek. Setting their horses into a quick gallop, they let their hair fly, disregarded every other thought and dashed across. Bliss did likewise.

"So far, so good."

Strange, but there was no sign of Taggart's men anywhere. Had she been marshal, Bliss would have posted guards everywhere. Could it be a trap? She had to keep that possibility at the back of her mind as she rode into Silver Bow.

"Almost like a ghost town." The streets of Butte had been teeming with traffic, but here they were nearly deserted despite the fact that it was the busy time of day. But then, perhaps there was a reason. Butte and Silver Bow had always been rivals until silver and copper were struck in Butte years ago. After that Silver Bow slowly declined while Butte built up. Now it was hardly a town at all, which was disturbing since it meant a stranger would be noteworthy. Was that why Travis had been noticed right from the first and set up to look like the guilty party in a holdup? It made sense.

Giving in to caution, Bliss didn't tie her horse to a hitching post on the street, but hid it in an alleyway behind one of the saloons. Then, keeping to the shadows, she sought out the general store. Without saying more than necessary to the proprietor, she gathered up the items from Travis' list, as well as a few other things she thought would be needed, paid for them with the money she had gotten for Travis' bounty, then hurried out the door. Looking behind her every few feet to make certain she wasn't being followed, she reclaimed her horse, then headed for the stable where the camera was hidden. Tying her horse to a pole inside, she quickly climbed up to the loft and started digging through the straw.

"Please be here! Please . . ." The thought beseiged her that perhaps Travis hadn't been as sly as he'd intended. What if someone else had found the camera? What if it wasn't here? She and Travis were counting on it so desperately, they had just assumed it would be waiting here when they came to reclaim it. But what if it wasn't? That her searching hands came up empty time and time again was frightening.

"Wait a minute. He said take ten steps from the pole then turn right—or maybe it was left—then go seven steps . . ." Bliss tried again, this time taking longer strides that would match Travis'. Bending down, she once more scratched about in the hay. Nothing. "Try one more time. Take ten steps from the pole, then turn left and go seven steps." Once more she frantically searched, digging until her

307

fingers were scratched and bleeding. This time she came up with something worth more than gold—the camera case.

Oh, but it was cumbersome! Much larger and heavier than she might have supposed. Clearly lugging this back to the Red Sign Mine was going to be much more difficult than she had thought. She missed Travis' muscles now. He would have hefted it up as if it weighed hardly anything, while she bent her back to the burden. Even so, she somehow managed to make it down the steps from the loft and to where her horse was tethered.

Suddenly the sounds of footsteps caused her to jump back and melt into the shadows. But it was only a boy with a hammer and nails. He was tacking something up to the entrance of the stable, right by the door. A handbill of some sort. Bliss chastised herself for being cowardly without cause. She did, however, wait until he had left before coming out of hiding.

"How in the hell am I going to take this damn camera case and the other junk back?" It was said in frustration. Travis hadn't mentioned anything about the weight or the bulk of these items. But then, she hadn't asked. Could it be that he knew she'd have trouble, and this was his way of teaching her a lesson? She didn't want to believe it, but that was a possibility. Well, she would show him. Oakwood Harrison's daughter never admitted defeat.

The problem was solved by tying a rope to the camera case and hoisting it up to the saddle. Then with thick, strong rope she secured the case to the saddle horn. So that the case would not injure her horse, she took an old blanket that was draped over the side of a stall, folded it and placed it on her horse, situating it so it would act as padding. Though it was going to make for some uncomfortable riding on the way back, Bliss knew this was the only way. Hell, hadn't she ridden with wolf hides piled deep in that very same spot? She had. Stepping into the stirrup, pulling herself up, she settled herself into the saddle for the return journey.

"And Travis said I'd be in danger." She couldn't wait to rub it in that she had managed to pull this off without a hitch. Taggart was so stupid, so blind he might never realize her involvement, she decided. Well, she wasn't worried about that. Even so, her eyes went to the handbill as she walked her horse out the stable door. Then they practically bugged out of her head as they took in a very unwelcome sight.

"A wanted poster!" But not one for Travis. To the contrary. Bliss's whole body went cold as she read the description of a red-haired woman that matched her to a tee. Wanted for Horse Stealing, Bliss Harrison, the poster read.

Chapter Thirty-One

Travis was so delighted to see his photographic equipment that he didn't ask about the details of her trip into Silver Bow and back. At least not yet. Running his hands over the camera case and tripod with nearly the same tenderness he showed her, he was in a world of his own. Thank God, Bliss thought. Though at some other time she might have been a bit put out at his lack of attention, it gave her some time to think of just how she was going to break the news to him that they were both in the same fix. Wanted.

She, who had always been on the side of the law, had been declared an outlaw. She was stunned. But should she have been surprised? In her usual daring manner she had thrust common sense aside. All she had thought about was saving Travis, escaping from Tom Barlow and the hotel. The truth was, however, that she had stolen a horse, a serious transgression in the West. Hell, people could be hung as horse thieves. The very thought brought a tightening to her throat.

"Oh, even Taggart wouldn't dare." Or would he? So far he had shown as much restraint as a vulture.

All this time she had thought that she knew exactly how Travis had felt being on the run, but only now did the true impact hit her. Being a bounty hunter, she knew what having a price on your head meant. Being mercilessly hunted. From this moment on, not only Travis, but she herself would not be safe anywhere. Nor could they trust any living soul. Bounty hunters and the marshal's men would be out there sniffing around like hounds after a fox. Lurking in the shadows would always be someone who had no qualms about turning them in for the reward. Just as she had done with Travis.

"Oh, I'm so sorry . . ." she said aloud. But at least she had tried to make it up to him by using the bounty money to help him.

Travis was bent down, examining his camera and tripod to make certain that everything was in good shape. "Oh, don't be. It wasn't your fault," he replied, misunderstanding her train of thought. "This stuff wasn't meant for a rough ride. But don't worry. It's a bit scuffed up and dirtied, but it looks like everything is intact."

Bliss watched as he removed the tripod, which had been broken down into four pieces, from its case, then a leather-covered box with polished brass fittings and a hinged front panel from another. How strange that this contraption could capture a person's image, Bliss thought, staring. It was a bit like sorcery.

"Can I help?" Hopefully she could at least do

311

something right. After the startling discovery she had just made in Silver Bow she felt the need to redeem herself.

"You can set out those chemicals I had you purchase. Put the items on that rock right there." He looked up from his attentions to his camera equipment to smile. "I owe you a real debt of gratitude, Bliss, and I have to say I'm sorry. All that talk about blundering into Silver Bow myself was just that. Talk. You were right all along. And now it looks as if I'm going to have to rely on you even more."

"Of course." She swallowed hard. His apology made her feel even worse. Silently she went about her task, neatly placing all the purchased things on a rock that had a flat top.

What were they going to do? How was she going to protect Travis when she was on the lam herself? Just how long could they hide out before they were caught? Oh, damn! She had made a mess of everything. Travis was right. She was headstrong and as stubborn as a mule, with no sense of delicacy at all. Well, she had blundered into serious trouble this time.

"Did you have any problems laying your hands on this?" At last Travis was ready to make conversation about her journey.

"Problems?" She started to confide in him, to tell him her shock at seeing her description posted and a price on her head, but instead she shook her head. "No. No problems at all," she said, reasserting her air of cockiness.

It wasn't a complete untruth. She had been

extremely lucky in getting in and getting out of Silver Bow without Taggart's posse and everyone else in town getting on her tail. Not that she could credit herself or her cunning for that. No, it was all a matter of timing. The posters alerting the townspeople to a woman with flaming red hair had just been going up. In another hour or maybe two she would have had the devil's own time of it.

"It was heavy and unwieldy, that's all," she did admit.

"That's because of the glass plate that's still in its holder. Let's hope it hasn't been broken." Carefully he checked. "Good. Good. Today really looks like my lucky day. And yours as well, Bliss."

"Yeah, our lucky day," she said, suddenly feeling as if the weight of the world had just been heaped on her shoulders. She tried to change the subject. "Just how does that thing work anyway?"

He was pleased by her interest in his profession. "This box has a mahogany interior where the film goes in a holder." He pointed to the hinged front panel. "This 'bed' drops and a bellows bearing the Bausch and Lomb lens and this shutter is pulled forward into operating position."

"Oh . . ." She didn't really understand, but she didn't want to admit it. "Uh-huh . . ." All the time he was explaining, her thoughts were elsewhere. Where on earth were they going to hide out? They couldn't stay in this mine forever.

"I use gelatin emulsions that contain light sensitive silver salts. I spread the gelatin on a glass plate, insert the plate in the camera, put the camera on the tripod, focus and . . . *voilà!*"

"Voilà!" she mimicked.

Travis shook his head. "How was I to know that one particular photograph would get me in such hot water? But that will soon be rectified, or so I hope."

"And what if it's not?" She wasn't in a mood to be optimistic. Not after what had happened that day. "What if the plate in your camera isn't the answer? What will we do then, Travis?"

It was obvious by the look on his face that he hadn't contemplated failure. "Well, I guess I'll just have to go on from there." Her question seemed to have made him more than a bit nervous because his fingers fumbled as he removed the glass plate from the holder. "Easy. Easy. I don't want to break it."

His nervousness was contagious. Bending down, Bliss held out the folds of her skirt to capture the precious negative. She watched as he went through the preliminaries of turning it into a picture, using the items she had gotten from the general store. "Now what?"

"I need to use the sun as my light source. I have to find a flat rock outside this tunnel."

Oh, how she hated to step outside, now of all times. The mine was the only place she felt safe. Nor was she comforted to learn that the entire process, from developing the negative to producing a finished print, would take more than a day to complete. Hours in the sun were needed just to bring out the photographic details on paper. Time was just something they didn't have in abundance. "The firelight won't do?"

"No, I need a brighter light." He nudged her

gently. "Come on. You can be my assistant."

Thus, Bliss was given a view of the photography business firsthand. Travis developed the print by leaving it in the sunlight until the image formed on the paper, then washed and "toned" it to a warm sepia color. He then fixed the print in a chemical solution that made the image insensitive to further exposure to light, washed it thoroughly in water and let it dry. And all the while he muttered, warning himself to be careful. Although he treated the exposed glass-plate negative with great care, accidents were inevitable and some images were lost.

The waiting time did have its advantages, however. Bliss did what she could to make the mine tunnel homey. Dried leaves were transformed into a comfortable bed, a large rock into their dining table. Their hideout became a love nest where she found it easy to laugh, to flirt, to be a little outrageous.

"Well, this isn't exactly a mansion, but it might prove to be interesting. We could pretend those mica-covered rocks up there are chandeliers, that the leaves are a satin coverlet."

"Any place is paradise when I'm with you," Travis answered. Now that this matter of the photograph was being taken care of, his thoughts turned to more amorous pursuits.

Leaning toward him, she stroked his neck, tangling her fingers in his hair. Travis closed his eyes, giving himself up to the rippling pleasure.

"Make love to me . . ." She leaned forward to brush his mouth with her lips. That simple gesture said all she wanted to say, that she loved him, that she desired him. Slowly his hands closed around

315

her shoulders, pulling her to him, and he responded to her kiss with a passion that made her gasp. Gathering her into his arms, he carried her to their makeshift bed.

"I do want you. So very much." His fingers slowly stripped off her garments, then his hands roamed gently over her body, lingering on the fullness of her ripe breasts, leaving no part of her free from his touch.

Bliss gave herself up to the fierce emotions that raced through her, answering his touch with searching hands, returning his caresses. Closing her arms around his neck, she offered herself to him, writhing against him in a slow delicate dance. She could feel the pulsating hardness of him through the fabric of his trousers and reached up to pull his breeches from him. If that was being overbold and brazen she didn't care.

Sweet hot desire fused their bodies together as he leaned against her. His strength mingled with her softness, his hands moving up her sides, warming her with their heat. Like a fire, his lips burned a path from one breast to the other, bringing forth spirals of pulsating sensations that swept over her.

Travis' mouth fused with hers, his kiss deepening as his touch grew bolder, and Bliss luxuriated in the pleasure of his lovemaking, stroking and kissing him back. He slid his hands between their bodies, poised above her. The tip of his maleness pressed against her, entered her softness in a slow but strong thrust, joining them in that most intimate of embraces. He kissed her as their naked bodies fused, and from the depths of her soul, her heart cried out. A tiny flicker of hope that all was not lost flickered within her breast.

Her legs went up around him, telling him she wanted him to move within her. He did, slowly at first, then with a sensual urgency. Travis filled her with his love, leaving her breathless. It was like falling and never quite hitting the ground. Her arms locked around him as she arched to meet his body in a sensuous dance, forgetting all her inhibitions as she expressed her love. A sensation burst through her, a warm explosion.

Even when the sensual magic was over, they clung to each other, unwilling to have the moment end. Bliss, reluctant to have him leave her body, felt that surely the fire they had ignited would meld them together forever. Smiling, she lay curled in the crook of Travis' arm, and he, his passion spent, lay close against her, his body pressing against hers. They were together. It was all she had for now. For the moment it had to be enough.

"Sleep now," he whispered, still holding her close. With a sigh, she snuggled up against him, burying her face in the warmth of his chest, breathing in the manly scent of him. She didn't want to sleep, not now. She wanted to savor this moment of being together, but suddenly she knew the time had come for her confession.

"Travis . . ."

He touched the tip of her nose. "Smile. Don't look so serious. We've just been to heaven and back. How can I have any worries now?"

"Well," she looked up at him, "everything didn't go as well today as I told you."

317

That got his notice. He sat up. "What happened?"

"Oh, I got into Silver Bow and back without being caught, as you can see. It's just that . . . just that . . ." Oh, damn! All she could do was blurt it out. "There's a wanted poster out on me for horse-stealing."

"What?" Frantically he ran his fingers through his hair. "I was afraid of something like this. I warned you. I feared—"

"And I didn't listen. I thought I was invincible. But now . . ." She waited for the lecture, but strangely it didn't come.

"It will be all right. I'll make it so!" He caressed her back, his fingers tracing her spine, comforting her until she drifted off.

Only when she was fast asleep did Travis get up. Slowly disentangling himself from her arms, he rose from the bed and moved about, gathering up his clothes. He had to get out of there. A long walk in the night air would aid him immensely. Tomorrow he would make some decisions. With agonizing clarity, he knew something must be done. He had to think of what to do to protect Bliss.

"Damn Taggart. Damn him to hell." But this whole ordeal wasn't over yet.

Early the next morning when Bliss awoke she found him busy at work on the photograph. Leaning over she watched as he made the finishing touch. He then pasted it onto a cardboard mount.

"The time has come."

Travis and Bliss breathlessly awaited the results, though they were counting on the picture so much, they were nearly afraid to study it. When at last he did, Travis gave a long drawn-out sigh. It was just as he had suspected. At the edge of the photograph, nearly out of the picture, was the marshal talking very amiably to one of the robbers as if approving of what was taking place. Or as if he was the leader of the gang. Travis mumbled, "Of course." It was the only thing that made sense. "Obviously Taggart thought I knew right from the very beginning about his involvement, so he intended to put me out of the way—permanently."

"And he nearly succeeded," Bliss whispered, once again regretting her part in thrusting Travis into the marshal's hands. "And look. Travis! It's him!"

"Who?"

"The one holding the gun is Tom Barlow. I'd know him anywhere, even if he does have a kerchief over his face. The hair. The lankiness. The way he's dressed. Tom Barlow!" It all fit in now, but how were they going to see the marshal brought to justice without endangering themselves.

The answer was simple, Travis provided it when she put the question into words.

"We're going to Helena! You see, I have some plans . . ."

"What are you going to do?"

"Put my talents to work," he said, smiling as mischievously as Bliss did when she was up to something. "I intend to write a story and print the photograph for everyone in Montana to see. These will be the epitaph of the man who so nearly took my life."

*   *   *

Butte was crawling with deputies. Every man on Sam Taggart's payroll. Hell, he thought, if they couldn't catch La Mont and Miss Harrison, then the bounty hunters would. Knowing that money speaks so loud it shouts, he had upped the ante, not only on Travis but on the woman as well. He'd beat that red-haired hellion at her own game. He'd set her own kind upon her. One hunter after another. A thrilling chase. And that wasn't the only thing he'd done. He'd confiscated the damn woman's dogs to use against her. He figured if anyone could locate her those huge gray beasts could.

"I say we ought to just shoot them. They're going to be more trouble than they are worth." Tom Barlow didn't make any pretense of how he felt about the dogs. Nor did the wolfhounds have any qualms about growling and showing their teeth.

"Just keep your hat on. We need those mutts right now. They're excellent trackers, and it seems to me they're anxious to be reunited with their owner." Bliss Harrison had left a neckerchief behind at the hotel, and Taggart held it in front of the dogs' noses like a carrot before a donkey. That sent the animals into a wild frenzy, had them pulling and straining at their leashes. "See. They miss her, Tom."

"Yeah, and ain't that sweet!"

"And aren't we obliging to enact a little reunion." Taggart's mood and health were steadily improving. For the first time since the bungled execution of La Mont he felt in control. He'd get him, the photograph and an added bonus—the woman.

"What are you going to do with *her?*" Tom Barlow seemed obsessively interested.

"Do with her? It all depends."

If he caught the two of them together he'd instigate a little "shooting" accident. If he caught her and not him he'd use her as bait to lure La Mont into turning loose that picture, that is, before he was permanently silenced. If he caught him and not her, he'd work on her strong feelings for La Mont to lure her into his clutches. No matter what happened, he couldn't let Bliss Harrison go free. Not now. She knew too much. Undoubtedly La Mont would have told her the whole story, thereby making her a danger to him.

As deputies, bounty hunters and dogs started off on their hunt Taggart clenched his jaw. Whatever happened now, the ending was cut in stone. He'd find them. And when he did there would be no other choice but to see both of them dead.

Chapter Thirty-Two

Everyone in the whole damned territory of Montana was after them, or so it seemed. Leaflets, dodgers and wanted posters were as plentiful in the towns and surrounding areas of Butte as fleas on a dog. Detailed flyers telling the color of their hair and eyes, estimating their height and weight, and cautioning that they were armed and should be considered dangerous floated around like snowflakes. A hopeless and inescapable situation some might have said, but not Bliss. Giving up just wasn't in her nature. Somehow they would make it to Helena outside the sphere of Marshal Taggart's influence. They had to; it was as simple as that. Travis's only chance was in exposing Taggart for what he was, and that meant he had to have a chance to write his article.

"We're trapped. Why not admit it?" Travis' mood was sour as he assessed the situation. They had retreated back to the tunnel after a narrow escape, when they had been spotted in Centersville and an alarm had been sounded. Somehow they had managed to lose their pursuers, but it had been a harrowingly close call. The mine was their salvation. Still, they couldn't stay in it forever. "The moment we set foot outside of here again, we'll be spotted and it will all be over."

"Then we'll just have to make sure no one sees us." Bliss realized she had to take charge in this situation. She carefully braided her hair and pinned it atop her head, so its color wouldn't give her away.

"Disguise ourselves you mean?" Travis shook his head, then quickly grew silent as he heard a sudden sound. "What was that?"

"I'll go see." Cocking her rifle, Bliss investigated. It was only a squirrel rustling about as it came into the mine entrance to look around for food. Its beady brown eyes were riveted on a large piece of bread, but Bliss quickly shooed it away. She couldn't afford to be generous. Not now. They had to make little food they had last. Going into any of the towns now for any reason was hazardous.

"Well?"

"Just a bushy-tailed, fur-faced varmint eyeing our supplies. I sent him scurrying."

She put her hand on his shoulder, a gesture calculated to calm him down. Travis had every right to be agitated. To him, it was a matter of life and death; to Bliss, it meant avoiding the chance of being used as bait to catch the man she loved. Oh, she understood Taggart's motive in putting her on the wanted list, all right. But it wouldn't work. She was determined not to fall into his hands. Not now. Not ever. Taggart might not realize it, but he'd soon find

323

he had bitten off more than he could chew when he'd tangled with Harrison and La Mont.

"An animal. The four-legged kind." Travis realized he was beginning to assume the furtive behavior of a fugitive, jumping at every noise. His nerves were on edge. Now that he had the incriminating photograph, he felt even more vulnerable. If Taggart got his hands on that, all would be lost.

"It's the two-legged type we have to avoid." Bliss sounded a lot more self-assured than she felt. "We'll do it. We'll get away. They aren't dealing with a novice you know. As I was saying, they can't catch what they don't see."

"Dressing like your Aunt What's-her-name isn't going to help me this time." Undoubtedly Taggart would now be on his guard for such trickery. "Besides, if that old nag I'm riding doesn't ensure my downfall, wearing a skirt would."

"We'll have to travel by night, that's what I meant. Use the darkness as our cover and sleep by day."

That was the only plan that made any sense; thus, after pilfering a horse from a nearby miner, they set out as soon as it was dark. The only hindrance was that, although they would have liked to ride at breakneck speed, they had to lessen their pace for safety's sake.

Bliss's father had always said you didn't really understand a man until you had walked in his shoes. Now she fully comprehended his meaning. She who had been the hunter now truly knew what it felt like to be the hunted, to have to constantly look over your shoulder, to always be on the alert, to travel by night and sleep by day, to have eyes in the back of your head.

Somehow Bliss and Travis stayed just one step ahead of their pursuers, however. For one thing they were both strong, agile and just about as skilled at horsemanship as any one could be. Travis told her of his days racing at the Kentucky Derby, and she was grateful for his know-how. It showed, enabling them both to manage their mounts skillfully, daring to perform normally unimagined maneuvers in their constant quest to stay free. And their mental prowess was another asset, Travis' intelligence tempered by education, Bliss's cunning sharpened by life's sometimes cruel training.

Using the night as cover, they doubled around, going in circles, retracing their steps, often purposely leaving hoof marks in the dirt in the hope of fooling Taggart into thinking they were headed to Bannack in Beaverhead or to Virginia City. Bliss and Travis both knew they had to lose the deputies before they could set out for their real destination— Helena. Only when they had shaken them would they even think of setting foot in that town.

Even so, their journey to Helena wasn't all panic and travail. Their mutual danger acted much like an aphrodisiac, making them passionate and making their moments of love all the more exciting. Bliss never tired of feeling Travis' hands on her skin, of tasting his kisses, of feeling the stiff flesh of his maleness buried deep within her. He taught her the secrets of his body as well as her own, dared her to be sexually brave in trying new positions and techniques and never ceased to make her feel truly loved. She gloried in her newfound knowledge, taking to lovemaking like a duck does to water, or so Travis said.

When they were nestled in each other's arms it seemed that love could conquer all. The rest of the time Bliss said over and over again, "Everything is going to be fine. Just fine, Travis," yet she came to believe it less and less. And there came a time when she knew she had to make a decision that was going to test the very core of her character.

She could hear the thundering of their horses' hooves as they plunged down the hillside, and strained her ears to hear an echoing sound that would mean they were being followed. She didn't, but as they crested the top of another hill the sight of campfires in the distance confirmed her suspicion of the worst.

"Travis, somehow they've found us! Look." The unthinkable had happened. Though she had used every trick in the book in trying to confuse their pursuers so they would tag off in the wrong direction, somehow their trail had been picked up.

"How?" Damn, Travis thought angrily. Taggart was sure hard to shake. "We'll ride all night and won't stop to rest during the day. It's the only way."

"No, there's another." Oh sure, they could evade them for another day or two or three, but eventually they'd be cornered. Worse yet, since Taggart was here, he knew right where they were headed. Helena wouldn't be a refuge, after all.

"You don't want to take a stand and fight them?" Travis knew he couldn't put Bliss in that kind of danger.

"No!" She swallowed hard, then taking a deep

breath, spoke quickly. "We've got to split up, Travis. It's the only way." She tried to make light of it, though the very thought of parting from him was troubling. "Divide and conquer as they say." She knew she wouldn't dare tell him her plan, but she intended to use herself as a decoy to draw them off of Travis' trail. If she could get Taggart to follow her, he could go on to Helena, unscathed. And if she got caught, her life would not be in jeopardy. Even Taggart wouldn't dare hang a woman.

"Split up?" The very idea was disturbing. Travis wanted to keep his eye on her, shield her from any onslaught. She'd gotten herself in a mess by helping him. How could he then just say thanks and goodbye, and ride away? He might never see her again.

"The truth is, if we stay together we're going to be caught. Eventually." Bliss could sense an argument brewing. Travis' pride would make him see himself as her protector.

"And if we part . . . ?" His mind whirled with arguments against such an idea. What if something happened to her when he wasn't there? What if Taggart caught her? What if he never saw her again? What if . . . ?

"If we part at least one of us has a chance." She knew it had to be him.

"No! If you think I'm throwing you to the wolves just to save my own hide, you can think again." He wasn't a coward. "We're in this together to sink or to swim."

"I knew you'd say that." Guiding her horse next to his, she leaned over and kissed him. "Being with you has meant more to me than I can ever say. It's been a hell of an adventure." And I'll remember you always no matter what happens, she thought. Forever. Quickly she pulled away before she lost her nerve and gave in to her selfish inclinations. "Goodbye, Travis."

"Goodbye, hell! You're not going anywhere." He maneuvered his horse in an attempt to block her horse's escape.

Unstrapping her saddlebags, the ones loaded with supplies, she let them drop to the ground. "The International Hotel, corner of State and Main streets. I'll meet you there." If all went well, that is. Guiding her horse to the right while he moved to the left, she easily escaped his one-man blockade.

"Bliss. Don't!" He couldn't let her go.

"Have to." With a feigned devil-may-care attitude, she touched the brim of her hat with her first two fingers and saluted as she rode past him. "The International Hotel! Remember." Then she was gone in a cloud of dust.

Chapter Thirty-Three

Like a mosquito or a gnat, Bliss began a series of ride-bys and near encounters with the deputies that were meant to annoy and slowly pull them away from the pathway she knew Travis would be taking. Scattering their horses, then riding quickly away she took personal satisfaction in knowing she had made Travis a bit more certain of reaching Helena. It was her way of thumbing her nose at Taggart and his boys, of saying catch me if you can. But he wouldn't catch her. She was much too clever in covering her tracks, or so she hoped. And all the while she lured her pursuers closer and closer to Watersville.

Bliss had it all planned, had calculated how long it would take Travis to reach Helena. Carefully she thought about her next moves in great detail. Just in case she was followed, she'd go south to Virginia City then change direction and head northwest to the mining camp of Laurin. It was about three miles north of Robbers Roost, a roadhouse used as a headquarters for outlaw groups twenty years ago.

The terrain was rough and rugged, just the kind of pathway to lose any tagalongs.

"We'll be meeting up again before you know it, Travis," she said, pausing briefly to get her bearings. She was near the fork formed by the joining of Silver Bow and Blacktail Creek. If she remembered right there was a small grove of trees, a perfect place to camp up ahead. She'd settle down for a few hours' sleep then head out for the long stretch of the journey she knew was coming.

There was a thick purple streak on the horizon. It was dusk, the time when she and Travis usually cuddled together, getting psychologically prepared for their nighttime traveling. She'd be hugging him tightly just about now, tempting him to just lie back and enjoy their closeness for a few minutes longer before they had to ride.

Her ears picked up a sound far in the distance. She was certain she had imagined it. It couldn't be. Not way out here.

Holding her breath, Bliss focused all her energy on listening. The breeze, that's all it was. Or something else? A strange high-pitched racket. Bliss's heart lurched.

"Dogs!" From experience she recognized the noise. Barking. But what were dogs doing way out here? There were no ranches, houses or places of human habitation. It could only mean one thing. Trackers. And just who did she imagine they were tracking? The baying of the animals grew louder. Bliss could hear the sound of a human voice urging the animals on.

She had to think clearly. Quickly. The fact that

her pursuers were using dogs changed the situation immensely. Men she could fool with her dodging about, but dogs went by their noses. She couldn't afford to be torn to shreds or forced to climb a tree while she was surrounded from below like a cornered squirrel.

The sound of the dogs was growing louder, more distinct. "Water!" That was it. The creek. Dogs couldn't track through water, she knew that from her experiences with Bard and Boru. The creek! She'd lead the horses through the gently turbulent water and the hounds would lose her scent. Nudging her horse with her heels Bliss guided it into a gallop.

Suddenly a tree branch seemed to reach out and hold her suspended in midair for the span of a heartbeat. Then she was falling. She hit the ground hard and rolled over and over several times into a tangle of bushes as her horse continued racing away.

For a moment she lay on the ground unmoving, trying to catch her breath, hidden by the undergrowth which was her only salvation. Strange how at that moment the silliest thing went through her head. She was glad that Travis hadn't seen her take such a fall. That would have been humiliating.

She lay in the bushes for only a moment longer; then she was up and running, heading for the creek and the safety of the water. On horseback she might have made it, but on foot she was steadily losing ground. And all the while the barking grew louder and louder.

Bliss reached the creek and grabbed for a low-hanging branch, but just as she was about to swing herself up onto it the dogs leaped through the

331

undergrowth. "Damn." She could well imagine herself being mauled and prepared herself for the pain, but the dogs weren't growling as they should have been. They were, in fact, happy to see her. Pulling her from the branch, pinning her to the ground, they planted sloppy kisses all over her face.

"Bard. Boru." Bliss recognized them in an instant and was struck by the irony of it all. To be tracked by her own dogs was a travesty of all that was right in the world. Who would do such a thing? "Bard. Boru. Heel." It took Bliss only an instant to gain control. Being well trained, the wolfhounds quickly responded to the forceful tone of her voice.

Escape. Looking to the right, then to the left, Bliss could see that she was lost. Though the wolfhounds had bounded ahead of those who were using them for their own purposes, the men were quickly closing in. Bliss scrambled to her feet, but before she could run a horseman cornered her.

Bliss stared at the man with the gun. He wore a worn and dirtied pair of jeans, an equally dusty and worn leather vest, a blue flannel shirt and a torn cotton neckerchief knotted around his neck. "Who?" He tilted back his head, revealing his face. "Barlow," she exclaimed, as if he were a disease.

He had a smug smile on his face and an ominous sparkle in his eyes. "I've been wanting to have you just where I wanted you, lady, ever since the first time you pointed that rifle at me. Now I've gotten my wish."

"To the contrary," she countered. "It's I who have you right where I want you." She knew he would never understand.

"Feisty as always." Wrapping his hands around his saddle horn, Tom Barlow dismounted.

Bliss reached for her gun.

"I wouldn't do that." There was menace in Barlow's voice, but the wolfhounds' barking kept him from physically assaulting her.

"So, despite the fact that you and my dogs have been in each other's company, they still didn't like you," she said under her breath. Slowly she regained her calm. It would be insanity to try anything else with eight of Barlow's men looking on. With a shrug, she tossed her firearm to the ground. "Can't blame me for trying."

"Well, we'll just see how spirited you are when you're looking at the world from behind bars." Motioning to two of his companions, he ordered that she be tied up. A riderless horse was led toward her. "Mount up."

"Where are you taking me?" As if she didn't know.

"To Taggart. He's going to be mighty pleased to see you." He bared his teeth. "Mighty pleased."

"I'm sure." Bliss had no intention of cowering. Even so, as she was roughly thrown back upon her horse, which had not gone far, and was made to ride off with Barlow and his men, she knew the taste of fear.

Part Three:
A Picture is Worth
a Thousand Words

Helena, Montana—Autumn, 1884

Justice is a machine that, when someone has given it a starting push, rolls on of itself.

—Galsworthy, *Justice*, II

Chapter Thirty-Four

Helena, a sprawling, gulch city whose buildings dotted the surrounding hills, beckoned to Travis in the morning sunlight with the promise of sanctuary. Out of habit he turned his head, wanting to comment on the sight before him, only to remember that he was all alone. It was an empty feeling.

He missed Bliss more than he could ever have foretold. He missed her energy, her zest for living, her smiles, her laughter, the way she wrinkled her brow when she was annoyed. Strange how quickly one person could get attached to another. In the short time they had been together she had become the most important person in his world. She held a permanent place in his heart, his soul, his every thought.

With each mile he had traveled, she had been on his mind. He had condemned himself a hundred times and more for not having ridden after her, telling himself that he should have forced her to stay with him. Until he saw the city he had fought the nagging guilt. At the same time he had recognized the wisdom in what she had done. Together they would have been caught. Bliss had given him a chance to survive. He hoped she would not suffer for her bravery, and he was determined that her noble gesture would not be in vain. It was said that the pen was mightier than the sword, and he intended to prove it. Only by doing so could he insure that they had a future.

"Bliss, we went through a lot together," he muttered softly. "I miss you like everything. Please watch out, and take care of yourself until we meet here as we planned." And they would. He should know by now that he shouldn't doubt her. If anyone could take care of herself it was Bliss. She was some woman.

Hoping to attract as little attention as possible upon arrival, Travis had not made the full journey on horseback. Just in case the authorities had been alerted to an incoming horseman, he had left his horse at a homestead along the way and hitched a ride on a heavily loaded wagon hauling supplies and machinery to Helena. He knew that he would never be found hidden away on such a dilapidated horse-drawn vehicle.

Helena was the easiest city in Montana to reach from all other places. Horses and buggies jammed the way into the city, stirring up a choking cloud of dust. Travis covered his nose and mouth, but nonetheless was struck by a fit of coughing. Fearing the noise would alert the wagon's driver to an unwanted passenger, he ducked down behind a piece of machinery only to realize the driver's attention was diverted to finding a place in the road wide enough to pass the other vehicles. At last the man did, passing a dusty stage and a heavily loaded wagon drawn by six mules with a whip-cracking driver.

"My compliments to the driver," Travis said beneath his breath. "Must be another alumni from the Kentucky Derby."

The wagon rocked back and forth, lulling him to sleep, but right at the outskirts he awakened with a start. He had to get off before the wagon was unloaded at the railroad station. With that thought in mind he pulled his hat down to hide his face and quickly leaped to the ground.

There was a brisk pace to Travis' walk despite the pinching of the too-tight boots Bliss had procured for him, but he didn't hurry out of a sense of fear. No, something else made him step lively. Now that he had arrived in Helena, his blood ran hot with the urge to scoop the other papers with a full account of Taggart's doings. In his mind he thought of a headline guaranteed to catch the readers' eyes— Marshal Caught With Pants Down. Under it, he would expose Taggart's duplicity in robbing the Silver Bow Bank.

Experience had taught Travis well that, human nature being what it was, people in all walks of life loved a scandal. It added spice to the usual list of marriages, births, deaths, celebrations, gold and silver strikes, and the society doings. Since editors seemed to relish lawlessness, some of them delighting in recording the outrageous doings of famous gunfighters, he doubted he would have any trouble finding a market for his story.

Helena wasn't like the smaller towns in Montana Territory. It was more sophisticated. As he walked along he took note that there was not one, there were several newspapers. The *Helena Journal*, the *Helana Herald*, the *Helena Weekly Herald*, the *Montana Post* and a few smaller papers. Comparing this city to the other towns he'd visited, he realized at once that the population in the outlying districts was leaner than it was here, and a large percentage of the people in the smaller towns could neither read nor write. Here in Helena, most people were well educated and literate. How good it felt to be among his own kind.

"Taggart, beware!" Strange, he thought, although every little jerkwater Western town had a newspaper, Silver Bow hadn't had one, nor had Watersville. The marshal obviously didn't want anyone nosing around. Now the reasons for the marshal's enmity and ferocity were all the more understandable. Taggart undoubtedly didn't like editors, reporters, photographers or anyone connected with the newspaper business. He was just a big fish in a little puddle. That was the reason. It might even go much farther. What if he was a wanted man who didn't desire any publicity?

Travis put Taggart temporarily out of his mind as he trudged along the boardwalk, getting lost among the crowd as he looked at the city with a critical eye.

340

Helena had electric lights, the first city in the territory to be so illuminated, and that made Travis feel right at home. There was even a streetcar to serve the outskirts. And the mansions built by mining magnates stood tall and proud. Some even had iron deer on their lawns and stone lions or other figures at their entrances. A few lawns were further adorned with fountains and carved stone hitching posts. Did such wealth represent honest earnings, or had some of these millionaires acquired it in the same manner as Taggart? He could only wonder.

Helena had the usual number of lumber yards, warehouses, taverns and saloons. It was an interesting place. A relatively large city. Varied in its architecture. Remains of abandoned gold diggings, gravel, beds of old ditches and huge excavations gave the city a ragged and uncouth look, in contrast to the other hillside, where picturesque buildings stood, ranging from log huts to a four-story brick hotel and a cut-stone palace of a bank.

He passed a street lined with homes surrounded by green yards, poplar trees and flowers while making his way to the area where the businesses were located. The first thing he had to do was get off a telegram to Farnham Tabor, editor of the *Rocky Mountain News* in Denver, Colorado. Farnham and his editor back East, Howard Vickery, were old cohorts. Friends as well as rivals. The more he had thought about it on his way to Helena, the more he had realized that Farnham was the key. Vickery was just too far away to come to Travis' aid, but Denver was close by. Farnham could help him clear his name and get his article circulated. He could also be a valuable link in getting the news to his Eastern audience.

"Farnham Tabor." A cantankerous and tough old buzzard if ever there was one, yet a man to admire. When Travis had been just an apprentice, that man had taught him everything he knew about the newspaper business. Once they had been almost as close as father and son. Over the years they had continued their friendship.

He remembered when Farnham had scooped all the other papers in his report of the great bonanza in the Black Hills. The owner of the mine had been a Montana millionaire, so Farnham wasn't exactly ignorant of Montana Territory. That would be of help.

Good old Farnham. Of all the men he knew, he admired Farnham the most. Tabor had traveled, from New York to Colorado and even as far west as California. As a matter-of-fact he had prompted Travis' wanderlust. Farnham had even become involved in politics in Colorado. If anyone had connections and knew how to skin that skunk of a marshal, Farnham would.

For just a moment Travis toyed with the idea of taking the railroad to Denver, but decided that was out. Bliss was a part of his life now. He couldn't just up and abandon her. In just a few days she was going to meet him at the International Hotel in Helena, and he couldn't chance not connecting with her. No, he'd have to rely on a telegram. The problem was, the telegrams Bliss had sent never reached their destination. Travis could only conclude that Taggart's tentacles extended to the telegrapher. Here, however, the man didn't have one iota of power.

Until Farnham responded he had to be careful. Even if it meant doing everything the hard way. His plan was to write a story exposing the marshal and to send it to the editor of the *Rocky Mountain News* immediately. In the article he would not only accuse Marshal Taggart, he would also let it be known that he had visual proof of the marshal's involvement and that the picture was in his possession, safely hidden away.

Travis located a telegraph office at the train station. As briefly as he could he highlighted the important details of the "Taggart matter" and closed by asking if Farnham could possibly arrange to come to Helena. A wild shot, yet Farnham just might do it. After sending the telegram, Travis settled back to await a reply, reading a copy of the *Helena Herald* to while away the time.

It took just about an hour to receive a return telegram, and Travis was pleased with the response. Even though a lot of time had passed since they'd been in each other's company, Farnham wasn't going to get him down. He was taking the evening train to Helena, the telegram said, and would meet him the next morning at the railroad station.

"Well, well, well . . ." Somehow it seemed like old times. Farnham made it clear that he would begin to enlist his own army of defenders once he arrived. As to his choice of newspapers it was the *Helena*

Herald. It was a good paper, he said in the telegram, the editor competent and a personal friend. No doubt Jim Erickson would be pleased to beat the *Helena Journal* in printing the first information exposing Taggart.

Smiling, Travis stuffed the telegram into his pocket and went on to the next item of business on his list, living quarters. He had to have a roof over his head while he brought about Marshal Samuel Taggart's downfall. The International Hotel, Bliss had said, corner of State and Main streets. Whistling, he started off in that direction, passing the public library at Park Avenue and Laurence and a museum on Wiley Street.

Travis had to hunt for the assay office in order to find the hotel, but find it he did at long last. The lobby was thronged with people, and had a cabinet full of specimens of gold and lead-silver ore from neighboring mines in the area. Helena was a prosperous, growing place with solid well-established businesses servicing an upright clientele. He got a comfortable room plus one meal for two dollars and fifty cents a day.

Visiting the library wasn't in Travis' plans, but remembering that it had loomed in his path on the way to the hotel, he found his steps taking him there now. Habit he supposed. Farnham had always told him that a good newspaper man did his research before tangling with any story. Besides, it would get his mind off of Bliss. It wouldn't hurt a bit to do a little detective work on his own, he thought as he climbed the stone stairs.

344

It was a small library compared to the ones back East, but surprisingly enough Travis soon found that it had numerous publications and leather-bound volumes. Shakespeare of course, due no doubt to the interest the theatrical companies and their performances had sparked in the Bard. *Jane Eyre. Wuthering Heights.* A tattered copy of *Ivanhoe. The Scarlet Letter.* Not to mention a large array of dime novels whose heros were local. As to magazines he found out-of-date issues of *Godey's Lady's Book, The North American Review, The Atlantic Monthly* and *Harper's New Monthly Magazine.*

It was old newspapers and their articles that Travis was interested in, however. There had to be a picture or article of Taggart somewhere in the stacks and stacks of newsprint. As a marshal he couldn't make himself totally invisible. Surely there was mention of him in his earlier years. Travis was determined to find something.

Taking a stack of papers, old issues of the *Helena Journal,* the *Anaconda Standard* and the *Butte Miner,* he headed for the table and chairs provided. Three hours later he was still in the library, having paused in his verbal gorging only to get himself a cup of coffee at a small cafe just next door.

"There has to be something. At least a paragraph, a sentence, a word." He even looked under marriages, hoping for something. In disappointment Travis put the papers back, replacing them with the issues of the *Helena Herald.* Nothing. He came up empty-handed again and again. "Damn, it's no use."

It was late. Travis knew he should get back to his hotel before they thought he'd changed his mind about the room. Hopefully they wouldn't ask for a deposit for the week. His finances were low due to his gentlemanly instincts. Although Bliss had wanted to give him half of her bounty money, he had politely declined, taking only ten dollars. It was all the money he had to his name, and fifty cents of it had already been used to send a telegram. He'd just have to ask Farnham Tabor for a loan.

Carefully Travis folded up the papers, scanning each once more as he put it back on its proper rack. He was putting the last newspaper in its place when the photograph of a striking woman caught his eye. Or was it the name that caught his attention. Josephine Taggart. Taggart. It was a short article detailing the philanthropic activities of one of Watersville's leading citizens, the daughter of a cattle baron from Virginia City and the wife of a renowned marshal. Samuel Taggart.

"Virginia City."

Travis searched for and found several newspapers from that area. "Come on. Come on!" He felt like a gambler hoping for a good hand, and when he least expected it he came up with aces. It was an article on Josephine's father, Richard G. Hammond, written eight years before. What interested Travis was the accompanying drawing of Hammond and his son-in-law. The artist's picture of a younger Taggart without mustache was amazingly lifelike. And Taggart looked strangely familiar.

"I've seen him somewhere. Somewhere before coming to Silver Bow." The question was where. It plagued Travis. "Given enough time I will remember," he said to himself. Just to make certain that he did, he "borrowed" the article. Carefully tearing it out, he folded it and put it underneath his shirt.

Chapter Thirty-Five

The hotel bed was large. Too big and empty without Bliss beside him, Travis thought as he lay awake and naked, staring up at the ceiling. Where was she? Lying on the ground somewhere, looking up at the stars? If so was she thinking of him? Most important, was she safe?

"Oh, sweetheart . . . !" The endearment was a caress on his lips. Closing his eyes, he put his arms around the pillow, pretending for a moment that it was she. Alas, the fantasy was nowhere near the actuality, and a sense of isolation washed over him. Despair. With Bliss he had felt whole; without her he was at loose ends. Like a song without a chorus, a day without the sun, a story without an ending.

Travis spent a restless night despite the comfort of the room. Was it because he was too hot? Too cold? Was the bed too hard? Too soft? Was it too quiet in the room? Too noisy outside? Kicking off the covers, he realized it wasn't any of those things. Oh, the tinkling of the saloon's piano down the street was loud, but that wasn't the reason he couldn't sleep. It was anxiety pure and simple. Over Bliss. Taggart. His being here in this city.

So much rested on his proving his own innocence and Taggart's guilt, but what if the plan backfired? What if Taggart's sphere of operation was much larger than he thought? Suppose it extended all the way here? Suppose he couldn't prove the truth in spite of the photograph. From experience he'd learned that people only believed what they wanted to believe. Could Taggart lie his way out of what he had done? If so, it wouldn't be the first time.

The springs on the mattress squeaked as Travis tossed from side to side. The picture, its reproduction achieved by a woodcut that Travis had torn from the *Montana Post* flashed before his eyes. Where had he seen Taggart before? Why did he get the feeling it had been back East?

"Oh, Damn!" Rolling out of bed, Travis paced up and down, cursing as he saw the early morning sun come up over the ridge.

Well, it didn't matter. There would be plenty of time to catch up on his slumber when this was all sorted out and he was reunited with the woman he loved. Bliss would give him one of her sensual massages, and he would drift off in her arms. In the meantime there was work to be done and a train to meet.

Hurriedly Travis shaved, remembering the time Bliss had extended him that courtesy. Touching his upper lip, he decided to leave the hair there unscathed. Luckily he had dark hair. It would show all the sooner there. A mustache, aside from being debonair would disguise his appearance, just in case a few of those wanted posters had landed here.

Wishing he had a change of clothing, Travis dressed, brushing the dust off shirt, pants and boots as best he could. As he headed for the train station, he quickly wolfed down a half-dozen biscuits bought from a bakery, keeping his Stetson pulled low and his head down.

It was a long, furtive wait, hiding in the shadows, but at last he heard the train clacking and hissing as it pulled into the station. Although the platform was crowded he spotted Farnham Tabor immediately. No one could miss that swagger, that stance or the cut of Farnham's gray pinstriped suit. Cigar chomping, balding, rotund and with a perpetual look of anger despite his rare smiles, Farnham was what might be called a tough customer, as rugged and untamed as the great sprawling terrain of Colorado that he was from. Having always been a journalist and having dabbled in politics once or twice, he was spunky, outspoken, had a way with words and was set in his ways. His was a highly personal style of journalism. He had withstood a blizzard, a flood and the threat of being kidnapped by a gang of outlaws who didn't like one of his editorials. To put it simply, Taggart would find he had met more than his match. And Farnham would learn, once he met Bliss, that she was every bit his equal.

"Goddamn. You're a sight for sore eyes." The minute Farnham saw Travis he pounded him on the back and let out that booming, hearty laugh of his.

"What took you so long?" Travis joked, knowing how careful Farnham was of keeping to schedule.

Seeing his old friend gave him an immense sense of relief, as if all would go well from now on. Perhaps that was because Farnham had believed in him right from the first and had let him know it. Travis was going to show that same faith in himself. Things simply had to get better sooner or later.

"Bah!" Farnham Tabor looked at his pocket watch. "Should have been here a half-hour ago, but the damned fool train was late. No excuse. I should personally have the engine master's head." He could be grouchy and gruff, yet Travis knew he had soft spots as well, particularly for children and animals. And one of his editorials had addressed the plight of the buffalo, influencing the decisions eventually made in Washington in their behalf.

"It doesn't matter. Just seeing you and knowing you're on my side means more than I can ever say." Loath to become too emotional, Travis turned away. "Let me help you with your bags. We'll talk as we walk back to the hotel."

In a monologue Travis poured out the whole story from start to finish. He told about taking the photograph, of being accused, of being on wanted posters, then ending up in jail. Though he tried not to show his emotions, it was hard not to smile when he told Farnham about Bliss, about her daring rescue, her loyalty, her sacrifice in making certain that he was able to get all the way to Helena.

"I owe her more than I can say."

"Even though she's the one who turned you in when you could have flown the coop!" Farnham clucked his tongue.

"I forgave her."

351

"From the tone of your voice it sounds like love."

Travis' smile was just a bit embarrassed. Speaking openly about his feelings was just something he wasn't used to. "I guess it is. Yes, I do love her. And you will too, the moment you meet her." Playfully he punched Farnham in the stomach. "She'll be the only one you've ever met who can set you on your ear."

"Yeah?" Farnham grumbled like an old bear.

Travis stared him down. "Yeah."

Farnham grinned. "Then I can't wait to meet her."

Chattering as happily as two squirrels who had just stumbled on a pile of nuts, the two men reminisced about old times and caught up on the latest news as they walked toward the hotel. Travis was surprised to find out that Farnham, an avowed bachelor, had recently married. A much younger wife.

"And are you happy?" Travis asked, taking a definite interest in the state of matrimony.

"Completely." Winking at Travis, he said, "I highly recommend it, but then something tells me you don't need me to have my say. Just when do you plan to wed?"

Travis held up his hand. "Whoa! Not so fast. At this very moment I'm still a wanted man. I've got to clear my name."

"And then?"

"I'll let you help me look for a preacher." Though Travis' tone was jovial, thinking of the trouble he was in sobered him. He was quiet as they rounded the corner and came to the hotel. He didn't speak again until they were safely sequestered in his room.

352

Pulling two chairs up to a small table, he showed Farnham a rough draft of the story he had toyed with late the night before.

"Sounds like this Marshal Taggart is a real bastard."

"And that's just the half of it. I have a gut feeling he's involved in more sins than Satan himself."

"Hmm. Could be. Could be." Taking out a second cigar to replace the one that was now just a stub, Farnham puffed on it as he put his feet up on the table. "And if so, then I'm just the one who can help you find out. I'll get started looking into his background this very day. You know me, I won't leave even a pebble unturned."

"I know you, Farnham. If Taggart has even one secret you'll find it out." That reminded Travis that he'd done a little looking into things himself. He pulled out the article. "He looks different now. Older. And he has a mustache. But the eyes. The nose. The slightly crooked slant to the mouth are very recognizable. The artist has captured his image as well as any camera. Damn, Farnham, I have the feeling I've seen him before. Could it be?"

Farnham Tabor looked carefully at the clipping. "It could. I've got the same feeling myself." Taking out a magnifying glass, Farnham was quiet for a long, long time as he stared. Suddenly he clicked his fingers. "I have it. I know who he is."

"Who?" Travis leaned over. Taking the magnifying glass from Farnham, he took another look.

"He's a man who served time in a Boston jail for larceny and worse. An escapee." Farnham's eyebrows formed a perfect V. "A Chicago newspaper carried the story when he skipped town. How could you forget? It happened right before you left the *Rocky Mountain News*. We even talked about it. Printed a story on it ourselves. It's no wonder this likeness gave you a start, Travis."

"Daniel Quentin Plummer." It came back to Travis in a surging tide of remembrance. "Taggart. Taggart is Plummer." Travis grinned. The future looked rosy after all. They had him. Taggart didn't know it yet, but his days were numbered.

Chapter Thirty-Six

Meticulously Bliss smoothed out the blanket atop the thin jail cot; then with an indignant huff, she sprawled out on her back, resting her head on her folded arms. "Well, I never thought I'd end up here," she said to herself.

It was the greatest of ironies. She might have laughed, but she was just too damned angry at the whole situation and the way she was being treated. Like some desperado. Of course, that might be because she had given Tom Barlow and his men a hard time all along the way.

Hellcat was what Barlow had called her when she'd scratched his face in retaliation for his unwarranted advances. Pulling out his gun, he had threatened to shoot her, but something—she supposed it was Taggart's orders—had kept him under control. Alive she was useful, dead she wasn't worth hay. Barlow knew that, so although he had blustered and tried to frighten her, he had been relatively harmless. Bliss had the feeling that she was safe, at least for the time being. Safe because she knew where Travis was and Marshal Taggart knew she did and was obsessed with getting the information.

The moment she had arrived in Watersville the marshal had plied her with dozens of questions. She had retorted with caustic remarks and quips. Would she tell Taggart where Travis was? Not on your life. She had more loyalty than that. She was willing to face anything to make certain that Travis was safe. Anything!

"Hell, what can they do?"

She knew they wouldn't dare hang her. When that had been done to a female cattle rustler just last year, it put the territory in such turmoil that it took months for the furor to die down. No, all they could do was threaten her. They already had as a matter of fact. She had merely laughed in their faces, telling them point-blank that she wasn't afraid. Knowing what a weasel Taggart was, however, she couldn't believe she'd seen the end of him. He just wasn't the type to let bygones be bygones.

"Oh, damn! I wish I could get out of here." She wanted to be with Travis. He'd be worried when she didn't show up at the International Hotel. He had enough things on his mind without fretting about her fate. Was there any escape?

There was if she could find a way to get out of her cell. The hole she and the blacksmith had blown in the jail's wall had been hastily patched, and she knew as she glanced in that direction that it was a botched-up job. There were cracks almost large enough to stick your head through and if she had a spoon, a fork or a knife perhaps . . .

The slamming of the connecting door startled her. She looked up to see Tom Barlow pushing his way inside, taking his turn at guard. His flashing eyes oozed hostility.

"Hello, bitch! I came to look in on you. Thought you might just be lonely."

Bitch! Bliss bristled, thinking of a few choice words she could call him. Words that weren't in the least polite. "Yeah, well I could never be lonely enough to want your company." Knowing that he was spoiling for an argument, she tried her best to ignore him and was successful until he brought up the subject of her dogs. She had a real soft spot for Bard and Boru.

"Got your mutts locked up too. Real nice and tight." Seeing her stiffen and knowing he had hit a nerve, he continued. "The marshal confiscated them."

"Stole them, you mean." Oh, that was loathsome, taking out their anger at her on two innocent animals. Trouble was, she didn't know just how low these bastards would stoop. She was soon to find out. "What do you intend to do with them?"

"Do with them?"

"You heard me." A gut feeling told her that the wolfhounds' future wasn't very secure at the moment. Right from the first Tom Barlow had shown his hatred of her dogs. Bard's and Boru's feelings had been mutual. Now he had his chance to harm them.

"Do with them." He leaned against the bars. "Well now, there's several choices. They could be shot."

"Shot!" The very thought of those noble animals

357

being struck by bullets made Bliss sick at heart.

"Or maybe we'll give them to the Orientals. Hear they rather favor dog meat."

"You wouldn't."

"It all depends."

"On what?" She could imagine. If she told them where Travis was and played their little game, then she'd be let out of jail, reunited with her wolfhounds and supposedly everyone would be happy. Wrong. Even to save her wolfhounds' lives she couldn't betray Travis.

"On your being cooperative."

"Cooperative." Pulling herself up into a sitting position, she crossed her legs. "Oh, I'm willing to be cooperative. I can be a model prisoner. Just as polite as I can be."

"Where's La Mont?"

She smiled. "Last time I saw him he was headed south to Virginia City."

"South?"

"Uh-huh!" And pigs could fly.

"You're lying. You answered too quickly." He pressed his face so hard against the bars it became contorted.

Bliss crossed her fingers behind her back. "That's because it's the truth. He went South." She could only hope that Barlow would believe her. It would buy Travis some extra time.

"We'll soon see." Going to the door, he shouted out instructions to form a posse to scour the area around Virginia City. To Bliss's dismay, however, he also sent a party of men north.

"Just in case you're trying to throw us off the

track." His expression told her that he thought that was exactly what she was doing.

"He's headed to Virginia City. We had a quarrel. That's why we split up." She tried hard to act nonchalant about the whole thing. "You'll find out I'm telling the truth, then maybe you'll let me out of here."

"Maybe." Something in his eyes told Bliss she wasn't as secure as she had first thought. Bard and Boru weren't the only ones in danger of their lives. Barlow was a killer who enjoyed his profession. Woman or not, she sensed she was in the gravest danger. It was only a matter of time. She had to get out of there.

Taggart sat with his feet propped up on his desk. He leaned forward as Barlow walked through the door. "Well . . . ? Did our canary sing?"

Barlow's expression answered him.

"No? Didn't your threat about the dogs frighten her?"

"Yeah, only she didn't react the way I thought. Instead she outright lied to me. Said La Mont went to Virginia City."

"Virginia City?" Taggart wasn't fooled by that. "Bull shit!"

"Said it blatantly. Cool as you please." Tom Barlow took out his anger on an inanimate object, a chair that just happened to be in his way. "I tell you that ain't no woman like any I've ever known. She's much too sure of herself. There's no softness about her. Tough as hard tack, that one."

"Don't be fooled. They're all the same!" Taggart thought about the arguments he'd had with Josephine. In the end she always gave in to him. "Pliable creatures that just love to be tamed."

"Yeah, well you just try. The only way I can see to loosen her tongue is take a bullwhip to her and beat the truth out of her!" As if he held one in his hands, Barlow slashed and struck out at the empty air. "Turn me loose on her. Just for an hour . . ."

Taggart shook his head. "Not yet. I want to try another strategy." He enjoyed playing games, matching wills and fortitude. Bliss Harrison suddenly seemed to be a most worthy opponent. Barlow was too physical, too bullying. Taggart intended to use another approach.

"And if that doesn't work?"

Taggart's jaw tensed. A bargain was a bargain. "I'll give her to you. For as long as you want her. To do with as you choose." Shaking hands on it, they formulated a gentlemen's agreement.

Chapter Thirty-Seven

It was great to be back in the newspaper business, Travis thought as he watched the printer apply ink to the type with a roller. He loved the sense of anticipation that crackled in the air, the smell of paper and ink, the clanking sound of the Washington Hand Press as the blank sheets of paper became newsprint. It made him feel invigorated. Useful. Alive! Powerful.

"Well, roll up your sleeves and let's get to work." Jim Erickson, the editor of the *Helena Herald* took off his coat and tie and did just that, keeping his white linen sleeves in place with elastic. He handed Travis and Farnham Tabor large aprons, then with both arms moving up and down like pump handles, he gave instructions to his staff to turn Travis' scribbling into print, into an article that was sure to raise more than just a few brows.

"I think Taggart is in for one big surprise," Farnham exclaimed, punctuating his sentence with a large puff of smoke.

"His game is up," Travis said with exultation. Jim Erickson wanted not just one article but several. An article a week. It was his plan to expose Taggart and his operation bit by bit, story by story, knowing it to be a way to increase his readership. Travis' paper back East would do the same, as would Tabor's.

This time Travis was letting it be known that Taggart was skimming money from the top. Dipping into the profits of saloons, gambling houses and other businesses, and even peddling laudanum to the houses of prostitution. His "boys" were terrorizing businessmen in and around Silver Bow and Watersville. Taggart was getting protection money for leaving them alone. A trick he learned somewhere back East, Travis supposed. Chicago more than likely.

Even the town undertaker was involved in Taggart's schemes. When it was discovered that he was stealing gold fillings from the teeth of the corpses, he would probably be driven out of town and tarred and feathered, Travis thought. Well, it served him right.

It was all a matter of timing in the newspaper business. A little slip here. A little slip there. This article would be a start. Later he would point out that Taggart was having financial problems and taking it out on innocent people. Farnham hoped that some of the townspeople would be brave enough to come forward with their stories. Next would come an article accompanied by the photograph, irrefutable proof of Taggart's perfidy. Lastly would come the article exploiting the use of Taggart's real name and exposing his true identity. If that didn't make the *Helena Herald* some money, then Travis didn't know what would.

"We'll let ole Travis here initiate. You get the honor of printing the first sheet." Farnham gave Travis a nudge toward the press. "'Course, now with these newfangled presses, this journalistic game is easy. Why, I remember a time on the frontier when our office was a tent. We had no presses and had to hand out handwritten copies. A powerful lot of writing. Twenty copies. That's all there was in circulation. Hell, a man would starve if he didn't make a better profit now."

Excitement surged within Travis as he joined in on the actual printing. He placed the sheet of paper on the hinged tympan and then slid the bed bearing the form into position beneath the cloth-covered platen. By pulling the lever, he caused the plate to press the paper against the type and produce an impression. A system of toggles kept the platen from moving and smudging the print when the bar's leverage forced it downward.

"There!" Taking the paper off the tympan he was careful not to ruin the ink. "The emblem looks great. A mountain scene. Mine is a front page story, eh." He read it carefully. Satisfied with its content, he handed it to Erickson.

"You're certain of all the facts." Having been a lawyer before going into the newspaper business, Erickson was always cautious.

Travis nodded. He had found out that all the territorial and monetary records had been moved in 1875 and were stored right here in Helena. It didn't take much to ferret out what Taggart had been doing if a man resorted to a simple matter of addition, multiplication and subtraction.

Taking into account Taggart's salary as marshal, minus his expenditures and the value of his properties and goods, he would have come out severely in the red. That he did not meant only one thing. Even so, Travis was wise enough to know you just can't call a man a thief unless you can prove that he is one. Thus, with the help of Farnham, he had employed a spy to do some nosing around in Watersville and Silver Bow. What the spy had come up with had proved him to be worth his weight in silver.

Erickson read the article carefully, then handed it to Farnham who had already sent the story on to Denver and his own newspaper. "When that son-of-a-bitch of a marshal reads this he'll pee his pants," Farnham snorted. Then he grew serious. "Of course, you know that once Taggart gets wind of this he'll know right where you are." Farnham looked worried.

"I don't care." Now that the truth was coming out Travis felt invincible. What could they do to him now that he had friends on his side? Incarcerate him? He would welcome the chance at a new trial. One that wasn't fixed.

The new courthouse was nearing completion. He might as well break it in. Besides, he would never be found in Helena if he decided to hide. The city was even larger than Butte, and the wealthy and educated who lived here wouldn't put up with Taggart's nonsense.

"Nevertheless, my boy, you need to use caution."

Farnham put a hand on his protégé's arm. "That wayward marshal didn't put together a crooked empire by being leery of killing. He's ruthless. Knowingly intending to hang an innocent man is proof of that. If I were you I wouldn't tangle with him. He'll play dirty if he gets riled enough."

"Let him." Travis was in a mood for a standoff. Bliss's example he supposed. He'd learned that when you lived in the West and came in contact with the lawless, you had to play by their rules. Well, if this was a game of poker he'd just placed his first bet, knowing all the while that having that photograph gave him an ace up his sleeve.

Chapter Thirty-Eight

It was Saturday night, a time for hooting and hollering as the townsmen kicked up their heels and celebrated the week's end by drinking and raising hell. Gunfire snapped and popped. The tromping of boots was as loud as a stampede. Music from the saloons blended in a discordant jumble. Boasting talk, laughing and chattering drifted through the jail window. Sitting on the small cot with her legs drawn up to her chest and her head resting on her knees, Bliss listened to the revelers.

"Have a nice time, boys," she mumbled irritably. Someone should be enjoying themselves. She certainly wasn't. Being locked up was getting to her, helplessness not being a feeling she enjoyed. Still she had to admit that the merriment kept Taggart's wolf pack at bay. It seemed only the little man named Ellis Jones didn't participate in the rowdiness. He had been left to guard her.

"How come you're in here? Did you draw the short straw or something?" Bliss quipped sarcastically, only to regret her huffiness. Her being here wasn't his fault.

"The boss gave me orders, that's why," he said proudly as he made his rounds. "Told me I should watch you."

"Watch me do what?"

The little man's eyes opened as wide as saucers. "Says you're dangerous."

That made Bliss laugh. How could she be when Taggart had clipped her wings so effectively? Still, she thought she'd have a little fun. "Oh, I'm dangerous all right. See my red hair. I'm a witch." Well, at least that rhymed with what Barlow and Taggart called her.

"A witch?" Jumping back, the little man made it obvious that he believed her.

"Yes, a witch. And I'll cast a spell on you if you don't behave." Playfully Bliss raised both arms as if beginning an incantation. It was enough to send her pint-sized guard scrambling for the door. Now perhaps she'd have a little peace. Tom Barlow, Jake Heath and the others had been hounding her unmercifully, trying to force her to tell them where Travis was, as if she'd spill the beans. Wild horses couldn't drag the information out of her. She might have her faults but she was loyal.

Resuming her position on the cot, Bliss closed her eyes, trying to fight the wave of depression that was threatening to crash over her. What if Barlow, Heath and the others meant to carry out their threats? What if she never saw Travis again? What if she just up and disappeared?

The door that connected the cells to the marshal's

office creaked open. Thinking it to be one of Taggart's henchmen, Bliss didn't even bother to turn around, but just said, "Leave me alone. I haven't anything more to say. Travis went south to Virginia City. Believe me or go to the devil!"

Her outbursts usually brought retribution, but it was strangely quiet. Looking up, Bliss saw to her surprise that it wasn't one of Taggart's men who stood before her but a woman so lovely she reminded Bliss of an angel.

"Hello." The voice was soft and soothing.

"Who are you?" One of the townswomen come to assuage their curiosity, she thought bitterly. She knew just how disheveled she was. Her hair was a tangled mass that fell into her eyes, there were smudges on her face, her clothes were dirty and her boots were scuffed from riding all over the country-side. She was hardly one to inspire awe, yet the woman was staring.

"My name is Josephine," the woman said with a courteous smile.

"Josephine?" Bliss was hardly in a mood to be social or to be stared at as if she were an oddity. "Come to take a look at the marshal's sideshow? Well, let me tell you lady I don't want to be on display."

"I'm sorry. I guess I deserved that, but please don't misunderstand. I don't think of you as a sideshow at all, only as a very interesting woman. One I've wanted to meet for some time."

"Really?" Bliss had always been suspicious of women like this one. Ladies usually turned up their noses at her way of dressing and manner of speech.

Yet, perhaps because she was tired or in need of a little company or longing for a sympathetic ear, she didn't try to get rid of this one.

"My father was a rancher. Even so, I've lived a quite ordinary life, afraid to do anything unusual."

Quickly Bliss's visitor told her about herself, about how she had always wanted to be like her Eastern mother, separating herself from her surroundings, contenting herself by traveling and buying pretty things. Lately, however, her way of life was becoming boring. Ever since she had heard about Bliss's adventures she had been determined to learn more about her and perhaps live a more adventuresome life vicariously.

"A woman such as yourself who has the strength of will and daring to do just as she pleases fascinates me." Josephine's slim-fingered hand traveled to her throat. "What would it be like to ride horseback instead of traveling about in carriages, to wear pants instead of skirts, to capture a man like Travis La Mont and spend so much time alone with him?"

"Heaven. Pure heaven," Bliss said dreamily, remembering.

Josephine was enthralled. "You weren't afraid of him?"

"Not at all. Unlike some men I've met he was honorable and decent. Not a killer. Not a robber. That's why I helped him." Why not admit it? She couldn't be in any more trouble than she was already. "I brought him in, so I figured it was up to me to let him go, seeing as how I was certain he was innocent."

"Yes, I heard all about it." The woman smiled.

"You captured him, though he gave the posse a terrible time. Imagine. A woman with the courage to be a bounty hunter."

"Yeah, a bounty hunter. The very thought of it must shock you all the way down to your proper little toes." Bliss could recognize "that look" in the woman's eyes. "Well, take a good gander and then get going."

"Oh, no!" Trying to placate Bliss's ire, the woman explained that she had recently met a few old-timers, who had told her about the early days in and around Silver Bow and Watersville, and she could now see that she had taken things too much for granted. Although she had done some philanthropic work occasionally, such as giving money to schools, churches and so forth, and had always been generous and benevolent in attitude, she needed something more in her life. "Perhaps you can be the key."

Throwing back her head, Bliss laughed. "Well, I could take you under my wing, train you in my profession." The very thought of this pristine, dainty woman becoming a bounty hunter was hilarious. "Of course now, I have to tell you that all that traipsing around might soil your gloves and shoes, and everything else in between."

"I don't think I'd care."

"Oh, I think you would. It even gets to me sometimes." Cradling her face with her hands, Bliss sobered. "Besides, just look where my daring got me. Prisoner of one of the most ruthless marshal's this side of the territorial boundary."

"Ruthless? Sam?"

"Yes, Sam!" Ignoring the woman's horrified look, Bliss rambled on. "Well, if you're thinking to mimic my adventuresome spirit, lady, I'll give you some good advice. Don't! It will only lead you into trouble. Just as it did me." Bliss looked earnestly at the beautiful young woman. "Truth is, my life is in danger here."

"No!"

Bliss shook her head vigorously. "It is." The thought that maybe this woman could be persuaded to help her gave Bliss the incentive to say, "You've lived in Montana for a long, long time. You must know then that the marshal of Silver Bow and Watersville is a scoundrel."

"He is not!" With an outraged gasp, Josephine Taggart defended her husband's reputation. "Sam is a decent man, as law abiding as the day is long. This town would be lost without him."

"Lost?" Bliss stood up so that she could look the woman in the eye. "Without him it would be a whole lot richer and healthier, I'd say. Truth is, lady, the marshal here is as crooked as a wolf's hind leg. Surely you must know. Why, he was even going to hang an innocent man just to save his own skin."

Showing far more spirit than her appearance suggested, Josephine Taggart bounded over to the bars like an enraged lioness. "How dare you! No wonder Sam warned me to stay away from you!"

Bliss raised her brows. "I can well imagine. Afraid you might find out the truth I'd say."

"The truth?" Haughtily raising her chin Josephine was adamant. "There has been a lot of blood spilled and many crimes have been committed but now the

371

territory has become more peaceful. It's become a civilized center in the Montana Territory since my husband has become marshal," she exclaimed.

"Your husband?" It was a startling revelation. "Josephine Taggart." Coming face to face with Taggart's missus made the hairs on the back of Bliss's neck stand on end. "Why of all the lowdown dirty . . ." So that was it. Get the little woman to come in here and make friends. A little woman-to-woman talk to loosen her tongue. "Well, I can tell you, lady. It just won't work. You can tell Taggart that for me. I won't tell anyone, especially him or you, where Travis is." Belligerently Bliss crossed her arms.

Josephine Taggart opened her mouth to reply, but the sound of the door opening quickly burst her bubble of bravado. Bliss watched in surprise as the young woman hid in the shadows behind the alcove, taking refuge behind the wooden door as it was flung open. It seemed she didn't want to be found there. Interesting.

"Well, well, well, if it isn't Marshal Taggart," Bliss said in greeting, all the while wondering if it was possible that the woman really didn't know of her husband's misdeeds. If that was the case she'd just have to find a way to make him incriminate himself.

"I thought I'd check in on you to see if you were comfortable." Like a mongoose charming a cobra Taggart was the epitome of consideration.

"Comfortable?" The very idea was ludicrous. What kind of game was being played now. "To come quite to the point, no."

"Too bad." Taggart held up the keys, allowing them to jingle temptingly. "Well, perhaps I can help you."

"Sure, if you'd like to try." Bliss licked her lips, and then said slowly. "For starters I'd like a feather mattress, some curtains at the window, a table cloth and a change of menu. How's that?"

Taggart chuckled. "Obviously you don't take me seriously, but I assure you, Miss Harrison, I am in deadly earnest."

"Deadly." Forming her fingers into a mock gun she pretended to fire. "Deadly. Now that's a key word."

Ignoring her, Taggart talked on. "Believe me. I am prepared to be benevolent if we can only come to an understanding. Tell me where Travis La Mont is."

"Understanding." Knowing that his wife was cloistered in the shadows Bliss decided to toy with him, arguing as usual. "All right, if you are serious, come to the point." A smile trembled on Bliss's lips. "Seems to me you could make it worth my while to give you the information you need."

"Money, is that what you want?" Taggart seemed reluctant to make any promises, but when Bliss seemed responsive he said, "All right, how much?" When she didn't answer he offered, "How about a cut?"

"A cut? Of what?" Bliss held her breath, hoping against hope that he would say something, anything to prove his guilt before he noticed his wife standing there.

"One percent of what I skim off the top in the

gambling halls," he hissed. "For a period of one year."

"Not enough!" Bliss's eyes darted to where Josephine Taggart was hiding, but not wanting to give her away, she quickly looked back at Taggart. She positioned herself so that when he looked at her he was looking in the opposite direction from where Josephine was hiding. "Try again."

"And one percent of the bawdy houses as well." His look of anger clearly told her that he knew she had him. He seemed prepared to do anything to get his hands on Travis.

"Gambling halls. Bawdy houses," she said loudly, just in case the man's wife hadn't heard. "What else do you have your greedy little hands into? Banks? I wouldn't be the least bit surprised." Taggart bristled, but didn't lose his temper. He was as cool as a cucumber, Bliss thought.

"I also get a percentage of the merchant's profits here and in the surrounding towns." His voice quieted to a near whisper. "A little insurance you might say, so they don't have any injuries, fires or unwelcome callers. I'll let you in on some of that too. Just tell me exactly where Travis La Mont went. I want to know the town. And don't say Virginia City, because I know that to be a damned lie! Tell me."

And as soon as I do I'm dead, Bliss thought. "Now, Marshal, don't be hasty." She didn't trust Taggart for a minute. He wouldn't want to give her a penny. "Let me think on your proposition for a while."

"A while?" He was incensed. "Well, don't think too long!" He stood watching her, tapping his foot, as if he expected her to ponder the matter, then come to a decision.

"I said, I'd think about it." Her eyes sparked fire, warning that she meant every word. She had to put him off for as long as she could in order to insure Travis' well-being as well as her own.

Taggart stood looking at her so fiercely she expected him to growl, but he didn't say a word, that is, until one of his deputies barged in waving a piece of paper in his hands. "What do you want, Withers? I thought I told you not to come in here."

"You did, but that was before the *Helena Herald* floated into town." Thrusting the newspaper into Taggart's hands, he stepped back, so busy looking at the marshal that he didn't even notice the fourth person in the room. "You'd better take a peek."

Shivers ran up and down Bliss's spine. He'd done it. Travis had printed his article. She felt proud and apprehensive at the same time. Just what did that mean for her? Looking toward Taggart, she watched the expression that played upon his face. He was damned mad.

"La Mont is in Helena!" Crumpling the newssheet up, he threw it on the ground. "Well, he'll pay for this. I'll make him sorry he was ever born." He looked like a rattlesnake about to strike. "And I'll make you regret that you ever tried to make a fool out of me. Barlow wants you. He can have you!" he said to Bliss. He stormed through the entranceway. "Come on, Withers, we've got to get the boys together." The door was slammed behind him with a resounding bang.

Bliss waited until he was gone before she spoke.

"You see, I didn't lie, Mrs. Taggart. Your husband isn't the hero you think him." She clung to the bars. "Please. You heard for yourself what kind of man he is. I'm in danger here."

Like a sleepwalker, Josephine Taggart slowly bent down and picked up the wrinkled newspaper and put it into her pocket, but she didn't say a word.

"Please help me."

"Help you?" In her eyes Bliss saw a flicker of compassion mingled with great sorrow, but no help came. Picking up her skirts, Josephine Taggart went out the door, leaving Bliss all alone.

Chapter Thirty-Nine

As usual Travis' first thought upon awakening was of Bliss. Where in hell was she? She'd had time to ride to Butte and then to Helena more than a couple of times. He had thought for sure that she would have arrived by now. He was worried. Restless. Last night he had tossed and turned, besieged with troubling dreams. Bliss had become so important to him that the thought of anything happening to her was like a knife wound, twisting and tearing at his insides. Still, there was little he could do. He didn't even know where she was, so he couldn't go after her. All he could do was sit tight, try to be patient and hope she would eventually show up at the International Hotel.

"She has to," he said aloud, forcing himself to calm down. "She will!" One thing he knew for sure, she could take care of herself. She was spunky, smart and brave. During their time on the run *he* had been dependent on *her*. That thought put his mind at ease, at least for the time being. Meanwhile he had an appointment this morning with Farnham.

Getting back to the business at hand, Travis slowly rose from the bed, dressed and started out the door to meet the editor of the *Rocky Mountain News*. They had decided to join up downstairs in the hotel's restaurant for breakfast. Work not pleasure. Even though the first article was barely off the press, they had already finished the second and had given it to Erickson and were at work on the third. The first article had been a success, and that meant there would be a fourth and a fifth. "Milking the story for all that it's worth," Farnham had said.

Grabbing the folded newspaper by his door, Travis sought out the headlines as he reflected on his masterpiece. Scanning the front page article in the Friday edition of the *Helena Herald*, he nodded his head. Couldn't have been done any better, he thought, even if he did say so himself. When Marshal Taggart read it, and he would eventually, he'd know his name was mud.

Travis found that he was becoming famous due to the story. Some folks even pointed him out as a celebrity. A wanted man with the grit to meet his adversary head-on. That kind of courage was respected in Helena. And little by little, people of influence were flocking to his banner, vowing to help him in his fight to right a serious wrong.

"I've come a long way in the newspaper business," he mumbled. The eagerness of his youth had been fulfilled, at least partially. His name was being bandied about, with respect. It was a far cry from being on a wanted poster. Would he enjoy his newfound fame? He doubted it. It seemed to put him

378

under a magnifying glass. He found himself longing to see a pair of huge blue eyes framed by bright red hair, of running away with her again. He had to admit that his days on the run with Bliss had been strangely exciting. Lovemaking and danger had gone hand in hand, had exhilarated him, made him feel alive.

"Well, Travis." As he entered the dining hall Farnham was all smiles, though he did look at his ornate pocketwatch as if to chastise. He had a carafe of coffee, a cup and saucer all ready for Travis. "Seems everyone in the hotel has read the first installment," he said, pouring some of the steaming coffee into Travis' cup.

"Seems so." Travis measured out half a teaspoon of sugar. "Even Taggart himself has undoubtedly seen it."

"It would seem so. News travels."

"Wonder what he'll do?" Travis didn't realize it, but he was stirring his coffee with his spoon over and over again. At last he took a cautious sip.

"It's hot. Just like our news." Taking a deep breath, Farnham blew on his coffee to cool it. "Seems it will no longer be necessary for you to be so secluded, in hiding so to speak. I've got a judge, three councilmen and the mayor on your side." His eyes glistened with laughter. Another smile crossed his face. "The worm has turned and Taggart will soon be the one on the run."

"Perhaps now I will become a hero and not the goat, that is, if a new marshal can be found who can run those towns without threats and bloodshed." Travis felt on top of the world, proud of himself.

"Why, who knows, maybe I can take a little vacation soon." A honeymoon with Bliss if he had his way.

"Vacation?" Farnham was horrified. "You've just begun."

Travis chuckled. "So let's get on with it." By the time the editorial exposing Taggart and some of his deputies finally appeared, Travis was certain that those of Taggart's "boys" who were seated on the Silver Bow town council wouldn't be anymore. Travis knew people would be up in arms. A movement to recall Taggart's "boys" had already been started in Helena, he had heard.

In between bites of steak and egg the third article took shape. By the fourth cup of coffee the rough draft was done. "So, that's it, at least for the moment."

Both Travis and Farnham had worked long and hard. Each felt the need for a little rest and relaxation. They had spent several hours mulling over old newspapers in the dark damp basement of the library building. Farnham complained that he had hardly had the chance to see Helena.

"Then by all means let's view it."

Leaving the restaurant, they walked up Main Street. "You're walking up Last Chance Gulch you know. Here's where some men took a chance and reaped a real bonanza," Travis said.

"Yes, I know that, but we've struck a bonanza of sorts ourselves in releasing that story." Farnham paused a moment to catch his breath, then started up again. Being a lover of beauty and elegant objects, it was his desire to see the architecture of the city. "Helena's growth is a continuous process, or so it

380

seems by looking at the various stages of building. Reminds me of Denver, you know."

Travis thought some of the houses were really quite beautiful. The miners certainly liked ornate design. Visible proof of their success. "There's an iron deer on the lawn over there and stone lions at the tops of those steps," he said, pointing.

"Looks a little different than when I was here last time, eating beans and sourdough." Farnham's eyes took on a faraway look that clearly said he was reminiscing. "I remember when the weekly *Herald* was first issued. It was on November fifteenth of eighteen sixty-six. I was here at that time. The first issue was on brown manilla paper sent all the way from Salt Lake City. It became a daily the next year. The residents of Helena have always had a nose for news."

"Be that as it may, perhaps we should get away from the news for a while. How about going up fishing?" Travis suggested. "We can rent a wagon or ride horses up those mountains. I've found that getting away once in a while helps to clear my head."

"Fishing?" Farnham thought about it. "Why not? And while we're relaxing we can work on a story of Helena's early days, a tie-in to your story. Why we could do a story a week and . . ." His voice droned on as he outlined his ideas, eliciting Travis' laughter.

After renting horses at the livery stable, they traveled about three miles and finally came upon an ideal spot. Hitching the horses to a nearby tree, they climbed up a slight incline to a bubbling creek. They made fishing poles for themselves with branches and string, and sat by a slow-running stream bowered by willow trees and some large cottonwoods. Travis and Farnham sat there for a long time saying nothing, just looking out at the white-tailed deer and watching the birds fly from branch to branch. If a man could find peace anywhere it was here.

"So what's she like, this new woman of yours?" Farnham's tone of voice seemed to hint that he thought this another passing fancy. "Pretty to be sure, and from what you have said spirited."

"She's intelligent, unpredictable and as fiery as her hair, yet with a soft, vulnerable side. A rainbow wrapped up in a firecracker is how I'd best describe her. A woman unlike any I've ever known before. One of a kind, Farnham." Feeling a tug on his pole, Travis pulled the line in only to find a boot at the other end. It seemed to exemplify his love life up until now. "This time what I feel is real."

Farnham was doubtful. "I remember when you said that before. The mayor's daughter as I recall."

"A woman I can't quite remember now. Bliss is the type of woman I could never forget. Once you meet her, you'll understand."

"A female bounty hunter." The wheels in Farnham's brain were turning. "Might be interesting to do a story on her. Why, with the right managing she could become a legend. Like Calamity Jane."

"No!" Travis felt protective. Possessive.

"No?" Seeing the look in Travis' eyes, Farnham quickly dropped the subject, trying to talk Travis into coming back to the *Rocky Mountain News* instead.

They really didn't have much luck fishing. But they had not cared that much about catching fish anyway. The whole idea had just been to leave their cares behind for a little while. As a red glow began to appear on the horizon the two men reluctantly left their utopia and headed back to town. Arriving in Helena, Travis stopped by the railroad station to pick up any messages he might have received. Because of the danger of being located, he had requested that any telegrams should be held at the train station telegraph office, where he would call for them in person. He understandably didn't want anyone to know the location of his hotel or anything about his living arrangements.

There were two messages waiting. Travis smiled as he read Howard Vickery's congratulatory telegram. "He wants more of the same, Farnham." He turned to the other message.

"Another felicitation, Travis?"

Travis' eyes held the look of a madman. "No! No!" He felt hot. Cold. His hands started trembling. "They've got Bliss," he choked out. "That damned devil can't do it, I won't let him." Suddenly Travis lost control as his worst fears were realized.

Farnham had to restrain him. When he had managed to calm him down a bit, he took the telegram and read the bold black letters.

WE ARE HOLDING BLISS HARRISON IN THE WATERSVILLE JAIL STOP IF YOU DO NOT GIVE YOURSELF UP WITHIN THE NEXT TWO DAYS SHE WILL BE TAKEN TO A DESTINATION UNKNOWN TO ANYONE OTHER THAN THE MAR-SHAL OF SILVER BOW AND WATERS-

VILLE STOP PERHAPS HER FATE WILL
BE EVEN MORE SERIOUS STOP MUCH
DEPENDS UPON WHAT ACTION YOU
TAKE IN DISCONTINUING THE RE-
LEASE OF YOUR DAMAGING NEWS-
PAPER STORIES AND IN PUBLICALLY
ADMITTING THEM TO BE A LIE STOP

Chapter Forty

It was dark in the jail cell except for the flickering light of one lone lantern at the end of the hall. The only sound was Boyd Withers' loud snoring. "My watchdog," Bliss whispered, thinking of him as Taggart's spaniel. Well, at least he was perferable to Barlow or Heath.

Sitting on her cot, Bliss stared into the lantern's flames. What was Taggart going to do with her now? Just what had he meant by saying if Barlow wanted her he could have her? Surely not what she feared. Barlow was an animal. Unprincipled. Violent. Cruel. To be at his mercy would be like being at a snake's.

"Taggart's anger talking, nothing more." For all his misdeeds Taggart was still a marshal. Surely he could be held accountable if something terrible happened to her or if she just up and disappeared. Taggart was angry with Travis, but there must be some limits on what he could do to retaliate, or so she hoped. If only she hadn't been caught . . .

Strange how one's whole life could enfold before one's eyes, perhaps because in solitude there was little to do but think. Her moments with Travis seemed all the more precious now. His passion, his caring, his gentleness. The way he tried to understand her even when she didn't fully understand herself. Their turbulent bickering in the first moments they'd been together made her smile. They had both met their match, it was as simple as that. She'd done just about everything she could to make him think she was strong, yet somehow he had sensed her vulnerability. Travis had taught her that being a female wasn't so bad after all, that it could be wonderful. For him she'd wanted to be all woman.

With her father it had been different, she realized now. Though he had never meant to hurt her, he had let it be known in many ways that he had wanted a son and not a daughter. A chip off the old block, he had laughingly called her; not a girl who wore frilly things and screamed at bugs and snakes. She had tried so hard to fill his shoes that she had nearly lost her own identity. Until Travis came along. He had made her feel appreciated, made her satisfied with who and what she was. Life just couldn't be so unfair that they wouldn't get back together. She refused to believe she'd never see Travis again.

"And when I do—"

Bliss's words were drowned out by the loud, violent thump of a slamming door. She looked up with a start as Tom Barlow stormed in. The way he swayed on his feet was proof that he had been drinking. "You. Withers. Get the hell out."

"What?" Withers sat up, scratching his ear and

trying to focus his eyes as he attempted to wake up.

"I said get out." If the devil had a twin it was Tom Barlow at that moment.

"For chrissakes, Tom, what the damned nuisance are you doing here? It's not your turn at guard until tomorrow morning."

"I'm not here to act as guard." Growing impatient, Barlow walked to the other man, picked him up by his arms and heaved him toward the connecting door. "Taggart said she's mine, and I intend to stake my claim."

"You mean . . . ?" Withers' mouth dropped open.

"You got it! Now get going." Withers did, without looking back or asking any more questions.

Bliss's heart thundered so loudly she was certain Barlow could hear the pounding. Her worst nightmare was about to become reality. Still, she refused to cower. Sometimes the only way to counteract a bully was to show strength.

"Well, well, well." He was cocky as he opened the cell door. That he locked it behind him was an ominous sign. "You've been asking for this for a long time."

Bliss took a step backward, careful not to trap herself in the corner of the cell. "Keep away from me." There had to be something she could use as a weapon. Anything.

"Keep away," he mocked, smirking as he strode forward. "Keep away, hell! I want what's between your legs."

She was angered by his crudity. "Never!" Bliss had nearly been raped once before and knew firsthand the feeling of degradation. She would never let

387

herself feel like a victim again. Bending down, she picked up a three-legged stool and raised it up to use as a weapon.

"That's right—fight. I like my women rough. Makes it all the more satisfying to force them into submission. And I will."

Like a stalking lion, he pounced, but Bliss forcefully pushed him back. What followed was a grotesque pantomime of a dance. He stepped forward, she stepped back, he stepped sideways, she moved to avert him; he lunged, she held him off. Over and over again the pattern was repeated as each tried to tire the other out. And all the while Bliss could think only of how much she wished she could run off. But Barlow had seen to that.

"I'll never let you touch me." She couldn't. If he did she would never feel clean again.

"Let me?" Barlow's eyes glinted with a spark that turned Bliss's blood to ice water. "I wouldn't want you to. The struggle makes it all the more fun." He laughed, emboldened by the refusal. It seemed the desire to hurt was even stronger than his lust.

Bliss wildly struck out with the stool, hitting him on the shoulder, on the thigh, on the leg. Bravely she held her own until he tripped her. Stumbling, she regained her balance before she fell, but in her brief moment of awkwardness he reached out and yanked the stool from her grip. Hurling it against the wall, he broke it into pieces.

"Now I've got you where I want you." Barlow was upon her in an instant, his hands gripping her shoulders, words that were unfit for any decent woman's ears coming out of his mouth. They were descriptions of what he intended to do to her. Bringing one knee up, she intended to aim a blow at his manhood, but he moved aside and rendered her assault harmless.

"Do that again and I will make you regret it," he threatened. Bliss had little doubt but that he would carry out his threat.

His hands seemed to be everywhere, bruising and burning. Bliss's shirt was torn from her shoulder, and she cringed in revulsion as she felt his fingers on her naked breast. He was going to rape her and there was nothing she could do to stop him! Bile rose in her throat as she smelled his alcohol-fouled breath. He had her, but she wasn't about to give up. Biting and scratching, she fought like a wildcat.

"Taggart doesn't know what he's missing! He was more generous than he could ever know in giving you to me." Pinioning her arms above her head, Barlow fumbled at the fastenings of his pants. "Go on. Fight. There's nobody here to help you."

"On the contrary." Josephine Taggart stepped into the light, holding a gun. "Let her go, Tom."

"No." Tom Barlow didn't loosen his hold on Bliss, didn't even turn around.

"I said let her go." There was firm resolve in the tone of the command.

This time Barlow turned his head. "This isn't any of your business, Mrs. Taggart. Now just go away and leave a man to his pleasures."

"Pleasures? Forcing yourself on a woman who has no chance of escape?" Holding the gun up with both hands, she carefully took aim, cocking the trigger. "Now put that away before you hurt yourself."

Giving Bliss a shove, Barlow moved toward the cell door. "Give me the gun, then go on your way. This is between her and me."

"Let her alone or I will shoot."

Bliss took advantage of the interruption to hastily rearrange her shirt. Wrapping her arms around herself, she tried to regain her composure. She had to find a way to get the keys. Josephine Taggart could only hold him off so long. Even now Barlow was threatening her in that intimidating way of his. She'd soon get spooked and run.

But Josephine Taggart didn't. It all happened quickly. Barlow made a grab for her through the bars and in that moment she pulled the trigger. Bliss heard the shot. It reverberated loudly in the cell. She looked down to see Barlow slumped on the floor, a darkening stain spreading over his chest.

"Oh dear, I hope I didn't kill him!"

"Rats don't die easily," Bliss retorted, her eyes narrowing as she fumbled for the key. The sound of the key turning in the lock was most welcome at that moment.

"I—I had to help you. Knowing what my husband has done, I suspected you must be innocent." Much like someone freeing a caged bird, Josephine Taggart opened the door wide. "I—I couldn't let someone like you be harmed by someone like him," she said, then looked down at Barlow with disgust. "It isn't right."

"And I thought you didn't really care what happened to me. I guess I misjudged you." Bliss had never really developed any strong friendships with women, but in that moment she could have hugged

Josephine Taggart. "Thank you. I don't know what else to say."

"You'd better hurry. The gunshot will bring someone." She held forth the gun like an offering. "Here, take this."

There were so many things Bliss wanted to say to this woman, but all she could manage to choke out was, "For a woman who claims to live a dull life, you're very courageous. I mean that." No one had to tell her what a predicament this had left Josephine in. "But you'll be in trouble." Bliss didn't want this lady to have to pay a harsh price for coming to her aid.

"I think I can handle it." That Tom Barlow was groaning was a welcome sign. As Bliss had said, rats were difficult to kill.

"Okay then." Bliss raised her hand in a signal of goodbye. Then she was gone, leaving the jail far behind.

Chapter Forty-One

Travis clutched the telegram as he stared out the window, but although he looked right at the New York Dry Goods' sign, he didn't really see the lettering. How could he when the words of the telegram were so imbedded in his mind? Taggart had Bliss and was threatening her well-being unless he stopped submitting his articles and wrote a retraction claiming his prior story to be a falsehood.

"I know what you're thinking, but you just can't do it!" Farnham was adamant. Since the telegram had come two days ago, he and Jim Erickson had been guarding Travis as diligently as Taggart ever had. "If you do Taggart will have the last laugh, and he'll go on laughing as he crams his pockets full. You just can't."

"That should be my decision," Travis shot back. He would put his life on the line for Bliss. Couldn't Farnham understand that? What did his own reputation matter? Or Taggart's duplicity?

"Your decision?" Farnham puffed so hard on his cigar, he looked as if he were on fire.

"They're my articles, damn it! It's my photograph. I was the one who started this thing in the first place." But even as he spoke Travis realized that what he'd said in fear and anger wasn't true. He had made a commitment to the *Helena Herald*, to Farnham Tabor, to the people of Montana and to his own newspaper back East. But how could he live with himself if because of his actions Bliss was the one to suffer?

"Yeah, you started it. But it's out of your hands now, my boy." Though his voice was gruff, Farnham's expression was sympathetic. "Knowing you'd be tempted to put a halt to the whole thing, Erickson already sent your second article to press. Truth is, the public is already reading it."

"Oh, God!" Travis sat down on the bed and put his face in his hands.

"Take it easy." Although Farnham's pat on the back was meant to be gentle it made Travis cough. "The whole city of Helena is rallying to your side. Hardly a man or woman in these parts hasn't come to respect you. We'll find your girl."

Travis crumpled the telegram and threw it on the floor. "No. *I* will." He'd been a fool to let Erickson and Farnham Tabor talk him out of it. The fear that he had already waited too long gnawed at him.

"Offer yourself up as a sacrifice, is that it? Throw yourself right into Taggart's hands?" As Travis headed for the door, Farnham blocked his way. "And do you think that would make Bliss Harrison happy? Do you think that's why she put herself in danger to help you? If you do then you're stupid!"

Travis glowered.

"Or in love. Sometimes it's the same thing." With a shrug of his shoulders, Farnham held up the key to the room. "That's why I've locked us in."

"What?" Travis grabbed for the key, but Farnham, belying his girth, hastily stepped out of the way.

"For your own good, my boy."

"My own . . ." A terrible blowup threatened to occur. "Taggart had me in his jail, but I'll be damned if I'll let you keep me locked up," Travis shouted. "It's my life. I can risk it."

"Your life or your death, Travis!" For just a moment it looked as if there might be a tussle, but Farnham threw him the key. "Here. But remember, I wash my hands of it. Whatever happens I don't want you to say I didn't tell you so."

Farnham's last words were ringing in Travis' ears as he bounded down the stairs. He'd get a horse and ride posthaste to Watersville. He'd make some kind of a deal with Taggart. Exchange himself for Bliss. Once she was safe he'd go on from there.

The lobby was crowded. The hotel was being advertised as a comfortable summer resort, and it appeared that there were those who wanted to investigate its facilities firsthand. Elbowing his way through the throng, Travis took a long time to get to the front door. That gave him enough time to think things over clearly. Farnham was right. He was making himself into a martyr—without knowing what results that would produce. But damn it all, what else could he do? He wasn't a gambler. He didn't want to chance that Bliss might be harmed.

"Papers. Get your copy of the *Helena Herald*. Hot off the press. Read about it!"

Travis paused, staring at the boy hawking the newspapers. The article that appeared in that issue might well be Bliss's death sentence. That thought gave him the shivers. Still, he was possessed with a need to see it. "Give me one," he said, throwing the boy a penny.

"WATERSVILLE MARSHAL EXPOSED," the headline read. "THE PRINCE IS A PAUPER."

Travis folded the paper up and put it in his coat pocket; Farnham had loaned him the money to buy a suit. Having written the article, he had no need to read it. He practically knew every word by heart. There was mention in it of his wrongful accusation, his incarceration in the Watersville jail, his near hanging and his interviews with some of the braver victims of Taggart's malice. Strong stuff. Just the kind of thing people loved to read. Perhaps that explained why the paper was selling like hotcakes.

"Damn! I should be on top of the world." Instead he was scared for Bliss. The only comforting thing was remembering her telling him that even Taggart wouldn't dare hang a woman.

Having walked down State Street at a brisk pace, Travis moved like a sleepwalker as he turned off for the stables. He was in such a deep trance, he might have missed the sight at the end of the block if the copy of the *Helena Herald* hadn't fallen out of his pocket. Stooping to pick it up, he spied a red-haired woman hurrying toward the International Hotel. A woman with two large gray wolfhounds tagging along behind her.

"Bliss!" Travis was certain it had to be a mirage, but the woman turned her head at hearing her name. "Bliss!" He jumped up and down, waving frantically. If it caused passersby to gawk he didn't care. Then he was running down the boardwalk as fast as his legs would carry him. Sweeping her up into his arms as the wolfhounds barked, he hugged her tight.

"I told you I'd meet you at the International Hotel, Travis. As you can see, I've kept my word." She didn't say a thing about the danger she'd been in nor did she tell him how she had escaped, but he didn't need to know that now. All he wanted to do was hold her.

"Taggart—" Was all he could say before her lips silenced any questions. His arms curled around her, he returned her passionate kisses with a ferocity of his own, and an unspoken need poured from them both as they clung to each other. Travis stroked her face as if committing it to memory once again. "How . . . ?"

"Later." Despite all that she had been through, Bliss turned up her lips in a smile. Then, taking his hand, she led him up the street toward the hotel.

Shoes, hats, dresses, coats and boots were scattered all across the bed and spilled over onto the floor. Four brightly colored carpetbags already bulging with clothes stood in the entryway. Josephine Taggart nearly stumbled over them as she hurried through the door.

"Oh, there you are. It's about time." For the first time Taggart's tone was sharp as he spoke to her.

"What are you doing?" Josephine eyed him warily.

"Packing." Sam Taggart's emotions were in turmoil. He was both frightened and angry. Someone had let La Mont's hellion out of jail, sealing his doom. "We have to get out of town."

"For a vacation, Sam?" she asked sarcastically. How many times had she begged him to go with her?

"No!" Seeing that she was just standing there, he took a large leather-bound trunk from the closet and crammed it full of her clothes. "A permanent change of location. Somewhere in California, I think." Before his whole world came crashing down. One thing was certain. He was through in Montana. Travis La Mont had seen to that, and he hated him.

"California." There was a strange glitter in her eyes.

"Yes, California." Perturbed by her lack of haste, he pushed a stack of garments her way. "Put these in the trunk." When she didn't do what he said he used a gentler tone of voice. "We must hurry, Josey."

"You perhaps. As for me, I'm not going." There she had said it.

"Not going?" Despite his desperation he laughed. She didn't understand, that was it. Well, he'd have to make her see that it was the only way he could save his neck, without letting her in on the true seriousness of the matter. "I'm in danger here, Josey. I think it's better that we move on. Tom Barlow was shot as you've probably heard, and that Harrison woman escaped."

There was a long drawn-out silence before she said softly, "I know."

Taggart was consumed by a nagging feeling. Something was wrong with his wife. She was acting so strangely. "Josey . . . ?"

"I shot Tom!"

His eyes bored into hers. "You. Why?" It must be some kind of a joke.

"He was . . . forcing himself on her. It wasn't right. I just couldn't let him do that."

Taggart realized she was serious. "You shot him. You?"

Josephine nodded.

Taggart tried to regain control of the situation. "Because Tom tried to rape her. Well, then I'm not surprised you came to her aid, although there were better ways to have handled it." He supposed there must have been a struggle for Tom's gun. Damned fool. Taggart had feared Barlow's lust for that little spitfire might ruin everything. "I've had my doubts about Tom, you know. Too hotheaded."

"Don't." The word came out in a sob.

"Don't what?" Sam took a step toward his wife, but she shrank away from his touch. "Josey . . . ?"

"I know Sam. I know."

He waved his hand. "That newspaper story is a fabrication. Travis La Mont is just being vindictive, paying me back for the time he spent in my jail by

398

weaving a web of lies."

"I heard you, Sam. Talking to her. Telling her you'd give her a cut of all your businesses. Like the bawdy house. I was there, hiding behind the door."

"Josey."

"It's over, Sam. Your little porcelain doll has finally evolved into a real person. One who can judge a man for what he really is."

"Listen, I can explain. You see I was trying to trick her and—"

"I just came to say goodbye."

Sam Taggart listened as his wife revealed her unhappiness. She had had money, nice clothes and lots of attention wherever she went, but she really hadn't been content. She didn't love him. Not really. It was just that he had been the only man she had met who'd been strong enough to stand up to her father. But she had mistaken deviousness for courage, cunning for intellect and the need to possess for love. She had been free to walk, to ride, to lounge, to feast, but Sam had never spent much time with her. She had been lonely.

"You're not the man I thought you to be, Sam. That man wouldn't have done the things you've done." Time had become her enemy. The only thing she had learned was how to kill it, how to idle away the hours, but Bliss Harrison had given her hope.

"Josey I . . ." Taggart couldn't just let her walk away. Helplessly he held out his hands. "I need you. Now more than ever." His voice took on the tone of a preacher. "For better or for worse."

"You don't need me, Sam. You never really did."

Her voice was a rasp. "Goodbye." Turning around, she walked through the door.

"Josey! Josey!" The sense of finality about the way she'd left was frightening. Taggart started to run after her, but then he realized that he had really lost her. Josephine was gone as was his empire. He had only himself to count on. It gave him an isolated feeling.

Chapter Forty-Two

Bliss luxuriated in the cool, clean feel of the sheets, and the soft feather mattress was a welcome change from the prickly straw of the jail cot. Having bathed, she felt fresh and invigorated as she nestled against Travis' strong form. "And then Josephine Taggart took aim and shot Tom Barlow, and that was the end of that," she said, coming to the end of her story. "I ducked out of the jail, rescued Bard and Boru from one of Taggart's storehouses and, "borrowing" a horse and wagon, came straight here."

"Just in the nick of time, I might say. As I told you, I was on my way to rescue you." Gently Travis brushed her hair out of her face, his fingers lingering at her temples. Something very precious had just been returned to him.

Her lips trembled in a smile. "I take that to mean you kind of missed me."

"That, Miss Harrison, is an understatement."

"Then I guess it's not out of line to ask for another

kiss." The fifteenth to be precise. He complied gladly, his lips soft and gentle. When he drew away he picked up his hairbrush and ran it through her tangled just-washed tresses, enjoying their silkiness. There was something very erotic about a woman's hair, particularly hers, he thought.

Bliss could feel the rhythmic movement of his fingers as he stroked the strands. The touch of his hands on her hair caused a shiver to dance up and down her spine. She leaned against his hand, giving in to the stirring sensations.

Travis' fingers left the softness of her hair. Putting down the brush, he clasped her shoulders, contenting himself with just looking at her. The hunger to be near her, to touch her, to make love to her, had been with him all the days they'd been parted. Now this moment seemed more dream than reality.

"Are you warm?" He touched her with his eyes before his hands went out to her. His voice was thick, the words catching in his throat. He worshipped the sleek lines of her neck and then let his gaze drop to her rosy-nippled full breasts. She was even more beautiful than he had remembered, her slender waist flaring into rounded, womanly hips. Breathing hard with his arousal, he swept her body with his hands—from shoulders to breasts to hipbones and thighs and back again.

"Mmmhmmm!" she answered, burying her face against his chest as he swept her up in his arms. Reaching up, she clung to him, drawing in his strength and giving hers to him in return. She could feel his heart pounding and knew that hers beat in matching rhythm.

"This is where I want you to be from now on. With me."

After what she had just been through, Bliss had no quarrel with that. "So do I," she said snuggling. For one blinding moment she was aware of every inch of his muscular body as they embraced. She could feel his desire throbbing against her, revealing his response to her nearness. Bliss's quickening body answered his, her awakened senses leaping wildly.

Gently he laid her back, his hands tracing the outlines of her breasts, his lips following his fingers downward, kissing the soft smoothness of her skin. He left no part of her free from his touch, and she responded with a natural passion that was kindled by his love. Her entire body quivered with the intoxicating sensations he always aroused in her. After time apart she wanted only one thing—to feel his hard warmth filling her. To share in his lovemaking.

He could feel the soft swell of her curves beneath his wandering hands. "You have flawless skin."

"So do you. Perfect for a man." She moved closer, leaning against him. Mimicking what he so often did to her, she let her lips run down to his chest. Her tongue explored his nipples, setting him afire. His breathing came faster and faster. Bliss wondered if she was even breathing at all.

Lying together in the sunlight, they let their hands roam over each other, touching, exploring. Travis was lost to the sensations she created. He loved the softness of her, the taste of her lips, the scent of her hair. Her body with its curving slenderness fully ignited his desire.

Bliss tingled with an arousing awareness of her own needs, discovering herself through Travis' touch. Her flesh was intensely sensitive. The lightest touch of his hands or mouth sent a shudder of pure sensation rippling deep within her. Reaching up, she tangled her fingers in his thick dark hair.

"Mmmmm, if this is the welcome I get when I've been away for a while, maybe I should go away again."

"I won't let you." He kissed her hard and long, but soon kissing alone couldn't satisfy him. A blazing hunger raged through him. If it was true that absence made the heart grow fonder, then it was true of another part of him too. "Bliss!" Desire raged like an inferno, pounding hotly in his veins. His whole body throbbed with the fierce compulsion to plunge himself into her sweet softness, and yet he held himself back. He wanted to find the perfect moment.

Bliss lay back, her eyes bright and glittering in the muted sunlight as his fingers trailed downward, tracing her spine. Travis kissed her stomach, moved up to caress her breasts with his lips. Then in a slow suspenseful gliding motion he moved on top of her. With a sudden, powerful grip he clutched the mounds of her buttocks, pressing her closer. He was gripped by the deepest, most powerful desire he had ever felt in his life.

"Bliss, oh, Bliss." This was the woman he loved. Sweet yet bold. Passionate, responsive and exciting.

His lips kept to their caressing, heated course, moving up her neck to devour her full, sweet mouth. Then he knelt, kissing the soft skin of her inner thighs. He felt her quiver as his tongue found her core and searched the soft inner petals. With wild abandon she opened herself up to new discoveries, sighing deeply as he savored the flesh of her secret place.

"Oh, Travis. Oh yes!" Her frantic desire for him was nearly unbearable. She warmed to him, making incoherent sounds as she fit her body to his. Her sensuous writhing motions drove him mad with wanting, but it was when she wrapped her fingers around his stiff flesh that he knew he couldn't wait a moment more.

Bliss opened up to him. Parting her thighs, she held them wide for his entry, then guided him to her. Writhing in pleasure, she was silken fire beneath him, rising and falling with him as he moved with the relentless rhythm of their love. Sweet, hot desire fused their bodies together, yet an aching sweetness mingled with the fire and the frenzy. In the final outpouring of their love, their hearts and hands and bodies spoke the words they had never uttered.

"I want to make love to you like this forever, without stopping. I want to touch you all over and love you." Which is exactly what he did. With masterful hands he brought her to a desperate longing, then to the edge of excitement.

Poised above her, he joined her in an explosion which erupted hotly through both their bodies. She was so tight, so smooth. The warmth of her flesh around him as she met his every thrust made him shudder. Her body arched and surged in a sensuous writhing motion that told him she was feeling the sensations too. Clinging to her fiercely, Travis whispered soft words of love.

In the aftermath of the storm, when all their passion had ebbed and they lay entwined, they sealed their vows of love with whispered words. Sighing with happiness, Bliss snuggled within the cradle of Travis' arms, happy and content.

"Welcome back . . ." Travis placed soft kisses on her forehead. She mumbled sleepily and stretched lazily, her soft thighs brushing against his hair-roughened ones in a motion which stirred him again. He touched her mouth with a kiss. "I love you."

Lying there, her flaming hair billowing out around her, she looked so fragile, so small, but he knew what strength and determination she possessed. The future might bring hardship, perhaps even more danger, but Bliss would find a way to survive. She was keen of mind, brave, loyal and filled with a resolve to make the best out of any situation. Perhaps in truth they had a lot to learn from each other in the days ahead.

They lay there a long time, bodies entwined, each one unwilling to be the first to bring reality crashing about them. Yet already sounds were clattering outside their doorway, reminding them that there were other people in the world. One in particular was showing extreme impatience.

"Travis. Travis." Farnham Tabor accompanied his intrusion with a gentle knocking.

"Go way." Travis was angered. Farnham knew very well that Bliss was back and that he wanted some time alone with her.

"I have some important information." Farnham's voice was insistent.

So was Travis'. "Not now."

"It's about Marshal Taggart."

Travis groaned. "Oh, have a heart." He intended to ignore Farnham, but as Bliss hurried to get dressed so did he. After several minutes he opened the door, holding it ajar only enough to talk through it. "What is it?"

"Taggart was caught with his hand in the candy jar. Trying to escape from Watersville with a carpetbag full of money."

"And you want to get the jump on the story."

"Precisely."

Travis knew it to be Farnham's due, and Erickson's. They had helped him when he needed friends. He couldn't turn away. Regretfully he turned to Bliss. "I'm going to leave for just a little while, but I'll be back." Jovially he blew her a kiss. "Don't go anywhere."

"I won't." She'd had her share of adventure. Padding to the door on bare feet, she locked it behind him, feeling more than just a little triumphant. She and Travis had beaten Taggart. It was only a matter of time until the happy ending she had envisioned became a reality.

Chapter Forty-Three

It should have been a perfect time in Bliss's life—
she and Travis were reunited, he was vindicated of
the charge of robbery and murder, Taggart was
sweating it out in his own jail as he awaited trial—
and yet it was not at all as she had imagined. Not a
happy-forever-after ending where she and Travis
walked off into the sunset together. They weren't
alone now. Other people had stormed into their
world, and she couldn't help resenting the intrusion
of the outspoken cigar-smoking man who made
himself so very visible.

Farnham reminded her of a bull—strong, stubborn and raging. He was opinionated, aggressive,
outspoken and condescending, the kind of man who
made it obvious that he thought all women should
be seen and not heard. Right from the first he and
Bliss had "locked horns" as her father would have
put it. Farnham Tabor expected everyone to give in
to him whether he was right or wrong. Bliss was the
only one who would not.

Nor was Farnham the only problem. The focus of attention had shifted from staying out of Taggart's clutches to putting the adventure into words. Though Bliss was the one who had actually been there, no one seemed to care about getting her side of it. She felt left out as Jim Erickson, Farnham Tabor and Travis toiled day and night on their "exclusive" stories without even once showing interest in her opinion of things. It was as if she had suddenly become invisible.

"I feel about as important as a flea on a dog's backside," she grumbled as Travis kissed her lightly on the cheek before leaving the room to meet Farnham and Erickson downstairs. "Noticed but unwelcome." She had gotten the impression that Farnham didn't like her. His mouth always had a disdainful turn at the edges when he looked at her.

"Unwelcome?" Travis shook his head, though he sensed that it was true. He'd so hoped Farnham and Bliss would hit it off but the opposite had happened. Still, he didn't want to hurt her feelings. "It has nothing to do with you. It's just that the opportunity of a lifetime has opened up to us, Bliss. Newspaper men are like that. They all have one-track minds."

"So I've noticed." The last few days Travis had come back to the room totally exhausted, too tired to make love.

There was a sad tone to her voice that made him feel more than a little guilty. He hadn't meant to ignore her, but he knew deep down that he had. It was just that everything was moving at such a hectic pace. "Things will settle down."

"And then what?" She had been so certain that

409

Travis intended marriage, that once they were together again they would make their union permanent, but he hadn't spoken one word about matrimony. Hadn't her father always said that a man didn't need to buy the honey pot when the honey was free?

"*Then* we'll talk." Travis picked up the pile of papers by the door. "I promise. Just be patient with me, Bliss." The door closed with a gentle slam.

"Patient. And in the meantime twiddle my thumbs."

She looked around the room with a critical eye. A large window with sapphire-colored drapes, a large bed with a blue velvet covering, a small table, a dresser, a settee and two small chairs, one of them upholstered to match the bedspread. The wallpaper was bright. Its blue-green- and gold-flecked pattern would have been called elegant. When she had first gotten here several days ago the room had seemed so big, so cheerful. Now she saw it as a gilded cage.

Bliss felt at odds with herself. She had reached a point in her life where things were at loose ends. Now that this episode had come to a head just what was she going to do? How was she going to make a living? Bounty hunting? That meant traveling around on the trail of some unlawful scoundrel or other. She just didn't want to be away from Travis for so long. Besides, to be truthful with herself that work just wasn't as appealing as it used to be. The pickings were getting slimmer and slimmer. If Bliss wanted to keep her independence, and she did, she knew she'd have to do something else.

"Bake. Knit. Sew?" Farnham had insinuated that

she should occupy her time that way, but Bliss knew there was little of a domestic side to her nature. It just hadn't been bred into her. What then? Even if Travis asked her, did she have it in her to be a wife?

Putting on her hat and boots, she left the hotel to wander aimlessly for a long, long time as she asked herself some serious questions. All fairy-tale musings aside, just what was the relationship between a man and a woman? Lovemaking, yes. Great physical interaction in fact—in that she was most fortunate. A great caring for each other when they were together. But it wasn't all roses, smiles and kisses. What about the time in between?

Like a ton of bricks she realized the truth. She and Travis had nothing in common. Not their backgrounds, not their likes and dislikes, not even their temperaments. They were two oh-so-very-different types strongly drawn to each other between the sheets. Bliss wanted more. Having been independent for so long, she needed a life of her own. Without really meaning to, Travis was denying her this.

"Stay put until I want you. Amuse yourself until then," she grumbled. "Turn down the sheets and warm the bed until I get there, darling." Ha! In a pig's eye.

There were times now when Travis seemed like a stranger to her. Sometimes she just couldn't tell what was really going on in his mind. All too often she felt so out of place in his world. Men had a certain bond between them that no woman could ever bridge. Not really. When Jim Erickson and Farnham Tabor were with Travis she vanished from Travis' heart and mind. He indulged in chatter about

411

the newspaper business with them. That talk was as incomprehensible to her as Chinese. Was it any wonder she wanted to do something to remind Travis that she existed. That she was alive?

Her steps took her to the hotel kitchen, then to the livery stable so she could give Bard and Boru some meaty bones. "Here you go, boys." She watched as they savored the treats.

The wolfhounds were housed in a large pen with plenty of running room, yet even so Bliss felt more than a little bit guilty. The dogs were just one more example of how her life had changed. Like them, she was now cooped up without the chance to roam free.

"Oh, damn!" There were times when she missed her wagon and the opportunity to just travel anywhere she wanted to go. Those had been hard times, lean times, lonely times, yet in spite of that there were fond memories. "Come on, boys."

Once a day she visited the dogs, taking them for a run through the streets of Helena for exercise, but it just wasn't good enough. Though she couldn't make Travis understand, the dogs were more than just animals to her. They were friends. Family. Hell, she'd even risked her chance of escaping to go and get them, had brought them all the way to Helena because she hadn't the heart to leave them behind. She wanted them with her. Wanted to have a permanent place to hang her hat alongside their collars. A house with a yard, even if it was a small one. Was that ever to be, or was she just fooling herself?

Opening the gate of the pen, she led Bard and

Boru on a merry chase. It felt good to be outside, to breathe in the fresh air. The sky, the flowers, the clouds and the company of her wolfhounds were soothing balms to her soul. She had always said that the best things in life were free, and today she really believed it. So much so that as she was at last returning to the hotel, she scolded herself for being so greedy in wanting it all. She had Travis, and she loved him. Wasn't that enough? Most women would have said that it should be.

The long hotel corridor was empty as she made her way back to the room, but she could hear voices coming from inside. Bliss gritted her teeth. They were both here again. Didn't their "men's business" ever cease? They ate, drank, talked and dreamed the *Helena Herald*. Enough. Squaring her shoulders, she tried to brace herself to be polite. It just wouldn't do to lose her temper again.

"You have to think of your future, your reputation, my boy," she heard Farnham's gruff voice saying. "Sow your wild oats, but for God's sake you can't think of marrying her. To put it quite bluntly, she just isn't wife material."

"Not the type for socials and teas you mean?" Bliss heard Travis reply.

"She's crude, undisciplined and wild. Not her fault, I suppose, considering her upbringing and parentage. But think, Travis, think. Your success here is only the beginning. The whole world can open up to you if you only make the right choice. The question is, will you?"

"Give Bliss up for the kind of woman who wears gloves and bonnets. A woman with influence who

413

can help me in my chosen career. Is that what you're saying?"

"In a word, yes! Bliss Harrison can only be a stone around your neck, dragging you to the bottom . . ."

Bliss stepped back, putting her hand to her mouth to block out an angry retort. Crude, undisciplined, wild! She wanted to march right in there and throw the words back in Farnham's face. He didn't think she was good enough for Travis. Well, she was what she was—and damned proud of it. She'd soon show him. Oakwood Harrison hadn't raised her to be a fighter for nothing.

Realization swept over her that there was another side to this whole matter of men and women. It took hard work, patience and perseverence to make it all work out. Maybe it wasn't supposed to be easy. Hadn't her father always said that anything of value was worth working hard for? Well, that was just what she was going to do. But there was another side to all of this. Travis needed to work to win her love as well. He'd taken her for granted the last few days. It was time to put an end to that! With that thought in mind, she marched into the room and gathered up her things without saying a word.

"Bliss! What on earth are you doing?" Travis followed after her, showing her he really did care. Though Farnham was blustering like a windy day, Travis wasn't showing his old friend any attention now. The thought made Bliss smile. "For God's sake, let's talk over whatever is wrong."

"Oh, nothing's wrong," Bliss said sweetly, looking in Farnham's direction. "Nothing at all. Just a conflict of interests. I think it's better if I have my own living quarters for a while."

"A conflict of interests?" Travis was baffled.

"Gentlemen, I'll be on the level. I think it's time you had a little competition." Like a lightning bolt, the idea came to her. Why not?

"Competition?" Now it was Farnham's turn to take note.

"I've decided that *I've* got quite a story to tell, and by damn, I'm going to tell it." Delighting in their look of confusion, she blurted it out. "I'm going to give an account of my experiences as a bounty hunter and of what I went through with Taggart." She paused. "To your rival, the *Helena Journal.*"

Farnham Tabor stared in pensive silence at the copy of the *Helena Journal* he held in his hand. He leaned forward in his chair, then his anger exploded. "Of all the double-dealing, traitorous things to do." Banging the hotel dining-room table with his fist he gave full vent to his outrage. "Imagine, Travis, betraying us like that. It's incomprehensible."

"I think it's great!" Far from being annoyed, Travis understood Bliss's motive perfectly. It was her way of thumbing her nose at Farnham, at Erickson and at him. Deep down he knew they all deserved it.

"I didn't think she'd do it," Jim Erickson interjected. "I didn't think she had the guts."

"That's because you don't know her very well." Travis smiled, remembering the time she had caught him in the tunnel when he was naked. Holding her gun on him, she hadn't even flinched. "Bliss Harrison is one of a kind."

"She's unprincipled—sneaky," Farnham shouted, his face turning red.

"And damned clever." Travis picked up his own copy of the *Journal*. To tell the truth he was amazed. All this time they'd been together he'd prided himself on his profession, but the truth was, Bliss had written an article that showed she was a fledgling journalist with a whole lot of talent. How had he been so blind not to have known she had it in her?

"We'll take her to court. We'll threaten to sue her and that damned paper. I'll talk to the editor of the *Journal* and make him understand that if he doesn't get rid of her at once he'll regret it. No little snip of a girl is going to best me. I'll clip her wings to bring her back to earth, I'll—"

"You'll do nothing of the kind. Not unless you want to answer to me." Travis' protective instincts surfaced with ferocity. He owed Farnham Tabor a great deal—more than he could ever repay—but he wouldn't allow anyone, not even him, to threaten to lift even one finger to cause Bliss harm. "Be truthful, Farnham. She isn't doing anything you haven't done time after time. She's giving us a little competition. It's good. It's healthy. That's what our business is all about. If she were one of your apprentices you'd be singing a far different tune."

"But she's a woman!" Erickson and Farnham echoed each other.

"More of a woman than you could ever know." Travis leaned back in his chair. Bliss Harrison had sent him into a topsy-turvy ride from the moment he'd met her, yet he wouldn't have traded one single moment with her for anything.

"Bah, the world is filled with pretty faces. Why, a man like you can have your pick. She isn't that unusual." Suddenly Farnham wasn't so sure. "Is she?"

Travis smiled. "I think you know the answer to that."

The muffled grumble said that Farnham did. "I suppose you want to marry her, eh?" Farnham raised his eyebrows, yet there wasn't the hostility usually present in his voice when he spoke about Bliss.

"Very much. Trouble is, I'm not certain she'll have me. Not now." Travis had to admit that he couldn't really blame her if she had changed her mind. "I guess I'll just have to see."

Chapter Forty-Four

Bliss Harrison was in the newspaper business! Now she didn't have time for Travis. Farnham Tabor be damned. Far from decrying her lack of sophistication, the people of Helena took Bliss to their hearts. They liked her daring, her honesty and the way she "told it like it was" with no artifice or pretense. Bliss told the story of Taggart, his rise to power and his downfall, from a different point of view than Travis'. That, coupled with her articles on wanted men of the West and the art of bounty hunting, soon made her rival Travis as a celebrity. Which only proved that anything was possible if you stuck to it.

Thinking about it now, she could only wonder at her nerve in marching straight into John River's office at the *Journal* and demanding to see the editor. Surprised at anyone with such grit, he had actually listened to her ideas. Though she was a novice to the newspaper business with no credentials, something about her had goaded River into giving her a chance. He insisted now that it was a decision he'd never regret. There was a journalistic war going on, pitting the *Helena Herald* against the *Journal*. And it had turned Travis and Bliss into rivals.

It was long after dusk when she returned to the International Hotel. She was exhausted as she climbed up the stairs but contented. There was a spark of admiration in Travis' eyes when he looked at her now, a special glow that hadn't been there before. Perhaps because she had proven to him that she could take him on in his own territory and hold her own.

"Bliss!" He was waiting for her when she came to the head of the stairs, pacing back and forth in front of her door. He hurried forward with a sheepish smile on his face. "Care to come in for a . . . a talk?"

- Yes, she wanted to say, but she choked the word back. "It's late, Travis. Tomorrow is going to be another long day."

"Yes, I suppose it is. For me too. No matter what anyone says, writing is hard work." He took a step toward her. "I read your account of my escape from jail and the part you and the blacksmith played in it. It was innovative and exciting. I liked the way you did it."

"It was John River's idea to write it as if it were a chapter from a dime novel, to slant all of my stories that way." She couldn't hide her excitement. "As a matter-of-fact he thinks I should change Taggart's name and try my hand at writing 'dimes.' Montana

Mary, bounty hunter of the West. How does that sound?"

He thought about it for a moment. "I like it."

Suddenly it seemed as if the conversation had come to an end. There was nothing more to say. They were strangely uncomfortable in each other's presence. "Good night, Travis," she whispered.

"Good night." He started to walk away, then turned back. "I miss you, Bliss. I miss going to sleep with you in my arms and waking up beside you. I thought when you came back from Watersville we'd be together like that forever. I guess I took that and you for granted. I got my priorities mixed up. I'm sorry."

"Don't be." He looked so regretful that for just a moment she almost weakened. "It wasn't just that. Not really. You have something to center your world around, and I was floundering. I guess I just didn't want to admit that bounty hunters are soon going to be a dying breed. I needed something, Travis. Needed to prove I could do more than shoot a gun or liven up your bed. I wanted you to see that I wasn't always wild and undisciplined." It wasn't really Travis she was angry with but Farnham and the kind of men he typified.

"You heard what Farnham said. That's it, isn't it, Bliss? The old grump hurt your feelings. Damn him!" He touched her arm. "Well, did you hear my answer?"

"Part of it." The gentle brush of his fingers deeply stirred her. So it wasn't just men who thrived on making love; she wanted him. Wanted him badly.

420

"I said I wouldn't trade you for any woman in the world, and I meant it, Bliss. I don't want a prim and proper miss who holds her little finger out when drinking tea. Farnham might, but not me. I want a woman who isn't afraid to show her temper once in a while, even if it's just to keep me in my place. A woman who isn't afraid to get dirt or gunpowder on her hands. A woman who keeps me on my toes. One who gets herself and me into trouble, then has the guts to get me out. Will you marry me?"

Bliss held her breath, then let it out slowly as she said, "I can't cook!" She had to be honest. "Hell, I don't even want to."

"Then we'll hire someone to broil, fry and bake."

"I can't sew. I always get stuck with the needles."

"There are seamstresses."

"My wolfhounds!"

Travis clenched his fists, rolling back his eyes. "I'll just have to learn how to make them like me. Or have Farnham teach me how to growl back."

It was so tempting to say yes, to throw everything else aside and just take a chance. She studied him keenly, her eyes searching his face. Everything was moving so fast.

"I swear. More often than anyone should." Why was she so afraid to tell him yes when it was what she really wanted to say?

"So do I." He laughed softly. "I learned it from you."

Bliss turned her large blue eyes up to meet his gaze. "I don't know, Travis. You love me and I love you, but there's more to it than that. I guess to be

421

honest I'm just plain scared." And she was. Wasn't that really why she'd gone running off? Marriage was forever, or so the vows said.

"Marry me anyway." His tone was stern. "Don't throw our chance for happiness away. Don't keep thinking up reasons why it just won't work. Love doesn't come along very often. Don't condemn us both to loneliness. That's all I ask." His fingers touched the wisps of hair that had escaped from her upswept braids. Bending down, he kissed her forehead. "Sleep on it." He was gone before she could tell him to stay.

Late that night Bliss knew full force what loneliness really was. An empty bed with no one beside you to hold you close. No one to keep you warm against the cool autumn breeze. No one to talk to or laugh with. She'd thought she needed to sort things out in her mind, but she'd been wrong. She *did* want to marry Travis. Had wanted that for a long, long time. In her heart she knew it was the right decision. If there were no guarantees, then she was willing to take a chance. Hadn't it been said by someone that love conquered all?

Putting on her robe, she opened the door, intending to tiptoe down the hall. The newspaper stuck under the door caused her to pause. Giving in to curiosity she bent over and picked it up, looking at the headline. "My God." In bold black letters it read, "CAN A FEMALE BOUNTY HUNTER AND STORYTELLER FIND HAPPINESS MARRIED TO A NEWSPAPER MAN?" Travis had chosen the best way of asking her to marry him that

422

a newspaper man could, by putting it in writing for all of Montana to see.

Padding down the hallway on bare feet, she knocked softly at his door and was surprised when he opened it on the second rap. Throwing her arms around him, she said the only word that needed to be spoken, "Yes."

Chapter Forty-Five

There was hardly a trace of cloud in the sky. A good omen for a wedding. And what a wedding it was. Unusual. Interesting. Completely unconventional. Outdoors, of course, with all the stores on Main Street decorated in honor of the occasion. Travis' and Bliss's wedding might not have been the social event of the year, but it did attract a lot of attention.

First of all, it was the only wedding in Helena's history at which the bride didn't wear a dress. Bliss just had never had much use for skirts, and wanting to feel comfortable, she had decided to wear a white silk shirt, white velvet pants and white leather boots. A touch of color was added by placing red and pink flowers in her hair. Second, there were two very important guests at the ceremony—the four-legged kind, Bard and Boru.

"This is bound to be the scandal of the year. Don't say I didn't warn you, my boy, but I think you are in

424

for a turbulent married life," Farnham Tabor said in a hushed tone as he fumbled for the ring, then handed it to Travis. He had let it be known from the first that he thought Travis was making a mistake.

"Turbulent." Travis grinned. "I would expect so. I'm looking forward to it." Looking at Bliss as she ambled down the pathway on the arm of her friend, the blacksmith, he knew in his heart he would never have one moment of regret. Living with Bliss was going to be anything but dull.

For one hushed moment Travis' eyes met Bliss's and he laughed softly. Even the marriage ceremony was going to be slightly different. Knowing that she couldn't always live up to promising to "obey," Bliss had insisted only the words "love" and "honor" be used.

"You really are pretty," Travis murmured, bending to take her hand as she stepped up beside him.

"Maybe. But not as fine looking as you." She whistled softly at the sight of his brand-new gray pinstriped suit. She'd nabbed a handsome devil.

It was a short ceremony without any fuss or frills, but a strangely beautiful one all the same. Bliss and Travis said their vows before a preacher as a large throng of invited guests looked on—Hattie Dodd, Jonathan Price and Josephine Taggart included. When at last the preacher pronounced them man and wife, Travis turned to his wife and was surprised to see that her eyes were misted.

"Happy tears, Travis."

Bliss felt the gold ring slide onto her finger and

425

knew in her heart that she would belong to Travis La Mont for the rest of her life. It was a potent realization.

When the ceremony was over and before all assembled, Travis kissed his bride, long and lingeringly. Bliss slid her arms around her husband's broad shoulders, relishing the ritual kiss and thrilled to know that this handsome, caring man belonged to her at last.

"And to think what I might have missed if I'd shot you," she said when he pulled away.

The wedding celebration was a lively affair, with whiskey by the barrel and an array of delicacies. Afterward there was dancing, then a giggling, lively group enthusiastically gave Travis and Bliss a loud send-off. Amidst jovial laughter and shouted congratulations, the newly wedded couple were escorted to a wagon, one Travis had had made up to look like the vehicle Bliss had sacrificed to get away from the posse's ambush. Bottles, tin cans and streamers floated from the "wolfer's" wagon, clattering as the equipage began to move.

"Thought this would be perfect for a honeymoon. What do you say?" He cringed as Bard and Boru jumped up beside him. Though he and the animals had tacitly declared a truce, he still didn't feel easy around them. But he would. He'd have to.

"Oh, Travis!" Of all the things he had given her this touched her most. She winked at him, then nestled against the curve of his arm. "Let's get going. It's a big, wide world. I say we'd better get started."

Picking up the reins, Travis flicked the horses' and sent the wagon rolling down Main. Man and wife waved to the assembled crowd. "When we get back I have a feeling we will have plenty to write about."

"I know so, Travis." The impish grin on her face was smothered by his kiss.

Author's Note

Printed publications that report and interpret current news events and print features intended to instruct, amuse or inform have long been important to civilizations. As a matter-of-fact, the first known sheet for such regular spreading of news, a daily bulletin posted in the public places of ancient Rome, contained reports of activities in the Senate, gladiatorial combats and official appointments.

The first American printing presses were set up in Cambridge, Massachusetts, in the mid 1600's. The newspapers of the American colonies were modeled after the daily papers popular in England and soon became a part of American life. As the settlers spread westward, among the top priorities of each new town was a newspaper. Indeed it was a rare town, no matter how small or how remote, that did not boast of at least one.

Many daring journalists toured the West to satisfy their readers' appetites for stories and news. Sporting pistols and carrying rifles, these chroniclers moved West to start publishing papers in cow towns and mining camps. With them came artists and photographers to contribute vivid pictures of life in the West.

At first photographs could not be transferred to the printed page, so drawings were reproduced by means of woodcuts, adding to the written story. In the mid 1880's, however, the perfection of halftone photoengraving allowed photographs to be mass-printed, and a new era of pictorial reporting had begun. It has often been said that a picture can say more than a thousand words.

Possession of firearms was commonplace on the frontier. Thus, newspapers across the West carried accounts of gunfights of every kind—brawls, shoot-outs, raids, robberies and vigilante reprisals. The guardians of law and order were county sheriffs, town marshals, state or territorial rangers and federal marshals. Their sense of right and wrong did not keep some of these lawmen from the pursuit of second careers as outlaws, however. Often law was the gun, and laws were written by those who were strongest and held the power. The label of gun-fighter applied to marshals and horse thieves alike. At times the line between bad men and good was blurred, for when there were scores to be settled it sometimes hardly mattered which side of the law a man was on.

With so many men breaking the law, there were a number of profitable ways of amassing money, bounty hunting being one of them. Wanted posters depicting outlaws and stating the amount of the rewards for their captures dead or alive could be seen on trees, fences, walls and even outhouses. Chasing and capturing gunfighters, murderers, robbers and miscreants for profit was a lucrative pursuit for many.